I0867914

ENCUENTRO

ENCUENTRO

Latinx Performance for the New American Theater

Edited by
Trevor Boffone, Teresa Marrero,
and Chantal Rodriguez

Northwestern University Press
Evanston, Illinois

Northwestern University Press
www.nupress.northwestern.edu

Printed in the United States of America

10 9 8 7 6 5 4 3 2 1

Library of Congress Cataloging-in-Publication Data

Names: Boffone, Trevor, editor. | Marrero, María Teresa, editor. | Rodriguez, Chantal, editor. | Container of (work): González, Rubén C. La Esquinita, U.S.A. | Container of (work): Torres-Tama, José. Aliens, immigrants & other evildoers. | Container of (work): Hinds, Rickerby. Dreamscape. | Container of (work): King, Mariana Carreno. Patience, fortitude, and other antidepressants. | Container of (work): González, Javier Antonio. Zoetrope: part 1. | Container of (work): Fernández, Evelina. Premeditation.
Title: Encuentro : Latinx performance for the new American theater / edited by Trevor Boffone, Teresa Marrero, and Chantal Rodriguez.
Other titles: Encuentro (Northwestern University Press)
Description: Evanston, Illinois : Northwestern University Press, 2019.
Identifiers: LCCN 2019003396 | ISBN 9780810140141 (paper text : alk. paper) | ISBN 9780810140158 (cloth text : alk. paper) | ISBN 9780810140165 (e-book)
Subjects: LCSH: American drama—Hispanic American authors—21st century. | American drama—Hispanic American authors—History and criticism. | Encuentro (Festival) (2014 : Los Angeles, Calif.)
Classification: LCC PS628.H57 E53 2019 | DDC 812.6080868073—dc23
LC record available at https://lccn.loc.gov/2019003396

This anthology is dedicated to the efforts of those who came before, those who sparked the individual talent of Latinx artists, and those who were there in the early days of the social and political struggles of our communities. We hold dear the groundbreaking works of El Teatro Campesino, Miriam Colón, María Irene Fornés, and Max Ferrá. Furthermore, we honor the contributions of past, present, and future generations of theatermakers and scholars who have sustained and will continue to nourish the Latinx Theater movement.

CONTENTS

FOREWORD
Encuentro 2014 Manifesto

José Luis Valenzuela

José Luis Valenzuela, Artistic Director of the Latino Theater Company and Los Angeles Theatre Center, delivered this manifesto three times throughout the Encuentro 2014 festival. Punctuated with the burning of sage, the invocation of this manifesto served as a welcoming ritual and as a form of communal intention setting, first on the arrival of the artists on October 12; again, on October 26 to mark the arrival of the second wave of festival artists; and lastly at the opening session of the Latinx Theatre Commons National Convening held at the Los Angeles Theatre Center November 6.

> Encuentro, encounter, a touch, a smile, a confrontation, a look, an embrace . . .
> And in the words of our ancestors:
> *Recuerda que no se vive fácilmente en esta tierra.*
> *Pero no olvides, que primeramente tú provienes de alguien,*
> *que tú desciendes desde alguien,*
> *que tú naciste por la gracia de alguien;*
> *que tú a la vez eres la espina y el retoño de nuestros antepasados,*
> *de aquellos que vinieron antes que nosotros,*
> *y de aquellas y aquellos que se han ido a vivir al más allá.**
> Remember, that one does not live easily upon this earth.
> But, do not forget that above all,

* These words come from the "Huehuetlatolli" ("The Ancient Word" or "The Sayings of the Old") which are found in the Florentine Codex Book #6; these codices are the only sources of pre-Columbian Aztec life, culture, and thought left.

you have come from someone;
that you are descended from someone;
that you were born by the grace of someone;
that you are both the spine and the offspring of our ancestors;
of those who came before us and of those who have gone on to live in the great beyond.
Welcome to Encuentro 2014.
We are here to inspire and to be inspired
We are here to meet and to know each other
To pollinate our artistic dreams and the dreams of the communities we come from
We are here to create and to be creative
We are here to see, without judgment,
But with enjoyment
We are here to help each other
To support each other
We are here to be generous with our knowledge
We are here to see, to touch, to provoke, to confront
We are the makers and the creators of an art form that speaks to us, that allows us to give, to engage,
To dialogue about our human experience
About our political ideals, about our dreams and our human needs.
We are here to create beauty and to be amazed by the beauty created by others
We are here to listen . . .
To the beat of the drum,
To the strumming of the guitar,
To the melodic notes of the piano
To the wail of the singer,
The verse of the poet,
The sound and cadence of the word,
To see the movement of the body.
We are here to cherish our accomplishments and to consider our missteps.
We are here to converge and to communicate our thoughts and ideas for the future.
We are here full of optimism, full of rage, full of pain, full of love, and joy.
We are here to look forward,
To move forward,
We are here to encounter ourselves, our audiences, and each other.
And we are claiming our history, our place and our presence.

We come from many places, like our ancestors;
We are here to continue the legacy of those that have come before us and to thank them with our work and to honor them with respect;
To recognize that we are not alone but that we come from somewhere.
That our history and our language should be held high and honored;
We hold high and honor the many colors of our skin, of our hair, of our eyes.
We come from somewhere and we are shaping our own destinies;
We are innovators, we are survivors;
We can adapt to the needs of the times;
We are thinkers and philosophers;
We engage intellectually and emotionally;
We laugh and cry;
We make you think and we make you angry;
We make you dance with our rhythms and our language.
We may confront you and our loudness may annoy you but that is who we are.
We embrace and honor all the elements that shape who we are.
We embrace our allies, those who recognize the importance of this gathering.
We elevate them, we celebrate them.
We are claiming our place here and now in the American theater, in the Latin American theater, in the global theater.
We live in the present and have great hope for the future, while honoring the past.
Bienvenidos al Encuentro 2014
Welcome to Encuentro 2014!

ACKNOWLEDGMENTS

This book would not exist without the artists. We give special thanks to the playwrights, directors, actors, dramaturgs, designers, producers, technicians, and all contributors who breathed life into these productions.

We are grateful for the immeasurable support from HowlRound and the Latinx Theatre Commons. The latter has coalesced formerly dispersed voices into a powerful network of Latinx theatermakers now leading the field. This anthology is just one example of the breadth of this work.

We give special thanks to Latinx Theatre Commons Producer Abigail Vega for her support and our editor Gianna Francesca Mosser, whose valuable counsel helped guide us through the publication process.

We honor the vision of the Latino Theater Company and the support of the staff of the Los Angeles Theatre Center in making the Encuentro Festival a reality.

This anthology has been made possible through generous funding from the Andrew W. Mellon Foundation and the Latinx Theatre Commons.

INTRODUCTION
Encuentro 2014: Encountering Latinx Theater and Performance

Trevor Boffone, Teresa Marrero, Chantal Rodriguez

What is the state of U.S. Latinx theater?[1] What would happen if theater companies could spend a month sharing and making work together? What could we learn about the breadth of the field? What would the new work look like, and how would it impact the collective aesthetic(s) of contemporary Latinx theater? These are the questions that informed the backbone of the 2014 Encuentro Festival. The aims of the festival were two-fold: to give artists and audiences the opportunity to explore a broad range of Latinx work and creative methodologies, and to reinvigorate professional relationships between Latinx artists and companies across the country.

Between October 12 and November 10, 2014, the Latino Theater Company, operators of the Los Angeles Theatre Center (LATC), in association with the Latinx Theatre Commons (LTC), created the largest national Latinx theater festival and convening of theater artists and scholars since the last TENAZ (Teatro Nacional de Aztlán) festival in 1992 at the Guadalupe Cultural Arts Center in San Antonio, Texas.[2] The 2014 Encuentro featured nineteen productions as well as a culminating performance of ten devised theater pieces, collectively created by the Encuentro artists. In addition to the productions, the festival included salons known as *tertulias,* and post-show discussions were offered throughout the month. Members of the LTC Steering Committee served on the festival selection and tertulia committees, and produced the second LTC National Convening during the final weekend of the festival. During this convening the festival's reach extended even further to over 100 attendees from across the country, and hundreds more via livestreaming of selected events, making it one of the most significant, large-scale events in recent Latinx theater history.

Encuentro is a Spanish word for an encounter, a meeting, a gathering. *Encuentro* also refers to a discovery or a finding. In the manifesto which prefaces this anthology, José Luis Valenzuela quite literally set the stage for the event: remembering the past, celebrating the present, and pointing toward the future. Encuentro was not only a theater festival, but a strategic, public event that proudly proclaims that Latinidad and Latinx theater are vital forces within American theater (and beyond) that deserve ongoing recognition.

HISTORY, HOPES, AND DREAMS: THE FESTIVAL TRADITION IN LATINX THEATER

Theater festivals have a long history in the Chicana/o and Latinx theater movement. In the late 1960s and early 1970s dozens of politically focused theater companies known as *teatros* sprung up across the United States and by 1972, a national organization, TENAZ, was created to support communication between the teatros, and to coordinate national and international festivals. TENAZ refers to El Teatro Nacional de Aztlán (The National Theater of Aztlán). The Spanish word *tenaz* also means tenacious. In 1973, TENAZ published its official manifesto, at a festival in San Jose, California, which stated in part that "the organization, TENAZ, will work with all oppressed people; it must develop a human and revolutionary alternative to commercial theater and mass media."[3] In addition to TENAZ, the annual International Hispanic Theatre Festival of Miami has formed an artistic bridge between Latin American and Latinx artists for over three decades. More recent festivals include the Goodman Theatre's Latino Theatre Festival, and Teatro Dallas International Theatre Festival, among many others. As Chicano theater scholar Jorge Huerta has noted, "A theatre festival is the natural manifestation of the collective desire to celebrate a people's history, myths, hopes, and dreams; to share ideas and quite simply to be renewed in one's mission as cultural workers. In the case of Latinx theatre, there is also the desire to question the status-quo."[4] The legacy of festivals and an umbrella organization to support these efforts is part of our theatrical past, as is balancing political and artistic aims within and outside of mainstream theater and the development of Latinx playwrights. This balancing act subsequently became evident in the decades to come.

Riding the wave of momentum from the historical Chicano and Puerto Rican civil rights movements, several significant regional theaters in the United States established outlets to develop Chicanx and Latinx playwrights. Although more existed, INTAR Hispanic Playwrights-in-Residence Laboratory (1978–1991), South Coast Repertory's Hispanic Playwright's Project (1986–2004), and Mark Taper Forum's Latino Theatre Initiative (1992–2005) became *the* prominent spaces for training, workshops, and collaboration which launched the careers of an entire generation of Chicanx and Latinx playwrights.[5]

According to Michael Wright, the underlying purpose of all new play development models is to cultivate playwrights' skills by providing them with a safe, supportive environment in which to develop as artists.[6] But this begs the question: What happens when these models cease to exist? In "Towards a Hub for Latina/o Theater Artists," Lisa Portes reminds us of the negative effects of the closing of seminal development projects such as the Hispanic Playwrights Project at South Coast Repertory Theatre (SCR) and the Latino Theatre Initiative at the Mark Taper Forum which folded in 2004 and 2005 respectively due to budget cuts. She claims that "Latina/o theater artists have been feeling the loss ever since."[7] The result of losing such centers of new play development for Latinx artists—actors, designers, directors, dramaturgs, writers—left a tremendous gap. Subsequently, the national network of Latinx playwrights became delimited by a sudden lack of institutional resources and established models of collaboration and support. The national network of Latinx theatermaking lost its "hubs" and, subsequently, longed for new models such as a "New Latino/a play festival that would use the work to ignite our national community."[8]

In 2003 Nilo Cruz's *Anna in the Tropics* became the first Latinx play to win the Pulitzer, with unexpected repercussions. David Emmes, then Artistic Director of SCR, went on record saying that Cruz's success proved "how far Latino writers have grown in their ability to be part of the fabric of American theater" and, thus, Latinx theater does not need "the spotlight and focus it's had in the past."[9] Supposedly, Cruz's landmark win signaled an "arrival" that justified the removal of support for Latinx theater from within the regional theater model.[10] However, in reality it did not signal an opening of the doors on a significant scale, nor did it fill the vacuum left by the development projects. Even though Quiara Alegría

Hudes (*Water by the Spoonful*, 2012) and Lin-Manuel Miranda (*Hamilton*, 2016) have won Pulitzer Prizes, the situation still remains.

¡YA BASTA! THE EMERGENCE OF THE LATINX THEATRE COMMONS

In 2011, Washington, D.C.'s Shakespeare Theatre Company (STC) produced a version of *Much Ado about Nothing*. Rather than a traditional take on Shakespeare, the play was set in Cuba and changed the characters Hugh Oatcake and George Seacoal to Juan Huevos and José Frijoles (the Spanish words for "eggs" and "beans"). Despite the Cuban setting, only three of the actors were Latinx, triggering a casting-related debate that continues to this day. Word of the production quickly spread throughout the artistic community both online and locally, STC hosted a town hall, STC artistic director Michael Kahn issued an apology, the characters' names were changed back to Hugh and George, and, most significantly, the growing Latinx theater community began to formally mobilize and publicly declare "*¡Ya basta!*/Enough!" In May 2012, using her position as playwright-in-residence at the Arena Stage in Washington, D.C., Karen Zacarías gathered a group of eight Latinx theatermakers (the "DC 8") under the sponsorship of what is now HowlRound, and the idea that would become the LTC was born.[11] The group—comprised of Zacarías, Kristoffer Diaz, Lisa Portes, Tlaloc Rivas, Antonio Sonera, Enrique Urueta, José Luis Valenzuela, and Anne García-Romero, gathered in a twenty-four-hour discussion with P. Carl, Jaime Gahlon, Vijay Mathew, David Dower, and Kevin Becerra from the American Voices New Play Institute. Together they devised a plan to revitalize the current state of Latinx theater. According to Zacarías, "It was time for Latina/o artists to discuss and design a viable, energetic, sustainable, inclusive 'something' that would serve a wide band of Latina/o artists nationally."[12]

In "Latina/o Theatre Commons: Updating the U.S. Narrative," Anne García-Romero recounts this landmark event. While it may seem obvious to some, the contemporary theater landscape does not reflect the cultural multiplicity that constitutes the twenty-first-century United States. According to García-Romero, "Contemporary Latina/o theatre updates the U.S. narrative through presenting diverse cultural worlds that allow theater audiences to more fully understand the U.S. experience."[13] Despite the lack of adequate representation in the American theater, Latinx theater artists have been creating new work that reflects the complexity of contemporary, multicultural Americans. For example, Latinx theater artists continued to mobilize after the loss of the labs through the development of regional alliances, networking through organizations such as Theater Communications Group (TCG), and the Association for Theatre in Higher Education (ATHE), and in their own long-standing, grassroots, ensemble, and community-based practices.

The DC 8 tapped into their networks of Latinx theater communities to establish an initial steering committee of over thirty practitioners who worked to produce the first LTC National Convening, held from October 31 to November 2, 2013, at Emerson College in Boston.[14] The Boston Convening was an historic event and the first such gathering of Latinx theatermakers since the last TENAZ festival in 1992. The DC 8 created an action plan that laid the foundation of what would become the Latinx Theatre Commons. According to García-Romero, the LTC would "build upon the foundation of the past and momentum of the present to create four initiatives that will continue to advance the field of US Latina/o theatre."[15] These initiatives included a national convening at, and support of, the Latino Theater Company's 2014 Encuentro festival, the 2015 Carnaval of New Plays at the Theatre School at DePaul University under the auspices of Lisa Portes's leadership, the LTC's digital platform and journal *Café Onda*, and the formation of the Latinx Theatre Commons Steering Committee. Since these initial events and efforts to draw national attention to Latinx theater, the LTC has continued to grow and adapt to the rapidly changing American theater landscape as evidenced in their work and mission statement:

> The Latinx Theatre Commons (LTC) is a national movement that uses a commons-based approach to transform the narrative of the American theatre, to amplify the visibility of Latinx performance making, and to champion equity through advocacy, art making, convening, and scholarship. The LTC is a flagship program of HowlRound.[16]

The LTC's values include service, radical inclusion, transparency, legacy and leadership cultivation, and advancement of the art form. The LTC fosters emergent national leadership through an organic organizing method of activating its networks and expanding its circles of connection.

The LTC celebrates diverse connections, honors the past with reflection, and envisions a future with optimism and enthusiasm. Using the collective forces of a volunteer steering committee made up of Latinx theatermakers, scholars, and allies from across the United States, the LTC has generated new momentum for multicultural art-making across the country since it began as an idea in DC.[17]

A COMMONS-BASED APPROACH AND THE LTC: AN HISTORICAL PERSPECTIVE

According to Indiana University's Digital Library of the Commons, "the commons is a general term for shared resources in which each stakeholder has an equal interest."[18] Historically, the term "*commons*" is derived from the medieval English legal term for land which was designated by the lord of the manor for use by common folk for their own sustenance. This was known as "*the commons*." The term "*commoner*" emerged from the idea of one who toils on commonly held lands.[19] The idea and practice of a commonwealth is predicated on the notion that all citizens assume a degree of responsibility for sharing labor, knowledge, natural resources, and contributing in public works for the common good of the community. In Great Britain the practice of commonly held land has eroded since the mid-nineteenth century, coinciding with the emergence of privatization, capitalism, and industrialization. The term was popularized as a shared resource term by the ecologist Garrett Hardin (1968).

There are several types of commons in practice today:

- Environmental commons are self-regulated systems by users of commonly-held resources such as forestry and fishing.
- Digital commons share information and knowledge resources that are collectively created and owned between or among a community that tends to be non-exclusive and shared freely to third parties. Wikipedia is an example, as is HowlRound's World Theatre Map, a user-generated directory and real time map of the global theater community.
- Cultural, social, and intellectual commons include literature, music, arts, design, film, video, television, radio, information, software, and sites of heritage. HowlRound and the Latinx Theatre Commons are examples.

Some of the important aspects of a commons-based approach are: shared leadership; everyone has a stake; it allows personal talent and cultural capital to organize around shared goals; it is task oriented and it does not depend upon the circulating models of top-down leadership, nor does it depend on notions of development and marketing strategies; it is not based on meritocracy (the system of career advancement both in academia and in the workplace); it uses free access technologies for the greater good. The beauty of the commons-based approach is its organizational flexibility. There are no top-down structures of hierarchy with which to contend. Hence, it fosters a discursive strategy based on peer-to-peer intercommunication and listening skills.

A commons-based approach not only stands in contrast to the enclosure and privatization of knowledge, but it creates opportunities for new ways of conceptualizing possibilities through collaborations using existing infrastructures. P. Carl, one of the cofounders of HowlRound, on the subject:

> The thing that most impresses me about the commons-based approach is that things get done as a result of it! The LTC has been the most impressive example of the power of the commons to activate people around shared goals and values to accomplish more than a single organization or person ever could. The commons is an intervention-based approach. . . . In this way, for me I always say the commons approach is revelatory. It makes possible what seemed impossible and what happens is usually much more than I could have imagined from my singular vantage point.[20]

The collective nature of the commons-based approach echoes the early Chicano theater movement, one which began with El Teatro Campesino at the grassroots level in 1965. Action- and intervention-oriented, both the historic and present Latinx theater movements emphasize the power of the collective.

COMMUNITY, CREATIVE COLLABORATION, AND CONVENING: ENCUENTRO 2014

The Encuentro festival grew out of the inspiration of the Latino Theater Company in Los Angeles. The ensemble has been together since

1985 and currently operates the Los Angeles Theatre Center (LATC), a multi-theater complex in downtown Los Angeles. After going on tour with their production of *Solitude* by Evelina Fernández in 2009, they realized how important it was for companies to share their work with other cities and other audiences, and also how rare these touring opportunities were. They were also struck by the need for artists to view one another's work and to understand the state of Latinx Theater on a national scale. Therefore, a festival was needed so that the work could be seen and shared. Having been active in the TENAZ festivals of the '70s and '80s, members of the company sought to honor the legacy of those festivals and create a vibrant space where multiple generations of theatermakers could encounter one another. The festival would differ from traditional festivals in that all artists could view one another's work, and engage in cross-company collaborations in the creation of new work, with the overarching goal of engaging in a national dialogue around aesthetics. With the development of the Latinx Theatre Commons, a partnership was formed and the LTC focused their participation on the festival selection committee, the *tertulia* committee, and producing the second national convening during the closing weekend of the festival.

Immediately following the LTC National Convening in Boston in 2013, steering committee members were invited to volunteer to serve on the selection committee for the Encuentro festival. The Selection Committee included: José Carrasquillo, Theater Director, Gala Hispanic Theatre; Jamie Gahlon, Associate Director, HowlRound; Amparo Garcia-Crow, Playwright; Daniel Jáquez, Theater Director; Alex Meda, Artistic Director, Teatro Luna; Richard Perez, Professor, Hope College; Chantal Rodriguez, Programming Director, Los Angeles Theatre Center; Mark Valdez, Executive Director, Network of Ensemble Theaters; José Luis Valenzuela, Artistic Director, Latino Theater Company/Los Angeles Theatre Center; and Karen Zacarías, Playwright, Arena Stage. Collectively they drafted the submission guidelines, and reviewed and scored the over seventy-five applications which included company histories, personal statements, and work samples. The selection committee subsequently met in Los Angeles for an in-person meeting to make their final selection. The festival was outlined with the following components:

> The Los Angeles Theatre Center, in association with the Latina/o Theatre Commons, is accepting submissions for participation in

> the 2014 Encuentro: A National Latina/o Theatre Festival. *Encuentro* translates to "an encounter," a theme that is a core component of this festival. This festival will celebrate the richness of contemporary Latina/o theater in the U.S. through presenting up to ten selected companies, in residence at The LATC, who will perform in repertory over four weeks. Each production will have up to twelve performances in the festival.
>
> In addition to presenting their work to the public, artists will work together during the month-long residency sharing creative methodologies in artistic workshops that will culminate in public performances of a co-created new work. This unique opportunity will allow participants and audiences to take an in depth look at the range of aesthetic diversity in the field. Public conversations about the work will include post-performance discussions, roundtable conversations, symposia, and distinguished speakers.[21]

Finalists were selected based on the following criteria: artistic merit, thematic content, logistical feasibility, cultural representation, and geographic representation. Speaking of Encuentro 2014, LTC Producer Abigail Vega notes, "The aim of Encuentro 2014 was to present a snapshot of Latinx theatermaking in the US and its varied aesthetics. Unlike a traditional festival, we were not curating strictly along the lines of traditional notions of artistic excellence. Rather, the goal of the selection committee was to gather a diverse group of theatermakers working in a myriad of ways (i.e. devisers, docu-theater creators, solo performers, ensembles, etc.), creating aesthetically diverse work from geographically diverse locales."[22] All finalists were asked to answer follow-up logistical questions; in some cases the logistics of a month-long residency in Los Angeles would prove too difficult and costly for several companies.[23] To accommodate some of these challenges, several companies were invited to participate in the festival for only two weeks, and another company would join for the second half of the festival. Ultimately, fifteen pieces were chosen for performances at the LATC, two for local productions at partner theaters, and two staged readings as part of the additional festival programming.[24] These productions and readings included:

- *Zoetrope: Part I* from Caborca Theatre (New York)
- *Enrique's Journey* from Su Teatro (Denver, Colorado)

- *Premeditation* from The Latino Theater Company (Los Angeles, California)
- *Your Problem with Men* from Teatro Luna (Chicago, Illinois)
- *Mariela en el Desierto* from Aurora Theater/Teatro del Sol (Atlanta, Georgia)
- *Juárez: A Documentary Mythology* from Theater Mitu (New York/ Dubai)
- *Dancing in My Cockroach Killers* from Pregones Theater (New York)
- *Agua a Cucharadas* from Tantai Teatro (Puerto Rico)
- *Patience, Fortitude, and Other Antidepressants* from INTAR/Unit 52 (New York)
- *Maria's Circular Dance* from Borderlands Theater (Tucson, Arizona)
- *Properties of Silence* from About Productions (Los Angeles, California)
- *Dreamscape* from Hindsight Productions (Riverside, California)
- *Aliens, Immigrants & Other Evildoers* from Arte Futuro Productions (New Orleans, Louisiana)
- *Daughter of a Cuban Revolutionary* from CalArts Center for New Performance (Valencia, California)
- *La Esquinita, U.S.A.* from El Teatro Campesino (San Juan Bautista, California)

Additional programming included:

- A staged reading of *The Long Road Today*, South Coast Repertory (Costa Mesa, California)
- A staged reading of *Alisal*, Cornerstone Theater (Los Angeles, California)

Off-site productions at local Latinx theaters:

- *Las Mujeres de Juárez* from Grupo de Teatro Sinergia at Frida Kahlo Theatre
- *Julius Caesar* from CASA 0101 Theater

In the spirit of inclusivity, the selection committee also recommended that a representative from each semi-finalist company be invited to attend the national convening with funding support from the LTC.

Another programmatic component of the festival was the tertulia programming. The central goal of these events was to not only engage the artists and audiences in dialogue around the Encuentro works, but also to connect with local artists to call upon the expertise of national and Los Angeles–based artists and scholars to engage audience members in panels, dialogues, speeches, and interactive events around diverse topics pertinent to the field. The nine tertulia events included:

- Harnessing the Power of YO—solo performance
- Performance & the Projected Image: Using Pre-Existing Video & Live Feed on Stage
- Translation & Presentation: ¿Por qué no en español?
- Exploring the Connection between Literature & Theatre: A Conversation and Book Signing with Sonia Nazario and Magdalena Gómez
- Activism in the Arts: A Life Journey (Dan Guerrero)
- The Art of Community-Engaged Theater
- Writing and Staging Stories of Violence
- Engendering Rebeldes: Exploring Radical Connections between Gender, Arts Leadership, Aesthetics and Organizational Models
- Celebrating Two California Ensembles: Culture Clash & El Teatro Campesino! Eighty Collective Years of Ensemble Work

Another concern for the Latino Theater Company, and for the field at large, was the issue of succession leadership. Recognizing the opportunities inherent in the festival, the company applied for and was awarded a grant from the Andrew W. Mellon Foundation to support an eight-week fellowship program that would host ten emerging arts leaders committed to careers as Artistic Directors. Through a rigorous application process, they selected ten fellows from across the country (Richard Azurdia, Mica García de Benavidez, Sylvia Blush, Arielle Brown, Adriana Gaviria, Alexandra Meda, David Mendizábal, Ricky Pak, Kinan Valdez, and Jecamiah Ybañez), who were instrumental in the success of the festival. Each fellow was assigned a company to shepherd through the festival and they also took the initiative to carve out space in the intensive schedule for artist-specific dialogues around aesthetics and the field at large. Additionally, each fellow led a diverse group of Encuentro artists through the process of creating a devised work.

The goal of these cross-company collaborations was to expose artists to a variety of artistic methodologies, culling from the approaches of the other participating artists in the festival. All artists, including non-performers, were divided into groups so that, as much as possible, they worked with people outside of their own company. Each group was issued an "inspiration packet," which included a news article, a song, a poem, and a piece of visual art related to a specific theme. Themes ranged from protests in Venezuela, to the drug cartels in Mexico, to immigration legislation in the United States, to the experience of women in prison, to name only a few. Throughout the month, these groups met during designated rehearsal periods and created a ten-minute response to their inspiration packet. The presentation of these devised works served as the closing performance of the Encuentro festival on November 9, 2014. The performance was also livestreamed via HowlRound TV and viewing parties were coordinated in Chicago and New York.

During the final weekend of the festival, the Latinx Theatre Commons produced their second National Convening. A concerted effort was made to make the convening as open as possible for participation to all who were interested. The convening, like the festival, was centered on the work. Conveners had an intense schedule mapped out for them that would allow them to see ten plays, and two readings/presentations of works in development. In addition, dedicated self-reflection sessions, a contemporary nod to the *autocríticas* of the TENAZ festivals, were planned so that each morning artists and conveners would gather to discuss the work they had seen the previous day.[25] With the arrival of 120 conveners, the LATC was once again reinvigorated with energy, and exciting conversations swirled in every corner.

LOS ANGELES LATINX THEATER *¡PRESENTE!*

In an effort to highlight the expansiveness of the Latinx Theater community in Los Angeles itself and to engage in a deeper dialogue with local artists, the selection committee extended the festival offerings to include off-site productions and two staged readings. As with all the other shows in the festival, the artists' schedules were accommodated to view all of these productions.

In addition to the host company's production of *Premeditation*, and Hindsight Productions' *Dreamscape*, Los Angeles was represented by productions with a wide range of aesthetic approaches and political concerns. For instance, CASA 0101 Theater's adaptation of *Julius Caesar* by William Shakespeare, directed by Robert Beltran, included a cast of professional and early-career Latinx actors. This classic play explores the human motivations behind the betrayal, assassination, and aftermath of Julius Caesar's death, which precipitated the end of the Roman Republic and the birth of the Roman Empire. Border issues continued to emerge through the work of Grupo de Teatro Sinergía/Frida Kahlo Theater's *Las Mujeres de Juárez/The Women of Juárez* written and directed by Rubén Amavizca-Murúra. Addressing the history of feminicide in the city of Juárez, this play is centered on the story of a mother searching for her missing daughter only to discover a web of misogyny and political corruption.

Testimonial performances were seen as solo and as community-devised pieces. CalArts Center for New Performance/Duende CalArts presented *Daughter of a Cuban Revolutionary*, a solo piece by Marissa Chibas, directed by Maria Kingsley. This tour de force zigzags through Chibas's own stories and key episodes in the history of her illustrious Cuban family amidst the Cuban Revolution and their subsequent migration to the United States. Cornerstone Theater's *Alisal* written by Juliette Carrillo, directed by Michael John Garcés, was developed with, for, and about the Alisal farm-working community in East Salinas, California.[26] *Alisal* tells the story of three generations of hard-working women, from the lettuce fields of 1963 to the present day, as they struggle to forge better lives and stronger bonds. And lastly, South Coast Repertory Theatre's *The Long Road Today* written by José Cruz González, directed by Armando Molina, was inspired by the stories and talent of more than a thousand Santa Ana residents. This large-scale, site-specific piece was presented as a staged reading with music. With no park in his neighborhood, Andrés plays ball in the street and chases it into tragedy. Two families and a community must confront the aftermath and take action to make change.

Ultimately, the festival explored avant-garde, community-based, ensemble-based, text-based, experimental, and autobiographical works. Adaptation and translation, whether from English to Spanish or from novels or poems to plays, became a technique and approach that was reflected in several of the festival offerings, thus reinforcing the variety of aesthetic and thematic choices of contemporary Latinx artists.

ENCUENTRO 2014: THE ANTHOLOGY

From its inception the LTC identified scholarship as a core value, and scholars have played an active role in all of the LTC's programming. A commons-based approach to Latinx Theater scholarship seeks to deepen and equalize the relationships between artists, companies, and scholars with the shared goal of advancing the field and documenting the ephemeral nature of the work and its tangible impact on communities and individuals. An example of this impulse can be seen in the Encuentro through the work of the Circle of Scholars.[27] The Latino Theater Company invited three local scholars whose work has been dedicated to the documentation and analysis of Latinx Theater to consider ways to honor and acknowledge the festival's place in the history of the Chicanx and Latinx Theater Movements. In the LATC's Vault, a vestige of the building's history as a bank in the early 1900s, Drs. Jorge Huerta, Tiffany Ana López, and Chantal Rodriguez created a gallery which honored the work of Latinx artists and scholars from the 1960s to the present. On prominent display was the timeline of Latinx Theater and Performance, collectively created by participants at the 2013 Boston Convening. In an act of collective scholarship, artists and audiences were encouraged to continue adding to the timeline by documenting their own contributions to the field. Additionally, archival production photos and programs were also displayed alongside published plays, anthologies, and volumes of scholarship on Latinx Theater. Ultimately, the Vault library became a space for collective reflection on where we as Latinx artists and scholars come from, and where we are going. The impulse to document and preserve our history also forms an act of resistance in the face of erasure from dominant narratives. This anthology lives within this trajectory and seeks not only to document this historic festival, but also to provide broader access to these works for students, artists, and scholars alike. While recent volumes such as *La Voz Latina: Contemporary Plays and Performance Pieces by Latinas* (2011) and *Goodman Theatre's Festival Latino: Six Plays* (2013) mark significant contributions to the field, the present anthology follows in the tradition of landmark publications which include a critical scholarship component such as *Out of the Fringe: Contemporary Latina/Latino Theatre and Performance* (2000), *Puro Teatro* (2000), and *Fronteras Vivientes: Eight Latina/o Canadian Plays* (2013).

Mirroring some of the central goals of the Encuentro festival, this anthology provides a snapshot of the festival and we, the coeditors, set about the task of curating a selection of plays that would highlight the festival's scope and exuberance. In the spirit of sharing the work itself, the process of curation began with discussion questions such as: Which works were already published elsewhere, thereby already enjoying circulation? Which pieces were ready for publication and production? While the issue of geographic diversity, one of the values of the Commons and the festival itself, was ever present in our minds, the realities of the submissions loomed large. Of the total Encuentro plays that made their way to the stage, five were from California, four were from the New York area, and the rest were spread from across the country. Admittedly, the selection of pieces for this anthology reflects an East and West Coast dominance: however, it is one that was reflected in the application pool and therefore the participating Encuentro companies themselves. Nevertheless, we recognize that many voices and approaches were not reflected in the festival, and are therefore also absent from this volume.

The six works anthologized here include: *Zoetrope: Part I*, written and directed by Javier Antonio González, produced by Caborca Theater (New York, New York); *Patience, Fortitude, and Other Antidepressants* by Mariana Carreño King, directed by Daniel Jáquez, produced by INTAR Theatre/Unit 52 (New York, New York); *Premeditation* by Evelina Fernández, directed by José Luis Valenzuela, presented by The Latino Theater Company (Los Angeles, California); *Dreamscape* written and directed by Rickerby Hinds, produced by Hindsight Productions (Riverside, California); *La Esquinita, U.S.A.* created by Rubén C. González, directed by Kinan Valdez, produced by El Teatro Campesino (San Juan Bautista, California); and *Aliens, Immigrants & Other Evildoers* written, performed, and directed by José Torres-Tama (New Orleans, Louisiana).

The pieces included in this anthology can be grouped into three general categories: solo pieces performed by their writers, a two-person piece centered on the experience of one character, and productions with a full cast. While *La Esquinita, U.S.A.* and *Aliens, Immigrants & Other Evildoers* are solo pieces, written and performed by their creators employing narrative structures that bridge personal experience grounded in our various communities, *Dreamscape* occupies the middle ground of centering on a biographical experience of a true historical instance with a second actor playing multiple roles. The full-length plays are *Premeditation*, *Zoetrope: Part I,* and *Patience, Fortitude, and Other Antidepressants.*

The first three pieces convey strong sociopolitical messages that address issues of racial/gender violence (*Dreamscape*), the ever-present U.S.-Mexico border politics (*Aliens*), and the recreation of the collective voice on an entire, now gentrified neighborhood (*La Esquinita, U.S.A.)* whose imprint surpasses time and space, much reminiscent of Mexican novelist Juan Rulfo's 1955 masterpiece, *Pedro Páramo*, in which the voices of the fictional town of Comala still murmur in the wind. These works also exhibit a wide range of aesthetic references, some from the visual/sound/dance experiences. *Dreamscape* embodies the choreographed story of one character's reenactment based on real-life events of her 1998 violent death at the hands of the Riverside, California, police, and it is reminiscent of Nilo Cruz's brilliant *Lorca in a Green Dress,* which reenacts the death of the famed Spanish poet at the hands of Franco fascists in 1936. As in *Lorca*, *Dreamscape*'s (post)dramatic action is a fait accompli from the beginning of the dramatic action; there is no plot tension to unravel, and all that is left is the retelling of a single event. *La Esquinita, U.S.A.*, while a tour de force solo piece, hails to the organizing principle of Thornton Wilder's canonic 1938 play, *Our Town*; and *Aliens, Immigrants & Other Evildoers* owes a tip of the hat to the seminal work of the paradigmatic Chicano *performero* Guillermo Gómez-Peña's *Border Brujo* of the 1990s.

On the other hand, the three full-length plays differ in significant ways, not only from the previously mentioned ones, but also from one another in format and aesthetics. Three unifying principles can be discerned in these: they weave their narrative threads around the common theme of marriage, they play with time, and their dramatic structures rely upon three types of visual arts traditions: the oil painting (*Patience, Fortitude, and Other Antidepressants*), the zoetrope (a pre-cinematic animation device that speeds up time to create the illusion of movement, in *Zoetrope: Part I*), and the Hollywood film noir tradition of the 1940s (*Premeditation*).

Patience, Fortitude, and Other Antidepressants centers on the dissatisfaction of a young, married woman with her police officer husband while she attempts to reclaim a sense of self through her paintings, which come to life in a similar way to Oscar Wilde's 1890 novel, *The Picture of Dorian Grey* (and later the 1945 Hollywood film), which entertains the notion of an alternate life of pleasure, the kind that deviates from standard mores. Unlike the Dorian Grey syndrome (the refusal to grow old), *Patience* shifts its message toward self-affirmation and independence of a young, traditional Latina character. Nevertheless, both pieces suggest escapism into an alternate reality to that of the quotidian and a suspension of time while engaged with the painting's images.

Likewise, *Zoetrope: Part I* shares the theme of marriage, but this time within a multi-generational scope that expands from 1951 to 1999, anchored in Puerto Rican history and its people's relationship to migrations back and forth to New York. It is a story made up of letters, themselves frozen in time, while the idea of the zoetrope offers the illusion of time passing. *Premeditation* centers on a middle-aged couple, jealousy and the ennui of a long-term marriage staged and costumed in the tradition of Hollywood, or as Evelina Fernández would have it, Chicano noir. *Premeditation* pays homage to Hollywood´s golden film era of the 1930s and 1940s, where strong female characters like Bette Davis, Joan Crawford, and Mexican stars such as María Felix and Katy Jurado played the gamut from the ironic, to the innocent, to the vindictive. The play self-consciously and successfully alludes to its Hollywood pedigree, and conveys—in high style—that appearances deceive and one evening can change the lives of four.

The six plays curated in this anthology offer a glimpse at the thematic, aesthetic sophistication, and variety of early twenty-first-century Latinx dramaturgy, one grounded in Latinx and American theater histories, yet not limited by it. By gathering six works presented during this singular event, alongside relevant critical essays for each, this anthology provides useful pedagogical and research tools. More importantly, it reaffirms the contribution of Latinx theater within the United States, as it updates and expands the archive of U.S. theater histories by filling a publication gap.

TO HONOR THE FULL BREADTH OF ENCUENTRO

It is essential to honor the full scope of the works that made up the festival, some of which share defining characteristics. For instance, there were several adaptations. Su Teatro's *Enrique's Journey*, written and directed by Tony García, was adapted from the Pulitzer-Prize-winning book by Sonia Nazario. *Enrique's Journey* depicts the contemporary odyssey of a Honduran boy who braves unimaginable hardship and peril to reunite with his mother in the United States. Pregones Theatre produced a stellar musical adaptation of Magdalena Gómez's poetic original *Dancing in My Cockroach Killers* with music composed by Desmar Guevara and directed by Rosalba Rolón. *Dancing in My Cockroach Killers* is an explosive mix of text, visuals, and live music based on Gomez's writings, delivering the rhythmic realism, humor, and hope found in her poetry. Characters face real life challenges and are openly inspired by friends, family, and Latino icons. Following the poetic vein, About Productions' *Properties of Silence*, written by Theresa Chavez, Rose Portillo, and Alan Pulner and directed by Teresa Chavez, revealed how poetry, science, and history spiral out of control as a contemporary Phoenix realtor, her pool contractor husband, and the famed seventeenth-century Mexican poet Sor Juana Inés de la Cruz meet in a multi-layered dreamscape.

Translated works included Tantai Teatro's *Agua a Cucharadas*, the Spanish translation of the 2012 Pulitzer-Prize-winning play, *Water by the Spoonful* by Quiara Alegría Hudes. Directed by Ismanuel Rodriguez, *Agua a Cucharadas* moves artfully from story to story unlocking an intimate portrait of both a family and the members of an online recovery community as they struggle with the harrowing consequences of addiction. Aurora Theater presented Karen Zacarías's *Mariela en el Desierto/Mariela in the Desert,* directed by Tlaloc Rivas. Performed in Spanish with English supertitles, the piece explores Mexico—its art, people, and history—through the isolated life of two celebrated Mexican painters after the death of their young son.

Border issues continued to surface. Borderlands Theater presented *Maria's Circular Dance* by Medardo Treviño, translated and directed by Eva Zorrilla Tessler, as a testimony to the violence in the U.S./Mexico border region. The play follows a Colombian migrant and her kidnapper during the Los Zetas drug cartel 2011 San Fernando massacre. Theater Mitu's poignant *Juárez: A Documentary Mythology*, directed by Rubén Polendo, is an artful portrait of a community in crisis. Drawn from research and interviews with citizens on both sides of the border, *Juárez* explores issues of gangs, cartels, corruption, NAFTA, feminicide, the

War on Drugs, fear, familial honor, mythology, and hope in this inventive theatrical work which maps the stories onto and through the bodies of the performers.

Finally, through absurdism and dazzling imagery, Teatro Luna's *Your Problem with Men*, written by Emilio Williams and directed by Alexandra Meda, dissects the expectations of modern women in a culture still clinging to patriarchal visions of love and marriage.

CONCLUDING THOUGHTS

As witnesses and participants in the event, it is the coeditors' most sincere hope that this anthology will provide a living document of a seminal event within Latinx and U.S. theater histories. This book is truly a collaborative effort, one that reflects brightly the spirit of a commons-based approach. All of the coeditors are active participants in the Latinx Theatre Commons steering and advisory committees, thus the perspectives and information offered here reflect the good fortune of being involved in this historic movement at the ground level. The works herein are a testimony of the wide range of thematic and artistic sophistication of Latinx theater and performance, and the power harnessed through commons-based collaborations.

NOTES

1. The coeditors note and support the emergence and evolution of the term "Latinx" in the U.S., as a gender-inclusive alternative to "Latina," "Latino," and "Latina/o" which acknowledges and makes room for people who are Trans, queer, agender, non-binary, gender nonconforming, or gender fluid. Even so, we acknowledge a lack of LGBTQ+ created and/or themed work in the Encuentro festival itself. Our aim is not to alter the history of the event in any way, but instead to acknowledge how the politics of Latinx self-identification have shifted in the years following the event. It is also important to note that the 2017 Encuentro de las Américas has replaced "Latina/o" with "Latinx" and included more LGBTQ+ created and themed work. The coeditors also respect individual contributors' choices regarding the use (or not) of Spanish accents and diacritical marks in proper names.
2. In January 2015, the LTC formally changed its name from the Latina/o Theatre Commons to the Latinx Theatre Commons.
3. Jorge Huerta, "Encuentro 2014: Moving Forward, Never Forgetting the Past," *Café Onda: Journal of the Latinx Theatre Commons*, November 2, 2014. Accessed September 12, 2016, http://howlround.com/encuentro-2014-moving-forward-never-forgetting-the-past.

4. Ibid.
5. In 1978, María Irene Fornés established the INTAR Hispanic Playwrights-in-Residence Laboratory where she would train many of the most widely produced Chicanx and Latinx playwrights. In 1986, José Cruz González founded the Hispanic Playwrights Project at South Coast Repertory in Costa Mesa, California. Later directed by Juliette Carrillo, this project held an annual playwriting festival in the summer that celebrated new works written by Latinx playwrights. In 1992, Los Angeles's Mark Taper Forum established the Latino Theatre Initiative, founded by José Luis Valenzuela and later codirected by Luis Alfaro and Diane Rodriguez. The project's aim was twofold: to diversify the audience base by offering programming that reflected the city's Latinx community and to grant access to young Latinx playwrights who reflected this diversity.
6. Michael Wright, *Playwriting at Work and Play: Developmental Programs and Their Processes* (Portsmouth, N.H.: Heinemann, 2005), xii.
7. Lisa Portes, "Towards a Hub for Latina/o Theater Artists," *Café Onda: Journal of the Latinx Theatre Commons*, November 1, 2013. Accessed September 12, 2016, http://howlround.com/towards-a-hub-for-latinao-theater-artists.
8. Ibid.
9. David Emmes quoted in Mike Boehm, "SCR disbands Latino showcase," *Los Angeles Times*, August 25, 2004. Accessed September 12, 2016, http://articles.latimes.com/2004/aug/25/entertainment/et-boehm25.
10. Caridad Svich, "Who Designates Arrival? As Latino Theatre Enters a New Phase, Its Playwrights and Practitioners Assess Their Evolution and Future," *American Theatre Magazine* 22, no. 4 (April 2005): 58–63.
11. HowlRound as an organization did not exist at this time, but was housed at Arena Stage as part of the American Voices New Play Institute. HowlRound emerged as an autonomous organization two months later when it moved to Emerson College.
12. Brian Eugenio Herrera, *The Latina/o Theatre Commons 2013 National Convening: A Narrative Report* (Boston, Mass.: HowlRound, 2015), 1.
13. Anne García-Romero, "Latina/o Theatre Commons: Updating the U.S. Narrative," *Café Onda: Journal of the Latina/o Theatre Commons*, August 8, 2012. Accessed September 10, 2014, http://howlround.com/latinoa-theater-commons-updating-the-us-narrative.
14. The Boston convening was organized through a process of invitation, with a goal of assembling a wide-ranging group of Latinx theatermakers and scholars from across the country and at various points of their careers. Ultimately, a group of seventy-seven people attended the event. The convening also aimed to widen the circle and engage in specific discussions with Latinx regional alliances nationwide, and held livestreamed conversations as part of the convening with alliances in Dallas, Miami, Los Angeles, New York, and Chicago. While all participants were called upon to attend as delegates of their respective theater communities, it is important to note that the process of invitation raised legitimate concerns about exclusivity and exclusion within the Latinx Theatre Commons. For a detailed account of this convening, please see Brian Herrera's *The Latina/o Theatre Commons 2013 National Convening: A Narrative Report.*
15. Ibid.
16. Latinx Theatre Commons, accessed December 16, 2018, http://howlround.com/latina/o-theatre-commons.

17. For a history of the LTC and a list of upcoming projects please visit http://howlround.com/latinx-theatre-commons.
18. "Digital Library of the Commons," Indiana University, accessed February 1, 2016, dlc.dlib.indiana.edu.
19. Frank Van Laerhoven and Elinor Ostrom, "Traditions and Trends in the Study of the Commons," *International Journal of the Commons* 1, no. 1 (2007): 3–28.
20. P. Carl, interview by Teresa Marrero, October 6, 2015.
21. Latino Theater Company, "Encuentro 2014 Festival Application and Guidelines," Latino Theater Company Archives, 2014.
22. Abigail Vega, "How a Commons Becomes a Selection Committee: 2017 Encuentro de las Américas," *Café Onda: Journal of the Latinx Theatre Commons*, August 1, 2017.
23. The month-long residency proved problematic for the overall applicant pool, and limited applications from companies whose membership work full-time elsewhere. The 2017 Encuentro reduced the festival to three weeks.
24. The decision to expand the number of participating companies from ten to nineteen was rooted in the desire to include as many companies as possible, and to highlight the diversity of Latinx theater in Los Angeles itself.
25. *Autocrítica* is the Spanish word for self-reflection or criticism. Philosophically, the notion is grounded in the Marxist dialectical praxis of thesis, antithesis, and synthesis. It came to Chicanx theater through the strong influence of post-Revolutionary Cuban theater and the New Latin American Theater movement starting in the 1960s.
26. *Alisal* was adapted from Carrillo's 2013 play, *Plumas Negras*, produced by Cornerstone Theatre Company.
27. Additional examples of the integral relationship between scholarship and the LTC is Brian Herrera's documentation of the 2013 Boston Convening and the scholar pairings for the El Fuego Initiative and *Café Onda*.

BIBLIOGRAPHY

Berry, David. "The Commons." *Free Software Magazine*. February 21, 2005. Accessed May 10, 2016. http://freesoftwaremagazine.com/articles/commons_as_ideas/.

Boehm, Mike. "SCR disbands Latino showcase." *Los Angeles Times*. August 25, 2004. Accessed September 12, 2016. http://articles.latimes.com/2004/aug/25/entertainment/et-boehm25.

Carl, P. Interview by Teresa Marrero. October 6, 2015.

"Digital Library of the Commons," Indiana University. Accessed February 1, 2016. dlc.dlib.indiana.edu.

García-Romero, Anne. "Latino/a Theater Commons: Updating the US Narrative." *Café Onda: Journal of the Latinx Theatre Commons*. August 8, 2012. Accessed September 10, 2014. http://howlround.com/latinoa-theater-commons-updating-the-us-narrative.

Hardin, Garret. "The Tragedy of the Commons." *Science* 162, Issue 3859 (1968): 1243–48.

Herrera, Brian Eugenio. "Evanescence: Three Tales of the Recent Queer Theatrical Past," *Theatre Topics* 26, Issue 1 (2016): 47–51.

Herrera, Brian Eugenio. *The Latina/o Theatre Commons 2013 National Convening: A Narrative Report*. Boston, Mass.: HowlRound, 2015.

Huerta, Jorge. "Encuentro 2014: Moving Forward, Never Forgetting the Past." *Café Onda: Journal of the Latinx Theatre Commons*. November 2, 2014. Accessed September 12, 2016. http://howlround.com/encuentro-2014-moving-forward-never-forgetting-the-past.

Latino Theater Company. "Encuentro 2014 Festival Application and Guidelines." Latino Theater Company Archives, 2014.

Portes, Lisa. "Towards a Hub for Latina/o Theatre Artists." *Café Onda: Journal of the Latinx Theatre Commons*. November 1, 2013. Accessed September 12, 2016. http://howlround.com/towards-a-hub-for-latinao-theater-artists.

Rodríguez, Chantal. "Living the Politics of *teatro* in Los Angeles: An Interview with Diane Rodriguez." *Latin American Theatre Review* 43, no.1 (2009): 143–49.

Svich, Caridad. "Who Designates Arrival? As Latino Theatre Enters a New Phase, Its Playwrights and Practitioners Assess Their Evolution and Future." *American Theatre Magazine* 22, no. 4 (April 2005): 58–63.

Tomás Ybarra-Frausto Papers. Benson Latin American Collection. University of Texas Libraries, the University of Texas at Austin.

Valdez, Luis. *Luis Valdez Early Works: Actos, Bernabé, Pensamiento Serpentino*. Houston, Tex.: Arte Público Press, 1994.

Van Laerhoven, Frank and Elinor Ostrom. "Traditions and Trends in the Study of the Commons." *International Journal of the Commons* 1, no. 1 (2007): 3–28.

Vega, Abigail. "How a Commons Becomes a Selection Committee: 2017 Encuentro de las Américas." *Café Onda: Journal of the Latinx Theatre Commons*. Aug. 1, 2017.

Wright, Michael. *Playwriting at Work and Play: Developmental Programs and Their Processes*. Portsmouth, N.H.: Heinemann, 2005.

ENCUENTRO

LA ESQUINITA, U.S.A.

Rubén C. González

Production photograph copyright © Salvador "Pocho" Sanchez

CRITICAL INTRODUCTION

Jorge Huerta

Since the birth of El Teatro Campesino (ETC) in 1965, Chicanx dramaturgy has focused on the working classes: people on the lowest rung of the economic ladder. Indeed, the original members of El Teatro Campesino were actual farmworkers, fighting for a union alongside Cesar Chavez and Dolores Huerta. From those humble beginnings ETC went on to inspire a national Chicano Theater Movement with *teatros* from the West Coast to the Midwest. A generation later, Rubén C. González became an Artist-in-Residence with ETC, where he wrote *La Esquinita, U.S.A.* This one-man play was first produced by ETC in 2010 featuring González under the direction of Kinan Valdez, then producing artistic director of El Teatro Campesino.[1] This play is a testament to the Chicanx Theater Movement's continuing commitment to theater and performance that exposes the struggles of marginalized peoples everywhere.

La Esquinita is "Every-town, U.S.A.," a microcosm of the global economy's devastating effects on the working classes. The performance of *La Esquinita, U.S.A.* at the Encuentro 2014 was a tour de force by the actor/playwright. I can still remember the magic in the room as we watched González transform, shifting between ages, genders, and nationalities; his voice changing in pitch, timbre, accent, and tone. The beauty of the writing is in the fact that each character speaks distinctly. In creating a one-person play, the actor, director, and designers are challenged to make these transformations understandable. Thus, it is important that the reader use their imagination as the narrator, Lencho, shifts into distinct personages. Try to visualize Lencho's transformations into the nine other characters he will embody as he changes right before the audience's eyes with a scarf, a cap, a shell necklace, a back pack, etc. Like the earliest Chicanx theater, this play is very portable, employing found objects to define a character or setting.

Because this piece is written to be played by one actor, it is crucial to pay close attention to the stage directions. And "listen" carefully to the sounds that underscore each transformation: street sounds, music, barrio noises, etc. To enhance the reading experience the reader might listen to some of the songs and music indicated in the script in order to help "hear" each character's musical backdrop. You, the reader, are the actor, director, set, costume, and prop designer. Most importantly, listen to the drumbeat of your and the characters' hearts.

This play is an actor's dream, emphasizing the importance of professional training. González has an impressive resume of training and experiences. When I asked what influences determined his acting style he told me, "As a Mexican, when I went to these Anglo institutions like Circle in the Square Theatre School in New York, I found myself stiffening up when I was asked to 'put it into the words,' but I was thinking, 'I'm Mexican, we talk with our whole bodies.' That was a fine-tuning lesson I learned."[2] Another important influence was working with Kinan Valdez and the Teatro Campesino ensemble members. In the actor's words, "Teatro helped me get into my body." The Teatro's legendary physical theater could be seen in González's wonderfully versatile use of body language.

In terms of his creative process, the playwright says, "I do not have a specific method. I am inspired by those who struggle to exist but are constantly going toward the light. Those who are on the margins/periphery." All artists can look for inspiration in the work of other artists, other art forms. When I asked him what were his other aesthetic influences, he told me that the iconic trio, Culture Clash, was one such inspiration for him. He saw *Bowl of Beings* at the Los Angeles Theatre Center in the 1980s and says, "It was the first professional play I had ever seen and I saw myself in them. I saw Latino actors talking about things that I was interested in." In the ensuing years González worked with a variety of directors and theater companies. He developed his first one-man show, *Diary of a Mad Mexican*, in 1999 and continued developing his playwriting voice which led to *La Esquinita, U.S.A.*

González creates his characters in a very individual way. In his words, "To be honest, my process is supernatural in some ways. I honestly have voices that speak to me and I write them down. They sort of speak through me." And when you witness the actor in performance, the characters, do, indeed, speak through him. Most writers will tell you that they hear voices and those voices become living human beings. When a Native American man asked him where he "got" these characters, González relates, "I answered him as I've answered you. I told him I was crazy. He chuckled and said, 'No, you are not crazy. In my culture what you have is a gift. You are a storyteller.' I guess I am not crazy."

This play is in the tradition of centuries of storytelling; an art form that is truly universal. Indeed, the spoken word preceded the written text as the earliest peoples related their histories, their truths through myths and re-creations of extraordinary events. Lencho is the story teller in this piece who invites us into his little corner of the world, a little town called "La Esquinita." He speaks directly to the audience, breaking the fourth wall from the beginning of his narrative, eager to relate Daniel's story. Daniel and his circle of friends (and enemies) are young and there is little hope in this town that has been shattered since the main form of employment moved to China. Like so many young people without other prospects Daniel is trying to finish high school so he can enlist in the Marines. His three older brothers have been killed in Desert Storms I and II. Sadly, when Lencho introduces us to Daniel, the young man is at the peak of his meth high—the scourge of so many communities.

Just before he transforms into Daniel, Lencho tells us, "Daniel was standing on the threshold between light and darkness," recalling Aeschylus's trilogy, *The Oresteia*, in which we follow the mythical characters as they go from the darkness of blood feud to the court of law; a metaphor for civilization's journey from the darkness into the light. In this play, however, justice means "just us," and the Law is represented by two despised policemen, one African American, the other Mexican American. Neither is a friend of the people we will encounter.

The characters seem mired in darkness with little hope of finding any light. What they do have is a sense of humor amidst all the darkness. From the beginning, comedy has been an essential part of the Teatro Campesino's aesthetic. Luis Valdez told an interviewer in 1967, " . . . we use comedy because it stems from a necessary situation—the necessity of lifting the morale of our strikers . . ."[3] In like manner, González has constructed his play of almost tragic circumstances with comic relief. Laughter is one of the few weapons the disenfranchised can use against their oppressors and the reader should not be afraid to laugh.

The young people's language was inspired by high school students González had taught. He listened to his students and transported their language and mannerisms into the young people he portrays. The older characters also have their distinct ways of speaking. The non-bilingual audience member might not understand some of the code-switching but body language or a prop can "translate" the term. So pay close attention to every word on the page as you "listen" and learn from these extraordinary characters, archetypes, really, who will take you on a journey of flight and fantasy. And miracles. Although the characters are fictional, González has created real people, giving voice to the voiceless.

NOTES

1. Kinan Valdez, son of Lupe and Luis Valdez, became the Teatro Campesino's Producing Artistic Director in 2009. His first major project was launching the ETC Teatro Lab in 2009 in order to give affiliated artists and ensemble members the resources to develop new works that re-imagined/re-defined what "the work" of "El Teatro Campesino" could be. *La Esquinita, U.S.A.* (2010) was the second "Teatro Lab" production developed through that initiative.
2. All quotes from Mr. González are from an email he sent me dated May 1, 2017.
3. Beth Bagby, "El Teatro Campesino: Interview with Luis Valdez," *Tulane Drama Review* 11 (Summer 1967): 77.

PRODUCTION HISTORY

La Esquinita, U.S.A. was developed at El Teatro Campesino in San Juan Bautista, California, under the New Works Lab in April 2010. It was directed by Kinan Valdez. All the characters were played by Rubén C. González.

La Esquinita, U.S.A. was produced at the Arizona Theatre Company in association with El Teatro Campesino in Tucson, opening on January 14, 2017. It was directed by Kinan Valdez, assistant directed by Alex Meda, with set design by Regina Garcia, lighting design by Michael Oesch, and sound design by Anahuac Valdez. Jennifer Smith was the production manager, and the production stage manager was Glenn Bruner. Again, all the characters were played by Rubén C. González.

CHARACTERS

Lencho, a shape-shifting, time-traveling narrator

Ravi, an Indian mystic

Daniel, a young man finding his way

Wilo, a revelation

Tweeker, an illusion

Skinny Black, a scapegoat

Sunshine, a portal between worlds

Mr. Jefferson, a good neighbor

Yolanda, a woman's worth

Grace, a peace within

PLACE

A bus stop corner and places in between.

TIME

The here and now.

[*Meditative music plays as the lights rise on a bus stop bench. Behind it is an abandoned tire factory. Litter is strewn all around. Old tires have been left in places. There is a shopping cart filled with knickknacks. A baseball cap hangs from the handle of a trashcan next to a bus stop sign. An old pair of jumper cables hang from a tire.* LENCHO, *in a flagger's vest and dark sunglasses and holding a trash picker, enters from inside a gate that closes off the bus stop from the abandoned factory. He surveys the place, then pulls out a bag and begins picking up trash.*]

LENCHO: We're here on a corner of a tiny town called La Esquinita, U.S.A. Land of the free, home of the brave, and all kinds of other *pedo.* A *pueblito* stuck between the here and now, the always and forever.

[*He picks up a child's worn teddy bear.*]

Tucked in the recess of your *macetas.* Ring a bell?

[*A tingsha bell rings.*]

No? *Pues,* OK. How 'bout . . .

[*He picks up another child's worn teddy bear that is dressed in an American flag.*]

La Esquinita, U.S.A.! The Big Red White and Blue! Where, who cares, what's next, who's winning? And all that jazz . . .? No? *Pues,* OK again. *Mira.*

[*He points toward the sky.*]

Above us we have *El Cielo. Está bien cuacha.* A melting sun.

Stars burned out for years hanging like wishes once filled with wonder. Below us, *La Tierra.* Crust. Mantle. Core. Well, that's after you get past all the wino piss, the doggie doodoo, and . . .

[*With a tissue from his pocket,* LENCHO *picks up a used heroin needle.*]

the *carga* needles.

[*He tosses the needle into the trash bag.*]

You see, the *barrio*'s been here throughout the illusion of time. Before childhood wonder became a program of good against evil. Before wars built walls out of ideas.

[*He uses his trash picker as a machine gun and fires.*]

Pop! Pop! Pop! Before the Great Fall from the hands of Grace.

[*He puts the trash picker in a trash can and stops in Rodin's* The Thinker *pose.*]

A time of Stillness. Peace. Space. A time when I could just dance.

[*He rips off his flagger's vest with sass.*]

I wanted to be the brown swan.

[*He dances like a ballerina across the stage. He stops and addresses the audience jovially.*]

Just kidding. *Puro* just messing around. I wouldn't want you to imagine me in tights. Or a dance belt. Imagine a little *tanga* going up my *nalga*? Just kidding. Relax. So you still don't remember this place? I guess not.

[*He approaches the bench and points to the bus stop sign.*]

40A Red Line. La Esquinita, U.S.A. A once-booming town but now forgotten like so many others. *Que gacho, no?* My name's Lencho. I've been living here for . . . let's just say a millennium. And let's just say I'm a neighbor who helps where he can. A voice between the here and now, the always and forever. Between what is seen and not.

[*He whirls like a dervish and stands in a pool of twirling light and becomes* RAVI.]

RAVI: A shape-shifting time traveler if you will. Your slum dog millionaire.

[*The light fades as* LENCHO *reappears.*]

LENCHO: So, let's go back and forth through the illusion of time.

[*He pulls out a cigarette and lighter.*]

Mind if I smoke?

[*He tries to light a cigarette. The lighter is useless.*]

Maybe it's better. Besides, the fire marshal may get all *encabronado* because the reality is we're in a theater not La Esquinita, U.S.A. But who knows. Maybe yes? Maybe no? Just play along. You paid for a show then that's what you're gonna get, a show! *Mira*!

[*He grabs his trash picker and points to the abandoned building.*]

Over here in this abandoned building is where the WorldMart Megastore promised to come and rescue the unemployed. Well, it's still just a vacant building filled with empty promises. Before that, it was home to the Thompson Tire Factory! A company that many *familias*, black and brown, had followed here many years ago. They were promised their old jobs, new homes, and a community. And they did keep their promise but not for long. You see, a couple of years after they moved here the Thompson's decided to move to China. That's where they assembled most of the products that were then supposed to be sold at the WorldMart Megastore where their motto was, "America First!" Don't you remember the commercial with the old white man in the blue smock? Damn, we forget so easily in this town. Well, the broken promise became La Esquinita, U.S.A.

[LENCHO *crosses to the bus stop.*]

Infrastructure got all *trasquilado.* The busses ran late and they still do. Hospitals went outta whack after the big business jack and there were two *placas* left to patrol all the locos who were running rampant. There was Cockeyed Ramirez the Mexican cop who hated Mexicans. It was tough being him. Imagine being Cockeyed and Mexican? That's a tough hill to climb. And a white cop named Whitey. *Serio pedo.* That was his real name. Need I say more?

[*He crosses to the abandoned tire with the jumper cables hanging from it. An oldie but goodie plays.*]

Now that abandoned *ranfla* over there . . . the lowrider in the ditch . . . that belonged to Wilo Juarez. A neighborhood *tecato.* A hype.

And a favorite of police abuse. A societal ill socially outcast in a town full of outcasts. One big happy *familia.*

[*He uses his trash picker as a heroin needle.*]

Well, Wilo dropped out. Doped up. Pushed to the outer limits.

[*He "shoots up" then begins to nod off.*]

Pushed to that place that makes a *vato* just wanna say, "forget it! I'm done!"

[*A hip-hop tune perks* LENCHO *up and out of the heroin effect.*]

Wilo's best friend was Skinny Black. Now Skinny was one of them *tilangudo* black *vatos* that runs with nothing but Mexicans. Now some homies called him Twizzler cuz he was skinny like a black piece of licorice. But he moved like a weasel. He was always on the lookout. Always on the run. Like scapegoats always have to be.

[*We hear the faint sound of men working on a chain gang.*]

Now Skinny Black, he lived on the other side of the railroad tracks. That's where most of the blacks had moved to since this town went bust. This once close-knit black-brown town had been divided by desperation. But like in all divisions . . .

[LENCHO *kneels and sprinkles seeds into the cracked concrete.*]

the cracks in the earth leave room for seeds of lost hope to fall through . . . giving them a chance to bloom.

[*A small weed grows from the cracks.* LENCHO *points toward a house.*]

Like that broke down *chante* over there with the barber's chair on the porch. Does the barber's chair ring a bell? You don't remember Mr. Jefferson our local barber? He gave the best fades in town. Five bucks a pop. He'd been living there for years and he refused to join the black exodus. Sixty-six years old. Four tours in Nam. Crazy *viejo.* Said he had nothin' to come home to so he kept re-enlisting until he did. Finally one time on leave he got his lady preggers and they gave birth to an angel. Yolanda. But I'll talk about Yolanda later.

[*Upbeat* conjunto *music plays. He dances joyfully, using the trash picker as his dance partner.*]

Now if you go down this road, 'bout six miles, you'll come to the White House! Actually, it's just a little white *chante*. That's where the Rodriguez's lived. An immigrant *familia* whose children signed the papers . . . to get their papers. Good old Uncle Sam's bait and switch! Four sons. The eldest killed in Iraq! Two more in Afghanistan. There was no saving Pvt. Rodriguez.

[*He dips the trash picker, abruptly ending the dance. Darkness falls as dissonant music plays.*]

Their youngest, Daniel. American born. He was chomping at the bit to join his brothers.

[*He grabs the baseball cap that hangs on the trash can handle.*]

Trying to find a way out of this graveyard—

[*He digs his trash picker into the trash can like a stake into a grave and pulls out a beat-up backpack from within.*]

just to step into another! He was searching for the truth! This is his story. Your story. Our story. An American tale. Daniel was standing at the threshold between light and darkness. Daniel. Your son. Your brother. Your friend. An after-thought!

[DANIEL, *at the peak of his meth high, appears on the bench. Gangsta rap plays in his ears. He spots* LENCHO *but then sees a friend passing by.* DANIEL *pulls out a cigarette.*]

DANIEL: Yo, spaz! Whaddup, homie? Gotta light? You neither? Na foo. Just waiting for the ghetto caddy. You know how we ride. Na, I ain't with G no more. Lucky can have my sloppy seconds. A'ight, foo. Catch you later. Peace!

[*He looks suspiciously at* LENCHO.]

Yo, Mister. Got a light? Yeah, that's what I thought. Nobody's got a light around here.

[*He reads an incoming text with disgust.*]

"I love you"? For real, G? Whatever!

[*He escapes back to his music. Suddenly, his batteries lose power. He pulls out an antiquated CD player from his pocket.*]

Damn! Nothing works around this broke-ass place! Yo, Mister. Got any batteries? That's what I thought.

[DANIEL *dejectedly shoves the CD player in his backpack. His cell phone rings. He still has a flip phone. He answers.*]

Yo, Toker. Yeah, Toker. I got the cash. I'm on my way to get it right now. I'll call you. Later. Coo. Later.

[*He hangs up. A stomach pang hits him. His phone rings again.*]

DANIEL: *Ama. Esperando.* What do you think? The bus is late again. *Ama, necesito mi dinero!* But it's my money, *Ama*! I'm not gonna tell you where I got it. *Mira*, if you don't give me the money, I'm gonna make that phone call! *Ya sabes* what I told you! So you better believe me. *Ama! Ama!*

[*He tries to call his mom but there's no reception.*]

Stupid phone!

[*He angrily puts his phone in his pocket. He paces like a caged animal. He opens up to the only person he can,* LENCHO.]

My parents are whack, Mister! My mom was creepin' 'round my room and found my *feria*. I made that money, you know! You do what you gotta do to make *feria* around here, *que no*? Just cuz my dad's been laid off they have to take my money? I'll help out, you know, but damn, that's whack! There's this guy Toker—forget it. That ain't even the beginning. I just found out my lady, G, cocked this homie, Lucky, from my class. Lucky used to be my homie, too, but I don't care! I only stayed with her cuz I felt bad cuz I was the first one to cock her. And no one can ever claim that shit. I landed on the moon. Planted my flag!

[*He grabs his aching head. He goes to the bench.*]

Damn, my eyes feel like they're gonna pop out of my head! I been all tweeked out since class today, Mister, and my stomach was doing donuts but I couldn't use the restroom to take a *masa* cuz my teacher Mr. Perez was on to me. Said he'd call my P.O. if I did it again but I had to you know. Cuz I been tryna make up these ten credits. That's like thirty packets of work. That's when I found out my lady G was with Lucky. Threw me for a loop so I spun. I just laid on my bed staring up at the ceiling like a zombie. But it was like a blessing, Mister, cuz check it out.

[*He takes out work packets from his backpack with pride.*]

I finished them packets, yo! Been up for three nights all tweeked out in pookieville but productive. And I checked all the work myself and it was all correct! So you see. It was for a good reason. My teacher Mr. Perez didn't like it when I finally told him how I did it but I had to you know cuz I felt sorta shameful cuz he's a'ight . . .

[*He begins to pace around, worried and lost as to what to do next.*]

but I know he ain't gonna call my P.O. cuz he's like a hippy or something. Makes us do yoga. I'm glad I'm gettin' outta here. Judge already told me I'm going to state if I don't graduate cuz I ain't no kid no more. Juvee ain't nothing compared to state. State's like a zoo. I don't even want to think about it.

[*He goes back to the bus stop bench and sits on the edge.*]

I just wanna graduate and join the Marines like my brothers did.

[*The reality of his brothers killed in war hits him like a ton of bricks.*]

I mean, they got killed and stuff, you know . . .

[*He springs to his feet, pushing off the weight of his pain.*]

but at least they went out in a blaze! Ain't nothin' left for me 'round here, Mister. And that's the truth!

[*Lights shift as a melodic tune plays.* LENCHO *whistles for his lost dog.*]

LENCHO: Truth! Truth! Truth! Come here, boy! Has anybody seen the Truth?

[*He runs to a trash can and calls into it.*]

Truth! Truth! Truth! Are you down there . . . down there . . . down there?

[*He pulls* DANIEL*'s hat from inside the trash can.*]

Ah, the truth. That illusive little thing in a world fed by misinformation. Untruths. Little white lies. Around here they were fed *La Carga!* Smack! Youngsters like Daniel, the pookie.

[DANIEL*'s hat becomes a pipe as* LENCHO *prepares to smoke it.*]

Crystal! Speed! Crank! A few rocks of cleaning products to pollute the mind. So they could not understand those who came to teach them.

[*He takes a drag from the pipe.*]

They saw the world through smokescreens of fear called goggles.

Some wore the pookie goggles. Anger goggles. Money goggles. War goggles. Hate goggles. Truth had become a mythological creature. Like Daniel's contorted vision.

[*Music fades.* DANIEL *notices* WILO *across the street.*]

DANIEL: Look at that foo Wilo over there begging. Someone should just blast that worthless tecato. [*Yelling to* WILO] Dirty Hype!

Nobody cares anymore, Mister. They blast foos like Wilo all the time. You know the hood. Your glock is all you got. Just like the "three hundred."

[*He looks around for suspicious activity.*]

The "three hundred," Mister. You know, the Spartans? Don't you know anything? Read a book. Watch a movie. Educate yourself. My teacher Mr. Perez has been teaching us 'bout the Spartans how they were conquering everywhere and these one Athenian foos who just kicked it and talked all day long like a bunch of sissies. But the Spartans, damn! They were trained to be warriors, Mister. Since they were little kids. Like little kids. And their parents couldn't do nothin' about it. Well maybe pray for their kid to be born with a messed up foot or something so the army wouldn't take them. Imagine praying for your own kid to be born with a messed up foot? But that's the way it was and that's the way it is. Foos like Wilo . . . they woulda been blasted just for being born messed up!

[*He suffers another stomach pang but fights it off.*]

Anyways, these other foos were called the Athenians. They were like the opposite of the Spartans. They were taught like art and philosophy. Kinda like thinking and talking all day long. Basically like when you blaze it but without having to blaze it. Kinda like rich people who have all that time and money to sit around and talk about mad shit. How do you expect to have time and money around here and just sit around and talk mad shit?

[*His stomach pain subsides for the moment.*]

Check out this scandalous thing, Mister. My teacher Mr. Perez did like this vote in class. He wanted to see who wanted to be a Spartan or who wanted to be Athenian. Like who wanted to fight all day long and who wanted to just kick it. And you know what they voted? Even the ladies, Mister! The ladies voted just like the homies did. They all voted to be Spartans. Can you believe that? Scandalous! This one foo in my class, they call him Animal cuz he's a huge sick foo. His dad hates him at home so he pounces on everyone at school. And Animal was like—

[*He jumps up on the bench with excitement.*]

"Forget that, Mister! I woulda been a Spartan! Bam! Cuz they were taxing bitches and they had all the spears and whatever!" And the whole class was like, yeah, yeah. They gave him a standing ovation, Mister! You know why? Cuz he was telling the truth! And you know it's the truth! And you know they got all the ladies too cuz that's what the ladies like. Man, those Spartans were rollin' . . .

[*He daydreams of Spartanhood.*]

Wait. Wait. Wait. Before you start getting all Obi-Wan Kenobi. Check this funny shit. There was these two rocker foos and an emo in the back of the class that voted to be Athenians. They were like, "We'd rather just chill with the homies, smoke some bomb-ass herb and do lines all day." I was like, damn. That don't sound too bad, *que no*? Just kicking it with homies all day long. Smoking some bomb herb and doing some mean o' lines.

[*Another stomach pang hits him.*]

Who, me? I voted to be a Spartan, Mister. I ain't got time for philosophy. Power talks and bull walks. The police can legally kill someone and get away with it. They run this town! Why are we on top, huh? U.S.A.! U.S.A.! U.S.A.! And all that? More fire power. Am I not right? You know I'm right. The Big Warden's got us all handled! And there ain't no going back! We've been studying all this in my history class and I was down in the hole all tweaked out and studying about the Spartans—I studied about the Americans, the Chinese, Russians, Arabs, Jews! It's all the same thing! I got the theories.

[*He leans in toward* LENCHO *to explain his conspiracy theory.*]

Peace ain't got nothin' on war. God has always been ruled by the killers and killed by the rulers. So I said forget it! I voted Spartans! Besides, I ain't got time for yoga! Why twist up my body if my brain's already in knots?

[*A tingsha bell rings followed by Indian sitar music as* LENCHO *whirls like a dervish into a pool of spinning light.*]

RAVI: Daniel had bought into the game of cat and mouse. He couldn't see that these wars were a fight for people's souls so I had to try and get Daniel's back. So I told him the story . . . of *Americo*.

[*Lights shift as the music fades.*]

LENCHO: Now *Americo* was a legend. We used to call *Americo* "Tree," cuz he was a "huge sick foo." Kinda like that Animal cat in Daniel's class. Well, Tree used to pick on everyone. He would make homies fight just to keep them mad at each other. He would even eat their food. No, *Serio*. He'd walk right into their *chantes*, make himself a bologna sangwich . . . walk into the middle of the street . . . stop traffic and eat his sangwich.

[TREE *eats his sandwich as he scans the neighborhood.*]

Kept the barrio in fear. That was his power. Until one day. All the homies he'd make fight got together and came up with a plan. The homies hid behind some bushes while this one *vato* Sleepy called out Tree.

[SLEEPY *appears from behind an old tire.*]

SLEEPY: *Orale*, Tree. Today I cut you down! Sleepy's awake!

[SLEEPY*'s eyes open wide. He's cross-eyed.*]

LENCHO: Nobody had ever seen his eyes before. Sleepy was cross-eyed. Well, Tree, he just dropped his sangwich. Looked over at Sleepy . . . and slowly made his way toward him. When he got close enough . . . Sleepy let out the *chifle.*

[SLEEPY *whistles, moving in slow motion.*]

In slow motion. Just like that. That's when the others came out from behind the bushes and jumped Tree.

[SLEEPY *lifts the tire and begins pummeling the imaginary* TREE, *who lies on the ground.*]

They cut him down. Uprooted him. They beat him up so bad . . .

[LENCHO *spins the tire in revolutions.*]

. . . he couldn't walk across the street anymore. No more free bologna. All his power, gone like that!

[*The tire stops spinning. Lights shift into a twirling pattern accompanied by Indian sitar music.*]

RAVI: Funny thing was, this is when *Americo* found his peace. He couldn't hide behind the fear that manifested into his punches.

[RAVI *bows to the audience respectfully, fist to open hand. An oldie but a goodie tune begins to play as the twirling lights shift.*]

LENCHO: The heat continued to beat down on Daniel. It was getting hotter and hotter. Almost to the point of burning out. This is when Wilo showed up.

[*He goes to the jumper cables and raises them to the audience.*]

The hype. The *Tecato*. A good time for a jump start.

[*Lights shift. A trembling* WILO *appears with jumper cables around his neck.*]

WILO: You *vatos* wanna buy some jumpers? They work good. I could use the *feria*. Hard times. OK. That's alright. That's alright.

[*He appears to notice* LENCHO *and* DANIEL *at the bus stop.*]

Orale, Lencho, I didn't even recognize you. You look good. What's up, little homie. Been out a month. No. I left *la carga* in the pen. Check it out?

[WILO *shows* LENCHO *the fading track marks on his arm.*]

I'm cleaning up. I mean just a little herb once in a while. Calm the shakes. Self-medicate. The hospitals won't help. But I don't wanna get into that right now cuz it gives me all willies. That's why you see me like this cuz I'm kicking it this time. *Si dios quiera. Te lo juro.*

[*Police sirens are heard.* WILO *tries to become invisible.*]

Trucha! Trucha! Act cool! Act cool!

[*The sirens fade in the distance.* WILO *reappears.*]

You think you leave the warden in the cage but them pig street wardens, Whitey and Ramirez, they don't let you forget. Check out my hands. That's like second degree.

[WILO *shows* LENCHO *and* DANIEL *his palms.*]

They pancaked me last night. They wouldn't let me take them off the car hood cuz Whitey kept beating me. And Skinny Black just ran off like a punk *chavala*. Thought we were homies. Thought we were tight but that's alright. He can stay on the other side of the tracks with the other *negros*. But I don't want to get into that right now. So you homies want the jumpers or not? Look, this is the *serio* truth. My lady, she's been sick at the *clínica* for two days and the doctors haven't seen her. You know, no cash, no Band-aids, right? So what do you say? Come on Lench, before the pigs come?

[*He sticks out his trembling hand. A tingsha bell denotes a coin deposited. His hand holds still a moment. The trembling returns.*]

Thanks, Lencho! Much appreciation. Hey, little homie. I'm gonna leave you the jumpers so you can give them to your *jefito* for the Father's Day!

[*He puts the jumper cables on bench then runs off with* DANIEL*'s bag.* DANIEL *gives chase then returns. He shouts at* WILO.]

DANIEL: I don't fight *tecatos*, I may get a disease!

[*He checks his backpack for his belongings. Everything is intact.*]

What did I tell you, Mister? Worthless! I'm telling you. Someone's gonna blast that worthless *tecato*. If a *negro* doesn't, one of his own will!

[DANIEL *begins to move around like a caged animal.*]

There's mad heat going down right now, Mister. It's a mad loot! People are scrambling for whatever. That's why we're blasting people all over the world cuz the world needs cleansing! Why not start here? Excess baggage taking up space!

[*He looks menacingly toward* WILO *as if he's going to shoot him.*]

Foos like Wilo . . . they just lie, steal, cheat, beg, and they always smell like piss! Pop!

[DANIEL *mimes shooting* WILO.]

Someone should just throw that worthless *tecato* into the empty factory and blow it up!

[*There is the sound of an explosion. The debris rains down as* DANIEL*'s hat flies through the air.* LENCHO *grabs it and cradles it tenderly. He places it on the bench, goes to the tall fence that surrounds the abandoned factory and touches it. He then turns to the audience.*]

LENCHO: Many years ago, a young man came from the other side of the *great wall.*

[*He gestures to the tall fence.*]

When he was a little boy, his father was a king. He had land, money. *Un ranchonón*. But then a war broke out caused by the grandfathers of those who had built the GREAT WALL. The war turned into a revolution and when the fighting was over, the boy's father found that he had been taken for everything. Pillaged. Time passed and the little boy grew up. And he realized the only thing he could do was to move closer to the man who had stolen his father's riches. That young man went from being the son of a king to cleaning toilets at the tire factory. That young man was Wilo's father. Well the tire factory decided to move here to La Esquinita. Brought all its workers. Promised them their old jobs, new homes, and a community. But then the factory closed down.

[*He closes the fence and is now standing behind it.*]

Wilo's father didn't know what to do. He couldn't find a job anywhere. It got so bad that he'd stand in front of the tire factory and just stare at it all day long. Empty. The same building Daniel wanted to throw Wilo into and ignite.

[*He comes out from behind the fence and stands by an old, beat-up chair.*]

One day, Wilo's father sat alone in his garage thinking about his own father. Wilo was just a boy then. A beautiful little baby boy.

[*He picks up the jumper cables as if they were a baby.*]

That day, Wilo's older brother picked him up and he took him into the garage, so they could call their father into the house. Their mother had just cooked their father's favorite meal to cheer him up.

[*He places the cables around his neck.*]

When the boys opened the door—

[*He kicks the chair and pulls the cables like a noose.*]

they were greeted by two legs dangling in the air. Wilo's father had hung himself. Wilo's mother was left with four children scrambling to exist in a place where you're worth your debt not your humanity. She never finished potty training Wilo. She had too much on her plate. Or not enough. Wilo grew up wetting his pants. Made fun of his whole life. A well-made hype.

[*He drops the jumper cables in the trash can. Lights up on Daniel's hat and backpack on the bench.*]

Daniel sat on the bench pondering this new information that began sucking the helium from his high. He began to drop. The "come-down." This is when Tweeker rolls up. Now, Tweeker is a different example of *barrio* negligence. A pure disregard for balance. A high, a pharmaceutical, a credit card, a savior, a delusion.

[*Lights up on* TWEEKER, *a dealer. He drives up in a car.*]

TWEEKER: Hey, Doggie. Wanna get high? Got some good shit here. Make you go, "Booya!" You'll fly high like a satellite. Like the kind that spies on you at night while you're thinking of all the crazy things going on in the world but that's why you got to get high, right? Tell you what I'm gonna do for you, right now!

[TWEEKER *gets out of his car. The sales pitch begins.*]

At this very moment, you gimme a ten spot, no coupon necessary, and I'll supersize sell you a radical superblast, dog! Make you forget your own name. Think of it as identity theft, only difference is your memory ripped you off but you won't remember even though it's your memory. Get it? You'll blank out. Think crazy and forget about the madness. And that's not all. This superblast will make you feel all tingly and no limpy side effects at all. Guaranteed!

[*He is receiving a message from the ether.*]

Whoa, I just went to that place you go to where you don't know what's next but you're right where you need to be because regardless of where you think you should be, you're never there. You're always here. [*Singing*] "Never there. You're never there. You're never ever, ever, there." Doggie! Did you know the universe is never ending? That means you're standing in the center all the time. Get it? The centah! You're never where you think you should be cuz you're always there. That's the secret! Where you're at is where you're at and this superblast can transport you just like that! Wait, Doggie! If you're in the center and

I'm in the center then I am you and you are me and whoa, Doggie, this just in! There can only be one center and this superblast will help you get there, guaranteed!

[*He produces another pill but there are no takers.*]

Nah? Well, suit yourself!

[TWEEKER *jumps in his car and speeds off. Lights shift.*]

LENCHO: Tweeker was off. Off his rocker. Off the charts. Off the axis and right back into Daniel's mind. Right back into that space where those around here looked for grace but could never find it cuz of the crutch of their addictions. The goggles they chose to look through were tweeked.

[DANIEL *looks out to where he last saw* TWEEKER *speed off.*]

DANIEL: He's gone, Mister. It's like he says some crazy things that, if you really listen to them, they make a whole lot of sense. I'm coming down, Mister.

[*He holds his aching stomach.*]

I should have scored off him. I don't wanna go home straight! It's kinda nice to light the pipe twenty-four-seven, spinning in heaven. Spinning so fast that the world goes right on by and I don't have to worry about nothing! Not my parents fighting about money or my lady getting cocked. Just high, you know. Exist like that foo who just left!

[*As if receiving a punch to his solar plexus,* DANIEL *takes a knee. A kaleidoscope of lights strike his body.*]

Disappear like sand from a hand

At that moment you realize

There was nothing left to hold on to.

Disappear like a song once sang

Like a cell phone ring that never rang

Like the pookie smoke long after the drag

Exist like that foo who just left

Who makes life a theft

Stealing it from mothers who've wept

Cuz their children distressed

Fathers under arrest and long been swept,

Up, up, up and away

Above the clouds and the flesh, where you mesh

alone in your own spin cycle

where you keep coming back

but never the same, it's all just a game.

[LENCHO *rises from* DANIEL*'s body and hovers over him. Like a referee in a boxing match, he begins giving* DANIEL *an eight count. The roar of a crowd is heard.*]

LENCHO: Daniel. A boy on a knee. A boy fighter taking an eight count. Dizzy from his cheap-ticket ride to a higher level. He couldn't see that his freedom was right then and there. That the center was everywhere and in everyone cuz it was in him.

[*A twirling pattern of light consumes him. Indian sitar music plays.*]

RAVI: This is the universal law of love that Daniel could not see because his vision was blurred. Body bruised. This is when Skinny Black showed up out of the blue.

[*Lights shift. A rap tune is heard as* SKINNY BLACK *peeks out from behind the bus stop bench.*]

SKINNY BLACK: Whaddup Lench? Yo, little homie. Y'all see Wilo around? He did? Right now, right now? Man! I been looking for that sucka all mornin'. All hell broke loose by the railroad tracks last night, Lencho. Is that what Wilo said, for real? I ain't run like no punk *chavala,* I'll tell you that much right now. Them pigs is tryin' to play us! Cockeyed Ramirez pulled me behind the old train depot where

Wilo couldn't see me. I had a gun in my mouth. Officer Whitey's tryna divide us cuz we the last of the Mohicans but we ain't gonna let no street wardens mess with us anymore. We been in chains too long! Look.

[*He jumps over from behind the bench.*]

Look. I risk it all comin' over here. *Eses* in their lowriders be chasing me down the block. Luckily, I lost them over on fourth street cuz I been workin' on my Jedi skills.

[*He gestures becoming invisible by swiping his hand over his face.*]

Invisible, dawg. Invisible. Now, I got some good news. My *'fita,* my moms, she just got a check in the mail. But it ain't no ordinary check cuz this ain't no ordinary day. Now, the check was for nine hundred and eleven dollars, dog. Nine-one-one. We're talking Emergency! Now nine plus one plus one equals eleven. Eleven! Eleven! That's downright synchronicity. Planetary alignment and sh—hold up!

[*He lies on the floor like a chameleon as a lowrider is heard passing by. As soon as it's gone, he swipes his hand across his face, gesturing his ability to become invisible.*]

Invisible, dog. Invisible. Now I know Wilo keeping it on the down down 'bout his lady being sick and all, but she real bad. Her *panza* be killin' her. I think it's too many trips to the *taco* truck. But who can blame her? I love me them *tacos de cabeza.* I don't know if they cow head, chicken head, hell, they may even be dog head, but they good. And I know she ain't preggers cuz Wilo got a starter pistol down there. He shootin' blanks. But don't tell him I told you! He liable to *loque* up on somebody!

[*A lowrider is heard approaching. He "disappears" behind the bus stop pole. The car passes. He "reappears." He swipes his hand across his face, gesturing his invisibility again.*]

I don't even have to tell you, dog. I don't even have to tell you. Now this is where I come in. My *'fita,* my mom, she kickin' me down with a thirty spot from the check she just got. And my *tito* and my *tata,* they gonna kick me down a thirty spot cuz they also my *nino* and my *nina* from my first Holy Communion. 'Member them days, Lench? Strolling to church in our clip ties and ugly-ass *zopatos* making our feet all stinky and sweaty? Thems the same *zopatos* that the *paisas* be wearing to the *quinceañeras*. I know about this, little homie, cuz I used to be a *paisa*. I mean, historically speaking and all but them was the days when we was all workin' together. Now look at this place. It's like Doomsday up in here. A'ight, I gotta get. If y'all see Wilo, tell him what's goin' on. And I didn't run like no punk *chavala*!

[SKINNY BLACK *runs off. Lights shift.*]

LENCHO: Skinny left on a mission. Daniel, the boy fighter . . . wasn't having any of it.

DANIEL: Forget that *negro*, Mister! We don't need his charity. And I ain't his homie. We'll never be one. It all starts in the inside. Warden makes sure we separate so we keep bashing each other's heads in. And when we on the outs, only difference is, everybody's set trippin'. So if they kill one of their own or the cops shoot 'em in the back like they did the other day, it don't matter to me. It's each man for himself! Ah!

[*A sudden pain pierces* DANIEL*'s heart. He grabs his chest.*]

What's happening to me, Mister? Aaahh! What's happening to me?

[*He goes to the bench and lies down.* LENCHO *rises out of* DANIEL*'s body and addresses the audience.*]

LENCHO: Daniel lay on the bench. He was going in and out of consciousness, looking for some sort of relief.

[*He picks up a crate filled with recyclables.*]

Ah, relieving yourself after holding it in for a long time is like the best feeling in the world. *¿Que no?* Ah, the relief. Never felt freer. But for Daniel. The freedom would be too much. You see, this warden had found his way into Daniel's mind.

[*He begins to separate the aluminum, plastic, and glass.*]

Before a time he knew existed. History. You see, this warden had Daniel believing that there was this white-bearded homeboy in the clouds who had scattered us all over different shades and sizes and said, "Go for it animals, it's each man for himself! Mwahahahaha!"

And this homie had an English accent. He was from Kensington or some place like that. *Puro pedo.* You see, most people think our spirits or souls, whatever you want to call it, come from a god. But science tells us, our bodies came from Africa. Whatever tickles your heinie. So regardless of how you look at it we're all related. We're all black down the line. Don't poop your pants, homie. Hold it in a moment. The relief will be oh so freeing. Now since you all believe in fairy tales, I got a good one for you about the first humans.

[*Lights shift as he plays out the following story using the cans and bottles as the early humans.*]

Let's just say that these hairy *peludos* lived on one gigantic piece of land. You all heard the theory, right? And they were some hairy homeboys, too. One day, after eating a bunch of dinosaur meat dipped in a little platypus sauce, they were chillin' in their caves scratching their hairy *nalgas.* When all of a sudden this *cochino* cave *vato* cut a mean ol' *pedo.* I mean, that fart was so loud it started an earthquake! The earth began to shake. Then it cracked! Then, it broke apart! Now some homies began floating away on their parts of land. Other homies reached out to loved ones who were drowning in the flood! Holding on to fingertips, all dramatic like in a James Cameron film. "I'll never let go, Jack. Never let go. I see you. Oh!" Now the ones that survived got a bad case of amnesia when their *macetas* hit the shaking earth. Ouch! It was such a *madrazo,* they forgot that they shared the same great, great, great, blah, blah, blah, grandparents. Amnesia. Well, time passed and they began to split into tribes and they began to concentrate on their own survival . . .

[*He begins to separate the recyclables.*]

and not that of the original *familia.* Amnesia. Time continued to pass and their features began to change.

[*He picks up a black can.*]

Some of them, their skin stayed dark to protect them from the sun.

[*He picks up a clear plastic bottle.*]

These *vatos*, their skin grew light because they had moved to the north and didn't need the dark pigmentation as much.

[*He holds up the black can.*]

These *vatos'* noses stayed wide to survive in the bush.

[*He holds up the clear bottle.*]

These *vatos'* noses grew thin to protect them from the cold.

[*He holds up a small brown coffee cup with lid.*]

And these *vatos* grew short . . . to survive in jungles . . .

[*He uses the lid as a steering wheel.*]

. . . and to drive lowriders. "GO RAIDERS"!

[*He begins putting the recyclables in their proper bags.*]

This separation was our first disconnect. We'd forgotten we came from the same seed. As time passed, chains were put on our seed.

[*Lights shift as the sound of an ocean is heard.* LENCHO *is handcuffed holding the bags. He slowly crosses the stage, dragging his feet. He raises his hands to his face, then they part as he stands, crucified. The sound of the ocean is accompanied by high winds.*]

RAVI: The warden put God in the clouds to keep the same story in the newspapers.

[*A Gregorian chant plays as the bags become spinning clouds.*]

LENCHO: Daniel was getting tired of the spin. He needed to see the world through different goggles.

[*He makes the sign of the cross on an imaginary body.*]

The warden had slipped him a roofie and was having his way with him in the shadowy confines of cell block D. Daniel needed a light.

[*Like a ray of sunlight, a light illuminates the old shopping cart.*]

Sunshine!

[*A tingsha bell rings. Ocean water can be heard dancing softly amid an African chant.* LENCHO *takes his recyclables and puts them in the shopping cart.*]

We called her Sunshine cuz she was always happy.

[*He takes a scarf and hat from the cart and begins transforming into* SUNSHINE *as soft music plays, drowning out the other sounds.*]

She'd been here before and after the companies had come and gone. A million years old. Timeless. An Island once enslaved. A portal between worlds. The cell that held the original seed.

[SUNSHINE *pushes her cart toward a sleeping* DANIEL *and sits next to him on the bench.*]

SUNSHINE: *Oye niño no has visto la guagua*? You no see the bus? Someday the three o'clock bus come when *es* three o'clock. It could happen . . . miracles.

[*She takes her hat and fans her feet.*]

Ay these feets. *Como plátano frito. Está tan caliente que se me hacen tostones. Fritos los tengo.*

[*Someone passes by on a bike.*]

Ahí va el flaquito on the bike. Every day I see him go back and forth, back and forth like he chasing a ghost. But you can't catch a ghost because you go right through it. One of these days he going to stop and find what he looking for. It could happen . . . miracles.

[*A bird crows on a wire overhead. She looks up to see it.*]

Ay mira que pajarito tan lindo. I like birds. You know why? Cuz *un* birds know he's a birds. No illusions. He no think he's a dog. He no say, "I'm dog. I'm dog." It's a bird. It's nice to know what you is. *Como en la isla.* When I was little girl on the island, every day we eat plantain, bean, rice. *Plátano, arroz, y habichuela.* No illusions. But you can makes many things with plantain. *Sí. Con el plátano se hace, tostones, plátano frito, pasteles. Como el Mexicano con el maiz; Taco, enchilada, tostada. Y el chino con el arroz; El sushi, pad thai, wontón. Pero lo Americano*

. . . everything in plastic bag. Illusion. Like the building. Sometime I wish everybody from La Esquinita bring whatever food they have in they house, on the Friday, and we go inside the building. And we have a big dinner. Together. We can eat. Laugh. Talk. Watch children play. Happy. It could happen . . . miracles.

[*She smiles peacefully, thinking of the possibilities.*]

You hear that, boy? *Silencio.* Silence. I like when city makes quiet like this. It's no crazy. It's like four in the morning and hear shhh. Silence. If you listen real close, you can hear the drum. That is the real *corazón* of the people *de La Esquinita*. It is the drumbeat they forget but never left. *Nunca se fue.* This is when I have the same dream but with my eyes open.

[*She rises with a new rejuvenation.*]

I can see everybody fly out of they houses. *Volando como espíritus. Desnudos. Despeinados.* They have no clothes. They naked. Then they begin to hear the drum.

[*African drums begin to play and she begins to dance.*]

And they begin to dancing. *Ahí todos bailando.* Then at the same time they eyes go—

[*A tingsha bell rings. Her eyes open wide with joy.*]

una luz, a light shine from they eyes. And they looks happy and alive because they not afraid like they is when they awake. Everybody alive and dancing! *Todos en candela!*

[*She sits next to* DANIEL.]

Listen in the silence, boy. Those too many voices are the bad *espíritus* this world make you believe in your *coco*. You must tell them "shhh, quiet. I no believe in you no more! I want peace!"

[*She pulls a seashell necklace from inside her cart and waves it over* DANIEL*'s sleeping body.*]

The Great ancestor is calling you home. The first spirit before all spirits. Your mother and father before they was two. When they was one. Listen, boy. Listen and you will know. Listen and you will know.

[*She returns her shell necklace, rises and disappears. The African drums fade softly in the distance.*]

LENCHO: Sunshine rose like a wave and left. She continued on her constant quest to collect and recycle that which others discard. Daniel rested on the bench as the ancient rhythm beckoned to him from somewhere far beyond his memory.

[*He approaches* DANIEL, *who sleeps on the bench.*]

You're ready for this now, little homie. Rise! The ancient rhythm is in you. Love is the only high there is. Receive the gift.

[DANIEL *awakens frazzled. He wipes the sleep from his eyes.*]

DANIEL: What the hell was that! Did I crash out or something, Mister?

[*His cell phone rings. He's worried.*]

It's Toker.

[*He answers his phone.*]

Toker?

[*His worry becomes anger.*]

Oh, it's you! What do you want? I told you it's over, G, a'ight? Nah, nah, nah. You cocked him! Lucky was my homie! Sure, it's a lie! It's all a lie! Well, I don't believe you!

[*He hangs up as he suffers another stomach pain.*]

I'm coming down hard, Mister!

[*Another call. He answers desparately.*]

Hey! What's up, Toker? Nah, foo. I got your cash. I'm not trying to avoid you. My phone just keeps going in and out

[*Dropped call. He becomes frantic.*]

Toker? Toker! Why is this happening to me, Mister!

[*Another call.*]

Ma, I need my money right now! They're coming for me but I ain't going down like this! Not me! *Mira, ama.* Listen! If you don't give me my money, *voy a llamar a* ICE! They'll deport you. *Te llevan.* What are you gonna do then, huh?

[*Dropped call. He moves about frantically, looking for reception.*]

Hey! Ma! Ma! MAAAAA!

[*He lets out a blood-curdling scream! Lights shift.*]

LENCHO: The *Indio* Scream. The *Indio* Scream was a call for salvation from an illusory world. It came when words could not describe the pain felt through the heart. A pain felt throughout the history of those who had been divided and conquered. We heard it here every night in La Esquinita. "The little corner." That kept getting smaller and smaller and smaller.

DANIEL: What's happening to me, Mister?

[DANIEL *goes to the trash can and vomits. Mongolian throat song is heard.*]

I can try to forget about the lies in my head, but I can't forget my mother's cries of dread.

What's happening to me, Mister?

I can hear the ancient song from somewhere far beyond the dawn.

But it doesn't drown out the moans,

the sand all over my brother's bones.

Their bodies left all alone . . . bodies left all alone.

[*He throws up one final time in the trash can. Lights shift.*]

LENCHO: Would Daniel slay the lion? Not the beautiful beast that roams African lands but that wretched one inside man. In reality, the *Indio* Scream was a call to love. I know. I had screamed before. It's an old story.

[*An old* Danzón *tune plays as a light comes up on a tire.*]

But my connection to Mr. Jefferson, our local barber, was a constant reminder. You see, lines had been drawn across that man so many times that the pain that once screamed the *Indio* Scream had become scars of understanding. He knew Daniel would drown in the scream so he extended an offering. In one fell swoop, a miracle proceeded.

[*The* Danzón *tune gives way to war news on a TV.* MR. JEFFERSON *is cutting a friend's hair. He calls out to* DANIEL.]

MR. JEFFERSON: Boy, you got the scream in ya! Come over and let old Charlie Jefferson clean you up a bit. I don't bite. 'Less you want me to. First cut's on me. Old Jimmy here used to polish his own pistol 'til Charlie Jefferson got a hold of his nappy head. Now he a coochy magnet. Ain't that right, Jimmy? Ain't you a bona fide coochy connoisseur? Like a playa from back in the day-a? Now he in love and all happy cuz he's no longer nappy.

[*He removes the barber's cloak off of* JIMMY.]

There you go, Jimmy. It's always good to see you. Save me a space at the bingo.

[*He turns his attention to the news on the TV as he cleans his clippers.*]

They should just call the news the "bad news." People love it and I can't shut the darn thing off myself. Well, well, well. Look who decided to show up. Get on up in the chair, boy. Yup, first cut's for free but then you gots to pay.

[*He puts the cloak on* DANIEL *and begins trimming his hair. Another war story comes from the television.*]

There we go killing the poor just so the rich can play on the tube. Kardashian. Miley Cyprus. Ivanka! It's that damn Paris Hilton started all this mess. Now what kinda parent name they kid after a city and hotel? Kinda messed up naming yo kid after the place you got buck nutty. Now, if my parents woulda done that, my name would be Eastside Motor Inn.

[MR. JEFFERSON *amuses himself.*]

Just a bunch of jokes, boy. A bunch of jokes. Let's turn this off and listen to some tunes better.

[*He claps his hands. The television turns off.*]

I got the clapper!

[*He claps again. Another* Danzón *tune plays, bringing him joy.*]

Oh, my! I like this one! I can't remember what they saying but I can sure feel it down deep in my bones.

[*He goes back to trimming* DANIEL*'s hair but he can't sit still.*]

Boy, stop moving around. Hell, if you need to use the restroom just go right on inside.

[DANIEL *doesn't respond.*]

OK. You poop in your panties if you want. That's alright by me. I'll just listen to my tunes . . . So how old are you, boy? 'Bout eighteen? What you screamin' about? I know it's rough out there but you got a lifetime ahead of you. Just don't blink cuz you liable to wake up and be as old as I am. You go to school? You ain't much for talking, are you? Well, that's all right by me. I'll just listen to my tunes. Hell, I'll even give you a dance if you want.

[*He dances.*]

You got to hold them close, boy, or they gonna get away from you.

[*His leg contorts. As he puts it back in place, he notices* DANIEL *staring at it.*]

You like my leg boy? Titanium plastic. Four tours. Sixty-four to sixty-eight. Compliments of Uncle Sam. But you probably don't know who Uncle Sam is, do you? Nah. They got them models recruiting you now, huh?. "Army of one" and all that bull. Breeds you then leaves you. Leg got blown right off. It was some fascinating stuff. So I'm lyin' in the jungle and I see this size ten staring right at me and I'm thinkin', "Boy, that foot sure looks familiar." I was like a beached whale staring at his fin. So I see my foot then I scc this little bug start crawlin' toward it. One of them roley polies. You know the kind. So this roly-poly crawls up the foot, gets to the top, then slowly turns to look at me. Behind it I can see mortar flying, bombs blastin', soldiers screamin'. And I swear that bug had the saddest look on its face. Then all of a sudden everything grew quiet. Then the little bug let out a tiny moan. It was so saddened by all the carnage that it began to curl itself up. Into itself. Rolled up into a ball, rolled up off the foot and disappeared. Killin' has never gotten anyone anywhere but right back to killin'. And you po' boys killin' each other out on the streets just so you can go kill some other po' boy out in the desert. We did the same thing only we killed them in the jungle. You know what that got me? Titanium plastic. Ain't no enemy on the outside, boy. Enemy's on the inside. Boy, stop squirming around. I told you, if you need to use the restroom just go right on inside my house.

LENCHO: Daniel stood up and walked away. When Daniel got back to the bus stop he put it to me like this.

[DANIEL *paces around the bus stop trying to shake off the shame in his heart and to hold back the chemicals his body is trying to release.*]

DANIEL: Why you trippin', Mister? Cuz I didn't use his toilet? You expect me to sit there and listen to his sorry story? I got my own. I only cut my hair cuz it was for free. I gotta see the judge tomorrow. Just getting mine just like they get theirs and believe me, they get theirs. They got their rap, their hoop, their flicks. What do we get? Wake up, Mister! It's an eye for an eye. We still Spartans!

LENCHO: Daniel wasn't gonna go down that easy. He wanted to throw blows. Go one-on-one in defense of his falsehoods. So I went deeper.

[*He whirls like a dervish as the lights shift into a twirling pool of illumination. Indian Sitar music plays.*]

RAVI: You see, Daniel, in these times, you think black is fine

because in pockets gold they line.

Basketball. A laugh. A song.

A dunk. A dash . . . one hundred yards long.

You think crime is fine,

when it's a black-on-black attack, a black-on-black jack.

But the connection is not made, Daniel-san,

That black on black is brown on brown

Town on town, state on state

You can't relate to see the fate of such hate.

You can't see the correlation that black on black

Is nation on nation, which makes for separation

of the power of unity, true divinity, the holy trinity

Between You, Mr. Jefferson, and the almighty WE!

[*Lights shift back to the bus stop.*]

DANIEL: I knew you were one of them Alleluias. You guys come out of nowhere! Nobody cares about any of that you're talking about or this place or us! There's *negros* blasting homies, homies blasting *negros*! There's no work! My dad hasn't worked in a year, Mister, and it ain't getting any better. And still the same rich foos stay rich and we keep praying! My mom's knees are bloody from praying. You think that's fair? That makes me wanna blast somebody's head off!

[*A sudden pain hits him in the gut. He doubles over on the bus stop bench holding his stomach. Finally, he gets enough strength to speak his truth.*]

I need cash. I live in a shack. My lady just got cocked and I can't do nothin' about that . . . cuz I'll get blasted. But one of these days . . . I'm gonna say forget it. I can't be nobody's punk no more.

[*His cell phone rings.*]

What's up, Toker?

[*An unbridled courage comes over him.*]

I already told you I got your money, so stop calling a'ight!

[*The reality of his false courage is realized.*]

No. No. No. Wait, Toker. Wait! I didn't mean it like that! I don't know why I said that! I'm just under a lotta pressure right now. Every thing's whack! No. Don't do anything crazy. Hey, Toker, how long have we known each other? Since we were like little dudes. Right? Toker? Toker!

[*Reception is lost.*]

What did I say that for, Mister . . . ? Sometimes you ain't got a choice.

[*Another call comes in. He answers.*]

Tok—oh, it's you! I told you to stop calling, G! Yeah, sure, Lucky was just joking! Just cuz you say you love me I'm supposed to believe you? You live in a different world, foo. I don't care what I promised. There is no US!

[*He hangs up the phone. He then experiences "the release." He grabs his butt. He has to use the toilet and let go of everything he's been holding in.*]

Its finally coming out, Mister! I gotta take a *masa*! Can I use your restroom? What do you mean you're not from around here?

[*He has nowhere to turn. He looks over to* MR. JEFFERSON*'s house, his only hope, and moves toward it. Lights shift.*]

LENCHO: Daniel swallowed his pride.

[DANIEL *sits on* MR. JEFFERSON*'s toilet.*]

He sat on Mr. Jefferson's toilet. As the chemicals flushed from his body his life flashed before him. He sank like a wish. A coin tossed in a well for luck . . .

[*A tingsha bell sounds.*]

. . . giving way to the truth.

[DANIEL *looks at his cell phone.*]

He loved his girlfriend, G. He loved G more than he let himself believe and it scared him to death.

[DANIEL *puts his phone away and looks at his hands.*]

He splashed cold water over his face. Looked at his hands. They shook. A realization he was still alive. He ran out of the bathroom.

[DANIEL *runs out of the bathroom. A wall of photos stops him.*]

He went down the hall and came to a wall full of pictures of Mr. Jefferson's mother as a little girl. An inscription read, "Veracruz, Mexico." There were more pictures of . . . a black woman and a brown man. "Lencho?" The pictures were of me and Mr. Jefferson's daughter, Yolanda. A feeling of wonder grew over Daniel. Then a confusion. Which suddenly turned to anger. Just the second wind he needed. The boy fighter returned with a flurry of punches.

[*Lights shift.* DANIEL *rushes to the bus stop like a ferocious lion.*]

DANIEL: Oh, I get it, Mister! I get it! Them "goggles" you've been talking about are from the *negro*'s point of view, *que no*? No wonder you're saying we're all black down the line. You got the jungle fever, huh? Is that why you been acting all calm cuz you're playing both sides? You can't be riding the fence, Mister. Not around here cuz if the homies find out, they'll rip out your heart. Damn! I'm slippin'! I can't believe I let that *negro* touch me!

[*Lights shift.* LENCHO *addresses the audience.*]

LENCHO: *Negro*? No. Mr. Jefferson . . . was actually Mr. Jimenez. Changed his name after the tire factory closed down. I mean, his people did come from Africa but through *Veracruz, México*. How do you like them *manzanas*? So what's a black? A brown? A wall? Just a bunch of ideas, *que no*?

DANIEL: Mr. Jefferson . . . a Mexican? Nah, nah, forget that . . .

[*Lights transform into a pool of twirling illumination.* RAVI *aims his bow and arrow at* DANIEL.]

RAVI: Like the master archer, Arjuna, my aim was keen. I hit a nerve right in his heart. But still the boy fighter staggered toward me. He pulled the arrow out. He wasn't ready for love.

[*Lights shift back to the bus stop.*]

DANIEL: Love?! Love ain't got nothin' to do with nothin', Mister! You can't love your way outta this! And you can't love whoever you want cuz the wolves will eat you alive! Can't do anything until the warden says so! This world is full of hypocrites, Mister. You, me, and everyone else! The hate sticks to our skin. To G's skin!

[*He stops. A secret has escaped. He grabs his backpack to leave.*]

Nah, nah, nah. I'm bouncing, Mister. You just tryna confuse me with all your voodoo talk. I don't believe in any of that you talkin', a'ight! I just know we live and we die!

[*He tries to leave. The lights flicker. He grabs his heart.*]

Argh!!! What's happening to me, Mister? What's happening?

[*A cacophony of sounds and lights. He looks into the distance. African drums call to him.*]

You hear that, Mister? Is that my lady love? Or the flapping wings of a dove?

Is that an *Indio* Scream? Or just a dream?

No, no, no, it's just the wind in the Arab sand.

Or is it a jungle or is it African?

Is that an *Indio* Scream in the distance?

Or is that the ancient rhythm Sunshine said was the sum of the sun.

What lies beyond?

Mister, what thoughts are you planting in my head

when all I see is red!

As it goes from brown to black and back to white.

And I'm losing this fight!

All I see are my dead brothers, cuts on knees of mothers,

bodies hanging from trees, killing dreams.

And bullets in glocks, time disappearing from clocks

running out on me!

[*He grabs hold of his backpack like a lifesaver. The drum sounds morph into the sound of African women chanting on an ocean shore. He looks toward the old tire. A glow comes from it. He is transfixed by the illumination and goes toward it.*]

And I hear the sea as she calls to me. Who is she? Who is she?

Nah, nah, nah. I ain't ready for this yet.

[*He collapses on the old tire.* LENCHO *rises from his body.*]

LENCHO: Daniel tried to step away from the light but I knew I had him, so I reeled him in with a story of forgiveness.

[*From the tire,* LENCHO *pulls out an identical seashell necklace that* SUNSHINE *shared earlier with* DANIEL *at the bench.*]

Yolanda.

[*Lights shift.*]

Yolanda and I were very happy in those pictures you saw, little homie. You should have seen the *Vera Cruzana*. African-*India*. A pure mixture of royal blood types that had known power and poverty but that time and time again reminded us of mother, earth, and Spirit. We used to chill at the local rec center back in the day. Black, brown, old, young. Joint was jumping but then the tire factory closed down . . . and I shut down with it. A fear filled the air and I got caught up in it, but Yolanda rose above it. I remember the night I broke up with her. We were at the rec center having a community meeting. Yolanda was trying to keep us all together. She spoke to the people.

[*Lights shift. Slow* Son Jarocho *music plays as* YOLANDA, *candle in hand, addresses the recently unemployed townsfolk.*]

YOLANDA: In these trying times, let's remember who we are and not what desperation is making us. We are not animals and we won't act as such! Remember we're neighbors. Yes, sir? I know it's hard but when has it ever been easy for us? We still here and we're still gonna be here because we a strong people! Yes, *señora*? No! We may be cracked but we're not broken. We're all family and we're gonna get through this but only if we do it together. Friends, talk to your kids. Hold them tight and tell them to remember love.

[*The candle goes out as the lights shift.*]

Hold on, Lencho. I know. I understand you have to go.

[*She caresses the seashell necklace around her neck.*]

These shells have been passed down from mother to daughter from before we were taken across the sea. They're given as a remembrance of love and forgiveness. I want you to have them.

[*She takes off the seashell necklace.*]

Baby, I know why this is happening and this town will rise again and you must stay here to shed light on them. Your heart is good. All hearts are good. It's when this is understood that the light will appear. You know, baby, men are men in this lifetime because they were bad mothers in their last one. Maybe next time you're a mother, you will remember this love I leave you with.

[*She offers* LENCHO *the necklace. Lights shift. He makes an altar with* YOLANDA'*s necklace, candle, and head scarf.*]

LENCHO: We became desperate, little homie. A community split into colors. This brokenhearted town forced me to pick sides and I believed the lies so I split up with her. I let Yolanda down cuz I let myself down. I felt sad and heavy for a long time after that. Then one quiet morning I woke up and I began to hear the ancient rhythm Yolanda had placed in my heart. Sunshine came through my window and warmed my face. And even though outside there was desperation and anger, inside I felt free.

[*Lights shift.*]

DANIEL: But I don't feel free, Mister. I feel trapped like a rat! Foos around here don't understand that, you talkin'. They just see right now and right now I need my three hundred! . . . Toker fronted me and my homie grip of meth and my homie sniffed it up his nose and left town and Toker wants his cash today! And Toker don't mess around. I just want to get outta here. Join the marines and blast some foos! Do what I gotta do! It's the only way outta here! That's my life! You can just stand around and talk all whack. It's easy to do nothing.

[*Lights shift.*]

LENCHO: Daniel's scars were deep.

[LENCHO *puts* DANIEL*'s hat into his backpack on the bench.*]

The lion fought hard to stay alive. On cue, Skinny Black shows up to the rescue. One eye open, one eye wide shut.

[*Sirens.* SKINNY BLACK *enters hurriedly. His left eye is shut.*]

SKINNY BLACK: Lencho! Come on, you got to get! Wilo finally lost it! His lady died waiting at the clinic! Now you two may be asking yourselves why my eye's like this. I was over at the taco truck eating a *taco de cabeza.* And I was surrounded by all these *Mexican paisas* so I sorta blended in cuz you know . . .

[SKINNY *swipes his hand over his face showing his Jedi skills of invisibility.*]

Then outta the corner of my eye, I see Whitey having a burrito with Cockeyed Ramirez. Then like a bat outta hell come Wilo with a machete in his hands and he let out the *Indio* Scream. AHHHH!!! All them years them pigs messed with him appeared in his eyes. Whitey put up his hands to block the blade but the blade came down and it was like Splat! Squirt! Like cherry Kool-Aid! *Tripas* and *carnitas* was flying everywhere. I look up and Whitey's finger went, BAM, right into my *taco.* Chile shot up into my eye. That's when Cockeyed Ramirez pulled out the heat! Bullets flyin' everywhere. Then I see this one stray bullet BAM! Hit poor Sunshine in the *panza.* But instead of blood squirting everywhere the sound of drums start comin' out her belly. Then she started to float up in the air like a balloon. And everyone just stood there looking up at the miracle float up in the sky as them drums kept gettin' louder and louder! That's when Wilo ran into Margarita's market and he's hulled up in there right now. Says he'll only talk to you cuz you the only one who helped him. Come on, Lench! We gotta get! We don't need any more people dyin' 'round here. This town's seen enough!

[SKINNY *runs off.* LENCHO *addresses the audience.*]

LENCHO: I was about to take off with Skinny, leaving Daniel to ponder his next move on his own. Wilo needed me. This town needed me. And I remembered Yolanda's words but there was Daniel without an answer to the question that kept burning up in his mind. "What am I gonna do?" kept ringing in his ear. Then a light appeared.

[*A tingsha bell rings. Lights come up on the old tire.*]

Grace.

[*He goes to the abandoned tire and dips his hands into it. He retrieves a hat, identical to* DANIEL*'s, with a lock of hair dangling from it. A tingsha bell rings.*]

G.

[*He dips his hand in again and takes out a pair of young women's sunglasses.*]

Daniel's love.

[LENCHO *dips his hands into the tire again and takes out a promise ring.*]

The truth.

[*Lights shift as R&B music plays.*]

[GRACE, *a young black woman, appears.*]

GRACE: D! D! There you are. Who you talkin' to? Ain't nobody around here? Spaz told me you be talkin' to yourself. You doin' them drugs again? I told you to stop! They gonna make you crazy! Now, we got to bounce cuz Toker's lookin' for you! I told you your homie Lucky is playing you cuz he always wanted to get with me! I'ma read you the truth? Hold up! I'm talking now!

[GRACE *takes out her cell phone and begins reading a text.*]

"Yo, it's Lucky. Hear u ain't wit D no more. I was just messin'. Oh, well. Wanna meet me in the park after dark? I hear the chocolate's good." You gonna let some triflin' foo get between us? Cuz this about you and what you want to believe and what you gonna do, Daniel. Now you promised me we was gonna get outta here together and I believed you and I'm standing right here. Don't that mean anything to you? D, you lettin' the pain make up your mind, that's why you scared. Now take my hand.

[GRACE *holds out her hand but* DANIEL *does not take it.*]

OK. You want to play it like that?

[GRACE *goes to leave. She stops and removes her promise ring.*]

I guess it's better than stayin' home wonderin' if you got shot in the streets or in the sand or wherever!

[GRACE *tosses the ring. It spins in the air.*]

LENCHO: Grace tossed her ring like a lifesaver. Daniel reached out for it.

[DANIEL *reaches out and catches the ring in midair.*]

Like the Ancient rhythm sound, Daniel's heart began to pound!

DANIEL: Don't go, Grace! Please! Don't go, G!

[*He goes to a knee. Exhausted.*]

I don't know what's gonna happen to me. The sky's falling on my head. I keep hearing these voices and they won't stop. I don't know what to believe anymore. I'm scared G . . . and I'm tired.

I'm tired of this lump in my throat. I'm tired of being thirsty.

[GRACE *holds him tenderly.*]

GRACE: It's OK, baby. It's OK. We all tired but we the love. You have to believe it. Can't nobody else do it for you.

[*A tingha bell rings.* LENCHO *places* GRACE*'s hat gently on the bench. He takes* DANIEL*'s hat from inside his backpack and places it on the bench next to* GRACE*'s.*]

LENCHO: They sat on the bench. Holding each other.

[LENCHO *watches over the two lovers on the bench. Suddenly, a car comes to a screeching halt.* DANIEL *looks up only to find* TOKER.]

DANIEL: What's up, Toker? Relax, foo. I got it! I told you I had it. I got your *feria.* She just came by to bring me the money. This is my lady. I got your cash. Let me get it. It's in my bag.

[*He pulls a handgun from his backpack and aims at* TOKER. *African drums begin to rise as* DANIEL *holds his aim.*]

What's up, Toker? Just keep your hands right there. So how we gonna do this, homie? Cuz I ain't got all the money. That's the truth. So we can keep doin' it like this, over and over again, killin' each other, or we can do it a different way.

[*He backs away as he loosens his aim. Lights shift.*]

There's another way, Toker. There's another way.

[*He puts down the gun, giving into his resolve as the sound of the African drums rise.* DANIEL *looks over at* GRACE *on the bench as a light consumes him. The African drums get louder and louder. He is blessed by the light. Lights fade to black.*]

ALIENS, IMMIGRANTS & OTHER EVILDOERS

José Torres-Tama

Production photograph copyright © Jonathan Traviesa

CRITICAL INTRODUCTION

Tiffany Ana López

José Torres-Tama's *Aliens, Immigrants & Other Evildoers* is a sci-fi Latino noir multimedia solo performance giving testament to the experiences of immigrants in the United States as they work to navigate a system that simultaneously depends upon their labor yet vilifies and denigrates them. Drawing inspiration from such conceptual mentors as Guillermo Gómez-Peña, Ntozake Shange, and Spalding Gray, Torres-Tama brings together visual aesthetics, improvisation, performance poetics, and satire with interview-based, character-driven storytelling that situates the audience as witnesses to the traumatic experiences of immigrants. Building from his training in pantomime, Torres-Tama "shape-shifts" into nine characters, including a Honduran day laborer, a Mexican minister, and El Pachuco of Interracial and Interplanetary Love of the Future. These stories expose the wounds immigrants carry, and serve to recover the humanity eclipsed by mainstream rhetoric that portrays immigrants as alien others. He invites us to see that the Nicaraguan woman was once a girl, hazarding everything to reunite with her father who had escaped the country's civil war in the 1980s: "I would have preferred to have my father for all of my eight birthdays instead of those dirty dollars he sent home." To facilitate the performance's mission to break down xenophobia in order to break through to a higher collective consciousness, Torres-Tama regularly traverses the fourth wall. As minister, he urges congregants to "see the Christ in the Immigrant" and espouses the mantra, "Love Is Radical; Hate Is Reactionary."

Torres-Tama affirms his stance as an artist: "If art does not challenge the power structure with well-crafted meaningful work, then it becomes an accomplice to the banal entertainment the system prefers to support."

Aliens, Immigrants & Other Evildoers was launched in response to the rise in hate crimes in the U.S. during the early 2000s, including the case of Marcelo Lucero, stabbed to death on Long Island in a "beaner hunt" a few days after the 2008 election of Barack Obama. The title of the work was inspired when George Bush, in the wake of 9/11, began to talk about "evildoers," language Torres-Tama was sensitized to, recognizing it as rooted in science fiction; entering the U.S. as a child, the artist was labeled a "permanent resident alien." Of his focus on docudrama and trauma stories, he explains: "The only way to challenge dehumanizations is making people human, showing that there is no such thing as aliens. My work is composed to visually and poetically engage the audience. I want to break your heart, make you laugh, have you walk away ready to take action."

With support from the National Performance Network Creation Fund and co-commissions by MECA (Houston) in partnership with the Ashé Cultural Arts Center (New Orleans), and GALA Hispanic Theatre (Washington, D.C.), an exploratory project began to take shape as a form of docudrama to bridge the gap between privately heard and publicly told stories about the experiences of immigrants. Over the course of a year, Torres-Tama traveled the country, focusing on Houston, New Orleans, and Washington, D.C., and collected more than thirty interviews, later deciding which ones to stage and dramaturgically inhabit. According to Torres-Tama, "The challenge was how to perform the stories in a way that conveyed the emotional power I experienced in how they were presented to me." In an early version of the script, Torres-Tama included a character named José. "I would tell his story exactly the way he told it to me, in the first person, with an audience member invited to come on stage and translate. I eventually took it out because it created a very heavy emotional flow. I had to bring in the humor much earlier. I started adding more filmic data and aspects of sci-fi, additionally morphing movement into the piece." His inclusion of multimedia "movements" between the characters' stories conveys the feelings of absurdity and dissonance other Latinx theater artists, such as Luis Valdez and Josefina López, also explore as a surreal juncture between the juridical language of citizenship and that of science fiction.

Of his methodology, Torres-Tama shares that when he teaches, he often asks artists to think of themselves as sculptures moving through space slowly to explore the nature of the body. He shares, "Sometimes, a simple prop, like a shawl, helps me to transform into another character. Sometimes, it is through a more devised transition of music and short films. The sci-fi score gives the piece a sort of X-Files/Mex-Files feel to it and adds to the science-fiction Latino noir aesthetic that I am cultivating through this hybrid performance genre." Notably, the artist never fully sets the script, but provides cues to allow for the role of improvisation: "while things are live, there is space for happy accidents to occur. I don't want to hit the same note each time. There has to be space for change because the audience changes with each show."

Throughout the performance, there is a sense of religiosity. Swamp Brujo paints his face with Native designs, and wears a bandana of the American flag with an elaborate leather cross sticking out through gloves painted green. "I want to use that space where the sacred and the profane intersect." Torres-Tama also draws from the elaborate costuming and face painting tradition of Mardi Gras culture. Within the performance, he smears his face with water, transforming his visage into that of a greenish, dirty alien. The performance visually juxtaposes the story with the ritual of cleaning off with towel and water to transform. While he washes his face, he tells the story of seventeen men living in one trailer, the character describing the overwhelming feeling of the need to wash. He uses details in performance to spotlight the atrocities, telling a story about the need to clean while engaged in that act.

Notably, Torres-Tama understands *Aliens, Immigrants & Other Evildoers* to be grounded by three archetypal immigration stories: the dawning of awareness of how one is defined by the dominant culture as "illegal"; the experience of gross human rights violations because one is an immigrant; the immigrant quest to make a difference in the world and forge a better path for future generations. He recounts, "When I interviewed Diana, as soon as she said, 'soy illegal,' I knew her story would find its way into the script." In his interviews with construction workers in New Orleans, Torres-Tama repeatedly heard testimony about laborers subjected to deplorable and inhumane working conditions, represented by a nineteen-year-old Honduran named Dennis, and his traumatic story about having his hand crushed in an accident while clearing through the wreckage of decimated homes. "When I performed an early version of the piece for the church of a Mexican minister, his response, 'I petition you to see the Christ in the immigrant,' called out to me for inclusion in the performance because it so powerfully invited a shift in perspective." Torres-Tama's minister testifies, "When I see an immigrant, I see a humble person, ready to work and contribute for all to benefit from his labor. I don't see a monster. I see a father working long hours to provide for his family. Just like all others, we have come here to dream."

Influences on the development of the work include events in Torres-Tama's adopted home of New Orleans, where he observed an influx of immigrant laborers to help rebuild the city following Hurricane Katrina: "It is the greatest untold story of the post-Katrina rebuilding, and Latin American immigrant workers were responsible for bringing the Big Easy back from the dead with a committed work force of epic proportions. Like a locust of reconstruction angels, they descended upon the fragile pueblo and restored the engines of the viable tourist industry by salvaging the many flooded hotels before they were condemned." One of his characters tells the story of how an encampment of more than three hundred immigrant workers were promised $3,600 for a three-week job, but the Thursday before their big pay day, the New Orleans police, acting as immigration officers, raided the abandoned warehouse where they slept. The police ran them all off, and not one worker was paid. In 2009, the Southern Poverty Law Center released data that 80 percent of the immigrants who reconstructed New Orleans were victims of wage theft. Torres-Tama's character recounts, "We remember . . . we urge others not to forget." Torres-Tama further observes that at this same moment, local citizenry was grateful for the new Mexican and Latino restaurants in town, but like elsewhere in the country, "some of the same people championing the food demonize the cooks." This prompted Torres-Tama to adopt the battle cry, "No guacamole for immigrant haters."

Torres-Tama sees *Aliens, Immigrants & Other Evildoers* as representing the apex of twenty years of work. In addition to Encuentro 2014, the performance history of *Aliens, Immigrants & Other Evildoers* includes: Baruch College in New York; GALA Hispanic Theatre in Washington, D.C.; Pangea World Theater in Minneapolis; Ashé Cultural Arts Center in New Orleans; Highways Performance Space in Santa Monica, California; and the University of Memphis, University of Arkansas, and Vanderbilt University, where it sold out a two-hundred-seat venue. His other performances have been presented internationally, in London, Liverpool, Wales, Poland, Slovenia, and Mexico City. Performances at colleges and universities across the United States include Duke, Cornell, Tulane, Louisiana State University, California State University, Northridge, and the University of California, Riverside. Torres-Tama's work has also been supported under the auspices of an NEA Regional Artist Project Award; Louisiana Theater Fellowship; National Association of Latino Arts & Culture 2016 grant for Taco Truck Theater Show; and MAP Fund 2015. From 2006 to 2011, Torres-Tama contributed commentaries to National Public Radio's *Latino USA*. Key collaborators for *Aliens, Immigrants & Other Evildoers* are John Grimsley, sci-fi lighting designer; Bruce France, satirical film/video shorts; Billy Atwell, original sci-fi music score; and Claudia Copeland, a classical vocalist whose operatic recordings are used in the production.

NOTE

All quotes from José Torres-Tama are from a discussion with the author in October 2014.

The performance text published in this anthology has been revised from the version performed at the 2014 Encuentro to include references to the 2016 election of Donald Trump and subsequent policies implemented by his administration.

PRODUCTION HISTORY

Aliens, Immigrants & Other Evildoers was developed through the support of a 2009 National Performance Network Creation Fund in collaboration with three commissioning partners that included Multicultural Education and Counseling through the Arts (MECA) in Houston, the Ashé Cultural Arts Center in New Orleans, and GALA Hispanic Theatre in Washington, D.C. The piece was developed through interviews with local immigrant communities in each of these sites. It is written, directed, and performed by José Torres-Tama, with lighting design by John Grimsley, film shorts and video graphics by Bruce France, and soundscapes by Billy Atwell featuring vocals by Claudia Copeland.

The first full stage production was developed at the Ashé Cultural Arts Center, September 16–19, 2010, followed by a three-week run at the Shadowbox Theater in New Orleans. It was staged in Houston at MECA on October 15 and 16, 2010. Pangea World Theater and Teatro del Publeo in Minneapolis presented it February 25 and 26, 2011. In the same year, *Aliens* had a university tour circuit that included Vanderbilt, the University of Arkansas, Xavier University, University of California at Riverside, California State University at Northridge, University of Memphis, and the University of North Carolina at Chapel Hill.

The production at the 2014 Encuentro was presented in partnership with Highways Performance Space in Santa Monica through a National Performance Network Residency. *Aliens* was performed at the Los Angeles Theatre Center October 16–19, before it moved to Highways October 24 and 25, 2014.

Post-Encuentro history includes a two-week run at Art Klub in New Orleans in 2016 and another at Touchstone Theater in Bethlehem, Pennsylvania, and in 2018 Sugarspace Arts Warehouse in Salt Lake City. As of 2019, *Aliens* is in its eighth year of touring to critical acclaim.

SETTING

The live art performance is set in a borderless space in the Hemispheric Americas.

TIME

It is the present, with a heightened era of post-9/11 anti-immigrant hysteria in FreedomLandia.

STAGE LANDSCAPE

The set is minimal but intriguing and has a magical realist feel to it, as a space where the sacred and profane will unfold.

Immediately striking are the two flags that are floating on opposite sides of stage center. They define the borderless space as symbolic representations of the migrant trajectory the protagonist has taken, and the conflict between North and South America that will be explored.

On stage right is a contemporary American flag with the fifty stars, and at stage left floats an Ecuadorian flag of similar size. Both flags are suspended by fishing wire that is not visible, and look like they are magically floating in the space. Each flag is lit with a haunting blue spotlight at 20 degrees throughout the show, and the minimalist set mirrors a temporary installation.

At downstage center on the stage floor are a number of props that will be used for the performer's shape-shifting from one character to another. Most noticeable is a large, oval-shaped tin basin filled with water that is flanked by various other props.

Two large skulls flank the perimeter on each side of the basin. At stage left is a plastic, purple-blue, glittery skull of less than human size, and at stage left is a more traditional skull, human-sized and bone-colored. Beside each skull is a green votive candle sitting in a glass. When the lights go to black, the candles will partly light the skulls for a haunting and spooky effect.

The bone skull is partly visible with a black top hat on its plastic cranium. The top hat is decorated with a green plastic snake protruding from its center and a green plastic rose decorating its side. It's the top hat for the Swamp Brujo character to come.

Other props surround the basin as if to suggest a sacred space for the ritualistic practices. A small round mirror is placed at an angle in front of the basin, and a spray can with an illustration of the Virgin of Guadalupe is to the right of the basin. The spray will be used by one of the characters to offer a "blessed" aroma to the space. Next to the can is a small white towel folded in fours.

On top of the towel is a set of silver-colored rabbit ear antennas from an old television set, which will be used as a comic prop for an "alien" spoof to come.

Behind the basin is a blue shawl that will be used for the Nicaraguan woman character, and it's covering a U.S. flag of the original thirteen colonies. Both props will be used for the various "Alien" characters to come. The set of props on the stage floor define the ritualistic space where the performance unfolds.

In front of the floating U.S. flag at upstage center right is a black music stand that contains a few pages of the script, which will be used for the conservative zealot character later in the show.

Not wholly visible at upstage left is an upright stand that contains a black tuxedo jacket and a vintage fire-red jacket, also for characters to come. At a small table next to the jackets sits a stylish red cowboy hat lit slightly by a candle, and a small rainstick.

At upstage center and a few feet from the 10' x 10' scrim is a black platform box that measures 2' x 2' and is about 2' in height. This will serve as a platform for the Alien character to stand for elevation for the final movement of the performance. The black box will also serve as a stand to prop the red cross against, and keep it standing at upstage center for the first two movements.

The *Aliens, Immigrants & Other Evildoers* performance begins with the first music track playing while the stage is black. A recording of classical vocalist Claudia Copeland's version of *Stella Splendens*, a fourteenth-century ode to the Black Madonna, plays. This operatic piece, sung in the original Latin, fills the darkness, and the song helps to create a religious, ritualistic tone for the opening movement.

The recorded music track plays for a total of 4:33, and it covers the duration of the entire first movement performed by the silent Alien character that appears through the darkened stage set.

At five seconds in, with the classical music piece filling the space and while the stage remains dark, the first video of text is projected upon the large 10' x 10' scrim upstage.

Video #1: Dirtiest Little Secret Text

In red bold letters against a black background, the first frame reads:

The dirtiest little secret of the post-Katrina reconstruction
of New Orleans is that the city owes a tremendous debt
to the thousands of Latin American immigrants who labored to rebuild her.

The second frame reads:

According to a Southern Poverty Law Center
study released in the summer of 2009,
80% of them were victims of wage theft by ruthless contractors.

The third frame reads:

The insidious tactic of employers calling
Immigration Agents instead of paying rightfully earned
and promised salaries is commonplace.

The fourth frame reads:

BIENVENIDOS
TO THE SLAVE LABOR FIESTA
OF 21ST CENTURY U.S.A.

As the last section of the projected videotext fades, the screen cyc is lit with an intense red wash, and JOSÉ enters as the enigmatic, silent Alien character. If possible in the theater venue, he enters through the audience for a very physical, Kabuki-like performance ritual.

MOVEMENT #1

Alien Intervention Ritual

[*The enigmatic Alien character* JOSÉ *enters and makes his way to center stage, carrying a large red wooden cross adorned with dollar bills propped over his right shoulder. His movements are stylized and pantomime-like, and the audience hears his breathing as he carries the wooden cross. Methodically, he makes his way through the audience, immediately informing the theater crowd that the border walls between performer and audience will be continuously challenged and broken.* Stella Splendens, *a fourteenth-century pilgrimage song to the Black Madonna, plays.*

This first movement creates the dynamic and haunting visual image of an enigmatic Alien character with a Christ-like blood-red cross. The cross is decorated with eight one-dollar bills and one five-dollar bill, placed exactly at the center where the wooden bars forming the cross intersect. All the bills hang from the horizontal bar of the cross.

As he approaches the stage, a host of green lights illuminate JOSÉ, *the Alien figure. He is wearing an eerie white mask that has a paper extension that elongates the blank visage. ALIEN is written in large green letters above the forehead of the mask.*

As the Alien character, JOSÉ*'s eyes are barely visible through the cut-out, vacant eyeholes of the mask, and it adds to the inhuman quality of the figure. A small slit on the mask outlines his mouth, but this character remains completely silent. It is symbolic of a voiceless Alien making his way through the minimal set and crossing the perilous border, burdened by a cross with the dreams of dollars.*

He is wearing a silvery sequined vest over a long-sleeved black shirt; white gloves adorn his hands to dramatize his exaggerated gestures. A bandana with a print of U.S. dollars is fashioned around his neck, and black trousers complete the Alien figure's apparel.

Draping the back wall of the stage, the 10' x 10' white cyc is lit by a bank of intense red lights. The red cross and the black-clothed Alien figure stand out in stark contrast to the red-lit scrim for a dramatic visual effect.

Once at center, JOSÉ *strikes the first tableau by coming to a halt with the cross directly visible to the audience.*

The following conceptual gestures are juxtaposed with operatic music:

Position #1: JOSÉ'S *whole body is positioned in dramatic silhouette with the cross over his right shoulder. He never looks at the audience, but the image echoes an art history visual of a Christ figure with cross. However, this tableau is charged with the sci-fi aesthetics of an enigmatic Alien character, and he appears detached yet burdened by the task of carrying this cross.*

He holds this position for seven seconds, and then transitions to the next posture.

Position #2: Removing the cross from his shoulders, JOSÉ *positions it in front of him at center stage. It is erected in full-frontal view for the audience to fully absorb the image. His white-gloved hands grip the cross below the intersecting wood pieces. The cross stands tall while he is behind it in a freeze position. It creates another bizarre and surreal juxtaposition of this Alien figure in front of this charged iconic symbol of a red cross with dollar bills.*

The cross is symbolic of the reason for the perilous journey that immigrants make across the border in search of dollars that become dolores ("painful") and elusive to earn for the undocumented and dehumanized immigrant border crosser. The cross is also symbolic of a U.S. culture that worships the almighty dollar as its one true religion, implying that all who enter its territories must succumb to the worship of El Dollar.

Position #3: In the most dramatic of early gestures, the Alien figure makes a loud guttural grunt while lifting the red cross some four feet above his head, and surprises all audience members while offering another dramatic visual tableau that is held still for some seven seconds.

He slowly breaks the pose and lifts the cross onto his shoulders again, moving toward the black platform at upstage center. He places the cross between two gold screws that have been attached to the box to secure it. The cross is held in place at the center of the box, standing erect against the small platform.

The cross serves as the backdrop for an additional sequence of gestures in relationship to the operatic piece that is still playing.

Position #4: With the cross behind him, the Alien figure makes a few hand gestures, beginning with the Star Trek Vulcan finger symbol made famous by Spock, where the two middle fingers are separated to create a "V" meaning "Live long and prosper." It alludes to a spoof of popular sci-fi TV and film culture, and from there, he makes the peace sign with his fingers, as if to note that he is an Alien that comes in peace. Finally, he defiantly raises his left fist-clenched hand with white glove to suggest his uprising Alien spirit against those willing to do him and his people harm. Each hand gesture is held for seven seconds.

Position #5: In front of the free-standing cross, the Alien figure drops slowly to his knees and puts his hands together in an act of worship for the fake religious symbol. This image, too, mirrors a scene from a Renaissance crucifixion scene. He holds this pose for seven seconds.

Position #6: The Alien slowly drops to his knees and places his hands above his head, appearing to be bound with the cross juxtaposed in the background. It alludes to the criminalized immigrant in the U.S. psyche.

This gesture suggests the silent torture that persecuted immigrants suffer in Immigration Detention Centers and jails across the country, and it suggests our general military condolence of torture as a means of a country at war with immigrants, who have also been vilified as akin to terrorists. His wrists are crossed as if bound, and with the red cross of dollar bills directly behind him, it should create a dramatic image of a tortured figure in front of the almighty money cross. He holds the pose for seven seconds.

Position #7: Continuing on his knees, he lowers his head and positions the Alien mask directly on top of his head for an odd visual effect that makes the mask's face protrude from his neck.

He has become a serpentine "Alien animal," symbolic of the dehumanization of immigrants. He sticks out his white-gloved left hand as far as possible, in the dramatic position of a distraught beggar, begging for help and mercy from the distant audience. He keeps his left arm extended in the dramatic begging position and holds this final pose for eleven seconds.

Once in this position, the vocal track begins fading normally, and the sequence of dramatic Kabuki gestures comes to an end. When the music finishes and the

Alien character is frozen in the extreme position of a supplicant beggar, the lights slowly fade to black.

In the dark, he gets up toward stage right, and the second recorded track plays to transition into the next character.

This track is a short recorded piece with sci-fi Mex/Files soundscapes, and José's voice. It notes that the first "illegal aliens" in the Hemispheric Americas were Columbus and his three ships, and that the Pilgrims, too, arrived without papers. It comically questions why the Pilgrims were not deported. The recorded voice emphatically and comically states that the Native Americans should have sent "all their asses back to Europe."

The following video projections are short film graphics of green-colored text about Columbus and the European "discovery" of America. These are very short text graphics that challenge the framing of near genocide of Native people as the "discovery" of the Americas.

Video #2: No Discovery

In green bold capital letters against a black background, the first frame reads:

How do you "discover" a people that already existed without you?

The second film frame reads:

Columbus thought he landed in India, and therefore called

all of the Native people of the Americas "Indians."

Third film frame reads:

It is one of the biggest misnomers in the history of the world.

Video #3: Thanksgiving Atrocity

The first frame reads:

Every time Thanksgiving is celebrated in the United States,

the near genocide of the Native people of North America

is turned into a national holiday.

The second film frame reads:

If you participate, you become an accomplice to that atrocity,

and the calendar you buy prepares you for it every year,

demanding the slaughter of millions of turkeys across the "land of the free."

On stage right in the dark, JOSÉ *transforms himself into the next character, El Swamp Brujo/Baron Samedi Shaman. He puts on a stylish tuxedo jacket and black gloves with green skeleton bones protruding from the fingers.*

JOSÉ *positions himself at center stage on his knees while the recorded track is playing.*

The lights fade in slowly, as the scrim backdrop is awash in green, and an amber spot lights him at center.

He puts on the top hat with the plastic snake decorating the center for the final prop used in the slow transformation into the Swamp Brujo character.

His face is beautifully painted with a "tribal alien" design, and it serves as another mask that is now revealed after the first "Alien" mask has been removed. It's symbolic of the many aliases that immigrants have to adopt as they negotiate living in the shadows of a sci-fi reality where they are ubiquitous and in hiding at the same time.]

MOVEMENT #2

El Swamp Brujo / Alien Green

[*Dressed as El Swamp Brujo/Baron Samedi Shaman, he performs the next piece with a sort of Louis Armstrong-dark-blues-throaty flair, and the slow dirge movements seen in a New Orleans jazz funeral.*]

JOSÉ: A Dirge for the Immigrant Worker at Saint James Infirmary

Sin Papeles Se Murió Trabajando

I went down to Saint James Infirmary,

saw my caramel-brown baby there.

She was an undocumented immigrant worker.
She had cleaned out the Superdome and Convention Center,
but nobody, nobody, nobody was there to cry for her.
Sin papeles se murió trabajando.
Por una miseria de dólares,
su sudor y su sangre regalando.
She was living in a parallel universe,
in a bizarre science-fiction reality,
ubiquitous and invisible simultaneously,
reconstructing the city that care and Bush forgot.
But like many of her brown Latino family,
her pain and suffering doesn't mean a lot
to the likes of you and you and *gringos* generally.
Era una mujer mestiza invisible
para los blancos en general,
como mucha de su gente indocumentada,
sufriendo en la plena oscuridad,
aguantando brutalidad policial,
y deportaciones de la pinche inmigración.
Sin comida y sin casa se encontraba,
combatiendo abusos, tristeza y soledad.
Se murió en la calle abandonada
en un país donde sobran el dinero y la libertad.
I went down to Saint James Infirmary,
my body overcome by grief.

But I am here to tell her story,

and those of my brown paper bag people

because it's my, my destiny,

after seeing my caramel-brown baby there,

dead at Saint James Infirmary.

I went down to the river and cried some more.

With tears, I plotted this performance for her revenge.

I went down to Saint James Infirmary

because I create from PAIN!

Ooohhh, another version for the lexicon.

[JOSÉ *pulls out a silver flask from his right jacket pocket, and offers up some to the Orisha Shango by spilling a bit on the stage floor.*]

Shango. Ashé! After an opening like that, I need a drink, so I bring my own.

[*He takes a good swig from the flask.*]

I don't even know what's in there anymore, but it's good fire water!

. . . *y esta rico y suave como yo.*

[JOSÉ *transitions to Spanish with a more exaggerated satirical cadence and a cabaret-like Joel Grey sassiness as El Alien Baron Samedi Brujo.*]

Verde Como Me Siento Verde / Green I Feel a Little Alien Green

Verde como me siento verde,

extraterrestre verde,

sin mi tarjeta verde

que me marca como verde ilegal.

Verde de gusano verde,

verde sospechoso,

verde odioso,

verde del brócoli verde

que lo recogemos con nuestras manos pa' tu cena.

Verde del aguacate dulce y sabroso

que lo comes sin mucha pena.

Verde de jalapeños verdes

y picantes como la rrrrrevolución que viene verde,

y rrrrrica como la salsita verde

de mi gente verde y orgullosa,

trabajando día y noche con manos

que se vuelven verdes y moradas

por el doloroso verde dólar.

¡AY, CARAMBA!

[*Switching deftly to English without skipping a beat*]

Green, I feel a little alien green,

extraterrestrial green, *My Favorite Martian* green,

supposedly illegal without a green card, undocumented green,

distrustful snake green,

odious Othello jealous thespian green,

broccoli of the many meals we pick for you green.

Guacamole you can't live without green!

Jalapeño rrrrrrevolution, here we come green!

[*In rapid fire rhythm like a possessed hip-hop rapper*]

Green of your painful greenbacks

that WE earn with our green veins flushed

because of our resilient cactus-green spirit
that will boycott the Arizona venom green inside
a law that leaks the puss green of infected minds
and polluted-battery-acid-green souls!
But I know not all of you *GRINGOS* hate like that,
like that green greed that exploits immigrant labor,
and our green alien vulnerability,
as endangered as our swamp-green of Louisiana,
threatened by British Petroleum logo green-black-oil-spill
transforming the green-blue waters of our gulf
into a Greenpeace emergency,
with their putrid green lies the oil has disappeared into
the green ecosphere just like that!
¡AY, CARAMBA!

[*In more of an MC, game-show-host voice directly speaking to the audience*]

Bienvenidos to the Hemispheric Americas,
a temporary borderless ethos without NSA security supervision,
without FOX propaganda bullshit-mountain television,
and without those vigilante minutemen whose desperate housewives
must be longing for HOT Latino interjections.
OOOHHH!
Maybe that's why they call themselves
the minutemen in the first place;
HUNTING DOWN LATINOS
because WE last longer than Duracell,

and the Energizer Bunny ain't got nothing

on my people's persistence because WE keep on going,

and going, and going, and crossing, and crossing, and crossing,

every day, every hour, every second

to reclaim what was ours in the first place

¡AY, CARAMBA!

Google the Guadalupe Hidalgo Treaty of 1848, after the U.S. invasion of Mexico,

and you will discover that all of its northern territories from Texas to California,

through Oklahoma and Utah, were appropriated by Uncle Sam's hunger

to manifest imperial destiny, and the thieves called themselves the New Freedom Republic

with cannons, rifles, and a pen to mark a redrawn border of more stolen lands.

The rightful Mexican landowners became a subjugated, segregated underclass,

foreigners in their own lands, and English the forced language

while Spanish was broken on the backs of every Mexican child

forbidden to speak it.

¡AY, CARAMBA!

Así que, venimos con las pilas puestas, cabrones,

y esto es un espacio experimental sin fronteras,

sin la pinche migra, y sin esos pendejos supuestamente

patriotas patrullando nuestros sueños con sus pesadillas de odio.

There's no translation for that!

[*He laughs maniacally.*]

But the latest statistics show that guacamole junkies are learning tango by the millions,

and salsa outsells Heinz Ketchup as the leading condiment every year,

and *Green-Go-Landia* is obsessed with tanning.

However, don't brown too much my amigo friends

because you'll experience the bittersweet surrender

of a marginalized existence if you have a permanent suntan,

speak with an accent, and visit Arizona

without a green card or a passport.

[*Performed with a rhythmic cadence, he stomps on the stage floor with his right foot, creating a percussive beat flowing with the sung verse of Spanish text. Then he switches to English with the same percussive beat. Depending on where he is performing, some audiences follow along and even clap their hands to the beat, as he invites their participation.*]

Porque me siento verde,

extraterrestre verde,

sin mi tarjeta verde

que me marca como verde ilegal.

Ooohhh!

I feel a little beat up, and black and blue, and green

because they call me *El Señor Boca Mucho Grande*

green, extraterrestrial green, *My Favorite Martian* green,

supposedly illegal without a green card,

undocumented here to stay green

like the first illegal aliens, Pilgrims, green.

Since the Pilgrims arrived without papers,

why were they not deported?

With Columbus and his three ships,

they, the Europeans, were the first illegal aliens in the Hemispheric Americas.

If you are a descendant of Pilgrims and other Europeans,

I recommend self-deportation because

unless you're Native American, you have no claims to these stolen lands

in these United States of Amnesia,

a nation that seduces its citizenry to embrace forgetting.

I am here to remember because NO HUMAN BEING IS ILLEGAL!

[*With maracas now accenting the rhythmic cadence further*]

No human being is illegal! No human being is illegal!

Ningún ser humano es ilegal! Ningún ser humano es ilegal! Ningún ser humano es ilegal!

And you, Agent Orange of Chaos, pimping hate and fear with your deplorable minions at your side, and your orange comb-over hiding the many crosses on fire that ignite to furor fever pitch every time you give another speech to make *America Hate Again*, with Jefferson Beauregard Sessions at your previous side, a living monument to the Confederacy, penning your Zero Tolerance border legislation to criminalize mothers and cage children—crossing a colonial scar, in search of bread and dreams.

Yes, you and your hateful minions. In my universe,

there is "NO GUACAMOLE for immigrant haters!"

And you, you can't even go near the CHIPS!

[*Making a wolf howl of a conceptual coyote!*]

Aaauuuggghhh!

[*Lights fade to black in a ghostly manner as* JOSÉ *takes a dramatic pose at the end of this section, then exits. He changes costumes during blackout and prepares to make an entrance while the next video is projected.*]

Video #4: *The Embassy Letter Video* (2:17)

[*The video details an actual U.S. Embassy letter given to* JOSÉ *when he lost his Green card while performing in Slovenia back in 1998. José performs the voice-over details of the letter's content with an official governmental and indifferent tone. It states, almost matter-of-factly, that* JOSÉ EDUARDO TORRES-TAMA *is a "legal alien" of the U.S.A., and that the letter comes from the Consulate Official at the United States Embassy in Ljubljana, Slovenia.*

It continually states that the "alien" can be allowed back into the U.S.A., and it is a satirical take on the "permanent resident alien" status and moniker assigned to José when he first entered the empire. The words ALIEN are repeated three times toward the end, and fill the screen in bold green letters against the black filmscape.

With the bold caps of ALIEN text, the short video finishes with five ring tones from an old phone. Offstage, JOSÉ *pulls out his cell phone and speaks into it, satirizing the film* The Matrix *where the protagonists confirm they entered the Matrix by answering the call.*]

I'm in.

Video #5: ALIEN *Matrix* film

[*Projected on the stage screen is a matrix-like wash of computer numbers with an image of* JOSÉ *as a young "alien" child when he first entered the U.S. The short video plays with no sound.* JOSÉ *enters from stage left, moving toward the center, and performs against the backdrop of this* Matrix *imagery. It offers a sci-fi visual dynamic, and* JOSÉ *performs the next section in cadence, accented by two maracas that he plays with a rhythmic beat.*]

MOVEMENT #3

Yo soy un inmigrante / I Am an Immigrant

Yo, yo soy un inmigrante también
con la piel de otra tierra lejana,
de Sur América, del Ecuador, de Guayaquil,
y yo crucé con mi madre por avión,
escapando un padre malhechor, egoísta, abusivo,
y por eso no había solución, mas que
cruzar como inmigrante que cruza
porque el sueño de cruzar siempre sabe más que tú.
Y yo, yo soy un inmigrante,
y por eso no hay traducción.
El inmigrante, el inmigrante
cruza por varias razones,
por necesidad económica,
por el sueño de otra vida mejor,
por evitar persecución política,
por libertad social y religiosa,
porque el acto, porque el acto, porque el acto
de cruzar es un poema,
es un poema, es un poema . . . físico
sin traducción.

[*He then speaks directly to the audience in English and in a more deliberate voice. He picks up the small rainstick next to the props on the stage floor while setting down the maracas. The rainstick is slowly moved back and forth, offering an engaging sound texture while he delivers this portion of the poetic text.*]

The immigrant crosses for various reasons,

for economical necessity,

for the dream of a better life,

to avoid political persecution,

for social and religious freedoms,

because the act of crossing is a physical poem,

a rebellious scream, a mythic undertaking,

because sometimes you simply have to cross.

[*He finishes and transitions into the next part of this movement. He drops to his knees in a supplicant posture and delivers this section in a more personal voice. Dramatically, he covers his eyes with his hands in a see-no-evil pose. The gesture symbolically represents the blind leap many immigrants make in their crossing to "the other side."*]

I arrived in the United States

at the tender age of seven with my mother.

She was brave enough to make the leap from Ecuador,

South America to New York City with a suitcase full of hope,

her only child, and barely a few words in English to negotiate our passage.

It was September 1968. We made our legal entry through the Port of Miami.

As we were held for customs inspection at the airport,

WE were transformed at the altar of the First World

because sacrifices were mandatory in order to enter the kingdom,

in order to enter the land of ah, ah, opportunity.

[*He lowers his arms and reaches to the audience as he continues.*]

The first new reality jolt came when my two last names were severed from each other because of a rather incomprehensible appetite for abbreviation in this English-only world dominated by monosyllabic name combinations such as John Smith, Bill King, and Tom Jones.

My full and more melodic birth name of José Eduardo Torres-Tama was reduced to José Torres, and for that there was no solution. It was the butchering of a metaphoric umbilical cord connecting me to the ghosts of all my dead relatives.

If you looked up José Torres in the New York phone book back then, you would find thousands of us stuck to those white pages, bound by an extremely common Spanish first name and a last one just as popular.

In the Latin cultural tradition, it is our two last names that help to distinguish our family history and archive our ancestry.

I was given a green card. I became a "permanent resident alien."

[*He begins to hum "America the Beautiful" through his nose in a rather haunting manner, and reaches for a set of old rabbit ears from an analog TV. He places the antennas on the back of his head, tying them to his American flag bandana to transform himself into an "alien." He continues the comic gestures while humming the patriotic tune.*

His hand gestures satirize his devotion to the flag of the United States, with his hand over his heart. He stops humming and addresses the audience, the antennas still on his head.]

Now, I normally leave my antennas at home because they scare people. But I've gone high def now in the digital age. I've had a little chip installed in the back of my neck, and it helps the NSA keep track of my subversive "alien" performance activities. On occasion, depending on where I am, I even get a little HBO.

[*He takes the antennas off, and continues to hum "America the Beautiful."*

Transitioning into the next character, he begins a ritual with the water in the tin basin, and uses it to smear the green tribal alien face paint all over.

He turns himself into a sort of green alien monster. His face is now completely smeared with this green paint, which transforms him into another type of scary and dirty "alien" character. Symbolically, it serves as a third mask for the "alien" in constant hiding and transition, covering his real face with the grime of labor in the shadows.

With his left arm raised in a gesture mimicking the Statue of Liberty, his left hand reaches for the air. He transforms into a Honduran day laborer, and begins speaking in Spanish, then shifts to broken English as he tells this story. This character is based on the interview of a young reconstruction worker in New Orleans.]

MOVEMENT #4

Honduran Day Laborer: *Mi mano* / My Hand

[*On his knees,* JOSÉ *begins with his left arm raised and his face grimacing in some kind of pain. The scrim is flushed with a bank of blue lights to offer a more somber backdrop to this character.*]

JOSÉ: *Yo me sentía como un extraterrestre, como alguien de otro planeta. Mi brazo todo hinchado, inflado como una llanta mala . . .*

I felt like alien monster. My arm swollen like bad balloon, fingers crooked pointing to sky. My arm, I keep up like this for six months.

Seis meses así con mis dedos apuntando para el cielo. No podía trabajar por dos años.

I not work for two years.

Yo llegue a Nueva Orleáns entusiasmado para trabajar aquí en la reconstrucción, mano de obra, arriesgando mi vida como miles otros por necesidad.

I arrive September 2005, two weeks after Katrina, to rebuild New Orleans. Many Latino people brought in to reconstruct flooded city, looked like apocalypse bomb had hit from a bad future movie. Strange silence of no people and everywhere smell of death . . . a lifeless city and no open food stores.

I was promised two hundred dollars for one day work, and make what I made in one week in Nashville doing busboy work. Good money for me.

Doscientos dólares al día, pero aguantando mucho, trabajando en la peste y mugre de una ciudad destruida.

[*He stands up at this point.*]

But everywhere dirty floodwater past my knees. I only have sneakers, no gloves, no masks and no protection. Contractors not give us proper equipment for our cleaning flooded houses.

Nomás tenía 19 años cuando me pasó esto.

I am nineteen years old when this happened in May 2006.

Era un día como todos los demás esperando en una esquina para trabajar y se presentó un señor que quería dos trabajadores.

Contractor comes to street corner where we wait for work. Two fingers for only two workers, and he look me and point . . . and *otro compañero*. My friend come, too.

We get in truck to go clean his house, *y se tiraba toda la basura en unos de esos,* dumpsters, *y se resbaló.* We throw flooded waste in huge dumpster, but we need to jack it up and move it closer. This is not work for two men to move this heavy dumpster, and jack slips.

[*As worker, he screams a silent scream of horror to dramatize the pain of a left hand crushed under the weight of the dumpster's tonnage. It's symbolic of the silent screams of millions of immigrant workers whose pain goes unnoticed because they suffer in the shadows due to their undocumented status.*]

Mi compañero me dijo que yo gritaba y gritaba como un animal.

My *compadre* say I scream like animal, pain like never before. My hand crushed under this metal dumpster for ten minutes . . . Contractor, not even call for help.

Mi compañero tenia un celular y llamó.

My friend calls for ambulance on his phone. He tries to lift out with jack . . . dumpster off my hand. I scream and scream.

Tenía los dedos colgando con la mano ya partida en dos pedazos.

. . . fingers hanging . . . hand crushed, cut in half . . . blood everywhere . . . bones open raw . . .

Los doctores que me vieron primero me dijeron que tenían que cortar mi brazo para evitar una infección. Yo pensando en este dolor que me tenía ya desvelado, como así yo vine a este país y ahora voy a tener que regresar a mi tierra sin un brazo. Que sueños que tenía para ayudar a mí familia y ahora esta pesadilla.

Hospital doctors and nurses say to cut off my arm because of infection. I think what dream I come for? Working here, and now go back to Honduras with one arm missing.

Pero como un milagro de dios había un doctor afroamericano que era el que mandaba y dijo que no. Vamos a salvar tu brazo porque es muy traumático para un muchacho tan joven como tú perder un brazo.

But black doctor sees me, and said "NO! We not cut your arm. We reconstruct your hand. I have son your age. Not good for you to be one-arm young man—too traumatic! He put back my hand. Three surgeries in two months . . . like a miracle.

I saw kind doctor man one year later at Walgreens, *el que está por hospital de la Universidad donde me operaron.*

I remember him. He remembered me, and point to my hand. I show him. He said, "Good for you. It's getting better." I never forget his kind eyes. He saved my arm, repaired my hand.

I am an activist now, *activista con el congreso de jornaleros*, with Congress of Day Laborers. *Peleamos por los derechos humanos para todos los trabajadores.*

We fight for human rights for all workers in New Orleans . . . for safety . . . dignity . . . for human treatment.

We are asking for respect of our right to feed our families. We are asking to go to our houses every day, sit with our children, our families, and eat without fear of Immigration coming, without fear of police coming, without fear a contractor boss not paying us.

We are asking to be respected. We are not aliens, but human beings. We have contributed to the reconstruction of a U.S. city.

Can you imagine? Contractor never, *nunca se lo vio mas* . . . never did nothing to help me . . . not even call an ambulance.

[*He slowly drops back to his knees, humming "America the Beautiful," and ritualistically washes all of the smeared green face paint off with a towel placed next to the basin. The washing ritual is slow, symbolic of the filth that workers endure in doing the jobs that no one else wants to do. He delivers his last lines while engaged in this moving ritual of washing himself clean.*]

Seventeen *compañeros* . . . seventeen men, we sleep like animals in one trailer.

Diecisiete durmiendo en unos de esos traileres con un baño, era inhumana las condiciones por estos dolorosos dólares.

Seventeen men sleeping in trailer for one person. They promised us housing and caged us like dirty rats.

[*He washes the green face paint off while delivering the lines about being dirty.*]

We wake up at four A.M. . . . *a las cuatro de la mañana nos despertamos para limpiarnos.*

Seventeen workers shoved in for one shower to clean to begin work at six A.M.

I hated being dirty. Covered with mold and dirty water every day.

We pulled dead people from some houses, and smell of rotted bodies caused terrible headaches. But we cleaned and repaired New Orleans. WE, thousands of Latino immigrants, and no one will tell you this story.

Anderson Cooper will not tell you this story, and ten years after the storm, it's the dirty secret of the reconstruction of New Orleans.

Sometimes, we worked for weeks, and instead of paychecks contractors call Immigration. No pay, and only dirt to remind us of work we do.

[*Hauntingly, he finishes by humming "American the Beautiful" while washing the remaining green paint off his face.*

Once all the green face paint is off, he shape-shifts into the next character, and reaches for the blue shawl placed on the stage floor. Rising from his knees, in a slow regal manner, he wraps the blue shawl around his body to transform into a woman.

The next character is inspired by the interview with a Nicaraguan woman who crossed the border when she was a little girl. She crossed without papers, and with her aunt and three sisters, crossed the Rio Grande to reunite with her father—fleeing the Nicaraguan Civil War of the '80s.]

MOVEMENT #5

Yo soy ilegal / I Am Illegal

[*As the female character draped in a blue shawl,* JOSÉ *begins in Spanish, addressing the audience directly. Not all the Spanish is directly translated, and it's done in part to challenge the pervasive monolingual paradigm in the U.S.*

Also, it strategically places the English-speaking audiences in the same language struggle with Spanish that the immigrant experiences with English.

The lighting is such that a purple aura is created on the upstage scrim around the character's head, and symbolically, it alludes to the woman being a Guadalupe-like goddess that crosses the border.

In a soft and tender female voice and hunched over like an older woman, José renders a gender transformation, and becomes an elderly Nicaraguan woman. He / she begins in Spanish, but switches effortlessly to English.]

Nosotros no venimos a robar, ni hacer maldades.

Venimos a trabajar, para contribuir a este país,

y nos tratan como basura.

Who repairs your cars and your houses?

Who washes the dishes in the many restaurants here?

Who prepares the guacamole you love so much?

Si, yo soy ilegal. Crucé ilegalmente cuando era una niña de ocho años con mis tres hermanitas. Cuatro niñas cruzando el rió grande con una tía por la media noche, en plena oscuridad con una luna llena como nuestro único testigo. No se lo deseo eso a nadie.

Yes, I'm illegal. I crossed "illegally" when I was a girl of eight years with my three sisters, four little girls crossing the Rio Grande with my aunt as our guide and only a full moon as our witness. I don't wish it upon anybody.

We were frightened, but we did not know what exactly was going on. Nobody told us that it was illegal. My aunt said we were crossing to reunite with our father, who had left Nicaragua to escape the war. He left before I was born, and I was going to see him for the first time. Eight long years he was gone from us.

Who landscapes your lovely lawns?

Who cleans your tall corporate office buildings at night?

Who picks up the garbage in the early morning?

Who are these invisible workers you don't even dare to make eye contact with?

"Illegal!" It's a disgusting term, but I embrace it because for many years it caused me great shame and pain. We have to take such words and remove their hatred, squeeze the poison out of them. Now, I use it to empower myself.

Many Latino people try to silence me when I say I'm "illegal" because they are frightened.

Ay, mi hija no lo digas tan fuerte, te puede oír alguien. Pues que lo oigan. Yo soy un ser humano refugiado de una guerra.

Let them hear me. Yes, I am illegal, but I am also a human being and a political refugee from a war-torn nation—a war the U.S. had much to do with.

Did you know the U.S. occupied Nicaragua for much of the early part of the twentieth century? Why would you want to know?

Your collective voluntary amnesia protects you.

You know why they called themselves the Sandinistas?

The rebels chose to honor the name of Augusto César Sandino, a revolutionary leader who led a rebellion against the U.S. military occupation of Nicaragua in the 1920s and '30s.

Sandino was assassinated by the *Guarda Nacional*—the U.S.-backed armed forces of the Somoza family dictatorships that ruled Nicaragua for over forty years . . .

Cuarenta años hasta que los Sandinistas los echaron a correr. Por diez años mi gente comió guerra para el desayuno, el almuerzo, y la merienda.

For a decade, my people, we ate war for breakfast.

We ate war for lunch.

We ate war for dinner.

A war between the U.S.-backed contra insurgents supplied covertly by your CIA and the Sandinista rebels who were Marxist, fighting for people's land rights.

WE, the people, the other we, are caught in between your bullets and your country's corporate interests.

I'm not blaming you, but the war took my father away for eight years because he did not want to fight, choosing to go north to work and send your dollars back home to our Nicaragua.

It's ironic. We benefited from the U.S. money because my mother had four little girls to feed and clothe, but I would have preferred to have my father for all of my eight birthdays instead of those dirty dollars.

[*At this moment the character gets highly emotional, and* JOSÉ *brings himself to tears as he delivers these lines.*]

I saw my father for the first time that night after we crossed the Rio Grande, and I would cross any border illegally—again and again to be with him.

I brought a mirror with me to this performance today.

[*As the Nicaraguan woman,* JOSÉ *leaves center stage and reaches behind the prop table at upstage left and retrieves an 18" x 24" mirror that has been kept hidden.*

In character as the Nicaraguan woman, JOSÉ *steps off stage with mirror in hands, and enters the audience—breaking the fourth wall. He approaches three different audience members in the front row, placing the mirror before each of their individual faces. It is a moment of great palpable live art drama beyond the borders of voyeuristic conventional theater.*

As he makes his way into the audience, a spotlight follows him. With the mirror in front of each individual audience member, he repeats the text below.]

I am here because you are there.

I am here because you are there.

I am here because you are there.

[*The Nicaraguan woman character makes her way back to the edge of the downstage area, and holds the mirror to the entire audience. She says the last lines in Spanish with her voice breaking from the emotional weight that consumes her, and tears flow from* JOSÉ*'s eyes.*]

Yo estoy aquí porque ustedes están allá.

[JOSÉ *holds the pose, and lights fade to black slowly to offer a ghostly image.*

The audience is in black for eleven seconds to let the drama of this moment breathe, and offer the performer and audience a respite.]

Video #6: Star Wars Sci-fi Satire—*The Dark Force Awakens*

[*This comical video short satirizes the Star Wars movie with text that floats into the infinity of space. Offering the premise of the current chapter of an Empire that has migrated deep into the "Dark Side," it outlines the persecution of immigrants as if it was taking place in a near sci-fi future, in a place called the Planet Seven. The sound track for the video is a sci-fi loop sounding much like a science-fiction 1960s B movie.*

The text reads:

The Future Today: In the most dangerous Reality TV Show the Empire has witnessed, the Aryan Asses of Evil reawaken and shake the Grand Ole Patriarchal Republican Guard with the birth

of a monster they themselves try to abort, and the KORPORATE KLANSMAN known by the monosyllable CHUMP pimps a message of FEAR that his minions embrace.

The CHUMP has an orange-hair comb-over hiding his many burning crosses that ignite at FUROR FEVER PITCH every time he gives another speech to make the EMPIRE HATE AGAIN! He becomes the new face of a White Supremacist Dark Force that even the GOP haters find over the top.

The CHUMP resembles a JABBA THE HUTT SUPER PIMP with three wives and a litter of SITH siblings who try to soften his appetite for incendiary hateful rhetoric as he tries to rise to the captain's chair to rule the empire like one of his many failed casinos on the Atlantic Coast.

CHUMP describes the immigrant rebel forces as criminals and rapists, and tries to seduce the "BLACK JEDIS" into his camp by selling them "What Do You Have to Lose with White Supremacy?" T-shirts. The Jedi Forces don't buy the bull and side rightfully with the day laborers and bilingual immigrants.

The immigrant rebel forces forge a rainbow coalition with like-minded progressives and try to establish a bilingual and multiracial colony on the Planet Pachamama. The rebel colony is temporarily named the Living La Vida Loca Free Zone.

The Elder Republican Guard who love to hate women and people of color now have an even bigger hater, and their revered and deceased Darth Sith Lord Ronald "MacDonald" Reagan is remembered for his famous words, "Bring down that wall, Mr. Gorbachev!" The wrath of KORPORATE KLANSMAN CHUMP makes his mantra, "Build that Wall!"

Even the channel Frightful Overt Xenophobes (FOX TV) run by bombastic pundits who push pure propaganda and lies, find the CHUMP bullshit mountain difficult to climb.

The rebels prepare for an epic battle led by their unshakable leader of the Jalapeño Revolution known as The Hot One, a.k.a El OBIE

JUAN KENOBI, and most commonly referred to as El Pachuco of Interracial and Interplanetary Love of the Future!

El Pachuco had been FEELING THE BERN, but now has to take on the dark forces with his message that hate is reactionary and "LOVE IS RADICAL!"

As the text fades into infinity, JOSÉ *enters stage right and positions himself before a music stand that has been placed in front of the red cross, which is standing erect before the floating U.S. flag. It makes for a dramatic backdrop, and rapidly switching voices from a TSA airport announcer voice to a Latino Radio voice to a Southern "redneck" voice, he delivers a satirical text about life under* Orange Alert.]

MOVEMENT #6

Orange Alert!

[*The sci-fi video continues, but the sci-fi sound track volume is lowered, and in the voice of a TSA airport authority figure,* JOSÉ *continues.*

Putting on a pair of glasses to give him a nerdy visage, and using a small bullhorn that he brings on stage, he begins emphatically, as if possessed by the urgency of the moment. He is lit with a dramatic orange spotlight.]

Attention please! Attention please!

We are under orange alert. Please make sure to wear your orange alert underwear at all times.

Attention please! Attention please!

All compliant and nationally conscious flag-waving citizenry of our esteemed republic who respect our credos and question nothing, we urge you to exercise your God-given rights to identify and report any suspicious **alien creatures,** who may look undocumented, illegal, and appear to be supported by not-for-profit, communist-leaning arts organizations and theaters [JOSÉ *names the theater he is in*] . . . looking to spread the subversive dogma of **"equality for all and diverse community engagement"** on their websites and propaganda literature.

We urge you to call "**one-eight-hundred-NO-ART-NOW!" Text or tweet, Tumblr, Instagram, and employ whatever other digital means you use to communicate** and denounce these instigators. Use Facebook only if you are over forty. Furthermore, we urge you to support meaningless abstract work that has no engagement with the community and clearly expresses high art values with no decipherable human concern.

Art for art's sake is the only art we support, pushing form for the sake of form, and artists oblivious to the political urgency of the moment.

We have engaged the highly touted institution of Creative Capitalism to support only conceptual experimental art being made by our mostly *gringo* brothers and sisters, who have graduated from M.F.A. theater programs WITH TREMENDOUS DEBT, and where art is regarded as a pure form not burdened by content, especially socially conscious content.

Please go to creativecapitalism.org to review the type of meaningless art we support.

[*He speaks the following in Spanish with a thick, funny* "gringo" *accent that mimics the recordings often heard as phone options to choose Spanish language translations.*]

Para escuchar estay mensajay en Español por fayvor oprima el numero dos.

[*He speaks the following in a redneck voice.*]

Ya see. They got ya talking that Spanish. Just the other day, I was ordering a medium-sized cup of coffee at that Starbucks, and I had to call it a GRANDE! Why can't we just call it BIG?

Then, ya go to that Taco Bell, and they got you ordering things like a chimichanga. That's that strange Mexican Spanish. What the hell is a chimichanga anyway?

Now, I heard it's the Mexican slang term for fornication with little dogs! Yes, I know. It's weird. They got you asking to have sex with little dogs because I heard "chimi" is Mexican slang for sex, and "changa" is the name of a little dog. In fact, the changa is the cousin of the chihuahua. Remember him, "Yo Quiero Taco Bell!"

You don't see him anymore. I heard he was working in Hollywood without papers, and Immigration Agents finally caught up with him. He got deported back to Mexico. Another Latino actor bites the dust.

But ya gotta watch them Latinos people. Hispanics! Yeah, they make me panic because they're growing in numbers. Dem' Latinos, they're having a lot of sex, and they're going to take over—not in 2050 but more like 2020.

And dem dere Cubans, they come in all kinds of colors. Just the other day, I discovered my neighbor is Cuban. I knew him as Peter, but his birth name is *Paydro.* He's white with reddish brown hair, and now that there are more open relations with Cuba, he had some kind of family reunion recently. Had a cousin that was black visiting him, and is apparently *Afro-Cuban.* Black and Latino—makes him doubly dangerous. Ya' gotta watch dem dere Latinos because they're taking over.

[*Speaking in an exaggerated Latino radio announcer's voice*]

¡Atención por favor! ¡Atención por favor!

Le pedimos a todos nuestros colegas que reporten a cualquier gringo que se vea sospechoso y de falta de ejercicio, que parece que ve mucha televisión y pasa mucho tiempo en los coffee shops tomando café con leche y disfrutando de living la vida loca mientras nosotros trabajamos como perros, como inmigrantes que trabajan sin descanso.

¡Atención por favor! ¡Atención por favor!

Le pedimos a nuestra gente Latina que reporten a cualquier gringo que está haciendo arte o teatro abstracto que no tiene ninguna razón y simplemente está creando arte para mantener el status de poder blanqueador, sin reconocer el dolor humano, y las condiciones de terror que sufren diariamente las comunidades de color porque son víctimas de brutalidad policial y marginalizadas históricamente aquí en los estados hundidos.

Si se encuentran con artistas así por favor mande los a la chingada, y díganle que dejen de ser pendejos y que crean arte revolucionario!

¡Atención por favor! ¡Atención por favor! ¡Por esto no hay traducción! ¡QUE SE JODAN!

[*Speaking in the voice of a game show announcer*]

Ladies and gentleman, at this point we want to announce that we will be considering developing an idea for **a new reality show called *"WHO WANTS TO BE A DAY LABORER?"*** where *gringo* contestants compete to be overworked and underpaid, even experience the heightened sensation of being victims of wage theft by their friendly neighborhood politically connected construction contractor exploiters. I mean employers.

[*Speaking in* Grigoñol *accent*]

¡No dinero aquí* for your *trabajo con más sabor!

[*Returning to generic game show host voice*] Contestants will also have no legal recourse for any injuries that may occur on the job and will be obligated to waive their rights to any claims against their exploiters, I mean employers, and will be engaged in the latest disaster to hit the Gulf: yes, cleaning toxic oil spills with no protective measures, no masks, no gloves, and certainly no lunch.

WHO WANTS TO BE A DAY LABORER? is brought to you by the corporate amigos who support slave labor in the twenty-first century, and they include Haliburton, the Shaw group, the highly secretive KRB, and of course our friends at Blackwater, who have all been repairing Iraq since we decimated it ten-plus years ago. Look at the mess they left behind, but making, shall we say it, "A killing for Dick Cheney and friends."

Good ole Dick being the dick that he has always been, looking out for *NUMERO UNO.*

[*Speaking in rapid-fire English like the announcements for side effects by drugs like Viagra*]

PLEASE NOTE that *gringo* contestants may be voted off the Day Laborers' show if they exhibit subversive behavior and begin demanding human treatment, human rights, and a living wage for their work.

NO WAY JOSÉ is our motto here at *WHO WANTS TO BE A DAY LABORER?*

GRASSYASS!

[*Lights fade to black here instantly. By this time, the* Star Wars *video has played out.*]

Video #7: Hate Crimes

[*This short film with another audio track by* JOSÉ *offering sections of a* New York Times *editorial with graphic charts that depict the rise in brutal racial violence and murders committed against Latin Americans since 2008, whether they are legal citizens, legal residents, or undocumented people.*

Offstage, JOSÉ *has prepared himself for the next character. He has transformed into El Pachuco of Interracial and Interplanetary Love of the Future, noted in the previous video as the stylish revolutionary leader of the Jalapeño Revolution. As the graphic noting the rise in hate crimes against Latinx people plays, he puts on a vintage red jacket made in New Orleans and a red cowboy hat. Video finishes.*]

MOVEMENT #7

El Pachuco of Interracial and Interplanetary Love of the Future

[JOSÉ *begins to speak as El Pachuco of Interracial and Interplanetary Love of the Future in an exaggerated East L.A. pachuco accent à la Edward James Olmos, mimicking the iconic Chicano character from Luis Valdez's "Zoot Suit" '70s play.*

Taking an exaggerated pachuco stylized pose, and holding a candle in his right hand with a skull in his left, he talks directly to the audience as the lights fade up on him.]

Órale, iconic Chicano image #59. ¿Que paso, mi gente?

[*No response from the audience, but he addresses them directly.*]

OK, iconic Chicano performance image #69.

[*He spreads out his arms with a badass look on his face, as if he was King of GringoLandia, and slowly kisses the skull on its mouth.*]

¿Qué pasó?

Here I am in [*says the city where the show is being performed*], and you people need to catch up on your iconic Chicano performance imagery.

I'll give you one more chance. Are you ready?

[*He waits for the probable tepid response.*]

Am I talking to myself again? Look, I'm here. You're there, and we're all in this together.

It's not like regular theater. It's not a voyeuristic experience. It's performance art. It's a sci-fi Latino noir solo, just like your program says, and this is the participatory performance part of the experience with lots of alliteration to boot. Look, look, I'm going to get conceptual on you, and break the fourth wall. Yes, I'm coming out to touch someone.

[*Moving toward the audience and approaching a man in the front row*]

Look, I'm touching you, and you're a man. I'm a man, too, and I cross all kind of borders. 'Cause I'm experimental like that. I'm not just macho for the ladies. I'm not just bilingual.

You know what I mean? You're looking good, *Vato.* You work out? No, *pues,* what vitamins are you taking?

People, it's not easy being a Latino man in the twenty-first century. We have to look good. We have to represent. We have to keep up with the Rodriguezes, and they're a big family.

[*Egging the audience on*] Am I looking good or what? Yes, I know.

[*Lifting his right leg to show off his suave* vato *shoes*] Check out the shoes, *Ese* Snakeskin! And let me hear it for the red jacket?

[*He waits for audience to respond strongly, as they begin to realize they can participate in this conceptual stand-up comedy movement of the show.*]

Vintage. Am I looking hot? I'm feeling hot, and not just because the candle wax is dripping on my hand. But it does offer a stimulating sensation. I like it because I'm kinky like that.

This is my outfit for my new HBO show called *Latino Eye for the White Guy*, where I offer clueless white boys the seductive strategies of Latino lovers. And in the Anglican patriarchal planation paradigm (big words, *ese*), there are two archetypal opposites assigned to the Latino male—Hispanic Killer or Latino Lover. I know you desire the latter, like an exquisite exotic high-end eatery enchilada! *Ay, que picante* verbal musings.

So now that we have established a relationship, I'm going to introduce myself again. Are you ready? I'm going to re-enter from stage right, like if I wasn't even here—like a holographic CGI image talking to you via Skype.

I'm going to put on a TV announcer's voice, and when I hit center stage again, you all break out in spontaneous prompted applause—just like on TV game shows where the signs say "APPLAUSE!"

[*Moving back to upstage left and in the shadows, and with an exaggerated, almost Elvis Presley–like game show host accent*]

Ladies and gentlemen, *damas y caballeros*, *enchiladas y burritos*, here he is all the way from the conceptual *barrio* of East L.A., the metaphoric mean streets of los *Vatos Bravos*, and inspired by Luis Valdez's *Zoot Suit*'s Chicano character originally performed with such exquisitely over-the-top ethnic exaggeration by Edward James Olmos in the movie that made that *carnal* super famous with his own home on map of the stars, I bring ***you a hybrid specimen, Mexican-born in the U.S.A., calls himself a Chicano (I don't even know what that means but it's in this invisible script), El Pachuco of Interracial and Interplanetary Love of the Future***.

[*He walks stylishly and slowly to center stage like a true pachuco of yesteryear. This time the audience goes wild.*]

Yes, go wild! This is live art *carnales*. If you are moved, take your clothes off, even, because it's performance art. It's a paradigm shift. You feel it?

And the future is going to look a lot like me, looking *caliente* good, and be better dressed.

[*Blowing kisses to all the men and women in the audience, and specially to anyone dressed in drag or with a non-binary look or attire.*]

I am here to talk about LOVE because there is too much hate in this country, right now! Right?

There's a lot of hate here in these United States of Amnesia, which seduces you to embrace forgetting. I'm here to remember.

And I am here to advocate for more love. *AMOR* people! Who likes more love to trump all this hate being spewed out? Yes, we need more condoms to go with all that love because we need protection as well. I'm here to advocate for interracial love, *amor interracial.* How many of you have made love recently to someone across the racial divide, from another country, who speaks another language other than your own. Let me see a show of hands.

[*Pachuco begins to improvise and ask specific questions of those audience members who raise their hands.*]

Over here, yes, you with your hand that went up immediately. I believe art is in the details, so give me some specifics, some juicy *caliente chisme* / gossip.

[*He continues, and it usually gets very funny, as he provocatively plays with the audience members about making love to the "alien others."*]

But you know what worries me the most? I'm talking to you all again.

The audience gets it now and asks collectively: What worries you the most, Pachuco?

Look at you, finally realized that this is not theater. I'm glad you asked.

I worry whenever I hear politicians say, "Let's take America back!"

I'm like, how far back do you want to go? We're not taking this bus back to 1950. No, it was not even a good time to be a white woman back then. Certainly, not a good time to be gay in 1950, and not even a good time to be a Jewish filmmaker in Hollywood back then.

Elia Kazan! No, I'm not naming any names, just name-dropping. Not a good time to be Native American in 1950 U.S.A. Not a good time to be Puerto Rican in New York or the Northeast. Not a good time to be Mexican in the Southwest. Not a good time to be Cuban in Miami, even. Certainly, not a good time to be African American in the Deep South with the ubiquitous lynchings of black boys, men, and women. Not unlike the killings of unarmed black citizens by white police today! Ouch, reality hurts.

And what your history books don't tell you in the United States of Amnesia is that after the Guadalupe Hidalgo Treaty of 1848, which forced Mexico to cede its entire northern territories from Texas to California to Uncle Sam, entire Mexican families were lynched if they refused to hand over their lands to the German and Irish immigrant settlers conscripted from Europe to take over the Southwest and segregate it like the South.

If you don't know this history, Google it! Yes, because Latinos, we love to Google. Google is an old Latin term. Actually, Google is an old AZTEC term from the tribal God Googlequetzalcoatl, which means, Look shit up! Know your history in the United States of Amnesia.

Let's look at some of your juicy laws like the Indian Removal Act of 1830. They weren't even trying to be subtle. They could have called it Operation Iraqi Freedom. Some jokes, I do just for me. Chinese Exclusion Act of 1882. Japanese Interment 1942. Operation Wetback 1954. I'm just saying. All built on fear. I'm just saying.

We need more love to trump the FEAR pimped by politicians who want to *MAKE AMERICA HATE AGAIN!* Refuse and resist.

We need to be there for each other. Just the other day, I was at a Mexican restaurant, near the front entrance, surveying the place in my pachuco-stylized way—like I do.

[*Taking a stylized pachuco pose, skull still in his hand*] This blonde girl comes over to me and says, [*speaking in a* gringo *Spanish accent*] *¿Donde esta el baño?*

And I'm like [*speaking in a* gringo *Spanish accent back*], *El baño esta allá.*

Yes, I wanted to show solidarity with her because she crossed over to *Bilingual-Landia*, and she didn't even need a passport. She spoke

Spanish to me, and later confessed that Spanish gets her hot, like the jalapeños she kept eating with her spicy guacamole right here in [*saying the name of town he is performing in*].

We need to cross over because we are always trapped in this monolingual paradigm. Who wants to make love in Spanish? Raise your hand.

[*Looking around for any hands raised*] OK, talk to me after the show, But don't talk to José. He's just too righteous. Talk to Pachuco because I do all the deep community outreach. I'm just saying!

Now, when I cross the border, my back gets wet sometimes, so they call us wetbacks. Well, I always cross with a Mickey Mouse towel to dry off on the other side because I'm Disney like that.

But my favorite is to cross with my low rider during low tide, and my flashy hood adorned with fifty U.S. flags . . . because I'm nationalistic like that. Fifty little U.S. flags made in China . . . because I'm global like that.

And let's make sure you all know that I don't get all romantic and choked up about previous president Barack Obama, like many on Facebook. No, because he migrated to the "Dark Side." Yes, he did. Who would have thought that the son of an African immigrant would rise to the captain's chair and become the "Deporter-in-Chief" after seducing a growing Latin American electorate to place him in power. Ouch!

He deported some three million of my immigrant people, mothers and fathers, and children and even DREAMERS. Let's not forget. I held my nose when I voted for him back in 2012. What was a *vato* to do, vote for self-deportation Mormon Romney?

So, I found myself between Barack and the GOP hard place on Immigration Reform! OK, let me say that again for those of you who missed it. I found myself between Barack and the GOP hard place on Immigration Reform. That's right! Some of you may get these jokes on your way back home. Some of you may never get them. You know who you are.

That Barack was a classic case of the tragic mulatto, and he never walked the talk of his Immigration Reform promise. But he left a well-oiled human expulsion apparatus for the billionaire thug to exploit to no end.

So my question to you all: Is the Eurocentric plantation paradigm getting you down? People of color in the house, I'm talking to you specially. OK, I'm going to ask all of you again for those of you that missed it. Is the Eurocentric plantation paradigm getting you down?

[*Audience responds with affirmatives.*]

Yes, me too.

I am brown, therefore I am suspect. I am Latino, therefore I am spicy. I studied art in college, therefore I am unemployed. You're laughing and I'm serious.

I often speak in Spanish to confuse my *gringo* audiences, therefore I'm a pain in the derriere of monolingual gatekeepers and hegemonic cultural epistemologies. I use big words, therefore I'm superfluous. I'm just saying!

But who reconstructs your cities after each hurricane and naturally manmade catastrophe? Us.

And in New Orleans, thousands of Latinos descended from all parts of the globe to transform Chocolate City into an Enchilada Village, but they suffered untold atrocities.

And here's a tale you won't hear anywhere else:

A U.S. citizen, with passport and no English,

from Puerto Rican farmlands,

accompanied by an even younger

Mexican boy seventeen, maybe sixteen,

who looked stunned without blood,

without remedy, without a floor to sleep

that night, or the night before,
in New Orleans at a bar during Halloween
October 2005 in the forsaken city,
this *Borinqueño* told me he worked
with a force of three hundred men
for three weeks from seven A.M. to seven P.M.
Promised twelve hundred dollars per week,
promised and promised to be paid
on the final Friday of the third week,
but on Thursday night before the much-awaited payday,
New Orleans Police raided their encampment,
an abandoned factory building with three hundred cots.
All of them ran, fled, the sound of sirens,
the chaos, the fright, *la migra,*
la policía, auxilio, socorro.
How convenient for the contractors, don't you think?
The benevolent NOPD just happened upon them,
and I wonder how much they got paid,
New Orleans' Finest, for their accidental raid
on *los invisibles* of the post-Katrina
reconstruction apocalypse blues.
This Puerto Rican youngblood
with commonwealth citizenship papers,
went back to the boss's trailer to collect
his thirty-six hundred owed.

He was told the company headquartered in Alabama,
and if he wanted his check,
he could walk to Birmingham.
Not a dime in his pocket and hunger in his belly
for three weeks' work of thirty-six hundred dollars his hurt back and blistered feet remembered.
Multiply by three hundred men,
and more than a million never paid
in one episode of twenty-first-century slave labor,
post-Katrina reconstruction apocalypse blues.
Hallelujah!
Can I get a witness?
We know this.
We remember.
We urge others not to forget.
Oh come, all ye faithful!
Oh come, let us explode you!
Oh, America, the beautiful, you make
my life a nightmare with such addiction to slave labor.
Oh, America, your underbelly is my undertow.
Do you remember?
Did you hire one?
Did you cheat one?
Así qué afilen los oídos,
despierten la subconciencia,

y ajusten sus cinturones filosóficos.

Do not be afraid, *amigos y amigas, porque se habla español aquí.*

Do not be afraid of the Spanish language

because *Tostitos* are here to *stay*!

In fact, we are new and improved, fat-free,

and *good* for the *economy*,

and we are *everywhere* you want to be,

doing what we do *best* to get a piece of the *rock*!

So, if you are *bilingually challenged*,

sharpen your ears, awake your subconscious,

and adjust your philosophical seatbelts,

because it's early in the dawn of the new millennium still.

Así qué,

A M E R I C A, as in South and Central *también,*

con huevos rancheros y salsita picante,

América por tus otros nombres,

wake up and smell the *café con leche.*

Do you know where your c o u n t r y is?

[*He takes a dramatic pose and lights fade slowly. He howls like an unleashed conceptual coyote, AAAAAOOOUUU! Before the lights are completely down, he states:*]

Bring the immigrants out of the shadows because no human being is illegal, carnales!

Video #8: Marcelo Lucero Long Island Hate Crime Short (1:13)

[*Another short hate crime video plays, and it depicts graphics from a* New York Times *article with a sound overlay of the brutal stabbing of Marcelo Lucero, an Ecuadorian legal resident. He was stabbed to death in Long Island a few days after Barack Obama was elected on November 7, 2008.* JOSÉ*'s voice with a haunting echo delay is heard as the official reporter offering details of the crime.*]

Marcelo Lucero, a thirty-seven-year-old Ecuadorian legal resident of the United States, was stabbed to death in Long Island by one of six teenagers who jumped him. The teens were out on a night of "beaner hopping," which is slang for the "sport" of beating Mexicans or Hispanics. "Beaner" is a derogatory term used against Latinos of Mexican descent, but it is applied generally as a racial term against all Latinos.

Marcelo Lucero was a law-abiding legal resident who had lived in the United States for sixteen years. He sent money home regularly from his dry-cleaning job to his mother in Ecuador who was a cancer survivor.

On a night of "beaner hopping," all Latinos regardless of specific ethnicity were open targets. Five of the six assailants were white, and one of the teens was of mixed race, Latino and African American.

[*The film sets the tone for the next character, a Mexican Methodist minister in New Orleans who advocates on behalf of immigrants under attack from both police and criminals.*]

MOVEMENT #8

El Cristo en el inmigrante / The Christ in the Immigrant

[*Speaking in a minister's cadence and switching back and forth from Spanish to English*]

Hay que ver a Jesús Cristo como un inmigrante,

Sufriendo y en la corrida, corriendo por su vida

Escapando el estado y la inmigración,

Cruzar el Rió Grande es como cruzar el Rió de Egipto.

If you recall, it was Herod who put the edict forth to kill the baby Jesus, the Messiah.

Immigrants are on the run like Christ, they are the sacrificial lambs of today.

Your Statue of Liberty, with its prophetic and compassionate words to the world, let's recall what it says, "Give us your poor, your wretched, your huddled masses yearning to breathe free!"

The immigrants are your huddled masses. Does it say in parentheses only the Irish immigrants, the Polish immigrants, the Italian immigrants? All immigrants have come to these shores under less than favorable conditions. I'm asking you [*expecting the audience to respond*].

I heard this was a lively congregation.

Cuando yo veo a un inmigrante, yo veo a una personal humilde

lista para trabajar y contribuir para el beneficio de todos.

When I see an immigrant, I see a humble person, ready to work and contribute for all to benefit from his labor. *Yo no veo a un monstruo.*

I don't see a monster. I see a father working long hours to provide for his family.

Just like all others who have come here to dream.

Les cuento sobre una ocasión donde un padre regresando de su trabajo

en su camioneta fue atacado afuera de su casa aquí en Chalmette.

I will share a story with you of an immigrant father returning home from work in Chalmette, a suburb of New Orleans.

Two men pulled up into his driveway, and they demanded money from him, knowing that immigrants carry cash on them more readily than others.

Sus hijos, sus tres hijos, gritando, no, no, déjenlo a mi papá.

His children screaming, *Leave my father alone*, screaming through the front window.

Leave my father alone! Leave my father alone!

El padre resistió. The father resisted.

Es un hombre y va resistir esa clase de ataque a su dignidad.

He's a man, and is going to resist this attack on his home in front of his children, crying through the window.

One man strikes him across the head. He drops to the cement, and his children screaming through the window, *Don't kill my father*, screaming and crying, and screaming and crying.

I am a Mexican Methodist minister here, and I came to New Orleans to serve my people. Sometimes, all I can do is just cry with them. So I cried with the family. I cried with the children. I cried with the mother and father.

The police . . . an immigrant life does not matter to them . . . especially if it is an undocumented immigrant . . .

La policía . . . mi gente le tiene miedo a la policía aquí como le tiene miedo a los criminales y a veces no se puede distinguir . . .

My people are afraid of the police as much as they are afraid of the criminals, and sometimes it is difficult to distinguish the difference in New Orleans.

Si fueron Afro Americanos . . . los dos muchachos.

The men were black. Yes, but here in my congregation, we have many African American people who support our cause, who relate to our pain, who stand in solidarity with us.

But on the streets of New Orleans—*en la calle llaman a nuestra gente cajas automáticas de dinero para violar día y noche*—our immigrant people are referred to as walking ATMs.

Walking ATM machines to violate and withdraw ready available cash. ATMs! Can you imagine that? We come here to be ATMs. *Es una desgracia.*

Love. Not hate. Love is radical.

Hate is reactionary. These people preaching hate on TV against immigrants. Do they go to church?

What Christ do they worship on Sunday who tells them to hate immigrants on Monday?

Jesus talked of love.

Jesús hablaba de amor.

El amor es radical.

El odio es reaccionario.

Ay, que amarnos.

Ay, que amar al inmigrante que viene acá a este país a trabajar, para soñar.

Love the immigrant who comes here to work? The contractor, who pulls a gun on the immigrant worker after two weeks of work, instead of paying him, does he go to church? He is just as much a criminal.

That is hate. Hate against the worker, the family, and all the people who depend on him to turn his labor into money. Love the immigrant as you love your Christ. My Christ speaks of love.

Love is radical.

AMOR, EL AMOR ES RADICAL.

[*The minister takes a dramatic pose with his hand on his heart as the lights fade.*]

Video #9: José Sucuzhanay Brooklyn Hate Crime Short (1:11)

[*The video offers a* New York Daily News *headline graphic about the violence exacted upon another Ecuadorian immigrant legal resident in Brooklyn.* JOSÉ*'s voice is heard as an official reporter for the sound track that accompanies the newspaper graphics and details the crime. The recorded voice track has a slight echo delay that gives it a haunting effect.*]

José Sucuzhanay, a thirty-one year-old Ecuadorian real estate broker, was beaten to death with an aluminum baseball bat on the streets of Brooklyn on December 7, 2008, exactly a month after Marcelo Lucero was killed.

> His three assailants kicked him and beat him with the baseball bat, shouting anti-Latino slurs and anti-gay slurs because he was walking arm-in-arm with his brother. They were tipsy and coming back from a party, and José and his brother had been mistaken for being gay.
>
> His brother managed to escape, but José died at the hospital. José was a legal resident and respected professional businessman in his community. His assailants were African American. Latinos and African American groups decried the murder as a hate crime.

[*It quickly fades into a news graphic of New Orleans reconstruction workers, and how they are referred to as walking ATMS, as referenced by the Mexican Minister.*

JOSÉ *is offstage, preparing. He drops the shawl and slowly transitions into the final Alien character, once more putting on the mask and outfit with silver sequence vest and white gloves.*

When this video short finishes, the music track of the classical piece from the opening movement, "Ode to the Black Madonna," is heard. This time the piece plays against a video montage of various U.S. flags, including the iconic image of the stars and stripes after the 1961 moon landing. It offers a dynamic set of visuals for the re-emergence of the masked Alien character.]

MOVEMENT #9

Alien Final Ritual with Flag

[JOSÉ *is at center stage dressed as the masked Alien character, and a red wash covers the stage. The recorded classical song re-creates the religious tone for the final movement. At upstage center, the Alien character climbs onto the black box that has been placed there to give him greater height.*

Juxtaposed against a large version of the U.S. flag, the Alien stretches his arms and hands out, resembling a Christ-like figure with the image hitting his body. It is symbolic of the "alien other" being crucified by blind nationalism that has overcome the "land of the free."

With the fourteenth-century "Ode to the Black Madonna" blaring through the sound system, the entire effect with sound and imagery and performance movements offers a dynamic and complicated live art diorama with a faux religiosity.

Meanwhile, the flag images are further complicated with various texts of the many anti-immigrant laws that are part of a dark U.S. legacy, and arise from the center of each flag image in bold graphic letters. The text exposes the hypocrisies of a "freedom-loving" country built on genocide, enslavement, and dehumanization of those outside a Eurocentric ideology that positions itself as the point of departure.

First flag image: A large projected version of the U.S. flag appears with the full fifty stars, and three seconds in, text emerges from the center of the flag that grows larger to read:

Since the Pilgrims arrived without papers, why were they not deported?

The next set of graphic text reads:

The Native People were branded as "savages" by "civilized" Europeans, who framed their genocide as "Discovery."

The next flag image is one of the flag waving in the winds, and the text reads:

The near extermination of Native People & appropriation

of their lands is the bedrock of the United States of Amnesia.

At this point the Alien character is on his knees on the black box, and folds his hands in prayer. He holds that pose, and then places his left arm on his heart and reaches for the audience with his right arm. The next film graphic reads:

Fugitive Slave Act of 1793

The Alien character is now standing on the black platform with his left arm raised and fist clenched in a defiant revolutionary gesture, and the black box gives him greater visual height while the flag image is projected layered on his body.

The large flag image changes to one where a shadowy stars and stripes stretches across the 10' scrim.

The text graphic that appears reads:

Indian Removal Act of 1830

The Alien character has now climbed off the black box and is on his knees on the stage floor. JOSÉ *arches his body back as far as physically possible to reflect an "alien" writhing in pain from invisible forces.*

The text film graphic now reads:

Chinese Exclusion Act 1882

This graphic floats above the head of the Alien character now, as he methodically makes his way downstage on his knees in a supplicant manner.

The projected flag image switches to the iconic photo of astronaut Neil Armstrong planting the U.S. flag on the moon, and the text that appears reads:

Japanese Interment 1942

While the iconic image remains, the next anti-immigrant law reads:

Operation Wetback 1954

The next graphic reads:

Arizona's SB 1070 2010

At center stage, JOSÉ *takes off the Alien mask in a ritualistic manner and deposits it as well as the white gloves on the stage floor. He picks up a U.S. flag that he has kept hidden behind the oval tin basin. It's a version of the early flag with the original thirteen colonies printed in a circle across the blue section. He rises to his feet from his knees.*

JOSÉ *takes out a black lipstick from his right pocket and begins to write across his forehead in a ritualistic manner. He writes "*ALIEN*" across his forehead and bald head, making dramatic black capital letters to mark himself as the dehumanized alien, like a sort of new scarlet letter "A" from Hawthorne's classic novel that branded women.*

He spreads out the U.S. thirteen colonies' flag across his body with arms outstretched, and holding a still pose with ALIEN *marking his forehead, he opens his mouth in an angry gesture with no scream erupting, resembling an iconic indigenous clay sculpture of warrior Aztec gods. Also, it alludes to the silent screams of immigrants by a system that persecutes them openly.*

In addition, it alludes to the violent alien immigrant portrayed in the media as a Mara gang member. It should frighten the audience and simultaneously make them realize that a monster is created through the political dehumanization of immigrants by politicians pimping fear.

He performs this rage three times, once each to stage right, stage left, and center, holding each open-tongue face of rage for some seven seconds. By this time, the final flag images appear, and the next to last one is of the bald eagle against the stars and stripes.

JOSÉ *begins the final ritual of gestures and wraps the flag across his head like a veil, with the word* "ALIEN" *visible on his forehead and face. His hands are also wrapped inside the flag so that half his body is encased within the stars and stripes, creating a dramatic visual image.*

He slowly drops to his knees like a sort of Guadalupe Madonna wrapped in the flag, and he rocks back and forth, as if in a deep mournful trance, almost weeping for the persecuted immigrants in the land of the free.

He picks up a small red wooden cross that has been lying on the stage floor with other props, and it's a petite version of the large red cross with a dollar bill centered and taped visibly to charge this object. He clutches the small wooden red cross with both hands and places it directly below his chin in front of his face, then speaking in a voice almost cracking with sorrow:

LATINO IMMIGRANTS ARE WE

the new evildoers in the land of the free,

or the cosmic hybrid race of a more hybrid future?

Hate is reactionary. Love is radical!

As he takes one last pose with the flag wrapped around his head, and the red cross below his chin, the lights slowly fade for the haunting final image.]

DREAMSCAPE

Rickerby Hinds

Production photograph copyright © Carrie Mikuls

CRITICAL INTRODUCTION

Olga Sánchez Saltveit

In the Luis Avalos Theatre of the LATC, an industrial-looking space with cement walls and floor, the low-hanging lights reveal a bare stage outfitted with only two metal folding chairs, upstage center. The venue is fitting for the spare production of Rickerby Hinds's *Dreamscape*, in which two actors bring an urban tragedy to life, slowing down the time it takes to die from gunshot wounds, and layering that time with hip-hop, beatbox, and modern dance. The performance begins with the two actors seated back to back; they will have each other's backs for the rest of the show, as they weave movement with stillness, gravity with humor, and rhymes with prose, embodying and voicing the different roles that constitute this *Dreamscape.*

Otis Redding's soulful rendition of Irving Berlin's *White Christmas* begins to play, and the actor playing Myeisha, sitting in the chair facing front, gestures and, reaching forward, launches into dance. Her graceful swaying and twirling, articulating limbs and torso, stretching and collapsing in slow motion and quick, are movements we will see repeated throughout the show. Each time they will take on new meaning; her right shoulder shrug will be seen again during the Coroner's report of "gunshot number three" and her leg kicks will reappear during his description of "gunshot number six." As the song ends, the final gestures of this dance propel her back into her chair. She looks stunned, as if struck, but then asks the audience, "Ever have one of those dreams / where nothing comes out when you try to scream?" Her performance will convey an omniscient, astral projection–like experience in which she comments on the world around her, though, to the world, she appears to be unconscious. Her body has a life of its own. Other times, she performs Myeisha's very grounded, very worried cousin Toni calling 911 from a corner of the stage, as if from a pay phone, reminding us that this is late 1998.

Likewise, the DJ/Beatboxer, her partner on stage, is at times a puppet master pulling the strings with his beatbox "skillz." Other times he is Officer Garland, submitting professional testimony of the fatal night his life and Myeisha's crossed paths. Most dispassionately, he is the Coroner, reciting autopsy findings. His handheld wireless mic is the only physical prop in the show, at times also representing a flashlight or a gun. More often, however, it is simply the instrument through which the DJ/Beatboxer underscores and punctuates Myeisha's rap with an encyclopedic virtuosity of sound effects that the script cannot begin to convey. Each of the twelve gunshot wound descriptions is accompanied by a unique series of beats, samples, or cuts from well-known hip-hop artists such as Kanye West and LL Cool J. The DJ/Beatboxer also vocalizes the dance music at the nightclub, the music video sound track, the taps at the window that try to wake Myeisha, and the fatal gunshots that take her life. While he may not have text he certainly has dialogue.

Myeisha may be "passed out" according to the story, but in her dream she is wide awake, optimistic, and charming. She strolls confidently across the stage in jeans, sneakers, T-shirt, and a checked flannel shirt, talking to the audience about her life. The rhythm and rhymes of her text drop casually: addressing the audience as friends, sharing secrets, encouraging a response. Following the Coroner's description of the impact of "gunshot number three," Myeisha demonstrates her sixty-five-mile-an-hour softball pitching form as well as her cheerleading routine. Her moves belie the wounds; her spirit is one thing, her body is another. A tension of the play that is amplified by its staging is the juxtaposition of Myeisha's vibrant life against the clinical chronicles of her death. When the Coroner begins the beatbox series that sonically heralds his reports, she tries to run off but is detained by his voice. As if hypnotized, she stands still while the Coroner begins the description of each bullet's location, depth, and impact.

Based on a true story, the circumstances of Tyisha Miller's death which inform Rickerby Hinds's *Dreamscape* have been well documented, and generated protests in the Riverside, California, community. However, Hinds was not interested in fanning the flames of political unrest nor in staging the details of Ms. Miller's life story.[1] Rather, the more important message to share was that the needless and avoidable death of a young woman full of history and potential reflects those of so many other young lives lost to law enforcement's history of racialized violence. While many of the events in *Dreamscape* echo Ms. Miller's life experiences, Hinds chose to maintain a respectful distance by creating the character of Myeisha Mills. In performance, time is slowed through sound, movement, and storytelling, engendering empathy for this full, young life and its potential. Myeisha is given time to share why her life matters, time that Tyisha Miller and too many others have not been given. Hinds's goal for *Dreamscape* has been to generate dialogue that provides a "different point of departure when it comes to discussing the very volatile subject of the relationship between the African American community and the police," presaging movements such as #BlackLivesMatter and #SayHerName.

As with most of his work, Hinds's aesthetic vision for *Dreamscape* begins with hip-hop. When Hinds began writing plays in the late '80s, he broke new dramaturgical ground by introducing hip-hop into the work. *Daze to Come,* which made its debut in 1989, is recognized as the first full-length play to use the foundational elements of hip-hop as its theatrical vocabulary.[2] "I wanted to create work for the stage that spoke and moved the way my friends and I did, and that meant creating work influenced by hip-hop culture. I didn't necessarily set out to create a new theatrical genre, I simply wanted to create theater that I found compelling."[3]

Hinds arrived in Los Angeles from the Bay Islands of Honduras as a thirteen-year-old. He and his family were soon immersed in the culture of the African American community. "My positioning in American society evolved more based on how 'Afro' I look than the fact that I was born in a Latin American country . . . One of the complexities in being AfroLatinx is that the 'Afro' part is the part that is seen first, and unless/until you reveal your 'Latinidad' you are treated like an 'Afro' with all that comes with it."[4] Back then rap was primarily an African American art form; hip-hop captured his imagination and became his mode of creative expression.[5] His subsequent works, including *Blackballin'* (1995), *Keep Hedz Ringin'* (2000), and *Dreamscape* (2005), have all included elements of hip-hop and have influenced his choice of collaborators. Actor John "Faahz" Merchant brought extensive expertise in beatboxing to his multiple roles. Natali Micciche originated the role of Myeisha, and still performs it, as does Rhaechyl Walker, both of whom performed the role at the 2014 Encuentro.

For many people in the United States, calling 911 in an emergency makes sense. However, for African Americans, Latinx, Native Americans, and other marginalized populations, encounters with law enforcement are notoriously and historically unsafe.[6] Racialized fear provokes swift responses, and the militarized approach is deadly.[7] Alive in body and spirit, reveling in the promise and potential of youth, *Dreamscape* opens the window that Tyisha Miller could not, to witness, if only briefly, the vision of a future beyond the gun.[8]

NOTES

1. Rickerby Hinds, email interview by Olga Sánchez Saltveit, August 18, 2014.
2. Ibid.
3. "Rickerby Hinds." *UCR Department of Theatre, Film, and Digital Production,* 2015, accessed May 14, 2017. http://theatre.ucr.edu/rickerby-hinds/.
4. Rickerby Hinds, email interview by Olga Sánchez Saltveit, August 18, 2014.
5. Rickerby Hinds, email interview by Olga Sánchez Saltveit, May 13, 2017.
6. Rickerby Hinds, email interview by Olga Sánchez Saltveit, August 18, 2014.
7. Brad W. Smith and Malcolm D. Holmes, "Police Use of Excessive Force in Minority Communities," *Social Problems* 61, no. 1, (2014): 86, accessed May 7, 2017, doi:10.1525/sp.2013.12056.
8. Smith and Holmes, 2014: 84.

BIBLIOGRAPHY

Bergner, Daniel. "Is Stop-and-Frisk Worth It?" *The Atlantic.* Atlantic Media Company, August 26, 2015. Accessed May 5, 2017. https://www.theatlantic.com/magazine/archive/2014/04/is-stop-and-frisk-worth-it/358644/

Dansky, Kara. "WAR COMES HOME—American Civil Liberties Union." *War Comes Home at America's Expense: The Excessive Militarization of American Policing.* 2014. Accessed Oct. 26, 2018. https://www.aclu.org/issues/criminal-law-reform/reforming-police-practices/war-comes-home

Donner, Christopher M. "Examining Officer and Citizen Accounts of Police Use-of-Force Incidents." *Policing: An International Journal of Police Strategies & Management* 35, no. 4 (2012): 301–27. doi:10.1108/pijpsm.2012.18135daa.006.

Gottbrath, Paul. "Suit kicks off battle over racial profiling." *Cincinnati Post Online Edition.* March 14, 2001. Accessed May 14, 2017. https://web.archive.org/web/20061020200910/http://www.cincypost.com/2001/mar/14/suit031401.html

Hermann, Peter, and Rachel Weiner. "Issues over Police Shooting in Ferguson Lead Push for Officers and Body Cameras." *Washington Post.* December 2, 2014. Accessed May 7, 2017. https://www.washingtonpost.com/local/crime/issues-over-police-shooting-in-ferguson-lead-push-for-officers-and-body-cameras/2014/12/02/dedcb2d8-7a58-11e4-84d4-7c896b90abdc_story.html?utm_term=.68dc9254d896

Leibovich, Lori. "The Mysterious Death of Tyisha Miller." *Salon.* February 8, 1999. Accessed May 1, 2017. http://www.salon.com/1999/02/08/cov_08news_2/.

McCabe, Bret. "Does the Militarization of American Police Help Them Serve and Protect?" *The Hub.* March 5, 2015. Accessed August 19, 20, 17. https://hub.jhu.edu/magazine/2015/spring/aclu-militarization-of-police/.

"Rickerby Hinds." UCR Department of Theatre, Film, and Digital Production. 2015. Accessed May 14, 2017. http://theatre.ucr.edu/rickerby-hinds/.

Rojek, Jeff, Geoffrey P. Alpert, and Hayden P. Smith. "Examining Officer and Citizen Accounts of Police Use-of-Force Incidents." *Crime & Delinquency* 58, no. 2 (November 11, 2010): 301–27. doi:10.1177/0011128710386206.

Smith, Brad W., and Malcolm D. Holmes. "Police Use of Excessive Force in Minority Communities." *Social Problems* 61, no. 1 (2014): 83–104. doi:10.1525/sp.2013.12056.

Terry, Don. "Unanswered Questions in a Fatal Police Shooting." *The New York Times.* January 8, 1999. Accessed May 1, 2017. http://www.nytimes.com/1999/01/09/us/unanswered-questions-in-a-fatal-police-shooting.html?ref=tyisha_miller.

PRODUCTION HISTORY

Dreamscape's development was a transient one, taking place primarily from 2005 to 2010 through workshops, festivals, and academic settings with the assistance of talented and visionary artists. The spaces and key artists contributing to its progress included: NYU, Daniel Banks (Director); New York Hip-Hop Theater Festival, Paola Mendoza (Director); New World Theater, Manu Mukasa (Director); Califest Hip-Hop Theater Festival, Daysha Broadway (Director), John Merchant (Beatboxer), Carrie Mikuls (Choreographer).

Dreamscape has toured five countries in addition to the United States—England, Honduras, Hungary, Poland, and Romania—and has been translated into four languages: Spanish, Hungarian, Polish, and Romanian. The lead role has been played by Janae Heard, Aisha Jordan, Natali Micciche, Rhaechyl Walker, and Jesse Sandoval. In 2016 *Dreamscape* was adapted as a film under the name *My Name Is Myeisha*, to be released in 2019.

CHARACTERS

Myeisha Mills, nineteen, female, African American

Toni, played by actor playing Myeisha

Beatboxer, provides the musical accompaniment, can be played by anyone (and change pronouns accordingly; referred to as "he" in the script)

Coroner, played by Beatboxer

Officer Garland, played by Beatboxer

911 operator, played by Beatboxer

Doctor, played by Myeisha and Beatboxer

Tattoo Artist

PROLOGUE

[*Otis Redding's "White Christmas" gently disquiets the darkness.*

Chalk outlines of MYEISHA MILLS *materialize.*

Lights rise to reveal MYEISHA *rising from the front seat of her aunt's Nissan Sentra.*

She dances the Twelve Mortal Moves dance as the music is spasmodically disrupted by twelve distortions—these are gunshots—each one finding its target in MYEISHA*'s body, transforming her movement into a dazzling life-and-death dance.*

She lands in the front seat of the car, closes her eyes for a moment, then awakens with a jolt.]

MYEISHA [*frightened*]: Ever have one of those dreams

Where nothing comes out when you try to scream

[*Commanding herself*] Scream

Screeam!

[MYEISHA *tries to scream but only a series of sampled "Hollas and Scream" are heard.*]

See what I mean?

One of those dreams

Christmas was three days ago

Jingle Bells and ho, ho, ho

Just so you know

This ain't gon' be one of them feel-good shows

Just so you know

So

Christmas was three days ago

Jingle Bells and [*party style*] ho-oh, ho-oh, ho-oh

Today's December 28th

Third day of Kwanzaa

Ujima

"To build and maintain our community together

And to make our brothers' and sisters' problems our problems

And to solve them together"

I know you didn't know

I didn't know till uncle Darnell told me so during one of his "black-outs"

Oh no, not that kind-a blackout

That's just what we call it when uncle "D" has one of his moments

And is compelled to bust you out 'cause of your lack of blackness

You'll see what I mean.

It's Ujima though

[*Proudly*] Umoja, Kujichagulia, Ujima

So

Me, Shy, and my cousin Toni dying to get our party on

Rollin' to L.A. though

Tired of Club Metro

Oh

For those of you who don't know me

See, I was born and raised in the I-E

That's the Inland Empire, the I-E

Sixty miles east of the City of Angels

So me, Shy, and my cousin Toni dying to get our party on

Rollin' to L.A. though

Tired of Club Metro

Four dance floors of Hip-Hop, Reggae, Rock en Español [*her tone says it's not her favorite*], and Retro

So

The Sentra starts to rattle and pull to the right

Ah man, I cannot believe we got a flat in the middle of the night

Not tonight

[*To the audience*] OK, let's just let me get the facts folks

What is the deal with automobiles and my Black folks

Fo real

And the fact that your spare is always flat folks?

Fo real

And do not get me started on a working jack, folks

My Black folks

So I wind up in a fix at the Spirit of Seventy-Six that sits on Central 'n Brockton

Gat in my lap case I get rocked on

Waiting for Shy and Toni to get back with the Triple-A card

One in the morning sittin' in my aunt Gwen's ride

I can't leave Aunt Gwen's Sentra sittin' on Central

If it gets stolen, scratched, towed, or broken into

Soon as I see her I'ma be the one get broken-in-two

Aunt Gwen gon' kill me

Well, maybe not kill

But I sho ain't gon' be rollin' the Sentra no more.

Feel?

Ever have one of those dreams

Where nothing comes out when you try to scream

Tap

So I'm sitting in the Sentra on Central sensing something

soundin' like rappin' like tappin'

Like . . .

[*Singin' along with* BEATBOXER] Who's that peepin' in my window

Sha-pow nobody now

Tap

I hear the tappin' again

Oh cool it's Toni

Hold on girl let me let you in, where you been? I'm lonely

Got me sittin' at this station in the middle of the night

One in the morning losing patience

Some'n just ain't right

Tap

[*To the audience*] Now before you trip

Let me go on and admit that

I'm strapped

Yeah, that's right

I'm strapped

[*Slowly starting to rhyme*] With my gat at Central 'n Brockton

Thirty-eight in my lap case I get rocked on

Yo that's nice

[*Spittin' with skillz this time*] So I'm strapped with my gat at Central 'n Brockton

Thirty-eight in my lap case I get rocked on

Late at night in my lap there it sat

there I sat

there it sat

there I sat

there it sat

there I sat

there it sat

there I sat

Took a nap

Rat-tah-tat-tat-tat-tah-tah

Tap

Tap

Tap

I put the gat in my lap 'cause I was a little terrified.

Ta-ta-ta-tappin' on the window cousin Toni outside.

So I say "hold on cuz, let me let you in"

But before I can . . .

Here comes that damn dream again

[*She tries to open door but can't move.*]

First I can't holla

Now I can't even move

Tryin' to open the door but I can't even move
Can't take this much more 'cause I can't even move
Feelin' like a prisoner of war and I can't even move
Can't move can't move can't move can't move
First I can't holla, now I can't even move
[*To self*] If you're dreamin' Myeisha, girl, wake up now fool!

[*She sees* TONI *walking away from car.*]

Toni, who you callin' this late on a pay phone
You better come on so we can get on and head on
Home
Toni, where are you goin' to?
Where the heck you been?
I'm opening the door least I'm tryin' to
Let me let you in
I know you're ready to go home girl, I'm dying to
We can just explain it all to Aunt Gwen
You can just explain it all to Aunt Gwen
I'll just explain it all to Aunt Gwen
We ain't fixin' no flat tonight forget that
Aunt Gwen's just gonna have to "get Black"
We ain't fixin' no flat tonight forget that
Aunt Gwen's just gonna have to "get Black."

[BEATBOXER *drops "911 Is a Joke" by Public Enemy.* BEATBOXER *becomes* 911 OPERATOR. MYEISHA *becomes* TONI. TONI *picks up the pay phone and dials 911.*]

BEATBOXER [*as* 911 OPERATOR]: Nine-one-one.

MYEISHA [*as* TONI]: Yes uh, could you guys come down to uhm, Central and Brockton to the seventy-six gas station because there's a um, my cousin's in a car and she has a gun on her, but she's passed out. We can't get in the car 'cause it's locked.

BEATBOXER [*as* 911 OPERATOR]: OK, who's inside the car?

MYEISHA [*as* TONI]: Uh, my cousin.

BEATBOXER [*as* 911 OPERATOR]: And she has a gun with her?

MYEISHA [*as* TONI]: Yes. It's sitting in her lap and uh, she's passed out.

BEATBOXER [*as* 911 OPERATOR]: She's passed out?

MYEISHA [*as* TONI]: She's passed out.

BEATBOXER [*as* 911 OPERATOR]: She has been drinking?

MYEISHA [*as* TONI]: I don't know. We just came—

BEATBOXER [*as* 911 OPERATOR]: Do you think she shot herself?

MYEISHA [*as* TONI]: Yeah, she has a flat. I don't know.

BEATBOXER [*as* 911 OPERATOR]: OK. What kind of car is she in?

MYEISHA [*as* TONI]: It's a Nissan Sentra.

BEATBOXER [*as* 911 OPERATOR]: Hold on. What color?

MYEISHA [*as* TONI]: White.

BEATBOXER [*as* 911 OPERATOR]: Is she in the passenger seat or . . .

MYEISHA [*as* TONI]: She was drive . . . she was driving. 'Cause we came to fix, she had a flat tire. We came to help her fix it and um, and we just found her like this.

BEATBOXER [*as* 911 OPERATOR]: OK so she's in the car by herself.

MYEISHA [*as* TONI]: By herself.

BEATBOXER [*as* 911 OPERATOR]: Have you tried to bang on the doors?

MYEISHA [*as* TONI]: Yeah, we banged on the window and everything. She's passed out. We cannot get her to wake up. The music is loud, so we can't do nothing.

BEATBOXER [*as* 911 OPERATOR]: OK. I'm gonna keep you on the phone until the officers are on their way. OK?

BEATBOXER [*as* OFFICER GARLAND]: On December 28, 1998, I was working the graveyard shift when I received a call from RPD Dispatch at approximately oh-one-fifty-five hours assigning me to proceed to the point of origin of a nine-one-one call which was Baines seventy-six Unocal gas station, located at sixty-five/seventy-five Brockton Avenue in the city of Riverside. The call conveyed that there was an unresponsive female locked in a white Nissan Sentra with a visible firearm on her lap.

MYEISHA [*rappin'*]: So I'm strapped with my gat at Central 'n Brockton

Thirty-eight in my lap case I get rocked on

BEATBOXER [*as* OFFICER GARLAND]: At approximately oh-two-hundred hours, I arrived on the scene and spoke with two females standing by the pay phone on the north side of the gas station's premises. The two females advised me that the female in the locked vehicle was a family member, that she appeared to be unconscious, and that she had a loaded firearm on her lap. I saw that the two females were very upset.

BEATBOXER [*as* 911 OPERATOR]: She been—I'm sorry—has she been drinking today?

MYEISHA [*as* TONI]: I don't, I don't know! That's what I'm telling you. I don't know. She had a flat tire and she called the house. So we're coming back to give her the Triple-A card—

BEATBOXER [*as* 911 OPERATOR]: Uh-huh.

MYEISHA [*as* TONI]:—so she can get the tire fixed. But this is how we found her. So we don't know.

BEATBOXER [*as* 911 OPERATOR]: You don't know what's going on.

MYEISHA [*as* TONI]: Uh-uh.

BEATBOXER [*as* OFFICER GARLAND]: Based on their demeanor and the occupant's non-responsiveness to her family members, I believed that the vehicle's occupant was necessarily in some sort of medical distress especially because her family members did not know what was wrong with her.

BEATBOXER [*as* 911 OPERATOR]: How long ago did she, did you talk to her?

MYEISHA [*as* TONI]: Um, I didn't talk to her. My aunt did.

BEATBOXER [*as* 911 OPERATOR]: How long ago was that?

MYEISHA [*as* TONI]: That was like twenty or thirty minutes ago.

Can you guys, can you guys send an ambulance with you?

BEATBOXER [*as* 911 OPERATOR]: Yeah.

MYEISHA [*as* TONI]: OK.

BEATBOXER [*as* 911 OPERATOR]: Yeah, since we don't actually know what's wrong with her—

MYEISHA [*as* TONI]: Uh-huh?

BEATBOXER [*as* 911 OPERATOR]: And . . . the gun, you can just see the gun?

MYEISHA [*as* TONI]: Yes. It's in her lap.

BEATBOXER [*as* 911 OPERATOR]: It's sitting in her lap?

MYEISHA [*as* TONI]: Uh-huh.

BEATBOXER [*as* 911 OPERATOR]: OK. And she's the only one in the vehicle?

MYEISHA [*as* TONI]: Yes.

[*Pause.*]

BEATBOXER [*as* 911 OPERATOR]: What is her name?

MYEISHA: My name is Myeisha.

Y'all know us E-shas: Myeisha, Moesha, Aisha, La'Resha, La'Creesha, Ta'Nesha, Tyisha.

We the E-shas we the first cousins to the Aw-nas.

You know the Aw-nas: LaJuana, Tiana, Shawana, Juwanna, Tawanna.

BEATBOXER [*as* 911 OPERATOR]: How old is she?

MYEISHA [*as* TONI]: Uhm, she's nineteen.

BEATBOXER [*as* 911 OPERATOR]: Nineteen years old?

MYEISHA [*as* TONI]: Uh-huh.

BEATBOXER [*as* 911 OPERATOR]: OK. And the car is just parked in the, in a parking lot?

MYEISHA [*as* TONI]: Yeah, at the gas station.

BEATBOXER [*as* 911 OPERATOR]: And when she called you twenty minutes ago she did, said she was alone?

MYEISHA [*as* TONI]: Uh, I don't know.

BEATBOXER [*as* 911 OPERATOR]: Oh she never did . . .

MYEISHA [*as* TONI]: 'Cause my aunt talked to her so I don't—

BEATBOXER [*as* 911 OPERATOR]: OK.

MYEISHA [*as* TONI]:—I don't know.

BEATBOXER [*as* OFFICER GARLAND]: As I finished speaking with the two witnesses, Officer Hobart arrived on the scene. I informed Officer Hobart that the vehicle's occupant was apparently unconscious and had a gun. Because the occupant had a gun, I knew that we would have to secure the area and make it safe for emergency medical personnel to render any aid the occupant required.

MYEISHA [*as* TONI]: How far is the um, police station from here?

BEATBOXER [*as* 911 OPERATOR]: Well they're just, they're in the city just driving around—

MYEISHA [*as* TONI]: Oh.

BEATBOXER [*as* 911 OPERATOR]:—But they're on their way there.

BEATBOXER [*as* OFFICER GARLAND]: Officer Hobart and I approached the vehicle with our guns drawn and pointed downward.

MYEISHA [*as* TONI]: Oh.

BEATBOXER [*as* 911 OPERATOR]: They don't sit at a police station, waiting . . .

MYEISHA [*as* TONI]: OK, here . . . I see one police officer. They found the, uh, the car right now. There's a police car right now.

BEATBOXER [*as* OFFICER GARLAND]: Officer Hobart approached along the passenger's side rear door as I approached along the driver's side door. From my position behind the driver's side rear door, I could see that the occupant's gun was on her lap pointed toward the driver's door.

BEATBOXER [*as* 911 OPERATOR]: OK. If they're coming—

MYEISHA [*as* TONI]: In the drive—

BEATBOXER [*as* OFFICER GARLAND]: The gun's magazine was in place and the weapon was readily accessible.

BEATBOXER [*as* 911 OPERATOR]: They're coming toward you?

BEATBOXER [*as* OFFICER GARLAND]: After Officer Hobart and I verified the occupant had a gun . . .

MYEISHA [*as* TONI]: Yes.

BEATBOXER [*as* OFFICER GARLAND]: I held that position until backup arrived.

BEATBOXER [*as* 911 OPERATOR]: Why don't you go talk to 'em?

MYEISHA [*as* TONI]: OK, thank you.

MYEISHA: Soon's I hear the cops' sirens the first thing pop in my mind

"Man I wish I was a white girl" or at least a little lighter than I am

Not white in the "I can flip my hair" and "I got blue eyes" kinda way

But in the "Officer, can you help me out" kinda way

In the "Young lady, are you OK? You look distressed" kinda way

In the "Are you OK, you need a ride? You look lost" kinda way

But not today

Tonight my name's Myeisha . . . and I am Black . . . mighta had a little to drink

Those are just the facts

But even still with all that I figure I should still be alright

I mean if Toni couldn't hear me I must be asleep, right

And if I'm sleepin' I'm dreamin' so it must be deep, right

And if I'm sleep and it's deep, then the police'll wake me up, right

Show a little care, help me find a spare, even help jack me up, right

[*She points out writing on Police Unit.*]

To Protect and to Serve

Written in black and white

Right?

BEATBOXER [*as* OFFICER GARLAND]: I observed that the occupant appeared to be in dire medical distress and in need of immediate medical assistance. I observed that the occupant's mouth was slightly open, her eyes were closed, her breathing appeared shallow, her lips were quivering, her body was shaking, and a white substance was accumulating around the sides of her mouth.

Based on my prior experience with persons overdosing on drugs, I believed Mills was experiencing many symptoms which were consistent with a drug overdose. Believing that time was of the essence, I thought we should use the quickest means available to remove the gun from her presence so that medical personnel could render the necessary aid.

I would attempt to break the window and retrieve the gun.

MYEISHA: So I'm strapped with my gat at Central 'n Brockton

Thirty-eight in my lap case I get rocked on

BEATBOXER [*as* OFFICER GARLAND]: After verifying all the officers were in position, I performed a silent three count and then broke the window on my first attempt using the ASP baton. I then dropped the baton and leaned to tuck my body into the front window and grab the occupant's gun. As I reached in to retrieve the weapon, I heard a "boom" which I believed to be a gunshot go off toward my right ear.

MYEISHA [*rappin'*]: So I'm strapped with my gat at Central 'n Brockton

Thirty-eight in my lap case I get rocked on

BEATBOXER [*as* OFFICER GARLAND]: Once I was inside the vehicle, I could no longer see the weapon.

I thought that the occupant had grabbed her weapon and shot me.

Once inside the vehicle I heard a boom which I believed to be a gun blast.

Once inside the vehicle I heard a boom which I believed to be a gun blast.

Once inside the vehicle I heard—

MYEISHA [*singing*]: Happy birthday to you

Happy birthday to you

Happy birthday dear officer

Happy birthday to you

[*She sings about* OFFICER GARLAND *on the ground.*]

Officer Garland, the one on the floor

It's his birthday today, he's turning twenty-four

[*She sings Stevie Wonder's "Happy Birthday."*]

Happy birthday to ya

Happy birthday to ya

Happy birthday

Happy birthday to ya

Happy birthday to ya

Happy birthday

Happy birthday—

You see the problem with this version?

Nobody knows how to end the thing

Happy birthday

Happy birthday to ya . . .

Yo wait

December twenty-eight

That would make the officer a Capricorn

Capricorns are supposed to be

Practical and prudent

Ambitious and disciplined

Careful and patient

Humorous and reserved

Pessimistic and fatalistic

December twenty-eighth.

That makes Officer Garland a Kwanzaa baby

Ujima baby

Well . . . maybe

December twenty-eight, nineteen ninety-eight

Means Y2K's only a year away

You heard of Y2K?

You ain't heard of Y2K?

OK

They say one second after twelve next New Year's Eve

After they drop the ball on New York

Right

Things are gonna go bananas, fo' real

End of the world

They say all the computers in the world are gonna lose their "megabites"

Like even banks and stuff are gonna lose grip on their cash

Of course nobody I know is so naive to believe

That some ATM's are gonna go crazy and start spittin' out twenties

[*She is still not convinced.*]

I ain't sayin' I believe and I ain't sayin I don't

But . . . you know . . . me, Toni, and Shy got the ATM on University and Main staked out

We just gon' be in the vicinity case cash starts to spit out

Think I won't?

Have no doubt

But a thousand years

That's crazy to even try to think

A thousand years of time

If we're lucky we get like seventy-nine

Like a blink

Like a wink

But at least I get to be one of the very few

In the history of the world to go from the old millennium to the new

Out of everybody in history to ever live

I get to be one of the ones who gets to go through from millennium one to millennium two

[*To audience*] You too

Know what I'm gonna do?

I'm gonna make the millennium that's next

My best

I'ma make M-two tha bomb

Might even make me an M-two resolution

Start me an M-two revolution

December twenty-eight, Y2K in a year

Makes Officer Garland a Capricorn over there

[BEATBOXER *drops "What's Your Sign" beat.* MYEISHA *gets audience hyped.*]

Let's see what other signs we got in the house tonight

[*To audience*] Say what's your sign!?

Say what's your sign!?

Do the Pisces run this motha for ya!

Do the Aries run this motha for ya!

Do the Libras run this motha for ya!

Do the Taurus run this motha for ya!

December twenty-eight, Y2K in a year

Makes Officer Garland a Capricorn over there

BEATBOXER [*as* OFFICER GARLAND]: Once inside the vehicle I heard a boom which I believed to be a gun blast. I immediately fell backwards onto the pavement, injuring my legs and wrists. I saw the occupant rise forward in her seat. While still thinking that I had been shot and believing that the occupant was attempting to shoot me again I began firing into the driver's side door of the vehicle.

MYEISHA [*trying to convince herself of the following*]: I mean if Toni couldn't hear me I must be asleep, right?

BEATBOXER [*as* OFFICER GARLAND]: I began firing into the driver's side door of the vehicle.

MYEISHA: And if I'm asleep and I'm dreamin' it must be deep, right?

BEATBOXER [*as* OFFICER GARLAND]: I began firing into the driver's side . . .

MYEISHA: And if I'm deep asleep the police'll just wake me up, right?

BEATBOXER [*as* OFFICER GARLAND]: I began firing into the driver . . .

MYEISHA: Help me find a spare, even help jack me up, right?

BEATBOXER [*as* OFFICER GARLAND]: I began firing—

MYEISHA: Right?

BEATBOXER [*as* OFFICER GARLAND]: I began firing—

MYEISHA: Right?

BEATBOXER [*as* OFFICER GARLAND]: I began firing—

MYEISHA: Right?

BEATBOXER [*as* OFFICER GARLAND]: I began firing—

MYEISHA: Right?

[*Beat.*]

Ever have one of those dreams

Where nothing comes out when you try to scream

[MYEISHA *tries to scream. Nothing comes out.* BEATBOXER *samples a series of "ones" which mix into the music for* MYEISHA*'s routine in the next scene.*]

SCENE 1

BEATBOXER [*as* CORONER]: The entrance to gunshot number one is located on the right upper arm.

This is a typical distant gunshot wound entrance. The course of the projectile is through the skin and soft tissue of the right arm, and perforates and fractures the right humerus.

This is a serious, however, non-fatal, gunshot wound to the right arm, fracturing the right humerus.

MYEISHA: Did he say humorous?

I think he/she said humorous.

[BEATBOXER *samples a series "humerus."*]

That's funny

What's not so funny is the fact that me, Shy, and Toni

Been workin' on our routine, you know, for when we hit the scene

[*Mildly defensive*] Yeah, that's right, we them girls, you know the ones

Get you out on the dance floor thinkin' you gon' have you some fun

Thinkin' you gon' get your freak on . . . your grind on . . . maybe even get you some

But as soon as we get you on the floor you realize you gets none

We bust out the routine we came here to do

Now we ain't tryin' to be mean, it's just how we do what we do

So you end up standing there bobbin' your head wondering if you're gonna get some attention . . . create a little tension

So when we see it in your face we give you a little taste, know what I mean

What you don't realize is that it's all built into the routine

Did I mention

[BEATBOXER *samples: Shai's Shy, Tony Toni Tone's Tony, Toni Tone has done it again and Another Bad Creations' Iesha.* MYEISHA *becomes* TONY, SHY, *and then* MYEISHA *again on cue when the* BEATBOXER *samples the following.*]

Like I said

We ain't mean, that's just how we play

We're Toni, Shy, Myeisha

We're three tha hard way!

So anyway, we workin' on a new routine, the old one's gettin' tired

'Bout time for it to be retired

So . . .

[*She dances, then stops in the middle of "humerus" move.*]

See the dilemma?

This is where we're supposed to hit this

[*She tries "humerus" move again.*]

It's cool an' all

Me myself personally

I think we should be doing more of Aaliyah's moves

Girl is bad . . . and so smooth

She's got that thing, you know

She should do some more movies or something, you know

I bet you she's gonna really blow up in a couple years or so

But I get the feeling she might wanna give the slip to R. Kelly

Maybe it's just me but he gives me the—

[*She does "he gives me the willies" shake.*]

Anyway, check out what we got so far on the routine down

Then you'll see why a fractured humerus is not such a funny bone

[MYEISHA *dances the routine, but can't hit the "humerus move." She battles the* CORONER *with the "humerus move" for control.* MYEISHA *wins this battle. Frustrated, she makes her way back to the front seat of the Nissan Sentra where she finishes the routine.*]

SCENE 2

[BEATBOXER *samples a series of "Twos."* MYEISHA *dances the "fractured jaw move" as the* CORONER *"cuts up" the following.*]

BEATBOXER [*as* CORONER]: The entrance to gunshot number two is located on the left posterior upper neck.

This is a typical distant gunshot wound entrance.

The course of the projectile is through the skin and soft tissue of the left upper neck; it courses through the mandible and exits the right side of the jaw.

The mandible is extensively fractured and there is some fragmentation of the teeth.

The exit to gunshot wound number two is on the right side of the jaw.

This is a very serious, however, not rapidly fatal, gunshot wound, fracturing the jaw.

MYEISHA: I heard that

Dreams about losing your teeth symbolize the loss of childhood innocence.

These dreams often occur at times of transition from one life stage to the next and can be a message that an important milestone is occurring and urging you to face the inevitable.

You know what I'm gonna miss

Gram's Mission Bar.B.Q.

Downtown on Main Street

Robert be puttin' his foot in his Q

Both feet

Oh, don't worry, that's a good thing, it's the same as sayin' mmm-mmuh!

That Q's slammin'

Beef tips

Coleslaw

Mac and cheese

Chicken

That's what I'ma be missin'

Pork ribs

Potato salad

Barbeque beans

Greens

Yams

Peach cobbler

I got something that needs to be said though

So, what's the deal with our barbeque folks and their bread?

Y'all heard what I said

The bread

The bread

The bread

If you can call it that

It's the same no matter where you're at

You can be at Graham's, Bobby Ray's in San Berdoo, Louisiana Seafood in Mo-Val, or M&M's in L.A.

Your meal's gonna come out the same way

Greens gonna be hooked, mac and cheese . . . pleeeease

Baked beans gon' be lip-smackin'

And the Q's gonna be slammin'

But sittin' on top of your order, off to the side

I guarantee there's gonna be some paper-thin, no-flavor, it-ain't-even-Roman-Meal white bread

You heard what I said

White bread

I'm tellin' you it's gonna be white

White bread

But if you accidentally luck out and get some wheat bread

Don't be lookin' for no wheat grains, wheat smell, wheat germ, or wheat taste

Nothin' like that found in this bread

This wheat bread is gonna be wheat only because that's what the bag said

What's really sad is that since the rest of the meal's so good

We forget about the bread, white or wheat

And when it's time to sop up that last bit of Q sauce out of the corners of that take-out Styrofoam container that you can't reach with your plastic fork

That paper-thin, flavorless, you-wish-it-was-Roman-Meal bread gets it done

That's what I'ma be missin

Barbeque

Fake wheat bread

And

Kissin'

Listen

Kissin'

OK

Wesley Snipes in *Sugar Hill* or Denzel in *Crimson Tide*

OK

Denzel in *The Hurricane* or Wesley Snipes in *White Men Can't Jump*

OK

Wesley Snipes in *Murder at 1600* or Denzel in *Devil in a Blue Dress*

OK

Denzel in *Glory* or Wesley in *Blade*

OK

Wesley in *Blade II* or Denzel in *The Preacher's Wife*

OK

Denzel in *Malcolm X* or Wesley in *Jungle Fever*

OK

Wesley in *Blade III* or Denzel in *Training Day*

OK

Denzel in *Mo' Better Blues* or Wesley in *Mo' Better Blues*

I heard that dreams about losing your teeth symbolize the loss of childhood innocence

These dreams often occur at times of transition from one life stage to the next

[MYEISHA *dances, but can't hit the "fractured jaw move." She battles the* CORONER *with the "fractured jaw move" for control of the turntables, trying to stop him from cutting the record, then letting it play.* MYEISHA *wins this battle.*]

SCENE 3

[BEATBOXER *samples a series of "threes."* MYEISHA *dances the "right shoulder move" as the* CORONER *"cuts up" the following.*]

BEATBOXER [*as* CORONER]: The entrance to gunshot number three is located on the right posterior shoulder on the right upper back. The course of the projectile is through the right posterior shoulder and through the wall of the back. This is a nonfatal distant gunshot wound to the back.

MYEISHA: I was always a tomboy

People used to say I must be gay 'cause I dressed this way

Baggy jeans, sneakers, and my shirt hangin' loose this way

Always a tomboy and if you don't like it you can kiss this . . . this way

Looked good playin' the field

And still had sex appeal

Played some basketball, but softball was my game

Got my pitch up to sixty-five my last year at Riverside High

even got a little fame

It's true

Got my picture in the Black Voice News, page B-2

My best pitch was the Quick-an'-Split

Had batters singin' the blues

See-ya!

Loved the sound of my pitch in the catcher's mitt when it hit the sweet spot

It's like, like,

[MYEISHA *pitches; the* BEATBOXER *makes the sound of the ball hitting the catcher's mitt.*]

It sounded good

Felt good

And I look good

OK, let me stop

I did look good though

[*On the pitcher's mound* MYEISHA *strikes her left hand with her right as if wearing a baseball glove. She blows a bubble, winds up, and pitches. We hear the pop. It's the gum, and it's also the ball in the catcher's mitt.*]

MYEISHA: I'm thinkin 'bout walkin' on at Cal State, or UCR., RCC, Valley, or Cal Poly

I messed up and didn't get my applications in on time

[*She pitches, then pops gum, self-congratulatory.*]

Tomboy

Shoot, I coulda been a cheerleader if I wanted to

Homeboy

[*Cheerleader style*] My name is My-e-sha

And I'm the best

Come get with me

Forget the rest . . .

My name is My-e-sha

You know my name

Wanna get with me

You betta step up your game

[*Hyped cheering*] I said, my name is My-e-sha

And I'm the best

Come get with me

Forget the rest . . .

My name is My-e-sha

You know my name

Wanna get with me

You betta step up your game

[MYEISHA *dances, but can't hit the "right shoulder move." She battles the* CORONER *with the "right shoulder move" for control.* MYEISHA *wins this battle.*]

SCENE 4

[BEATBOXER *samples a series of "Fours."* MYEISHA *dances the "scalp move" as the* CORONER *"cuts up" the following.*]

BEATBOXER [*as* CORONER]: The entrance to gunshot wound number four is on the left posterior side of the head. This is a typical distant gunshot wound entrance. The course of the projectile is through the scalp and exits the right posterior side of the scalp. The projectile does not enter or fracture the cranium, and the course is only through the scalp. The exit on the right posterior scalp is a half-inch, irregular, stellate hole without abrasion. This is a non-fatal distant gunshot wound perforating the scalp only.

MYEISHA: Hold up . . .

[BEATBOXER *samples "wait a minute . . ."*]

I know he did not just say only through the scalp

I know she did not just say only talkin' 'bout my scalp!

She must not realize that the only place my hair grows is on that scalp

You know what

I'm not even gonna get into the whole Black women and their hair conversation right now

Not with a coroner anyhow

[*Beat.*]

[*Reluctantly*] All I'm gon' say is Sarah Breedlove

Aka Madam C. J. Walker

Aka first self-made American woman millionaire

Built on Black hair care

[*To* CORONER] You hear!

[*Beat.*]

Hot iron burns on your forehead, scars on your neck

Highlights, lowlights, frostin', tintin'

Sleepin' sittin' up so your new style don't get wrecked

Kitchen sink perms

Combing through them naps

Baby hair pumpin'

Getting your dandruff scratched

Now I know some of my sistas you all gone natural and I ain't hatin'

All I'm sayin' is you don't wanna go there unless you are aware of the hair

[BEATBOXER *samples LL Cool J's "Around The Way Girl."*]

Only through the scalp

Lemme give you, Mr. Coroner, some advice when addressing a Black woman's hair

The only time you wanna let "only" come out your mouth is if you're sayin

If only I could get my flip to flip as good as yours

If only I could get my goddess braids to rock as good as yours

If only I could get my wrap to drop as good as yours

If only I could get my micro braids to hold as good as yours

If only I could get my streaks to blend as good as yours

If only I could get my bob to hold as good as yours

If only I could get my Farrah Fawcett feather to layer as good as yours

If only I could get my quick weave to blend as good as yours

Only through the scalp

And since I'm handing out advice

Let me give the men a little slice

You know me

I'ma be nice

Brothas should already be aware of this fact

But if you ain't a brotha and you like your coffee black

Here's a little insight to help you with your mack

Do not touch the hair

Permed, relaxed, crimped, slicked, braided, dreaded, or 'fro

Please

Just let the hair go

Do not grab the hair

Do not stroke the hair

Do not caress the hair

Do not clutch the hair

Do not fondle the hair

Do not fiddle with the hair

Do not twiddle with the hair

Do not absentmindedly twirl the hair or swirl the hair or curl the hair

Do not pensively seize the hair

Do not passionately grip the hair

Do not attempt to run your fingers through the hair

Do not kiss the hair

Do not lick the hair

Just

Did I make it clear

Hands off the hair

But if you care to get near the hair then be aware of when hair's just been done

When sista's just come from Ebony Crest, Shear Elegance, or Miss Ellison

Make it very clear that you see the hair, you feel the hair

And if allowed to

You would stroke the hair

You would caress the hair

You would clutch the hair

You would grab the hair

You would fondle, fiddle, twiddle, and twirl the hair

I know it's not fair

But hey, hair's not fair

So if you really care

Do not touch the hair

And, oh yeah, when you see a sista goin' like this

[*Pats hair*] Don't be fazed

Ain't nothin' wrong with her, she's only scratchin' her scalp through her braids

[*Facetiously, 'bout the* CORONER] I know she/he did not say only through the scalp

Only through the scalp.

[MYEISHA *dances, but can't hit the "scalp move."* MYEISHA *wins this battle.*]

SCENE 5

[BEATBOXER *samples a series of "Fives."* MYEISHA *dances the "lower back move" as the* CORONER *"cuts up" the following.*]

BEATBOXER [*as* CORONER]: The entrance to gunshot number five is located on the central lower back.

The course of the projectile is through the skin and soft tissue of the left lower back and exits the left anterior lateral hip.

This is a non-fatal gunshot wound to the left lower back.

MYEISHA: I was in a video
Nah, fo' real
I was in a video
I was in this video
It was even on TV
OK, so it was just like on channel twenty-three
Exclusively local to the IE
OK, see, this emcee from Mo-Val got signed by Mo-Val Records
Local label, think his name was MC D-Lo
And they about to release his first single and they 'bout to shoot the video
So me, Shy, and Toni are at Club Metro lettin' ourselves go
This kid sees us, says he's shootin' a video
Sees us doin' our old routine
Not even the new one you just seen
Says he's lookin' for some females to represent the IE
So naturally, you know . . . Toni, Shy, and me—
[*She mimics the kid*] "You guys heard of Empire Records, right?"
No
"Well, we shootin' a video"
So?!
But we still show up for the shoot
Shoot, we just down to get our groove on
They were for real, had a director, a crew, an' everything
So on "action" we did our thing

OK, so you probably won't recognize us, you know

I thought they were serious

But when I saw the video all they showed was the angle on the gluteus

I mean, I like my posterior, but I like my face too

I think they showed it once on *BET: Uncut*

But in the final cut you *don't see me*

Least not from any angle where you could see me

All they showed was what me, Shy, and Toni called the "ho shot"

All bottom, no top

OK, so this is how Mo-Val Records shot me

[*She gives audience the* BET: Uncut–*angle on the posterior shot. The smirk on her face turns to disappointment to anger to sadness.* MYEISHA *dances, but can't hit the "lower back move." She battles the* CORONER *with the "lower back move."* MYEISHA *wins this battle.*]

SCENE 6

[BEATBOXER *samples a series of "sixes."* MYEISHA *dances "fractured femur move" as the* CORONER *"cuts up" the following.*]

BEATBOXER [*as* CORONER]: The entrance to gunshot wound number six is located on the left thigh. The course of the projectile is through the skin and soft tissue of the left thigh, perforating, fracturing, and fragmenting the left femur. This is a non-fatal, however, serious gunshot wound to the left thigh, fracturing the left femur.

MYEISHA: My cousin died once, well . . . almost died

No, not Toni, my cousin Freddie

Well, he kinda died

OK, so if you know me and you know I got sports skills

When it came to Freddie, sports kills

He's uncoordinated like a mug, I mean like a mug

So when I heard he broke his leg I was like

Yeah

And?

Of course he broke his leg, it's Fred, that's what he does

You know how you got that one cousin who always gets hurt

You could be playin' tag, hide-and-seek, jump rope, or diggin' in the dirt

You know you played diggin' in the dirt

No matter what though

Guaranteed . . . Freddie was gonna get hurt

Dropped a brick on his head . . . that was funny

That one bled

Broke his left arm twice

Broke his right arm once

Ankles always sprained

Usually the left, but the right one too

Always something caught in his eyes, even though he wore glasses

Over a hundred stitches, no lie

Had to sleep on the bottom bunk 'cause he would fall out the bed

That was Fred

So then he gets hurt and starts cryin'

We're like "shhh, come on man, you act like you dyin' or something"

Thing was

If one of our aunties heard Freddie's boo-hoo our game was through

Toni used to get so mad at him she didn't know what to do

[MYEISHA *as* TONI *in the moment*] Damn Fred, shut up!

You act like a little girl

Long as there was no blood flow though

Freddie was usually good to go

So

They take him to Kaiser—

Oh wait, let me break down the break

This fool goes out to Devil's Canyon out by Cal State

Rollin' on a moped

A moped

That's a motorcycle that you pedal

So full speed ahead goes Fred

Crashes the moped

They take him to Kaiser Fontana

Soon's I find out I am on my way to the hospital

To have some fun

Get my bag on

When I get there he's like

"They just wanna keep me overnight then I'ma go home"

Next day I'm learning about fat embolism syndrome

And Freddie's not at home

He's in a coma

It was induced

That's how it was introduced

Doctors explained it this way . . .

MYEISHA AND BEATBOXER [*in unison, as* DOCTOR]: Fat embolism syndrome is a symptom complex of acute respiratory failure after long-bone fractures. It is thought to be caused by deposition of embolic fat within the pulmonary capillaries, resulting in a capillary leak within the lung. The source of the embolic fat appears to be marrow fat.

MYEISHA: Freddie broke his femur

The fat was headed to his lungs

Got stuck in his throat

So he's put into an induced coma for two weeks

'Cause he was too weak to breathe or speak

Two weeks

Too weak to even eat

Like he was dead

In a hospital bed

They said

Told us it was good for him to hear familiar voices

So I showed up just about every day

Aunt Dee moved in to Kaiser Permanente

Per-ma-nent-lay

My Aunt Dee, Freddie's mom, had always been the auntie with faith

You know, the religious aunt who made sure you prayed in you car 'fore a long ride

Or dropped a "stay on the Lord's side" if she thought you were starting to backslide

Aunt Dee moved into the ICU

I-kid-you not

Prayin' my cousin back to this side

Sayin'

"This coma ain't nothing but a comma in my son's life story"

After sixteen days Freddie woke up in a haze

First thing he says is

"Cuz, I went to New York City"

And I'm thinkin'

Not pretty

Shame

The fat emboli got his brain

How sad

And he's gettin' mad

'Cause nobody's believin' his New York City dream

Starts to scream about the weather, what he ate, where he went, cash he spent

Talkin' 'bout he was

[BEATBOXER *samples "Déjà Vu (Uptown Baby)."*]

Talkin' 'bout he was in

[BEATBOXER *samples "Brooklyn's in the House."*]

Talkin' 'bout he was in

[BEATBOXER *samples "Strong Island."*]

Talkin' 'bout he was in

[BEATBOXER *samples "South Bronx."*]

Talkin' 'bout he was in

[BEATBOXER *samples "The Bridge."* BEATBOXER *goes into a serious "South Bronx"/"The Bridge" mix.*]

MYEISHA: I'm like, fool, you were right here in

Fontana baby, Fontana baby

With yo' mama baby

With yo' mama baby

Freddie didn't think that was too funny

Anyways . . . who knows?

Maybe Freddie did go to the city

I sure hope Aunt Dee has some of her prayer power left over for me

[*Beat.*]

I ain't never been to New York

[MYEISHA *dances, hits the "fractured femur move." She battles the* CORONER *with the "fractured femur move."* MYEISHA *wins this battle.*]

SCENE 7

[BEATBOXER *samples a series of "sevens."* MYEISHA *dances the "lower back move" as the* CORONER *"cuts up" the following.*]

BEATBOXER [*as* CORONER]: The entrance of gunshot number seven is located on the right middle back. The course of the projectile is through the subcutaneous tissue of the right central back. The bullet did not enter the chest. This is a non-fatal gunshot wound to the chest.

[MYEISHA *is at the tattoo spot with* TONI.]

MYEISHA: Toni, you sure 'bout this spot?

"Yeah girl, this is where I got mine done and you know mine's hot"

Yeah, I'm here for a tat. My cousin tells me you got skills. You got a problem with that?

My lower back

Nefertiti

Queen

Black

Here, Toni, where's the one you drew?

[MYEISHA *shows* TONI'S *Nefertiti drawing to* TATTOO ARTIST.]

My cousin got skills, huh?

You told me forty, not sixty-five. Let's go

What?

[*To* TONI] That's all I got

Let me get twenty-five, I'll pay you back

I know I ain't got no job

You don't have to bust me out

Just do me this favor I'll get you back. Just like I got your back last month

Don't front

Awright, let's see what you can do

[*She positions herself in tattoo chair.*]

Hold up, wait

Is it gonna hurt?

[*Beat.*]

TATTOO ARTIST: "Do pigs like dirt?"

MYEISHA: [*Not amused*] That's funny. But fo' real though

Tiny pieces of fire tappin' your skin. But then . . .

Numb, that'll work

Awright

Begin

She was powerful, beautiful, and smart like me

Her name means "the beautiful woman has come"

I'm heeere!

I'm puttin' her there 'cause only kings get to see the queen. Know what I mean?

Trust me, it'll be the last time you see her

Two hours?!

I told Uncle Darnell I was thinkin' 'bout gettin' a tattoo

I can be just like you

He says: First of all, ain't nobody gon' see it dark as you are

Second, a tattoo ain't nothin' but a scar

You can get a scar if you want

From me

For free

The pain'll be the same

Just won't take as long. Then he starts going into one of his "blackouts"

[*Imitating Uncle Darnell*] "You woulda never made it as no slave

It'll be a hundred degrees . . . IE heat"

And if I forget and say, "Man, it is hot"

[*Imitating Uncle Darnell*] "You woulda never made it as no slave

This ain't nothin' but dry heat

Down South they got that humid heat, plus massa wasn't givin you much to eat"

I get me some new tennis shoes

[*Imitating Uncle Darnell*] "You woulda never made it as a slave

They didn't even have shoes

You'd just be steppin' with your bare feet on the hard concrete"

He always tried to throw in some lame hip-hop to prove he was cool

Even when I did something right, like help him move our couch

[*Imitating Uncle Darnell*] "You woulda never made it as a slave

Don't you know that once you let 'em know how hard you could work, that's how hard you would work"

So I dropped the couch

[MYEISHA *dances, hits the "lower back move." She battles the* CORONER *with the "lower back move."* MYEISHA *wins this battle.*]

SCENE 8

[BEATBOXER *samples a series of "eights."* MYEISHA *dances the "lower back move" as the* CORONER *"cuts up" the following.*]

BEATBOXER [*as* CORONER]: The entrance to gunshot number eight is located on the right lower back. The course of the projectile is through the skin and soft tissue of the right lower back, perforating and fracturing the third lumbar vertebra.

This is a non-fatal gunshot wound to the right lower back.

MYEISHA: They found my "C" in junior high

[*Showing lower back*] See? Here's how

There was a screening one day that seemed to be pretty benign

They drew a line, we stood in line, they took a look at our spine

A few days later came a letter saying I needed further testing

After X-rays the doctor says he didn't like the way my spine was resting

The diagnosis . . . scoliosis, a lower "C" curve

Not like Becca who had an "S," hers was an internal swerve

Told I had to wear that brace for two years in my case

This thing went all the way from my chest down to my waist

I'd have to be encased in this brace to prevent improper alignment

Since I didn't embrace the exercises the doctor gave me as my assignment

[MYEISHA *demonstrates exercise using chair, as the* BEATBOXER *narrates instructions in a monotone voice.*]

BEATBOXER: This exercise aims to align the spine and activate underused muscles. Stand next to an elevated bench so that the edge of the bench is near your hip. The leg on the same side as the thoracic concavity should be against the bench. Lean to the side over the bench and bring up your leg to form a straight line with your body. The foot should point up. The shoulder and the hip that are on the same side as the rib hump should be slightly back. The palm on the same arm should face up. Your other arm should push against the surface of the bench, so that the shoulder above the thoracic concavity is as high as possible. Try to lengthen your neck as far as you can, in the direction of your thoracic curve. Also try to reach as far as you can with the raised leg. Feel your spine straightening and lengthening. Breathe into the thoracic concavity while maintaining this position. Feel the thoracic concavity getting wider and larger. Continue breathing slowly deeper and deeper.

MYEISHA: Since I didn't embrace the exercises the doctor gave me as my assignment

I'd have to be encased in this brace to prevent improper alignment

Told I was gonna have to wear it for two years straight, eighth grade and ninth

The first year wasn't too bad, but the second we were gonna have a fight

Ninth grade, first year of high school

Now you know that was not cool

I wasn't 'bout to show up as a freshman looking like a fresh fool

Like some kinda geek

Like some kinda freak

All grotesque

A whole year-an'-a-half 'fore I got my second-base chest

So I was like, forget it, I figured I might as well just

Take the chance, take the risk

I mean the worst thing that could happen to me, I guess, is that I'd have some back pain when I got old, like fifty-six

Worst thing . . . I guess . . . back pain at fifty-six

[MYEISHA *dances, hits the "lower back move." She battles the* CORONER *with the "lower back move."* MYEISHA *wins this battle.*]

SCENE 9

[BEATBOXER *samples a series of "nines."* MYEISHA *dances "left breast move" as the* CORONER *"cuts up" the following.*]

BEATBOXER [*as* CORONER]: The entrance to gunshot number nine is through the left breast. The wound is located five inches to the left of the anterior midline and fourteen inches down from the top of the head. This is a typical distant gunshot wound entrance. The course of the projectile is through the soft tissue of the left breast, through the anterior chest wall, and exits below the right breast. The exit to gunshot wound six is located below the right breast. This is a non-fatal gunshot wound perforating the left breast.

MYEISHA: If you know me you know I wasn't

One of the early bloomers like my cousin

'Til I was like sixteen it seemed like "A" was gonna be the only letter on my bra ever

Clever Ricky and his friends got to callin' me "Manchester"

Wanna know what I called their sorry behinds?

Never mind

But then I turned sixteen

And bam

I mean boom!

I mean pow!

I mean wow!

I got mine

See

[*She does a chest pop.*]

Second base all in yo' face

Now it wasn't like I was easy . . . or fast or loose

But that don't mean I didn't let loose when I let loose

I guess if I wanted to I could tell you that I'm a virgin

But that wouldn't be the honest version

Waited 'til I was sixteen though

I didn't know if we were even doin' it right

No lights

Dontrey kept talkin' 'bout how the time was right

How he was the last of his boys in line

How that wasn't right
Thing was, Dontrey was foine
And once we did it we did it all night long
[BEATBOXER *drops Kurtis Blow–style*] 'Til the break-a-dawn
Well, at least that's Dontrey's version
But let's just say that dawn came with a quickness
can I get a witness . . .
But
It was still awright
It was still awright
[*Back in the moment*] Mouth was slightly open . . .
Eyes were closed . . .
Breathing shallow . . .
Lips quivering . . .
Body shaking
Dontrey liked my lips, he dug my hips,
But yes, he loved my chest
Confessed my chest was the best
Good guess
He was a breast man
And at sixteen, like I said, I had the best, man
Forget the rest, come caress
Why settle for less, man
Just stop right there

Do not touch the hair

At sixteen stopped wondering, found out for sure

At seventeen stopped accepting and started wanting more

At eighteen declared myself a woman, grown . . . mature

At nineteen awaiting twenty . . . knockin' on heaven's door

Awaiting twenty

A weight in twenty

I wait for twenty

At sixteen stopped wondering, found out for sure

At seventeen stopped accepting and started wanting more

At eighteen declared myself a woman, grown . . . mature

At nineteen awaiting twenty . . . knockin' on heaven's door

At twenty a teenager no more . . . grown

I'm gon' learn to moan

At twenty a teenager no more . . . grown

I'm gon' learn to moan

But looks like twenty's getting out of reach

And I'm running out of time

Half a dozen on one hand, six on the other, figure of speech

And I'm running out of rhyme

Seems like a crime

To waste all that I bring to the table

So why don't we agree to make this tale a fable

Let's agree to make this a fable

Seems like a crime

To waste all that I bring to the table

So why don't we agree to make this tale a fable

[*Rappin'*] Once upon a time in the Inland Empire

There lived a young girl wanted to spit fire

There lived a young girl wanted to spit fire

There lived a young girl . . .

Why don't we agree to make this tale a fable

Then if you're able, if you can

If it's not too much to ask

When they finish singing your happy nineteenth birthday before you make your wish and blow

Put a candle on your cake for me to add to the glow

Close your eyes and wish that what you're seeing ain't nothin' but a dream-fable

And I'm gonna wake up nineteen at your birthday table

Close your eyes and wish that what you're seeing ain't nothin' but a dream-fable

And I'm gonna wake up nineteen at your birthday table

Put another candle on to add to the glow

Now make your wish and blow

BEATBOXER [*as* OFFICER GARLAND]: Miller's mouth was slightly open, her eyes were closed, her breathing appeared shallow, her lips were quivering, her body was shaking, and a white substance was accumulating around the sides of her mouth.

MYEISHA: At nineteen . . .

Knockin' on heaven's door.

[MYEISHA *dances, hits the "left breast move." She battles the* CORONER *with the "left breast move."* MYEISHA *wins this battle.*]

SCENE 10

[BEATBOXER *samples a series of "tens."* MYEISHA *does the "upper left forehead move."*]

BEATBOXER [*as* CORONER]: The entrance to gunshot number ten is located on the left upper forehead. This is a typical distant gunshot wound entrance. The course of the projectile is through the skin of the forehead, entering the cranium through the left frontal bone, through the left and right frontal lobes of the brain, through the right orbit, perforating and rupturing the right ocular globe, and exiting the right orbit. The direction of the projectile is back to front, left to right, and downward forty-five degrees. This is a fatal distant gunshot wound to the head.

[MYEISHA*'s lifeless body stands and is moved by the invisible touch as he examines her wound. The* CORONER *wins this battle.*]

SCENE 11

[BEATBOXER *samples a series of "elevens."* MYEISHA *does the "left ear move."*]

BEATBOXER [*as* CORONER]: The entrance of gunshot wound number eleven is above and behind the left ear on the left side of the head. This is a typical distant gunshot wound entrance. The course of the projectile is through the scalp, entering the cranium through the left occipital bone, perforating the left cerebellum, perforating the pons of the brain stem, and penetrating into the anterior base of the cranium. This is a fatal distant gunshot wound to the head.

[MYEISHA's *lifeless body stands and is moved by the invisible touch as he examines her wound. The* CORONER *wins this battle.*]

SCENE 12

[BEATBOXER *samples a series of "twelves."* MYEISHA *does the "right central back move."*]

BEATBOXER [*as* CORONER]: The entrance to gunshot number twelve is located on the right central back. This is a typical distant gunshot wound entrance. The direction of the projectile is back to front, left to right, and slightly upward three degrees. This is a fatal distant gunshot wound to the chest, perforating the right lung.

[MYEISHA's *lifeless body stands and is moved by the invisible touch as he examines her wound. The* CORONER *wins this battle.* MYEISHA *holds headphones to left ear, as if in recording studio.*]

MYEISHA: One-to-the-chest

One-to-the-arm

One-to-the-leg

One-to-the-neck

One-to-the-dome

One-to-the-dome

One-to-the-dome

One-to-the-back

One-to-the-back

One-to-the-back

One-to-the-back

One-to-the-back

I bet you ain't seen no female MC who's been shot as many times as me

Not since Supersonic has a female MC from the west put it down with the best

You know, one of the J's from J. J. Fad lives in the IE
For a minute I was thinkin' of rappin' in Pig Latin
But that ain't hap'nin'
This is the key right here
It's been a year since they shot Biggie
Since Tupac was killed it's been two
It just makes sense that this should happen to me now
I gotta live
I'll be the first female MC ever
Ever
Before me MCs only been shot a couple times
And lived
I got a dozen and I'll still be spittin' rhymes
You can't stop me, this is my time to shine
One-to-the-chest
One-to-the-arm
One-to-the-leg
One-to-the-neck
One-to-the-dome
One-to-the-dome
One-to-the-dome
One-to-the-back
One-to-the-back
One-to-the-back

One-to-the-back

One-to-the-back

[MYEISHA *battles* CORONER. *The* CORONER *wins this battle.*]

BEATBOXER: The average person can hold their breath for sixty to ninety seconds

The lungs take in oxygen-enriched air first and get rid of carbon dioxide second

The average person breathes in and out fifteen to twenty-five times every sixty seconds

Breath enters through the nose and mouth first, pharynx and larynx second

[MYEISHA *exhales.*]

There are two phases to the process of breathing

Inspiration

Expiration

[MYEISHA *"inspires" and "expires" twenty-five times.* BEATBOXER *speaks the following on her breaths. Breaths should be taken meditatively, gradually slowing, then coming to a stop.*]

BEATBOXER: Creativity

Release

Insight

Conclusion

Inventiveness

Completion

Ingenuity

Closure

Imagination

Exhalation

Revelation

Cessation

Stimulation

Departure

Arousal

Eradication

Muse

Expelled

Motivation

Termination

Vision

Discontinuance

Illumination

Extinction

Elevation

Execution

Enthusiasm

Closure

Invigoration

Obliteration

Exuberance

Collapse

Excitement

Finale

Fervor

Finish

Elation

Termination

Vivification

Death

Awakening

Passing

Uplift

Exit

Rapture

Deceased

Alpha

Omega

Beginning

MYEISHA [*rushing to get to bed, in one breath*]: Now I lay me down to sleep

I pray the Lord my soul to keep

If I should die before I wake

I pray the Lord my soul to take

Bless Mommy and Daddy, Shy, Freddie, Aunt Dee, and my cousin Toni

This is Myeisha

You know me.

BEATBOXER: End.

[MYEISHA'S *breathing stops. The* CORONER *wins the battle.* MYEISHA *dances the "twelve mortal moves" to Otis Redding's "White Christmas." The* BEATBOXER *repeats the following until the end of the dance.*]

BEATBOXER [*as* CORONER]: Right lung weighed two hundred seventy grams

Left lung weighed three hundred twenty-five grams

Liver weighed nine hundred seventy-five grams

Spleen weighed one hundred grams

Kidneys weighed one hundred grams each

Brain weighed one thousand twenty-five grams

Heart weighed two hundred seventy-five grams and was smooth and glistening

[MYEISHA *finishes her dance, then gets back into the white Nissan Sentra.*]

MYEISHA: Ever have one of those dreams

Where nothing comes out when you try to scream

[MYEISHA *falls into her final sleep.*]

PATIENCE, FORTITUDE, AND OTHER ANTIDEPRESSANTS

Mariana Carreño King

In collaboration with Daniel Jáquez and Intar Theatre's Unit 52

Inspired by *Yerma*, by Federico García Lorca

CRITICAL INTRODUCTION

Beatriz J. Rizk

The process at work in women's writing, often perceived as cyclical in nature, is nowhere more evident than in Mariana Carreño King's *Patience, Fortitude, and Other Antidepressants,* based on *Yerma* (1934), one of Federico Garcia Lorca's rural Andalusian tragedies. In this modern version, Carreño King forms a collectivity of women characters. The conflation of women trapped between society and personal desire, with the expression of same-sex love, also harkens to the beginning of the Chicana writing tradition with the pioneering work of Estela Portillo-Trambley in her play *The Day of the Swallows* (1971), also loosely based on Lorca's play. Juxtaposing female precursors' texts with those of later writers no doubt highlights and reinforces the female tradition but also denotes that, despite significant changes, progress has been slow. This is corroborated by the need to rewrite and/or address the same issues facing women in general and which becomes more pronounced for women of color.

Commissioned to write a play for the New York INTAR's Unit 52, an emerging artists company founded in 2010 by Lou Moreno, Daniel Jáquez, and other INTAR artists, Carreño King—also a Unit 52 cofounding member—wrote a piece that provides dialogue and action to twenty-three actors by adapting Lorca's universal worldview, his passionate defense of the imagination, and his penchant for detail. Carreño King began working with the ensemble after a six-month training period looking for a balanced theatrical piece. According to Jáquez, who directed the play, the process was "about challenging the actors and matching that with INTAR's mission of helping develop Latina/o writers in English."[1] After three weeks of intensive rehearsals, the play opened in 2012, and it was subsequently selected to participate in the 2014 Encuentro.

Changing the setting from Lorca's rural environment to New York's urban barrio stoops was a significant one. Working collectively with the theater troupe, "extracting and distilling" *Yerma*'s different scenes that were of interest, the basic storyline still centers upon a barren woman who longs for a child to fill the void of what she feels is an empty life.[2] The other characters, on the contrary, undergo considerable transformations. Reflecting some of the most serious social problems plaguing contemporary society such as sexism, police brutality, and homophobia, they were molded according to the dramatic significance the overall repressive system has upon them.

Yerma and Carreño King's Isabella feel that they are stuck in loveless marriages that they are unable to end. They both live in worlds based on strict conventions wherein women reach a sacrosanct status only by marriage and procreation, in the case of the former, and conjoined to stability, in the case of the latter. Interacting with her gender construction and perception, there is also a distinctive culture of poverty that surrounds Isabella, emphasized by her inability to escape it. Painting becomes her emotional outlet, as her husband Juan is happy to remind her: "You have your paintings, a roof over your head. You don't have to worry about food or making a living." Cultural ideology thus turns into cultural determinism as the importance of familyism, invoked by both Yerma's and Isabella's husbands, becomes the rule of the land in their universes.

Reading the female characters through a feminist lens, the play can be perceived as a study on the distinct functions associated with womanhood. Isabella's role wholly corresponds to the expected gender and sexual behavior of men and women conceptualized in terms of "metaphorically associated binary oppositions," such as "nature/culture, self-interest/social good,"[3] passivity/activity, etc. Cornered by the restrictions established at home to forsake her chances of becoming anything other than a properly trained housewife (Juan even suggests that she should take cooking lessons from his sisters), she is placed in a defenseless limbo for her inability to procreate, suggested in the play due to Juan's indifference, which nevertheless compromises her place in the patriarchy. Isabella's struggle to restore equilibrium results in dissimilar measures from that of Yerma. One of them is to look for affection to soothe her feelings of isolation by engaging in same-sex lovemaking with her friend Jess (maybe the "other antidepressant" suggested in the title). Another clear escapist strategy is found in her own creations: her paintings, which could be seen as extensions of her personality. Representing a ritualistic repetition of gender accentuated by their names—Fortitude, Patience, and the unfinished Bella—they embody parallel beings that allow Isabella to vent her resentment and anger at her inability to break free. Watching her life from the sidelines, Fortitude tries to instill resilience in Isabella by bringing to her attention to the fact that "This is about control. Control of our body, your life." Patience's role, in turn, consists of appeasing her frustration by reciting her duties as a wife and family member. As to the unfinished rendition of Bella, she is the symbol of the woman-object-trophy from whom not much is expected ("I'm beautiful. I'm just another version of yourself"). The repetitive list of medications associated with Isabella throughout the play suggests a schism, an inability to navigate her circumstances: "Propranolol to ease out of reality," "Bromazepam for the anxiety," "Dietilamida to induce erotic dreams," and "Cimetidina to inhabit an alternate dimension." An optimistic note at the end of *Patience* is represented by Isabella's decision to finish the Bella painting once and for all, which suggests that perhaps recovering wholeness of body, mind, and spirit is possible even amid chaos.

Theatrically speaking, the paintings provide a surreal touch suggesting the allure of a hidden world to an otherwise realistic scenic design. The production utilized three large frames, in one of the lateral rooms, from which the painting-characters are brought to life, addressing the other characters and sometimes even interacting with them but always returning to their initial static condition. Other than the seemingly antagonistic private and public spheres divided along gender lines, the production questions the divisibility of space by placing the occupants of tight enclaves among the inhabitants of exterior spaces. The feeling is contrasted and simultaneously reinforced by the choice to highlight the street dominating the stage as the geographic locus representing the main artery of the barrio. It is the space where social interactions take place, designated as the distinctive site where community happens, but it is also the location where rituals find reenactment. One such instance is the carnival block party celebrating the summer solstice for which the characters are preparing. As it happened in Lorca's play, in which a *romería* (a pilgrimage to a shrine) takes place, these commemorative traditions are necessary for the development of the tragedy. It is on the eve of these rituals, which ironically are meant to celebrate the propagation of life, that the male protagonists meet their tragic end, carrying with them the seeds of life into death.

To bring the circle to fruition, mention should be made to other Latinas who have ventured down a similar path as Carreño King with promising results. One case is Josefina López; in *Simply María or the American Dream* (1987) the protagonist metaphorically develops split personalities, called Graces, for exactly the same reasons as Isabella: to escape reality. They are depicted as evocations of self-knowledge, perhaps a necessary step in the process of breaking loose from María's repressive surroundings. In a Chicana narrative, Sandra Cisneros also conjured them in her celebrated novel *The House on Mango Street* (1984) through the "three *comadres*" who represent the "gift of prophesy" as well as the "gift of identity."[4] The three Graces or Fates have a long history which has been a part of "Western literature since the Spanish Roman poet Catullus in his 'The Marriage of Peleus and Thetis' describes the wedding gift of the three sisters, the Fates, all dressed in white, spinning their prophesy."[5]

Patience, Fortitude, and Other Antidepressants is a welcome addition to the growing body of work by Latina playwrights. It is an understatement to say that more plays reflecting women's experiences beyond the usual stereotypical characterizations are necessary.

NOTES

1. Daniel Jáquez, interviewed by the author, Los Angeles, November 12, 2017.
2. Mariana Carreño King, in *Alyson Mead*, "Interview with Mariana Carreño King," for LA FPI Podcast: "What She Said," November 2014. http:// lafpi.com.
3. Gayle. Austin, *Feminist Theories for Dramatic Criticism* (Ann Arbor, Mich.: University of Michigan Press, 1990), 42.
4. Ibid, 228.
5. María Elena De Valdés, *The Shattered Mirror: Representations of Women in Mexican Literature* (Austin, Tex.: University of Texas Press, 1998), 223.

BIBLIOGRAPHY

Austin, Gayle. *Feminist Theories for Dramatic Criticism*. Ann Arbor, Mich.: University of Michigan Press, 1990.

Cisneros, Sandra. *The House on Mango Street*. Houston: Arte Público Press, 1984.

García Lorca, Federico. *Blood Wedding and Yerma*. New York: Theatre Communications Group Inc., 1994.

De Valdés, María Elena. *The Shattered Mirror: Representations of Women in Mexican Literature.* Austin, Tex.: University of Texas Press, 1998.

López, Josefina. *Simply María or the American Dream.* In *Shattering the Myth: Plays by Hispanic Women.* Linda Feyder, ed. Houston, Tex.: Arte Público Press, 1992.

Mead, Alyson. Interview with Mariana Carreño King, for LA FPI Podcast: "What She Said," November 2014. http:// lafpi.com.

Portillo-Trambley, Estela. *The Day of the Swallows.* Ypsilanti, Michigan: Bilingual Press, 1971.

PRODUCTION HISTORY

Patience, Fortitude, and Other Antidepressants was commissioned, developed, and produced by Intar Theatre for Unit 52's 2013 company of actors. It was subsequently produced for Encuentro 2014 at the Los Angeles Theatre Center with the following cast:

Patience . . . . Tiffany Esteb
Fortitude . . . . Jenniffer Díaz
Isabella . . . . Diomargy Nuñez
Juan . . . . Orlando Rivera
Jess. . . . . Mariana Carreño King
Maria. . . . . Ashley Marie Ortiz
Victor . . . . Aldo Uribe
Bella . . . . Hara Zi
Jordan . . . . Oscar Cabrera
Agnes . . . . .Martina Potratz
Grace. . . . . Lori Felipe-Barkin
Joy . . . . Christin Eve Cato

Both productions were directed by Daniel Jáquez and designed by Thomas Ontiveros, Marios Aristopoulos, Stefan Martin, and Lou Moreno; Rebecca Martinez was the choreographer and an assistant director and Ngozi Anyanwu was the stage manager and assistant director.

CHARACTERS

(Although there are no specifications on the ethnicity or skin color of the characters, all of them are people of color.)

Patience, Isabella's early painting

Fortitude, Isabella's early painting

Isabella, early twenties

Juan, early twenties, Isabella's husband

Jess, late twenties

Maria, early twenties

Victor, late twenties

Bella, Isabella's unfinished painting

Jordan, early twenties

Agnes, Juan's sister, thirties

Grace, Juan's sister, late twenties

Joy, Juan's sister, early twenties

TIME

The present.

PLACE

A gritty, urban neighborhood in an American city. The action takes place in Isabella and Juan's apartment, the stoop of their building, a laundromat, a hospital room, and the streets.

PROLOGUE

[*Penumbra. All we hear is heavy breathing and the beeping of a medical contraption attached to* JUAN*'s body.* ISABELLA *sits center stage. There are three "paintings" above her:* PATIENCE, FORTITUDE, *and* BELLA. *After a moment,* PATIENCE *and* FORTITUDE *step out of their frames.*]

PATIENCE: The incessant beep-beep-beeping of the machine—

FORTITUDE: Keeps me awake.

PATIENCE: My body registers random smells—

FORTITUDE: Sensations.

PATIENCE: People who come to visit.

FORTITUDE: Family members who blame me for this.

PATIENCE: And who else can they blame?

FORTITUDE: I'm where I've always been.

PATIENCE: The doctor tells me that I don't know what happened. That I just don't know.

FORTITUDE: But I do know.

PATIENCE: I did what was expected of me.

FORTITUDE: I died once. A few times.

PATIENCE: But I came back.

[JUAN *gets up. He puts on a police uniform methodically, slipping into each piece of clothing with reverence, like a ritual. The hospital room becomes an apartment.* JUAN *and* ISABELLA *are in the bedroom. Outside the bedroom, in* ISABELLA*'s work area, is a painting of a woman,* BELLA, *along with the paintings of* PATIENCE *and* FORTITUDE; *they witness the scene.*]

PATIENCE: Hello!

FORTITUDE: Am I not here?

ISABELLA: Juan, are you listening to me?

JUAN: I don't have time for this nonsense.

ISABELLA: But you're getting ready to leave and we haven't talked—

JUAN: We can always make time to talk later.

ISABELLA: You always say that and we never do.

JUAN: We talk all the time.

ISABELLA: Not like we used to.

JUAN: Of course not. We have different responsibilities now, interests, tastes. But we still talk. What's the matter?

ISABELLA: I'm invisible.

JUAN: Don't be silly.

ISABELLA: We don't do anything together anymore. I wish we could go out sometimes, maybe go dancing, take walks. Remember when we would just walk around the neighborhood, holding hands, talking to our friends?

JUAN: We were younger.

ISABELLA: We're still young. I feel like I'm missing out on something.

JUAN: On what?

ISABELLA: We've been married three years and you only get sadder. You don't talk to me. I feel like we're growing apart.

JUAN: Jesus.

ISABELLA: I feel so lonely sometimes . . .

JUAN: You have your paintings, a roof over your head. You don't have to worry about food or making a living—

ISABELLA: I make a living.

JUAN: How much do you make at the laundromat?

ISABELLA: I could get another job.

JUAN: Doing what? Nobody is hiring, and you said yourself that painting is the only thing you want to do. I am happy to provide.

ISABELLA: But I feel like a ghost. You're never here and when you are it's like you don't see me.

JUAN: I have to work nights, you know that. My sisters will keep you company soon.

ISABELLA: That's a whole other matter.

JUAN: What? You don't want them here?

ISABELLA: Of course I do, but—

JUAN: But what?

ISABELLA: Forget it.

[*Beat.*]

JUAN: Look, this is what growing up means. To have stability. You always wanted that.

ISABELLA: Stability, yes. But not loneliness. You know I love you.

JUAN: I do. And I love you too.

ISABELLA: Juan, I want a family, a child, a baby.

JUAN: We've been through this before. Maybe we're just not meant to.

ISABELLA: How do you know if we don't even try?

JUAN: I don't like it when you talk like that.

ISABELLA: Why? Sometimes I feel my blood boiling and a tornado tearing through my insides. Do something about it.

JUAN: I have too much work and too much on my mind. We'll talk about this later. If you need anything just let me know.

[JUAN *kisses* ISABELLA *on the forehead and exits. Transition: we return to the hospital.*]

PATIENCE: He suffers. He's hurt. He's dizzy. His head palpitates like his heart—

FORTITUDE: But I know his heart doesn't palpitate much.

ISABELLA: What do I do now?

FORTITUDE: Buprenorfina for the pain.

PATIENCE: Bromazepam for the anxiety.

FORTITUDE: Nimodipina for high blood pressure.

PATIENCE: Profenid—

FORTITUDE: An anti-inflammatory—

PATIENCE: Analgesic—

FORTITUDE: And antipyretic.

ISABELLA: I try to match his breathing, to blend with him, to become him. I see his chest moving up and down. But I see nothing in his eyes.

PATIENCE: Propranolol to ease out of reality.

FORTITUDE: Dietilamida to induce erotic dreams.

PATIENCE: Cimetidina to inhabit an alternate dimension.

ISABELLA [*to* PATIENCE *and* FORTITUDE]: Thank you.

[ISABELLA *looks at a painting of* BELLA, *a woman she has been working on.* ISABELLA *touches* BELLA*'s face.* BELLA *caresses* ISABELLA*'s face back.*]

SCENE 1

[*Transition.* MARIA *and* JESS *yell at* ISABELLA*'s window from the street.*]

JESS: Isabella!

MARIA: Come outside!

[ISABELLA *looks out the window.*]

ISABELLA: What are you guys doing here?

JESS: Girl, we would've come earlier, but we waited for Mr. Charming to leave.

ISABELLA: Don't be mean.

MARIA: Guess what I got?

ISABELLA: I don't know. Nail polish?

MARIA [*taking a joint out of her purse*]: Ha!

ISABELLA: Put that away! If Juan sees it he'll kill me!

JESS: He won't be back until morning.

ISABELLA: But the smell lingers—

MARIA: What do you think stoops were invented for? Come on! I have big news.

ISABELLA: Alright . . .

[ISABELLA *disappears from the window.*]

JESS: Can I tell her?

MARIA: It's my news.

JESS: Alright.

[ISABELLA *comes out to the stoop.* MARIA *takes a long drag from the joint.*]

ISABELLA: Well . . . ?

JESS: Can't you tell?

ISABELLA: No. What?

JESS: My mom knew the minute she saw her, the witch.

MARIA: I guess it doesn't show a lot yet.

ISABELLA: What?

MARIA: There's this little thingy growing inside me.

ISABELLA: What? Congratulations!

MARIA: Thank you!

ISABELLA: Wait—why are you smoking this shit?

MARIA: I think it's OK to smoke during the first trimester.

JESS: I've heard that too.

ISABELLA: Where do you get your information?

MARIA: Alright, alright.

[MARIA *is about to put the joint out.* JESS *grabs it from her.*]

JESS: Wait! I'm not pregnant! I don't even have a boyfriend anymore.

ISABELLA: What happened?

JESS: Dumped the good-for-nothing.

ISABELLA: Why?

JESS: Why not?

ISABELLA: Let's go in. I don't want the neighbors to start talking.

MARIA: You'll have to cut their vocal cords for that.

ISABELLA: I can't believe you're fucking pregnant. How did that happen?

MARIA: Do you really need me to explain that?

ISABELLA: No. I mean, did you actually want to?

MARIA: Sure! I mean, why not? What else is there to do around here?

JESS: I can think of a couple of things that don't involve changing diapers.

ISABELLA: I just thought you'd wait.

MARIA: For what?

ISABELLA: I don't know. I always thought I'd be the first. But with Juan working nights now . . .

JESS: Don't tell me you're not having sex.

MARIA: You can have sex during the day, you know? It's not like there's a law.

ISABELLA: I am! Just—

JESS: By yourself?

ISABELLA: Alright already! Enough about me. How do you feel? What does it feel like?

MARIA: It sucks! Your body gets bloated, you're nauseous all the time, you're dead tired and want to pee like crazy, and then when the damn creature finally pops out I hear it hurts like dying a thousand deaths at once.

ISABELLA: You make it sound so easy.

MARIA: You know the husband. He really wanted one.

JESS: He was running out of time!

MARIA: He's not that old.

JESS: He looks it.

ISABELLA: He's obviously still got something down there. Do you, like, enjoy doing it with him?

MARIA: Hell yeah!

JESS: With that old man?

MARIA: Older dudes know how to please a woman.

JESS: It's pro'ly all wrinkled and nasty.

MARIA: The good ones are always a little wrinkled and nasty.

JESS: I still like 'em young and circumcised.

ISABELLA: How do you know they're circumcised?

JESS: You really need to go out more.

ISABELLA: Well, I've only been with Juan!

MARIA: I bet he isn't circumcised.

JESS: Child, you've gotta take the initiative. If Juan doesn't know what to do, you have to teach him. If he still doesn't get it, at least play with yourself.

MARIA: You might not get pregnant, but you'd feel better.

JESS: Have you ever cum, like had orgasms and stuff?

ISABELLA: I think so.

MARIA: If you just think so you probably haven't.

ISABELLA: I've felt good . . . warm. Inside. Is that what you're talking about?

MARIA: You are missing out.

ISABELLA: Do you ever sing?

MARIA: Like, while doing it?

JESS: What kind of question is that?

ISABELLA: I feel like singing. Sometimes.

JESS: Maybe you should focus more on the task at hand instead of singing karaoke in your head.

ISABELLA: I don't know what's wrong with me.

MARIA: There's nothing wrong with you. [*Giving her the joint*] Here. You keep it. When Juan returns in the morning give him some.

ISABELLA: Are you crazy?

JESS: Or you smoke it. Maybe it helps. When Juan comes back just embrace him and whisper something sexy like—

[JESS *embraces* ISABELLA *and whispers something in her ear.* ISABELLA'S *body tenses.*]

MARIA [*tickling her*]: You have to relax!

[*They all laugh.*]

MARIA: I have to go now. Gotta get my hair done before the salon closes.

ISABELLA: Are you going out tonight?

MARIA: Of course! I'm celebrating. Come!

ISABELLA: Nah. I don't feel like going out. Saving myself for carnival.

JESS: Oh shit, yeah. When is that?

ISABELLA: Day after tomorrow. Summer solstice.

MARIA: Yeah, it'll be the baby's first carnival!

ISABELLA: Plus, Juan's sisters are coming tomorrow too.

JESS: Oh god. They're back.

MARIA: All the more reason to go out tonight!

ISABELLA: Really, no. I'm tired.

JESS: You never go out anymore.

ISABELLA: I know. God, I'm getting old.

JESS: I'm old. That's what Mom says. But if you enjoyed yourself more you wouldn't grow old. That's what I say.

ISABELLA: Nonsense.

JESS: Call me if you change your mind.

ISABELLA: I doubt it, but yeah . . .

[ISABELLA *is about to go back in when* VICTOR *enters.*]

VICTOR [*to* JESS]: Just the person I was looking for! I was waiting.

ISABELLA: Hi, Victor.

JESS: Sorry, we were celebrating. Maria, you know?

VICTOR: Congrats, girl. I hope it's healthy . . . and beautiful.

MARIA: Of course he'll be healthy.

ISABELLA: You know it's a boy already?

MARIA: Right now it's just an it. But Jess's mom said it'll be a boy, and I trust her.

VICTOR: Great! Bring another unemployed dude to the hood.

MARIA: No, he'll inherit his dad's hair salons.

JESS: Another potential asshole in the hood.

MARIA: You're such a bitch.

JESS: Sorry, you know I'm kidding. I'm going to be the best aunt that critter will ever know.

MARIA: I know. He'll love you too, the little, potentially ungrateful fuck!

ISABELLA: He's going to be one lucky boy.

JESS: Anyway, Vic, my old Vic, do you have my stuff?

VICTOR: Yeah, but do you have cash? I can't do credit no more.

JESS: Come on!

VICTOR: Sorry, Jess, times are tough. Gotta pay for the shit myself, you know? I'll share my own stash with you, but that's about it.

JESS: Fuck. Isa, can I borrow a twenty?

ISABELLA: Are you going to pay me back?

JESS: Pro'ly not.

VICTOR: Come on, Isa, it's all good, ain't it? You guys have jobs.

ISABELLA: I guess. But I still don't like you selling it. If Juan knew—

JESS: He doesn't have to know, right?

VICTOR: It's just weed, it's almost legal.

ISABELLA: Almost.

[ISABELLA *gives a twenty dollar bill to* VICTOR, *who gives a baggie to* JESS.]

JESS: Isa, I owe you big time.

ISABELLA: I know.

MARIA: We should go.

ISABELLA: You kids have fun!

[MARIA *and* JESS *say good-bye and exit.*]

VICTOR: Is Juan around?

ISABELLA: He left already.

VICTOR: Right. He's doing nights now. At least he's got a real job.

ISABELLA: Yes, he does.

[ISABELLA *goes to straighten her paintings.*]

VICTOR: How's that working out for you?

PATIENCE: He comes back sweaty, dirty, and exhausted.

FORTITUDE: When he goes to bed I smell his bitter breath and I freeze.

PATIENCE: Maybe he'll touch me, I think.

FORTITUDE: But he never does.

VICTOR: Hello? Planet Earth to Isa?

ISABELLA: Sorry. It's great. Now I get to spend time with him during the day.

VICTOR: That's good.

ISABELLA: Funny how you two grew up to be so different.

VICTOR: All of us. Look at Maria.

ISABELLA: I know, at least she's not lonely.

VICTOR: Are you lonely?

ISABELLA: I'm just saying. Kids keep you busy.

VICTOR: If you want to be busy, have one.

ISABELLA: It's not that easy.

VICTOR: Tell your husband to think less about work.

ISABELLA: Yeah, any other advice I should give him?

VICTOR: Just tell him I said hi. I'll catch up with him later.

ISABELLA: Alright then. Be well.

VICTOR: Thank you. You too.

[VICTOR *exits.* ISABELLA *watches him leave, takes out the joint, lights it, and takes a long, deep puff.* ISABELLA *goes to her easel and begins to work on the painting of* BELLA.]

SCENE 2

[ISABELLA *works on the painting of the woman. The woman in the painting begins to breathe.* ISABELLA *steps back. The woman,* BELLA, *steps out of the painting, stretches.*]

BELLA: It's tight in there.

ISABELLA: I haven't finished you!

BELLA: Loosen up! You're way too serious. Smile!

ISABELLA: Don't tell me to smile! What should I be smiling about?

BELLA: There are many things!

ISABELLA: What do you know?

BELLA: Would you give me a smile?

ISABELLA: Why would I give you anything?

BELLA: Because you're painting me.

FORTITUDE: She creates you and then ignores you. That's her MO.

PATIENCE: We're still here.

ISABELLA: And you still don't stop the burning.

FORTITUDE: The pain.

PATIENCE: The anxiety.

BELLA: I get it. Come. Rest your head on my lap.

[ISABELLA *hesitates.*]

BELLA: Come on, I'm not going to bite you.

[ISABELLA *rests her head on* BELLA*'s lap.*]

ISABELLA: It feels warm.

FORTITUDE: Comfortable.

PATIENCE: Safe.

BELLA: You're still a child, that's your problem. And your blessing. Me? I'm old.

ISABELLA: I don't want you to be old.

BELLA: At this point it doesn't matter. But you did make me feel old.

ISABELLA: I can fix you. I want you to be beautiful and perfect—

BELLA: I am beautiful! I'm just another version of yourself.

PATIENCE: And another.

FORTITUDE: And another.

ISABELLA: You're not me.

BELLA: I'm the tornado tearing through your insides.

ISABELLA: I just feel numb.

PATIENCE: Empty.

FORTITUDE: Like I don't exist.

ISABELLA: Is this it? This life?

BELLA: What do you mean?

ISABELLA: You grow up, you go to school, you marry, you settle down, and then what?

PATIENCE: And then what? What else do you want?

ISABELLA: A project. Something to hold on to.

BELLA: We are your projects.

ISABELLA: It's not the same. I'm not the same.

PATIENCE AND FORTITUDE: I'm drowning.

FORTITUDE: The fumes make me dizzy.

PATIENCE: The paint hurts my skin.

ISABELLA: I feel like I paint the same thing over and over again. And I just grow sadder.

BELLA: Why did you marry him?

ISABELLA: Juan? Because he asked me to. I was in love.

BELLA: Was?

ISABELLA: I love him.

PATIENCE: It was the right thing to do.

ISABELLA: He's a good man.

FORTITUDE: I thought I'd be content.

PATIENCE: Happy even.

ISABELLA: I thought with him I would have a better life.

FORTITUDE: I thought that's what I wanted.

PATIENCE: A traditional family with a traditional man. Juan the policeman. Juan the responsible man.

FORTITUDE: I thought we would keep laughing.

ISABELLA: I thought maybe I'd become a great painter and travel the world and drink wine from his mouth on rooftops overlooking infinity.

PATIENCE: I thought I would get used to this life.

FORTITUDE: I thought we would be happy.

BELLA: I thought, I thought, I thought. But what are you actually doing?

FORTITUDE: Trying to escape.

PATIENCE: Pretending I'm OK.

ISABELLA: Surviving.

BELLA: You're talking like an old woman.

FORTITUDE: I don't think I can do this much longer.

PATIENCE: It hurts too much.

ISABELLA: I can't do this alone. I want a child.

BELLA: A child to keep you company?

ISABELLA: Yes!

BELLA: Get a dog.

ISABELLA: A child to laugh with. To play. To sing.

FORTITUDE: Kids are overrated.

ISABELLA: So what do I do now?

BELLA: Create.

ISABELLA: What about love?

BELLA: What about it? It comes and goes.

ISABELLA: Where does it go?

PATIENCE: To patrol the streets at night.

FORTITUDE: That's not really love.

BELLA: How do you feel when you see him?

PATIENCE: A knot in my stomach.

FORTITUDE: A void in my heart.

ISABELLA: Like I'm not there.

PATIENCE: It wasn't always like this.

FORTITUDE: We used to dance.

PATIENCE: And talk. And dream.

ISABELLA: Yes, it was love. A long time ago.

FORTITUDE: But it wasn't Juan.

PATIENCE: Yes, it was.

FORTITUDE: The first to make you tremble? To make you want to dance.

[*Outside, on the stoop,* VICTOR, MARIA, JESS, *and* JORDAN *drink beer and smoke a joint on the stoop. They sing the first few lines of Sublime's "Smoke Two Joints."* ISABELLA *follows the music outside, takes the scene in from the window. The song ends.*]

ISABELLA: I see that the party moved to the stoop.

JORDAN: Hi Isabella! I miss you! You never come out no more.

ISABELLA: What's up, Jordan? Miss you too. What you guys doing here?

VICTOR: We were just walking the ladies home. What are you doing up so early in the A.M.?

JESS: We danced all night!

MARIA: You did! You were on fire tonight!

JESS: I was celebrating.

JORDAN: Jess finally broke up with that dude she was with.

ISABELLA: I heard.

JESS: A toast to singlehood! Again.

EVERYBODY: Cheers!

ISABELLA: Maria, should you be drinking?

MARIA: Loosen up! I just had a beer and tons of apple juice.

ISABELLA: And your husband?

JORDAN: We're not mentioning husbands or wives or boyfriends or girlfriends tonight. Tonight everybody is single.

VICTOR: Come join us for a little while.

ISABELLA: The sun will come up soon.

JORDAN: Not yet. Come on!

MARIA: Juan is not coming back any time soon.

JESS: We said we weren't going to mention in-significant others tonight! We're celebrating freedom!

JORDAN: To freedom!

EVERYBODY: To freedom!

VICTOR: This is for you, Isabella!

[VICTOR *sings the first verse of Sublime's "Perfect World." Everybody joins in.* JESS *sits on* JORDAN*'s lap.* ISABELLA *comes out to the stoop.*]

JESS: It's so good to be single.

JORDAN: I second that.

ISABELLA: You're not afraid to be lonely?

JESS: I like my freedom.

JORDAN: I like your freedom too.

VICTOR: And you can feel lonely even if you're with someone.

JESS: Even lonelier if you're actually not alone.

JORDAN: Word.

JESS: I can go to the parties I want. I can dance and sing until the sun comes up. I have no kids and no worries.

JORDAN: Yeah, tell that to your mom.

JESS: Don't mention her. That witch.

JORDAN: She always knows where you are and what you do.

JESS: Don't believe everything you hear about her. She's dying for grandchildren, but I tell her to wait for my baby brothers, 'cause I ain't going down that road.

VICTOR: Never?

JESS: Why would I? Look at her! [*Pointing to* MARIA] In a few months she'll hardly be able to walk.

VICTOR: At least she has help! When my sister had her first baby she moved back in with Mom and life is hell in that apartment ever since.

ISABELLA: Nobody here wants a family?

JORDAN: I might want a kid someday . . .

MARIA: You do?

JORDAN: Why not? A little monkey to follow me around?

JESS: A monkey, yes!

VICTOR: Hehehehe. Monkeys.

JORDAN: Shut up! You probably already have one or two monkeys running around and you don't even know it.

VICTOR: Of course that's a possibility.

ISABELLA: Really?

VICTOR: Nah. But we are a family. Who needs more than this? These friends, this stoop?

JESS: I toast to that!

VICTOR: To family!

EVERYBODY: To family!

MARIA: I don't know what I'd do without you guys, really. I mean, I really love you, you are my real family.

ISABELLA: You're drunk.

JORDAN: Loosen up, Isabella! Juan's bitterness is rubbing off on you.

ISABELLA: He's not bitter.

VICTOR: Just sad.

ISABELLA: He's got a job. He's got responsibilities.

JORDAN: He's a cop. With all due respect, once you cross that line, you can't be a member of this family.

VICTOR: That's not true. Isabella is right. At least he's got a job. Almost nobody else here can say the same.

JORDAN: Well, why don't you enlist?

VICTOR: I'd never pass the pot test.

JORDAN: He could've become anything. A cop? In this neighborhood? That's like joining the enemy.

ISABELLA: Cops don't have to be the enemy. And you know Juan means well.

VICTOR: He's still our brother, and he has a job.

JORDAN: I have a job too.

VICTOR: Bagging groceries for loose change doesn't count.

JORDAN: Neither does selling weed. And I just got another good gig walking dogs.

JESS: That's a job?

JORDAN: Cleaning their shit is.

MARIA: I offered to recommend you all to my husband.

VICTOR: That man scares me.

MARIA: Why? Alright, he's a little older than us, but he's a good man.

JORDAN: Who carries a big gun.

MARIA: It's only for self-defense.

JESS: There's no such thing as a good man in the long term.

JORDAN: He looks like the Godfather.

MARIA: Which one?

JORDAN: What do you mean, which one?

MARIA: Marlon Brando or the one from the Grimms's fairy tale?

JESS: The Grimms's fairy tale?

MARIA: Isn't there a fairy tale where there is a godfather who is actually death?

JORDAN: Which godfather do you think your husband looks like?

MARIA: Well, at least he has his businesses. He's a real grown-up.

ISABELLA: We should all grow up.

JORDAN: This city don't let you grow up. This city beats you into submission, and then spits you out, broke and unemployed.

VICTOR: This city is my home.

ISABELLA: This city is my jail.

MARIA: Stop it. You're going through a rough time, but it'll pass.

VICTOR: Why, what's going on?

JESS: She's horny.

ISABELLA: Shut up!

JORDAN: Welcome to the club!

ISABELLA: Stop it.

[JUAN *enters.*]

JUAN: Good morning everybody.

ISABELLA: Juan! You came home early . . .

JUAN: I got a noise complaint.

VICTOR: Sorry bro, I guess we got a little carried away.

JUAN: Don't apologize to me. Apologize to the hard-working neighbors that have to deal with this bullshit.

JESS: The neighbors have jobs?

JORDAN: Alright. Party's over everyone! Ladies, allow me to walk you home.

MARIA: I'm going the other way. Good night.

JORDAN: We'll walk you.

MARIA: Don't worry. The night is beautiful. You guys go.

JORDAN: She's going back to the bar.

MARIA: Nah, just walking home. See you tomorrow.

JORDAN: Officer, it's always a pleasure.

JESS: I could keep going. Wanna go somewhere else?

JORDAN: I'm going home. Gotta walk those damn dogs in a couple of hours.

VICTOR: I'll walk with you, Jess.

JORDAN AND MARIA: 'Night everybody! [*To each other*] You owe me a beer!

[JORDAN *and* MARIA *exit in opposite directions.*]

JUAN: Did you go out?

JESS: She didn't.

JUAN: She can answer herself.

ISABELLA: I didn't.

VICTOR [*to* JUAN]: Are you done with work? You want to grab a beer or something?

JUAN: I'm tired. [*To* ISABELLA] What are you doing out here?

ISABELLA: I couldn't sleep. I heard Victor and these guys on the stoop. The night was nice. I wanted to get out.

VICTOR: We were coming back from the bar, just walking the girls home.

JUAN: Is that beer you're drinking?

JESS: Oh, come on Juan, I know it's "illegal," but there's no one around.

JUAN: I'm around.

JESS: Fine. [*She chugs her beer.*] Have a trash can around here? I would hate to contaminate.

ISABELLA: I'll take that. Go home you guys.

VICTOR: Alright, bro. We get it. We'll go. Come on, Jess. Good night, Isabella, Juan.

ISABELLA: Good night.

JESS: See you tomorrow.

[ISABELLA *watches them leave.* JUAN *walks to the door.*]

JUAN: Are you coming?

ISABELLA: Don't you want to stay out a little? The sun is about to come out. Why don't we see it together?

JUAN: I'm tired. I don't like these streets at night.

ISABELLA: But these are our streets.

JUAN: You don't see what I see at work. You don't know.

ISABELLA: Because you don't tell me.

JUAN: I don't want to scare you. But you and your friends shouldn't be out here in the middle of the night.

ISABELLA: They're your friends too. They're like our family.

JUAN: Families grow apart. Some people grow up and some don't.

ISABELLA: You used to like seeing the sun come out with us. With me.

[JUAN *embraces* ISABELLA.]

JUAN: We have a different life now.

FORTITUDE: This life is no life.

PATIENCE: It's the life you chose.

JUAN: I know you're upset, but we can work things out. I'm just tired now. And I don't want to bother the neighbors.

ISABELLA: We'll be quiet.

JUAN: I just want to go to bed.

PATIENCE: Maybe it'll be different tonight.

FORTITUDE: It's already morning.

ISABELLA: Sure. Sorry.

[JUAN *and* ISABELLA *walk into the apartment.* ISABELLA *tries to kiss* JUAN. *He lets her for a moment. She tries to unbutton his shirt.* JUAN *pushes her away.*]

ISABELLA: What's the matter?

JUAN: I don't know. I'm just tired, I guess.

ISABELLA: It's OK.

[*Beat. They look at each other.*]

JUAN: Isa, you still love me?

ISABELLA: Of course!

JUAN: I'm sorry.

ISABELLA: It's OK.

[*As* ISABELLA *and* JUAN *exit toward the bedroom, in another area of the stage, his sisters,* AGNES, GRACE, *and* JOY *pack their suitcases.*]

AGNES: Repellent for bugs.

GRACE: Bed bugs?

JOY: Mosquitoes.

AGNES: We should be ready for the worst.

GRACE: Let's take our own sheets and towels. I don't trust Isabella.

JOY: She works at a laundromat!

AGNES: We will do our own laundry.

GRACE: I hate laundry.

AGNES: Girls, focus, for god's sake.

JOY: On what?

GRACE: Packing.

JOY: I'm done.

GRACE: This is actually exciting!

AGNES: This is temporary. Don't forget the Pepto.

GRACE: Yes, she's a horrible cook.

JOY: Is Victor still around, you think? He was so cute.

AGNES: I'm sure. All the losers stay in that neighborhood.

GRACE: So we're losers for going back?

JOY: Juan is no loser.

AGNES: Of course he's not. I was speaking metaphorically.

GRACE: That was not a metaphor.

AGNES: This is a temporary solution. An obstacle we shall overcome.

[*Back in the apartment,* PATIENCE *and* FORTITUDE *bring* ISABELLA *out from the bedroom and to her easel where* BELLA *is waiting.*]

FORTITUDE: Trimipramina to endure.

PATIENCE: Donepezilo to forget.

GRACE: I can't believe that you sent me away for two years and lost the house.

AGNES: You were up to no good. Mother was worried.

GRACE: And then she died.

PATIENCE: Fenelzina to ignore reality.

FORTITUDE: Selegilina to fight back.

[*The sisters disappear.*]

SCENE 3

[ISABELLA *continues to paint* BELLA. PATIENCE *and* FORTITUDE *watch.* BELLA *gets out of the painting and stretches. The scene becomes a dream.*]

BELLA: How do you want to paint me?

FORTITUDE: Naked!

PATIENCE: As a friend. Just a friend.

BELLA: You can't control it. You have to paint me how I wish to be painted.

ISABELLA: And how's that?

BELLA: With blood.

ISABELLA: Whose blood?

PATIENCE: Let's stop this now.

ISABELLA: No, tell me.

PATIENCE: LALALALALALALALALALALALA!

FORTITUDE: Shut up. Bella, bring it on!

[ISABELLA *paints. The three sisters sing a children's song in the background, something in the style of "Miss Mary Mack."* ISABELLA *doesn't see them and continues to paint, first within the canvas, but slowly making broader strokes with her brush, then with her hands.* PATIENCE, FORTITUDE, *and* BELLA *join her. The sisters enter, still singing and dancing, towering over* ISABELLA.]

AGNES: You are ruining everything.

ISABELLA: Leave me alone.

FORTITUDE: We're creating.

AGNES: Creating a mess.

ISABELLA: Shut up.

PATIENCE: Art is messy.

BELLA: So is life.

AGNES: Three years into the marriage and no kids.

JOY: You didn't have kids either.

AGNES: I never married.

BELLA: Lots of people don't marry, lots of people never have children. Who cares!

JOY: Why are the paintings talking?

ISABELLA: Paintings talk.

GRACE: I was once married to God, but he didn't give me any kids either.

JOY: God can't give you kids, only a man can.

AGNES: God can give you anything!

GRACE: Only if you ask nicely.

BELLA: God is overrated.

AGNES: Blasphemy!

ISABELLA: I just want to paint.

PATIENCE AND FORTITUDE: Let her paint.

BELLA: Cover everything with paint.

AGNES: Hide behind your so-called art while the apartment crumbles.

BELLA: Yes, hide.

JOY: Like when we were kids! Let's play hide and seek!

AGNES: Everything is falling apart.

GRACE: This building, this city—

AGNES: This family.

[JESS, MARIA, VICTOR, *and* JORDAN *enter.* VICTOR *covers* ISABELLA*'s eyes.*]

JORDAN: Guess who it is.

ISABELLA: Stop playing, Jordan, I'm trying to work.

VICTOR [*laughing*]: Guess again!

EVERYBODY: Oh, hi Victor.

AGNES: That man will ruin you!

FORTITUDE: That man could give you an orgasm.

ISABELLA: We're just playing.

PATIENCE: He is a player.

JORDAN: Playin' like players play.

JESS: Playin' like we mean it.

MARIA: Playin' like platypuses.

JOY: How do platypuses play?

JESS: Pooping peripatetically.

FORTITUDE: Stupid.

MARIA: Pooping peripatetically playful pallets for pleasure.

GRACE: I want to play too!

ISABELLA: I can't hear my thoughts.

BELLA: We are your thoughts.

AGNES: You are a painting.

JESS: A portrait—

MARIA: With a capital *P*!

VICTOR: What are you thinking now, Isabella?

JESS: Sex!

ISABELLA: No I'm not.

JORDAN: Why not?

VICTOR: I'm always thinking about sex.

[JUAN *gets out of the bedroom.*]

JUAN: Perverts. All of you, perverts!

MARIA: Loosen up, Juan.

JESS: Yes, Juan, you're always ruining the party.

AGNES: This is not a party.

GRACE: We can make it one.

JOY: Yeah, a party!

ISABELLA: I'm painting.

BELLA: You're dreaming.

VICTOR: You're dreaming that I touch you like this.

[VICTOR *embraces* ISABELLA.]

JESS: You don't know how to do it. Let me—

[JESS *embraces* ISABELLA.]

JUAN: Why is everyone touching my wife?

GRACE: Because she wants to be touched.

AGNES: Whore.

FORTITUDE: Iceberg.

JORDAN: This is your chance to say and do anything you want.

JESS: It's a dream.

MARIA: You'll wake up and we'll be gone.

JUAN: Not all of us.

JOY: We're not even here!

BELLA: Just paint.

PATIENCE: Concentrate on the canvas.

FORTITUDE: Forget the canvas. Paint the whole world!

JORDAN: More blue!

JESS: More gold!

[*Everybody but the sisters and* JUAN *are painting the whole apartment with their hands, frantically, with broad strokes. Colors are everywhere.*]

AGNES: What a waste of time. You should worry about your marriage.

JUAN: There's nothing wrong with our marriage.

JESS: You should go out more often.

MARIA: You should have more fun.

JORDAN: You need to do this or that or something else.

FORTITUDE: That's a good idea.

PATIENCE: You should listen. Concentrate.

ISABELLA: There's so much noise.

AGNES: Why aren't you in bed with your husband? What kind of marriage is this?

JOY: You're so, like, twentieth century. Nobody has a husband anymore.

GRACE: They're a nuisance.

JORDAN: You still could fuck more.

JUAN: Thanks for the advice, but—

GRACE: Do you want to come to the convent with me? There's a surprising amount of sex going on there.

AGNES: How dare you!

JESS: Makes sense, if you think about it.

ISABELLA: Let me paint!

PATIENCE AND FORTITUDE: Let her paint!

AGNES: I thought you would be the one to help us preserve our name for future generations.

JOY: I can still have kids.

AGNES: But they wouldn't have your last name.

GRACE: What's in a name?

JUAN: My name is a lie. It might not even be my name.

AGNES: Of course it is. Your father was a bum but you still have his last name.

JOY: I think it was Mom he was talking about.

GRACE: She was the one sleeping around.

FORTITUDE: I heard his "dad" gave his name to anything he wanted to control. But he couldn't . . . You know . . .

EVERYBODY: Shhhhhh!

ISABELLA: I will paint my son and my daughter and myself in another city in another country in another world—

BELLA: Paint the children!

JESS: They're not children, they're evil creatures!

JORDAN: They're not evil creatures, they're crayons!

GRACE: Yes! They're colors!

JOY: Primary colors!

JUAN: Stop this nonsense and go to sleep!

[*Everybody exits but* ISABELLA *and* JUAN. *The dream ends. They're both awake.*]

JUAN: Is that too much to ask? For you to come to bed?

ISABELLA: Sorry. I couldn't sleep.

JUAN: Every night, as soon as I fall asleep you get up and walk away.

ISABELLA: I get restless.

JUAN: Just lie there with me.

PATIENCE: To cuddle?

FORTITUDE: To clench my jaw. To stare at the ceiling.

ISABELLA: There's too much noise in my head.

JUAN: I know. Come. Let's get some rest.

[JUAN *and* ISABELLA *exit to the bedroom.*]

SCENE 4

[*Lights on* MARIA *sleeping on a stoop.* JESS *and* VICTOR *walk toward her, singing, fresh out of a bar.*]

JESS: Oh shit. Maria . . . Maria, wake up!

MARIA: What!

JESS: Why are you sleeping outside?

MARIA: Leave me alone.

VICTOR: The sun is out. You need to go home.

MARIA: I'm home now.

VICTOR: No, you're on the stoop of Isabella's building.

MARIA: Same thing.

JESS: You gotta go home. Your husband will be pissed.

MARIA: Exactly. That's why I can't go.

JESS: Do you want to go to my place?

MARIA: Nah . . . I'm fine here. Really. He'll go to work and then he'll forget. It's happened before.

VICTOR: You're not fine. You're drunk.

MARIA: I'm not. I'm just tired.

JESS: Where did you go after you left?

MARIA: The where is relative . . . I mean, irrelevant.

VICTOR: We're not going to leave you here.

JESS: Let's go to my place. Mom can give you something to sober up.

MARIA: No witchcraft!

JESS: Just tea. Or something.

MARIA: Oh man . . . alright.

[*They exit. In another area of the stage, dogs are barking and playing in a dog run.* JORDAN *carries about seven different leashes. Dogs keep barking. He lets his dogs loose as he speaks.*]

JORDAN: Shut up already! It's too early for this shit, damn it . . .

Didn't know you could drink "too much" beer. Shit . . . [*To the dogs*] Yo, stop it. For reals. Go run, or whatever. You're so annoying. [*Thinking*] Dogs are just like people. Nah . . . Dogs are not like people. Dogs are like dogs. They suck like people sometimes . . .

Suck . . . I like that . . .

No, dogs don't "suck" suck like that—Why am I even picturing that?

Dogs are mean, unpredictable, stubborn.

[*To dogs*] Hey! Stop that! You can't hump that . . .

You can't even reason with dogs . . .

Well, I guess they are like people.

Jesus. I hope they're neutered . . .

This is a really stupid job.

Come on, you guys! Do whatever you need to do, 'cause I need to get going.

I need a nap.

SCENE 5

[*The laundromat.* JESS *and* ISABELLA *fold clothes.* PATIENCE *and* FORTITUDE *hang around.*]

JESS: Today's the day . . .

ISABELLA: Yep.

JESS: How exciting.

ISABELLA: Yep.

JESS: How long are they staying?

ISABELLA: Who knows.

JESS: Is Agnes still a bitch?

ISABELLA: I haven't seen them in years.

JESS: But JUAN talks to them, doesn't he?

ISABELLA: When their mom died. And when her dad died. And then when his dad died. Other than that . . .

JESS: That's so weird.

ISABELLA: That they're all dead?

JESS: I guess. And that they're all getting together again. I mean, they really have nothing to do with each other.

ISABELLA: They're still family.

JESS: Family from hell.

ISABELLA: Just old-fashioned. They stick together and keep appearances no matter what.

JESS: Their mom was really poisonous.

ISABELLA: Yeah, scary.

JESS: It rubbed off on his sisters.

ISABELLA: Nah, they're fine. Agnes may be a little stiff, but Grace and Joy are fine. They're like my sisters, really.

JESS: I know. They were really nice to you.

[JORDAN *and* VICTOR *enter.*]

VICTOR: Where are the special guests?

ISABELLA: Juan is picking them up at the train station.

JORDAN: But they're coming here first, right?

ISABELLA: I don't know. What do you care?

JORDAN: It'll be like a family reunion!

JESS: Like a dysfunctional family reunion.

VICTOR: They'll fit right in. Hey, what did your mom give Maria?

JESS: I don't know. She went home.

JORDAN: What happened to her?

VICTOR: She probably went back to the bar after we left.

JORDAN: Wow. That girl can drink.

ISABELLA: She shouldn't be drinking.

JORDAN: I think it's OK during the first trimester.

ISABELLA: Where do you guys get your information?

JESS: My mom thinks there's something wrong with her.

JORDAN: Yeah, her husband.

ISABELLA: What are you guys doing here?

JORDAN: Where else can we go?

VICTOR: I'm here for my laundry.

JESS: Yeah, right.

JORDAN: I'm here for the gossip.

VICTOR: I did drop off my laundry yesterday.

[ISABELLA *retrieves a laundry bag.*]

ISABELLA: Funny timing. Here.

VICTOR: Thank you. So . . . I hear they lost the house and everything.

ISABELLA: Yup. And since none of them married . . .

JORDAN: How long has it been?

ISABELLA: Since they left? I don't know. Five years? Their mother wouldn't let them come back.

JESS: Wasn't one of them a nun or something?

ISABELLA: Grace. She got kicked out of the convent.

VICTOR: Do you guys want to smoke?

ISABELLA: We're working.

JORDAN: I'm not.

ISABELLA: Juan could show up.

JORDAN: Exactly.

VICTOR: With the sisters.

JORDAN: And they're creepy.

[JESS *hums the intro to* The Addams Family.]

VICTOR: Not all of them. I remember Joy fondly.

JORDAN: Fondly! Ha! You wanted to bag her since you were fifteen.

VICTOR: No, I really liked her.

ISABELLA: You did?

VICTOR: She was very sweet and super hot.

ISABELLA: You're talking about my sisters-in-law.

JESS: Let's be honest.

JORDAN: Let's . . . shut up now.

[JUAN *enters with* AGNES, GRACE, *and* JOY. PATIENCE *and* FORTITUDE *talk over (or under) everybody else.*]

JUAN: They're here.

[JOY *and* GRACE *hug everybody.* AGNES *is more reserved.*]

AGNES: Hello everyone.

JOY: Isabella! Jess!

GRACE: Wow. Everything looks the same.

ISABELLA: Welcome home. You remember Jordan and Victor, right?

GRACE AND JOY: Of course!

AGNES [*to* JUAN]: Why is she still friends with them?

VICTOR: Wow, Joy. You look amazing.

JOY: Thank you, you too!

JUAN: Did you get their room ready?

ISABELLA: Of course.

[*The following is a moment in* ISABELLA'*s head, a daydream.*]

PATIENCE: I washed the sheets and ironed the pillowcases. I swept and mopped. I scrubbed the floors on my knees.

FORTITUDE: I dreamed that I laced the curtains with cyanide, and that I Krazy-glued their door shut, and that I poured Drano in their morning coffee, and that I smothered them with a clean pillow wrapped in a just-ironed pillowcase.

[*Returning to the laundromat*]

GRACE: It's going to be crowded.

JOY: Like the old times!

JORDAN: I thought I'd never see you again.

AGNES: The sentiment is mutual.

JORDAN: I didn't mean it like that. Welcome! I'm glad you're back. It's just that your mom never liked me.

GRACE: I'm glad to be back.

JUAN: Did you ask if they're hiring?

JESS: We're not.

AGNES: I don't know if I'd like to work here.

FORTITUDE: Nobody would hire you. You're lazy, bitter, and mean.

JORDAN: What line of work are you interested in?

JESS: What kind of experience do you have?

JORDAN: Grace, what did you learn at the convent?

GRACE: A lot, but nothing that I can really apply here.

JORDAN: I can imagine. I can't wait to see the skills you acquired.

GRACE: Ha! I'm sure you would. The convent was Agnes's idea anyway. I knew I wouldn't last.

VICTOR: How long are you staying?

JUAN: As long as they want.

PATIENCE AND FORTITUDE: What?!

JOY: I'm hungry.

JUAN: Isabella, come upstairs with us so you can help them settle in.

ISABELLA: But I'm working.

JUAN: So?

FORTITUDE: So I can't.

PATIENCE: So this sucks.

ISABELLA: Everything is ready up there.

JUAN: Please? It would mean a lot.

ISABELLA: Jess, can you cover for me?

JESS: Sure.

[*As* JUAN *and his family exit to the apartment area,* JESS, JORDAN, *and* VICTOR *clear the laundry and exit.*]

SCENE 6

[ISABELLA *and* JUAN*'s apartment.* BELLA, PATIENCE, and FORTITUDE *witness the scene.*]

AGNES: So . . . the three of us in the same room.

JOY: Like when we were little!

AGNES: We'll be fine. This is temporary.

GRACE: But you said—

AGNES: We don't discuss family business in front of strangers.

[AGNES *starts rearranging furniture right away. She looks at the paintings with suspicion.*]

ISABELLA: Feel at home. You know where everything is . . .

GRACE: Wow. The apartment looks great.

ISABELLA: Thank you.

GRACE: Oh my god, Isa, the paintings . . . patience . . . fortitude . . . they're really cool.

ISABELLA: Thank you.

AGNES: What are they supposed to be . . . ?

JUAN: So . . . How was the trip?

JOY: Long! And we haven't eaten since the morning.

ISABELLA: I'll get dinner ready.

[ISABELLA *exits to the kitchen.*]

AGNES: Is she still a horrible cook?

JUAN: It's really not that bad.

GRACE: It was pretty bad . . .

JUAN: Well, maybe while you're here you can show her some of Mom's recipes.

AGNES: We'll see. And about the sleeping arrangements—

JOY: It's tight in that room—

JUAN: That's the room you shared before and it's all we have.

AGNES: But we're grown-ups now. What about that space? We could convert it into a semiprivate room.

JUAN: That's where Isabella paints now.

AGNES: You work nights, now, right?

JUAN: Yes . . .

AGNES: So maybe Isabella can sleep with the girls and I can take your bed at night.

JUAN: Why?

AGNES: So I can be more comfortable?

GRACE: What about us?

JOY: It'll be like the old times, like a slumber party every night!

JUAN: I don't know if Isabella would like that.

GRACE: What about you, Juan? Would you like that?

JOY: What's not to like? Do you really want to sleep with Agnes?

AGNES [*to* JUAN]: You're not even sleeping with Isabella.

JUAN: Don't say that. You don't know.

AGNES: Please. Nothing to be ashamed of. It runs in the family.

GRACE: I don't think it's a good idea, this reshuffling of roommates.

JOY: Why? The three of us used to have so much fun!

GRACE: No, the two of you did. You and Isa never included me.

JOY: You had fun too!

AGNES: It wasn't easy for us to come back here. We all have to make some adjustments.

JUAN: It wasn't easy for me to take you back. Can you make do with what we have?

AGNES: Isabella is so selfish to take all that space for her hobby.

JOY: It's not just a hobby.

GRACE: It wasn't Isabella's fault that you lost the house . . .

AGNES: That's not the point. Juan doesn't like her friends anymore—

GRACE: Are you talking about Jess, Jordan, Victor, and all those guys?

JOY: We grew up with them!

JUAN: It's not that I don't like them. It's just that—

AGNES: They're stuck here.

GRACE: Like us?

AGNES: We're different. We have an education. We are going places.

JOY: Where are we going?

AGNES: The point is, we are blood and we help each other. We needed a place to get back on our feet and Isabella needed company.

[ISABELLA *enters*.]

ISABELLA: I didn't say I needed—

PATIENCE: Stop!

FORTITUDE: No, go ahead. You don't need company. You have us!

ISABELLA: I mean, this is not what this is about.

FORTITUDE: This is about control. Control of your body, your life.

PATIENCE: It might be fun to have Joy around.

AGNES: Let's unpack.

JOY: Can we eat first?

GRACE: Maybe we should eat out.

AGNES: No, we're having supper here like a real family.

JUAN: Yes, like a family. We are family.

FORTITUDE AND PATIENCE: Are we?

JOY: We're sharing the bedroom!

ISABELLA: We are?

GRACE: Well, since Juan works nights and Princess Agnes here doesn't want to share . . .

ISABELLA: But Juan sleeps there during the day, and the sheets—

AGNES: We'll wash them. I mean, you work at the laundromat downstairs.

JOY: I want to work there.

ISABELLA: But, wait. Why would I give you my bedroom?

AGNES: Well, I don't know. Because my family took you in as a teenager, and you paid us back by seducing my brother, and now you're living in his father's house, and—

JUAN: Isabella, let's not make a big deal about this.

AGNES: Besides, you girls used to have so much fun together. Take it as an opportunity to reconnect.

JOY: This is going to be fun.

JUAN: It's temporary.

ISABELLA: It's temporary.

JUAN [*to* AGNES]: So what's your plan? Do you have a plan?

AGNES: I'm not going from management to folding clothes.

ISABELLA: They're not hiring.

GRACE: And you managed the house and our inheritance so well . . .

AGNES: It wasn't my fault.

GRACE: Face it. You spent Mom's inheritance and lost her house.

JOY: Yeah, you suck at business.

AGNES: I do not!

JUAN: You're going to drive me crazy.

FORTITUDE: Drive *you* crazy?

PATIENCE: Keep calm. Relax your muscles. Try to smile.

FORTITUDE: Fuck that!

JOY: Can we eat?

ISABELLA: Yes. Why don't we talk about this calmly over food.

AGNES: Joy, Grace, help Isabella set the table.

[ISABELLA, GRACE, *and* JOY *exit.*]

JUAN: Can you explain to me what happened to the house?

AGNES: It got foreclosed.

JUAN: Why?

AGNES: You know, the economy.

JUAN: What happened to your job?

AGNES: I was laid off.

JUAN: Why?

AGNES: Look, that's a long story. Let's eat. We'll feel better afterwards and we'll have plenty of time to talk.

JUAN: You never want to talk. You never have the time.

AGNES: Well, I'm a busy woman.

JUAN: You're unemployed.

AGNES: Let's just eat.

JUAN: Fine. But we will talk.

[JUAN *exits toward the kitchen.* BELLA *catches* AGNES*'s attention. They stare at each other.*]

JUAN [*offstage*]: We're starting without you!

AGNES: Wait! What about Grace?

GRACE: What did I do now?!

[AGNES *exits.* BELLA *steps out of her frame and sticks her tongue out at* AGNES*'s back.* BELLA *then smells the sisters' belongings left behind.*]

SCENE 7

[*On the stoop,* VICTOR *plays guitar.* JESS *and* JORDAN *share a joint.* JESS *keeps looking around her.*]

JORDAN: Hey, Jess. You OK?

JESS: My mom is sending her little fucking demons to check on my ass. She's fucking spying on me. I'm so tired of her shit.

JORDAN: Relax. They're not demons. I've see them.

JESS: You have? Where?!

JORDAN: Hehehehe. Nah.

JESS: Jesus.

JORDAN: I don't see any demons. I mean, I don't believe in any of that stuff, but your mom's always been pretty spot on.

VICTOR: Yeah, everything that's gone down. Marriages and deaths and stuff. She's always known in advance.

JESS: The fucking little demons.

JORDAN: Forget about the demons. Fuck them. Let's think about the important stuff. Let's think about the now. How are we going to make a living? Can we have better jobs? Can she predict that?

JESS: It doesn't work like that. And I'm fucking tired of her shit.

VICTOR: Well, you're still living in her house.

JESS: And where else can I go?

JORDAN: You could move in with me.

JESS: Yes, with you and your seven roommates.

VICTOR: Your mom ain't that bad, Jess.

JESS: Yes, she is. She really is a witch. A demon. Demanding and demeaning.

JORDAN: Dabbling daftly in dumb deals.

VICTOR: Diverting devils daily.

JESS: And dourly!

JORDAN: To Dakota!

JESS: To Dakota?

JORDAN: Well, isn't that like a really fucked up place?

JESS: I don't know. Never been. But can't be worse than this dump.

VICTOR: Don't exaggerate. We don't have it that bad.

JESS: Are you kidding me? No jobs, no men, and nothing to do.

JORDAN: You have your health, your family—

JESS: Yeah, my stupid little brother and my mom, always looking at people's "auras" and seeing spirits everywhere.

VICTOR: So what do you want?

JESS: Something else. Something better than this. This life.

VICTOR: Now you're being overly dramatic.

JESS: Seriously guys. I listen to Isabella talking about how she feels a burning in the insides. And I used to make fun of her, because I thought it was just about getting laid, but it's about more than that.

JORDAN: Let it out.

JESS: My mom says they're my own demons.

JORDAN: Devious demons?

VICTOR: Duh!

JESS: Seriously. We all have some sort of demons inside. Some are good, some are bad. Mine are just noisy and annoying.

JORDAN: Seriously. Let them out. Whatever they are, let them out.

JESS: How?

JORDAN: Like this: [*howling*] Awoooooooooooooooooooooo!!!!!!!!

JESS: Stupid . . .

VICTOR: Come on, try it! Awoooooooooooooooooooooo!!!!!!

JORDAN AND VICTOR: Awoooooooooooooooooooooo!!!!!

[VICTOR AND JORDAN *continue howling. Eventually* JESS *joins them.*]

JORDAN, VICTOR, AND JESS: Awoooooooooooooooooooooo!!!!! Awoooooooooooooooooooooo!!!!!

[BELLA, PATIENCE, *and* FORTITUDE *howl from the apartment.*]

[AGNES, GRACE, *and* JOY *step out.*]

AGNES: What is going on?

[VICTOR, JORDAN, *and* JESS *crack up.*]

VICTOR: Sorry, Agnes. We were letting our demons out.

JOY: Can I try it?

AGNES: Don't even think about it.

VICTOR: Come on, Agnes, let Joy howl a little. Just for the sake of the demons.

JORDAN: Jess's mom says we all have demons inside.

AGNES: Her mom is a demon.

JESS: That's what I've always said.

AGNES: Unsurprisingly, you sound like animals.

VICTOR: We apologize if we disturbed you.

JORDAN: Speak for yourself.

JESS: Is Isabella around?

JOY: Isabella!!!!

[JUAN *enters from the house. He's in full uniform.* ISABELLA, PATIENCE, *and* FORTITUDE *follow.*]

JUAN: Why is everybody yelling?

JOY: They were howling.

JUAN: And you were just yelling.

VICTOR [*to* JOY]: I can take you out howling any time you want.

JUAN: Stay away from my little sis, Victor.

VICTOR: Relax, bro, I'm just joking.

JUAN: I don't like how you joke.

ISABELLA: Juan, please.

JORDAN: Come on, Juan, he didn't mean anything.

JOY: And what if he did?

JUAN: Joy, go to your room.

JOY: Make me.

AGNES: Come on, Grace, Joy, we do have to unpack.

JOY: Fine. See you guys later.

GRACE: Bye.

[*The sisters exit.*]

JUAN: Please don't flirt with my baby sister. It's hard enough as it is.

VICTOR: It's all cool, bro. I won't even look at her.

JESS: What if she likes Victor?

JUAN: She doesn't.

JESS: Seriously. Why can't she decide?

JUAN: I don't have time for this.

[JUAN *kisses* ISABELLA.]

JUAN: Please make sure they're comfortable.

ISABELLA: Don't worry. And please be safe.

JUAN: Stay out of trouble.

JORDAN: Will do, officer.

[JUAN *exits.*]

JESS: Something about men in uniforms . . .

JORDAN: I know, right?

JESS: No, not like that. They terrify me.

VICTOR: How are the sisters treating you?

ISABELLA: They're OK, I guess.

JESS: They just got here.

VICTOR: Joy hasn't changed a bit.

JORDAN: None of them have.

ISABELLA: You do like Joy, huh?

VICTOR: It's an old crush.

ISABELLA: But do you "like her" like really like her?

VICTOR: I hadn't seen her in so long, but yes. I mean—

ISABELLA: Just remember that she is like a sister to me.

VICTOR: Isa, I would never hurt you or anyone in your family.

JORDAN: She's too good for you anyway.

JESS: And you don't want to get involved with that family.

ISABELLA: Jess!

JESS: No offense!

VICTOR: Shut up, Jess.

ISABELLA [*laughing*]: It's OK. I know exactly what she means.

VICTOR: Juan is a good man.

ISABELLA: Yeah, he is.

JORDAN: I have to get going.

JESS: Where?

JORDAN: Gotta walk the dogs.

VICTOR: I'll walk with you. Coming, Jess?

JESS: Nah. I'll catch up with you later.

VICTOR: Alright. See you later, Isabella.

[JORDAN *and* VICTOR *exit.*]

[PATIENCE *and* FORTITUDE *will sometimes pop out of a window, fire escape, or door to speak over or under* JESS *and* ISABELLA.]

JESS: Are you OK?

FORTITUDE: I'm terrified. I'm nauseous. I can't breathe. I'm drowning.

ISABELLA: Sure.

JESS: How are things with Juan?

ISABELLA: You know, the usual. And now with the sisters . . .

JESS: Yeah, I know. It sucks to be you right now.

ISABELLA: You always manage to make me feel better.

JESS: Sorry. I can't help it. But something is dying inside you.

PATIENCE: What are you talking about? I have a roof over my head, a room to paint, a job . . . a husband.

JESS: I can see you fading. Damn. I don't ever want to be like her, but Mom says that I have it. Her gift.

ISABELLA: Are *you* OK?

JESS: Yes, of course.

ISABELLA: Come in.

JESS: No, I gotta go. I gotta pick up some juju for Mom.

ISABELLA: Can I go see her?

JESS: Really? When?

ISABELLA: Tonight?

JESS: Yes. I'll tell her. She'll be happy.

[JESS *exits.* ISABELLA *goes inside.*]

PATIENCE: Count my blessings. I know what it is to be alone. Really, truly alone. It's better this way. I can get used to this life. I'm adaptable. I have everything I need.

FORTITUDE: What happened to traveling the world, painting the world, drinking wine overlooking infinity?

PATIENCE: Juan means well.

FORTITUDE: He wants to trap me. Suffocate me.

PATIENCE: He loves me.

FORTITUDE: He owns me.

PATIENCE: He wants the best for me.

FORTITUDE: He wants to control my every move.

PATIENCE: It's part of growing up.

FORTITUDE: How can misery be part of growing up? Why can't you say how you really feel, not even to your friends?

ISABELLA: Stop it!

[AGNES *comes out of* JUAN *and* ISABELLA*'s room*, GRACE *and* JOY *from their room.*]

AGNES: Still talking to yourself?

GRACE: What happened?

JOY: Is Victor still around?

ISABELLA: No, sorry. I was just . . . Jess just left.

AGNES: Of course. I'm glad it's OK with you that I take Juan's bedroom while he's at work.

ISABELLA: It's my bedroom too.

AGNES: I'll move in with the girls when Juan comes home. It's just that I have a terrible time falling asleep and Grace snores.

GRACE: I do not.

JOY: You do too.

AGNES: I'll bring the sheets to the laundromat every time it's your turn in the bedroom.

FORTITUDE: This is fucked up.

PATIENCE: I don't sleep much anyway.

ISABELLA: I guess it's OK.

FORTITUDE: When are you going to learn to say no?

PATIENCE: It's OK, it's OK, it's OK, it's OK.

GRACE: Do I even get to have an opinion?

JOY: Ha ha! Come on, Isabella, let's get ready for bed.

ISABELLA: But it's early. I still need to—

GRACE: Juan said you hardly ever sleep.

ISABELLA: Of course I sleep. It's just that—this is usually the time when I paint.

AGNES: Of course. We have to give space to "the artist."

JOY: What are you working on?

AGNES: Is that even considered work?

GRACE: Of course it is!

JOY: Just because you could never even color inside the lines doesn't mean it's not work.

GRACE [*to* ISABELLA]: I always loved your work.

ISABELLA: Thank you.

AGNES: I'm tired. Please be quiet. Good night.

[AGNES *exits.*]

ISABELLA: What time do you usually go to bed?

GRACE: I'm going soon. Joy can stare at the stars all night. It's like she doesn't need to sleep.

ISABELLA: Yeah, I'm still like that too sometimes.

JOY: Remember when we were kids and we'd stay up until the sun came up?

ISABELLA: We could talk for hours.

GRACE: You could.

JOY: You did too.

GRACE: It was hard to keep up with you guys. But it was fun. The convent was too quiet.

ISABELLA: I can't believe you went to a convent.

JOY: That was Agnes's idea. I never saw a nun in her.

GRACE: I know, I know. That convent plan was pretty ill conceived.

ISABELLA: How long were you there?

GRACE: Just a couple of years.

ISABELLA: "Just."

JOY: I wouldn't last a day.

GRACE: I don't know. Time goes by pretty fast.

ISABELLA: Really? Time here is slow.

JOY: Today's been pretty fast. I mean, I feel like we just got here, and now the day's gone.

ISABELLA: Things have changed since you left.

GRACE: Everything looks the same to me. Same people. Same old, dilapidated buildings. Same—

ISABELLA: We're older. A lot older it seems.

GRACE: But it's like we've traveled in time. Like we came back to a weird, distorted past.

JOY: Yup. Here we are again.

ISABELLA: But you left for a while. And in that time you lived a little, you went places.

GRACE: Mom had a pretty tight grip.

JOY: My dad was more fun.

GRACE: Your dad was a deadbeat and Mom was right to take us away.

JOY: Juan turned out OK, and he stayed with him. And he wasn't even his dad.

GRACE: Your dad, my dad, his dad, our mom. They were all alcoholics with delusions of grandeur.

JOY: And Agnes is heading in that direction.

ISABELLA: She drinks?

JOY: No. She's just bitter.

GRACE: Yes. She got worse when Mom died.

AGNES [*offstage*]: I can hear you!

GRACE: Jesus.

JOY: Show us your paintings.

AGNES [*offstage*]: Go to bed.

GRACE: We're going, Agnes!

JOY: Damn.

[ISABELLA *puts a coat on and motions them to be quiet.*]

ISABELLA [*loudly*]: I guess we should go to bed now.

GRACE [*whispering*]: Where are you going?

ISABELLA: Shhhh.

JOY [*loudly*]: Yes, let's go to bed now. I'm so tired!

ISABELLA [*whispering*]: I'll be back soon.

JOY: This is exciting!

ISABELLA: Nothing exciting about it. I'm just meeting Jess. I'll be back soon.

[ISABELLA *exits.* JOY *and* GRACE *see her go.*]

GRACE: Is she cheating on Juan?

JOY: God, I hope so. He's such a bore.

GRACE: Joy, it's your brother!

JOY: So what? He is a bore.

BELLA: Go to bed.

GRACE: Who said that? Agnes?

JOY: Don't call her back!

BELLA: Shut up and go to bed.

JOY: This is creepy. Like an echo.

GRACE: Come on. It's late.

JOY: I bet she's cheating on him.

GRACE: Let's go to bed.

JOY: You go! I'm out of here too!

GRACE: Where?

[VICTOR *walks to the stoop and whistles.*]

GRACE: Joy . . .

JOY: He's just a friend. And you know I always liked him.

GRACE: Right. Have fun, little sis, but come back before Agnes wakes up.

[JOY *meets* VICTOR *outside and they exit.*]

[GRACE *looks at* BELLA. BELLA *smiles.* GRACE *smiles back.* GRACE *looks closer at the painting, sees the title.*]

GRACE: Bella . . . man, Isa is good. [*Beat.*] Good night, Bella.

[GRACE *exits to the bedroom.*]

BELLA: Some go, some come back. Life goes on. Nothing changes. Until everything does.

SCENE 8

[*The stage is empty.* BELLA *steps out of her frame.* PATIENCE *and* FORTITUDE *follow her. The dialogue continues.*]

BELLA: I hope she finishes painting me.

PATIENCE: She will. She finished her [*indicating* FORTITUDE].

FORTITUDE: I'm an early one. And she really didn't—

PATIENCE: She used to finish all of us. I don't know what happened. I still have some blurry spots.

FORTITUDE: She got married. I'm surprised she keeps me out. All the paintings from my period are in some box somewhere.

PATIENCE: I know. Sad. But you're still here.

FORTITUDE: That's because I'm really not finished either.

PATIENCE: You look done to me.

FORTITUDE: Fortitude? Are you kidding me? If she wanted to do justice to my name she could have made me, I don't know—

BELLA: Stronger?

FORTITUDE: She would've left Juan. That's what she wanted when she created me.

PATIENCE: It was a phase. She got over it. She's happier now.

BELLA: She's numb and growing miserable.

FORTITUDE: Just going through the motions. Reacting to whatever happens to her.

BELLA: Not taking control. The reins—

FORTITUDE: Of her own life! What the fuck! She was never like that!

BELLA: She's aging before her time.

PATIENCE: She's gone through her own hell. She did the right thing. She chose the right man.

FORTITUDE: The right man she chose changed too. What happened?

PATIENCE: Juan the policeman. Juan the responsible man.

FORTITUDE: Juan, whose touch is as cold as a bucket of ice.

BELLA: Juan, who's so worried about doing the right thing he forgets that life is passing him by.

PATIENCE: Juan, who cared for her, who bought paints and canvases for her, who put her on a pedestal and took care of her every need.

BELLA: You can't love anybody on a pedestal. A pedestal is also a cage. You don't love a pedestal. You admire it from afar.

FORTITUDE: And now he resents her.

BELLA: And now she resents him.

FORTITUDE: I hope she finishes me.

BELLA: She has to keep painting. She has no choice.

PATIENCE: She could stop, and then what . . .

BELLA: She won't. It's stronger than her.

FORTITUDE: She should leave Juan.

BELLA: Some things she can't control.

FORTITUDE: She can control her own destiny . . .

BELLA: But not other people's.

PATIENCE: I just wish her to be happy. Us. To be happy.

FORTITUDE: And you're just waiting for that to happen?

PATIENCE: "Patience" is my name.

FORTITUDE: And your name is your penance.

BELLA: There is no such a thing as destiny. She's learning this now. Free will—

FORTITUDE: Free will is limited by our circumstances.

PATIENCE: She exercised her own free will to marry Juan, whether she really loved him or not.

BELLA: She must use that free will to change course.

[JESS *and* ISABELLA *enter.*]

[BELLA, PATIENCE, *and* FORTITUDE *go back to their frames.*]

JESS: There's no such a thing as destiny. And Mom is not always right.

ISABELLA: There is and she is right.

JESS: What about free will? You can choose your own path.

ISABELLA: Exactly. She said I should leave. But where am I going to go? How? My circumstances dictate my destiny.

JESS: And then there are the "forces." I don't think the sisters are "the forces" Mom was talking about.

ISABELLA: I don't know. I love Grace and Joy. But Juan has changed so much . . .

[*As they walk home, they find* MARIA *slumped on the stoop. She has a mean black eye.*]

MARIA: Hey . . .

JESS: Fuck. Maria.

ISABELLA: What happened?

JESS: That motherfucker.

MARIA: I lost it. The baby.

ISABELLA: What?

MARIA: He said he was sorry.

ISABELLA: We need to get you to the hospital.

MARIA: I just got out of there. I'm fine. It looks worse than what it is.

JESS: Call Juan.

MARIA: Don't!

JESS: Your husband is an asshole and needs to be held accountable.

MARIA: No, please. Don't call the cops. Don't call Juan. I just need a place to rest up for a bit. I'm just tired. I can't go home now. Not now. I just need to rest. I'll be fine.

JESS: You have options. I know he pays for everything, but really, is this worth it?

MARIA: I'll be fine. Really. I'm just tired. I don't want to talk about it.

JESS: But you have to! This is just dumb.

ISABELLA: We should call Juan.

MARIA: Please, don't.

JESS: Does your husband know you're here?

MARIA: No. I don't think so. He left. I don't know where he is. He took me to the hospital and said I'd fallen down the stairs. And then he left. Just like that.

ISABELLA: That bastard.

MARIA: Then I went home. But home was empty. He took everything. I don't know what I'm going to do.

ISABELLA: You need to rest.

[JOY *enters.*]

JOY: What's going on?

ISABELLA: What were you doing out?

JOY: I just went for a walk. With Victor . . .

[ISABELLA shoots her a look.]

We just walked! [*To* MARIA] What happened to you?

ISABELLA: Maria is spending the night with us. And your brother's going to kill you.

JOY: A walk. Whatever. Is she OK?

JESS: She got beat up.

JOY: No shit.

ISABELLA: She just needs some rest. Let's take her in.

JOY: Let me help you.

[ISABELLA, JESS, *and* JOY *take* MARIA *into the apartment.*]

MARIA: I'm fine. Maybe I should just go.

JESS: Where?

ISABELLA: You're spending the night here.

[ISABELLA *takes* MARIA *to the bedroom.*]

JOY: Jesus. She looks awful.

JESS: I know.

JOY: Has this been going on for long?

JESS: Not this bad.

JOY: Why did she marry him?

JESS: Why do people marry? Beats me. So . . . Victor?

JOY: You know we always liked each other.

JESS: Yeah, yeah. I love the guy. But, really?

JOY: We're just friends. I haven't seen you guys since I was, like, a teenager. It's good to be back. Give me a break.

JESS: Welcome back, Joy.

[ISABELLA *enters from the bedroom.*]

ISABELLA: I put her in my bed. I'll sleep out here. You can go to bed now, Joy.

JOY: Really? You're sending me to bed now?

JESS: Please don't wake up Agnes.

ISABELLA: I don't mean it like that. We just—

JESS: I should go.

ISABELLA: No, wait. I just want to . . .

[ISABELLA *and* JESS *look at each other. Beat.*]

JOY: It's alright. Good night, guys.

ISABELLA AND JESS: Good night, Joy.

[JOY *exits to the bedroom.*]

ISABELLA: Well . . . so you were saying . . .

JESS: What Mom told you. It doesn't have to be a prophecy.

ISABELLA: I know.

JESS: You have options.

ISABELLA: I know.

JESS: Just saying. Look into my eyes.

ISABELLA: Why?

JESS: Just do it.

[ISABELLA *does.* JESS *kisses her.*]

ISABELLA: Wow. What was that?

[JESS *kisses her again.*]

JESS: You don't have to live like this.

ISABELLA: Like what.

JESS: Without pleasure.

ISABELLA: Pleasure?

JESS: That thing that makes your heart flutter.

ISABELLA: YES.

[ISABELLA *kisses* JESS. BELLA *steps out of the painting.*]

BELLA: I'm a witness made of paint and words and anguish and love. I've seen it all and also taken part in it all. The hardship and the pain and the destruction. But also the joy. Remember the joy, Isabella. The joy of just being alive. Take it back. Own it.

[BELLA *puts a blanket over* JESS *and* ISABELLA.]

No matter what it takes.

SCENE 9

[*Lights on* VICTOR, *handcuffed, standing between* JUAN *and* JORDAN.]

JUAN: You're such a fuckup.

VICTOR: Look, bro—

JUAN: Don't call me bro.

JORDAN: Come on, Juan, it's just weed.

JUAN: It's not just that.

VICTOR: You know there are no jobs. I had to do something.

JORDAN: It's really hard out here, Juan. Come on, give him a break.

JUAN: I'm just doing my job.

VICTOR: Exactly. You have a job. You don't know what it's like to—

JUAN: I know what it's like. I sucked it up. I worked my ass off. And now look at me.

JORDAN: Now you're arresting your best friend over a joint.

VICTOR: You've changed so much.

JUAN: Some of us grow up.

VICTOR: You wanted to be an astronaut, remember? Always looking at the stars.

JORDAN: What happened to you?

JUAN: I'm just doing my job.

JORDAN: Sending another brown guy to jail?

JUAN: You don't know what you're talking about.

VICTOR: Look around you, man. Weed is the least of our problems.

JORDAN: You're filling your monthly quota, Officer Asshole?

JUAN: Shut the fuck up or I'll take you in too.

VICTOR: OK. I get it. You don't want me around. How about, if you let me go, I'll go away?

JUAN: You got nowhere to go.

VICTOR: I swear, bro. I'll never come back.

JORDAN: Where the fuck will you go?

VICTOR: I don't know. North, south, it don't matter. But I'll go away.

JUAN: I don't believe you.

JORDAN: Come on!

JUAN: I see how you look at Isabella. And now Joy.

JORDAN: He looks at every woman like that!

VICTOR: No, I don't! Isabella is like my sister, dude.

JORDAN: You do like Joy, though.

VICTOR: Shut up, Jordan.

JUAN: Motherfucker.

VICTOR: Look, I'm tired of this hellhole. I might as well try my luck somewhere else. Just let me go.

JORDAN: You can't leave.

VICTOR: I have nothing here.

JUAN: You leave tomorrow.

VICTOR: After carnival. After the party. During.

JUAN: Deal.

JORDAN: This is insane. You're forcing another guy out of the neighborhood.

JUAN: Another criminal.

JORDAN: Juan, please. Don't do that to him. To us.

JUAN: He did it to himself. He's got to go.

VICTOR: I am leaving. I swear.

[JUAN *takes off* VICTOR*'s handcuffs.*]

JUAN: Get the fuck out of here. I can still give you a ticket for loitering.

JORDAN: We're going.

[JORDAN *and* VICTOR *exit.* JUAN *clenches his fists, looks up.*]

JUAN: The moon . . . it's beautiful. [*Beat. He snaps out of the moment.*] I've got to get back to work.

[JUAN *exits. Lights on* BELLA, *looking at* JESS *and* ISABELLA. JESS *and* ISABELLA *wake up.*]

BELLA: I'm a two-dimensional witness in a three-dimensional world. I observe. I learn. I make things happen. I'm here to stay. I'm here to make things change. The one who created me, gave me that power.

JESS: Let it out. Whatever it is.

ISABELLA: How?

[JESS *howls.*]

ISABELLA: Silly.

JESS: Come on, let it out!

BELLA: I can do things. BOOM! Just like that.

[JESS *and* ISABELLA *howl.* BELLA *goes back to her frame.*]

SCENE 10

[*It is morning in the living room.* AGNES *does yoga.* ISABELLA *paints.* JESS *watches over her shoulder.* GRACE *and* JOY *paint their nails or toenails.* BELLA, PATIENCE, *and* FORTITUDE *are quiet, resting at last.*]

AGNES: I hope your pajama party was fun. I couldn't sleep all night.

GRACE: I could hear you snoring.

JOY: That didn't sound like snoring to me.

ISABELLA: Ha! You're right. It wasn't.

AGNES: You woke up in a good mood.

JESS: We had a good night's sleep for a change.

GRACE: I did hear something weird last night. What was that noise?

JOY: Like an explosion?

ISABELLA: I just heard music.

JESS: Yeah. I heard that too.

ISABELLA: I thought it was a dream.

[MARIA *enters sipping coffee.*]

AGNES: What are we going to do with your friend, here?

ISABELLA: Maria? How are you?

MARIA: I'm fine. Couldn't sleep much.

AGNES: Animals. All men . . .

GRACE: Not all—

AGNES: How do you know?

GRACE: I read.

JOY: Why do you think they kicked her out of the convent?

GRACE: I wasn't kicked out. I decided that that lifestyle wasn't for me.

AGNES: What a pity. Mom and I worked so hard to get you in.

JESS: Poor thing. It must have been a traumatic experience.

AGNES: Yes, it was.

JESS: I was talking to Grace.

JOY: I could never join a convent.

AGNES: That's an understatement. So, Maria. What are your plans for the future?

MARIA: I don't know.

AGNES: We're crowded in this apartment.

ISABELLA: Agnes, Maria can stay here for as long as she needs to.

JESS: She's coming with me. Mom can help her.

AGNES: That witch.

JESS: She's a healer.

ISABELLA: And Jess too.

JESS: Nah . . .

ISABELLA: I think you can heal.

JOY: Can I go see her? I want to be healed.

ISABELLA: You are not sick.

JOY: Neither are you, and you went to see her.

AGNES: When?

ISABELLA: I've visited her many times. We all have.

GRACE: Yes, Agnes, even we went to see her a few times when we were kids.

AGNES: Only because of Joy and Juan's father. He was so ignorant.

GRACE: And ours wasn't?

AGNES: Ours was a drunk. Theirs was a hick.

JOY: They both chose Mom. What does that say about her?

AGNES: In any case, Maria doesn't need a witch, she needs the police.

MARIA: My husband . . . he's a powerful man.

JESS: And what he did is still a criminal act.

JOY: There's always divorce, orders of protection, hired killers—

AGNES: Joy! The things you say.

JOY: I learned everything I know from Dad.

GRACE [*about her nails*]: There! Don't they look pretty?

JOY: Let's see how long they last.

GRACE: I'm not like you. Mine always last longer.

JOY: What time does carnival start?

AGNES: We're not going.

GRACE: What?

JOY: Why?

ISABELLA: Oh, yes we are. And we are going to have a good time.

AGNES: People get rowdy in street parties. Don't you remember?

JOY: Yes, I do! People dress up and wear masks, and there are fireworks and music and laughter and—

AGNES: I never understood why you liked that party. Summer solstice? What are we, pagan?

ISABELLA: We're going. And Joy and Grace too, if they want.

AGNES: Mother would never approve of that.

GRACE: Mother never approved of anything and she is not here anymore and we're all grown-ups now.

JOY: Yes, we are.

GRACE: At least age-wise.

JESS: Come on, Agnes. You used to like it. It's carnival. The whole community comes together to celebrate.

AGNES: To celebrate what? Poverty? Unemployment? What are we celebrating?

JOY: I am actually happy to be back. I want to celebrate that.

GRACE: You like Victor! That's why you're happy to be here.

JOY: Shut up!

[JUAN *enters.*]

JUAN: I see we have a full house.

EVERYBODY: Good morning.

JUAN [*to* MARIA]: What happened to you?

JESS: Guess.

JUAN: Bastard.

JESS: Come, Maria, let's go home. Let's get ready for the party.

MARIA: I don't feel like going to the party.

JESS: Come on, you'll get distracted. See all you guys later.

[*To* ISABELLA] Hope you're feeling better.

ISABELLA: Yes, lots better. Thank you. See you later?

JESS: Sure.

[JESS *and* MARIA *leave.*]

JUAN: What's wrong with you?

ISABELLA: Nothing. Do you want breakfast?

GRACE: I'm cooking! I don't mean to be rude, but—

ISABELLA: I know. You can take over the kitchen if you want.

AGNES: At least she learned something at the convent.

JOY: If you only knew what else she learned . . .

GRACE: There was a lot of prayer and meditation and that kind of thing.

JOY: Right.

GRACE: Help me in the kitchen, Joy. You have Mom's touch.

AGNES: And her father's head.

ISABELLA: I'll watch. Maybe I'll learn something.

[GRACE, JOY, *and* ISABELLA *exit.*]

JUAN: So . . . how was your first night back home?

AGNES: Uneventful, as far as I can tell.

JUAN: Are you going to the party?

AGNES: Just to watch over the girls.

JUAN: I'll be working, but I'll see you there. I need to rest now.

[JUAN *exits.* AGNES *stares at* BELLA. BELLA *stares back.*]

AGNES: I don't like you.

[BELLA *sticks her tongue out.*]

AGNES: What the . . . ?

[BELLA *gives her the finger.*]

AGNES: This is not real.

BELLA: Ha!

[AGNES *tries to destroy* BELLA*'s painting, but* BELLA *somehow defends herself.* AGNES *runs out.*]

AGNES: This is ridiculous. Juan! Juan!

[*Lights change.*]

SCENE 11

[*Carnival. The ensemble wears masks. There is music. Everybody is drinking.* JORDAN *enters, agitated, looking for* VICTOR, *and approaches a couple of masked people.*]

JORDAN: Victor! Where are you, bro! Excuse me, are you . . . ? Sorry. Victor!

[VICTOR *finds him.*]

VICTOR: What's going on?

JORDAN: Something horrible. I . . . I don't know what to do. They're coming after me.

VICTOR: Who?

JORDAN: The dogs—

VICTOR: The dogs are coming after you?

JORDAN: I lost the dogs. Their owners are going to kill me.

VICTOR: How did you lose a pack of dogs?

JORDAN: It was horrible. I had them on leashes. All of them tied up together. I was crossing the pedestrian bridge over the highway and this big-ass dog with a fucking attitude and a suicide mission just jumped over the railing, taking all the little fuckers with him.

VICTOR [*laughing*]: That's fucked up!

JORDAN: Don't laugh! This is serious! A couple of cars crashed and the dogs just got . . .

VICTOR: I can see the headlines: "It's Raining Dogs" over the highway!

JORDAN: I caused a terrible traffic accident that killed, like, at least seven dogs and you're joking!

VICTOR: It's funny, man.

JORDAN: Are you high?

VICTOR: Dude, let's get a drink. It's my last night in town.

JORDAN: I'm leaving with you.

VICTOR: Sure. But we're not going alone.

[JOY *approaches.*]

JOY: I'm ready when you are.

JORDAN: You're such a dog.

VICTOR: Ha! A dog!

JORDAN: Juan is going to kill you!

JOY: Relax, he'll come to his senses.

[ISABELLA *approaches.*]

ISABELLA: Jordan, what's going on? Juan is looking for you.

JORDAN: Fuck. Fuck. Fuck! I . . .

VICTOR: His dogs committed suicide. Ha!

JORDAN: It's not funny.

ISABELLA: Where are you going?

JORDAN: Don't have time to explain. Victor, let's go.

[JORDAN *runs off.*]

ISABELLA: Where are you going? Why is everyone leaving?

[JUAN *enters.*]

JUAN: Party's over.

JOY: No, it's not.

JUAN: It is. Go home now.

JOY: You can't make me.

JUAN: Victor. You said—

VICTOR: I know what I said and I will.

ISABELLA: What's going on?

VICTOR: Nothing. Juan's right. Party will be over soon.

JOY: I'm going to get a drink.

JUAN: I said—

JOY: Oh, look! They're getting the fireworks ready.

[JOY *runs off.*]

ISABELLA: What are you talking about?

VICTOR: Your husband is kicking me out of the hood.

ISABELLA: He can't do that.

JUAN: If he doesn't leave I'm going to have to arrest him. And now Jordan too.

ISABELLA: What did they do?

JUAN: Where's Jordan?

ISABELLA: Wait. Tell me what's going on.

JUAN: Your friends are criminals.

ISABELLA: They're not. They're your friends, too.

JUAN: They were. Until they chose to break the law.

ISABELLA: I smoke too. It's only weed. It's legal in most places.

JUAN: Not here.

VICTOR: It's OK. I'm going.

[*The ensemble slowly gathers around* JUAN *and* ISABELLA.]

ISABELLA: No! This is crazy! Why are you doing this to me?

JUAN: I'm protecting you.

ISABELLA: You're isolating me.

JUAN: I do it because I love you.

ISABELLA: You just want to control me and everyone around you.

JUAN: I'm doing my job. As a policeman and as your husband.

ISABELLA: You're certainly not doing your job as my husband.

JUAN: Don't say that.

ISABELLA: Why not? When was the last time you touched me? The last time we made love?

JUAN: We're not discussing this in public.

ISABELLA: It's like I lost you after the wedding. Like you just wanted to take me away from my friends, from everything I love.

JUAN: You love to paint and I support you.

ISABELLA: You treat me like a thing.

JUAN: I treat you like you deserve.

VICTOR: Cool it, Juan.

JUAN: This is none of your business.

ISABELLA: I deserve better than this.

JUAN: I should arrest you too.

ISABELLA: For what?

JUAN: You don't think that I notice? The night escapades, the drugs. How you look at Victor.

ISABELLA: Is that it? You're jealous of Victor?

VICTOR: Juan, please.

JUAN: I see how you treat him.

ISABELLA: How? What have I ever done to make you jealous?

JUAN: You've always liked him.

ISABELLA: I only want you. But you don't let me. Two years it's been since we made love. Two years—

JUAN: Shut up!

ISABELLA: I can't anymore. I haven't said anything for two years!

JUAN: You are such a whore!

VICTOR: Juan!

ISABELLA: Because I want to be kissed and desired by my husband? Because I want to be touched? Does that make me a whore? You are the one with the problem, not me. You're the one who can't get it up!

[JUAN *slaps* ISABELLA. VICTOR *pushes* JUAN, *who loses his balance and falls back.* PATIENCE *and* FORTITUDE *pin* JUAN *to the ground.* VICTOR *gets on top of him. Fireworks go off. The ensemble reacts.* VICTOR *stands up.* JUAN *is unresponsive.*]

GRACE: What happened?

AGNES: I'm calling an ambulance.

PATIENCE: Oh my god.

FORTITUDE: Holy shit.

ISABELLA: Come on, Juan. Get up.

VICTOR: Fuck. Juan, brother. Come on.

MARIA: I saw him fall back. He probably hit his head.

JESS: Yes, he lost balance. Victor was trying to help him.

[*They hear the sound of an ambulance approaching.*]

EPILOGUE

[*Lights are on* ISABELLA, PATIENCE, FORTITUDE, *and* BELLA.]

BELLA: She thinks there is such a thing as destiny. But there isn't. She painted her own world in primary colors, not in blood, like she painted me.

PATIENCE: Vital signs stable. But he suffers. He's hurt. He's dizzy. His head palpitates like his heart—

FORTITUDE: But I know his heart doesn't palpitate much.

ISABELLA: What do I do now?

FORTITUDE: Buprenorfina for the pain.

PATIENCE: Bromazepam for the anxiety.

FORTITUDE: Nimodipina for high blood pressure.

PATIENCE: Profenid—

FORTITUDE: An anti-inflammatory—

PATIENCE: Analgesic—

FORTITUDE: And antipyretic.

ISABELLA: I try to match his breathing, to blend with him, to become him. I see his chest moving up and down, his hands resting at his sides. I hear the bubbling of the oxygen cup and the beep-beep-beep-beeping that keeps him alive.

PATIENCE: Propranolol to ease out of reality.

FORTITUDE: Dietilamida to induce erotic dreams.

PATIENCE: Cimetidina to inhabit an alternate dimension.

[*With a simple gesture,* BELLA *pulls the plug on* JUAN*'s machine. There follows a continuous, incessant beep.*]

ISABELLA: I killed my child . . . I killed my child . . . I killed all hope.

BELLA [*leading* ISABELLA *away*]: Nonsense. You have to finish painting me.

[*As they walk away, scene goes to blackout.*]

ZOETROPE: PART I

Javier Antonio González

Photograph from Caborca Theater production copyright © Hunter Canning

CRITICAL INTRODUCTION

Irma Mayorga

As performed at Encuentro 2014, near the end of *Zoetrope: Part I*'s first act, the play stages an uncanny wedding ceremony emblematic of the potent anti-realist, epic theater techniques that fuel the play in performance. A bride (Inés), groom (Severino), and priest (Padre Aurelio) take up separate locations across the field of a stripped-down proscenium stage—the theater's exposed back wall and wings are the mise-en-scène. Inés sits with her sister Francisca downstage right where they primp her hair and makeup. Severino and his sister Celeste rehearse his vows stage left. Suspended between the two families in this disjointed spatiality, Padre Aurelio stands center stage; he will proctor the ceremony from this midpoint to humorous effect, facing the audience. Moreover, to manifest the mesmerizing visual dramaturgy that saturated *Zoetrope's* staging, a "videographer" with camera atop tripod, camped center stage, trains his camera on Inés and Francisca's intimate preparations. As it will do throughout the performance, the camera captures details of the stage action—a hand's languor, an eyebrow's impatient arch, bodies spooned on a bed—and projects them onto a large screen (at least fifteen feet high) that dominates stage left. Notably, the nervous Severino and his sister stand directly in front of the screen's fragmented close-ups of Inés. Throughout the performance, as with this moment, the stage picture assiduously composes provocative interanimations between corporeality and filmic image. Crafting a beguiling visual discourse about presence and absence, it suggests the material, affective, and psychic texture of the characters' lives in mid-twentieth-century Puerto Rico.

The disjointed ceremony takes one further non-naturalistic turn. As Severino recites his vows, two wedding guests invade the stage's minimalist landscape, gyrating with abandon. Inés crosses to join her groom as hypnotic, electro-industrial music rises, forming an anachronistic soundscape for the couple's 1951 wedding in Lares, Puerto Rico. The entire company executes an ebullient, precisely choreographed group dance. The camera's projection amplifies the wedding party's jubilation even as it is estranged when written large onto the screen: the multi-perspective visuality is sublime. Inés and Severino are hoisted into the air, transported to an air mattress laid center stage, and tumbled into it. As with the most powerful deployments of epic theater's techniques, this form of theatricality folds wrinkles into the fabric of realism, generating critical distance between the play and its spectators, and for this scene of *Zoetrope: Part I,* they productively roil the well-known protocols of a wedding.

Regrettably, representation of this raucous, audacious, and gloriously weird theatricality eludes the schematic of the play as script offered here. Instead, only a modicum of its arresting composition finds notation in the text: "A wedding dance unlike anything we could possibly imagine a Puerto Rican wedding dance to be."[1] The fault is not the script's; a play's text is always and only the architectonics of a play performed. The staging operations described above—temporal-spatial collapse, videography and projection, an emulsion made of the surreal in the quotidian, and joy—braid themselves throughout the play in performance. As such, I offer the account above to foreground the stylistic adventurousness of Caborca's enactment of *Zoetrope: Part I.*

Puerto Rican playwright Javier Antonio González's *Zoetrope: Part I* becomes performance in the hands of New York–based theater company Caborca, where González as artistic director shapes wondrous manifestations of his works.[2] Caborca was formed by a group of young theatermakers who first collaborated as students at the University of Puerto Rico in 2002. The collective continued together at Columbia University's interdisciplinary M.F.A. Theatre Program as they gathered more collaborators over the years, and formally established Caborca in 2009.[3] Continuously mining Brechtian epic theater techniques, Caborca describes itself as an "experimental theatre company" determined to create "plays that move seamlessly between the irreverent and poetic, the personal and political, and the highly entertaining and intellectually challenging."[4]

Zoetrope: Part I is the first of an ambitious two-play saga that travels across forty years, from the 1950s to the 1990s, in the lives of a Puerto Rican family. Subtitled *Severino e Inés*, part one concentrates wholly on the young couple's courtship, marriage, and the birth of their son Claudio. It concludes with Severino's untimely death in New York City. Importantly, the play also prioritizes the stories of Severino's sister Celeste and Inés's sister Francisca, who each serve as sharp interpellators of the trials the newlyweds face.

During the tumultuous early years of the 1950s, Puerto Rico drafted, voted on, and adopted its own constitution in order to conceive itself as a commonwealth—actions which simultaneously stoked a fierce pro-independence movement. Although Puerto Rico officially became a commonwealth in 1952, this designation does not supersede the fact that the island remains an unincorporated U.S. territory, that is, a U.S. colony. Neither a fully enfranchised U.S. state nor an independent nation, Puerto Rico's frustrating ambiguous status promulgates complexity: identic, geographic, political, and economic. Congressional legislation in the early twentieth century extended federal laws to the territory, allowed a civilian government, and granted Puerto Ricans a representative in the U.S. Congress. Puerto Ricans were also given U.S. citizenship.[5] However, indicative of the arm's length governance the U.S. exerts on its colony, the territory's congressional representative cannot vote on legislation; likewise, Puerto Rican citizens cannot vote in presidential elections. Combined with the virulent anti-Latinx and anti-Black racism Puerto Ricans have endured, as journalist Juan González offers, and in the constraints of U.S. possession, Puerto Ricans negotiate a stalemated existence as "citizens yet foreigners."[6]

Even as the love story between Severino and Inés serves as *Zoetrope: Part I*'s spine, the political miasma that describes Puerto Rico's untenable history as a U.S. colony finds expression in the minutiae of each character's lived conditions; as a result, Puerto Rico's stasis profoundly shapes their conflicts. Severino enlists in the army and subsequently migrates to New York City; this dislocation not only erodes his marriage, his migration also articulates the political and material consequences of Puerto Ricans' massive mid-century diaspora to the U.S. The play thrives on scenes where the women grapple with how to salvage the couple's long distance marriage even as they attempt to fathom the territory's existential crisis on the eve of its shift to a commonwealth. As clear-cut answers to personal or political dilemmas fail to arrive in an alternation of scenes that pivot between the women in Puerto Rico and Severino in New York, a sense of ennui saturates the characters' lives, strongly suggesting the stalemate that is Puerto Rico itself. In the dialectics fomented by this form of geographic back and forth dramaturgy, the play proposes that the story of Puerto Rico cannot unfold in one singular protagonist's story, nor within the bounds of one location. Rather, like the optical toy that is a zoetrope, the story of Puerto Rico is found in "a series of figures representing successive positions of a moving object."[7] That is, seemingly static images—the snapshot each scene offers of the characters' lives—become animate, and therefore descriptive, when considered in a perception of vision that affords connections between them to yield a whole.

Importantly, Severino never returns to Puerto Rico, nor does Inés follow his migration—another stalemate. He dies from an unidentified wasting illness in New York which seems brought on, in part, by his dislocation. Here, the play's end in performance also escapes the script's notation, yet adumbrating a final deployment of Brechtian *Gestus* more clearly illuminates the political work embedded in the play's enactment.

Severino's body is returned to Puerto Rico, and, as the script describes, the final scene dramatizes his military funeral where Inés and Celeste engage in a heated dispute. Celeste and members of the pro-independence movement had planned to seize the U.S. flag from her brother's coffin and burn it as protest. The plan goes awry: when the military honor guard offers the flag to Inés, Celeste demands she repudiate it. Inés will not; despite all that it avows—Puerto Rico's complete subjection by the U.S—it nevertheless also signifies the life Severino lived within and despite the U.S. "It represents him . . . So even though I hate it I am keeping it."[8] This conflict profoundly describes Puerto Ricans' existential Gordian knot as "citizens yet foreigners." The script concludes with Celeste's final plea for her sister's concession to burn the flag. But in Caborca's performance, as the women's argument subsides, the production's stage manager, visible onstage throughout as another device of epic staging, lays out a tarp and paint can. With solemnity, she retrieves the flag from Inés's lap, unfurls it on the tarp, and scrolls white paint across it—a desecration, like incineration, that signifies rejection of the U.S.

At first glance, *Zoetrope: Part I* presents as a family drama, an enduring tradition of Latinx theater. Yet by seizing epic theater's anti-realist strategies, Javier Antonio González and Caborca's creative capaciousness reconceives the Latinx family drama, and in this way, they expand the aesthetic horizons of Latinx theater in extraordinary new directions even as their bold experimentation takes up an important theatrical discourse that ardently attends to Puerto Rico's embittered history of colonization and possession.

NOTES

1. Javier Antonio González, *Zoetrope: Part I*, 287.
2. An excellent collection of video trailers that offers a visual sense of Caborca's theatrical works can be accessed from their Vimeo site: https://vimeo.com/user12046771.
3. "2014 Theatre Co. Residency Recipient: Caborca," *The Loisaida Center*, http://loisaida.org/caborca/. Caborca also maintains a rich website with descriptions and images of its theater works at http://www.caborca.org/.
4. Ibid.
5. Specifically, legislation enacted through the Foraker Act of 1900 and the Jones Act of 1917.
6. Juan González, *Harvest of Empire: A History of Latinos in America* (New York: Penguin Books, 2011), 81.
7. *OED Online*. March 2017. http:// www.oed.com, s.v. "zoetrope, n.".
8. González, *Zoetrope: Part I*, 314.

PRODUCTION HISTORY

Zoetrope: Part I was first presented by Caborca as part of an ASAP Residency at Pregones Theater in December of 2013. It was directed by Javier Antonio González, with set and costume design by Jian Jung, lighting design by Jeanette Oi-Suk Yew, sound design by Elizabeth Rhodes, and choreography by Veraalba Santa. The stage manager was Brooke Bell and the assistant stage manager was Melissa Hudson.

The cast was as follows:

Padre Aurelio	David Skeist
Francisca	Tania Molina
Inés	Laura Butler Rivera
Severino	Marcos Toledo
Celeste	Yaremis Félix
Susan	Veraalba Santa
Russ	Michael Barringer
Gutiérrez/Esmeraldo	Pedro Leopoldo Sánchez Tormes
Genoveva	Brooke Bell

Zoetrope: Part I premiered at Encuentro Festival in Los Angeles Theatre Center in 2014. The cast was the same, with the exception that the role of Russ was played by Timothy French.

Zoetrope premiered in full (parts 1 & 2) at Pregones Theater in January 2015. It was first developed at the Emerging Writers group at The Public Theater in New York City.

CHARACTERS

Padre Aurelio

Francisca

Inés

Severino

Celeste

Susan

Russ

Gutiérrez

Genoveva

Esmeraldo

SETTING

Lares, Puerto Rico, and New York City.

A note on the passage of time: A zoetrope is a device that produces the illusion of action from a rapid succession of static pictures. This play is written as a series of scenes that skip back and forth through years and settings. The passage of time, like its characters, is conveyed through language. It is important not to "represent" or "describe" time passing with tricks such as extreme use of makeup, too many costume changes, or imitations of senility. Instead actors should not be shy to use the characters' remarks on time as what they are: exposition. The scenes should be performed fast and furious, creating a carousel effect, where gestures change meaning and where words both hurt and delight.

Likewise, rather than a descriptive set, the world of *Zoetrope* should be an imaginary space created from elements of all the settings in the play: a red carpet, a patch of grass, school desks, a bed.

A note on language: Unless specifically noted, characters in Lares are understood to be speaking in Spanish and characters in New York, in English. There is also a bilingual version of the play.

ACT 1: INÉS AND SEVERINO (1951 TO 1952)

1.1 *SEPTEMBER 1951*

[PADRE AURELIO *stands alone in the center of the stage. When he enumerates, he waits a fraction of a second for each word to sink in; when he speaks in Latin, he does so with full awareness that no one understands him. He talks as if he were talking to a crowd of illiterates.*]

PADRE AURELIO: Wedding... Funeral... Baptism... Communion... Four words. Same meaning. In that order or not. Baptism. Communion. Wedding. Funeral. Different names. Different clothes. Different music. Different hors d'oeuvres. All. Meaning. The same. Thanking God Almighty, creator of Heaven and Earth, etcetera. *Dixitque Deus: fiat lux. Et facta est lux.* Some of you might wonder, if it's true that He created the Earth, why is there evil, why hunger, why earthquakes? [*Smiling*] The littlest doubt hurts my feelings. None of those things was created by God! God did no more than create light, and by default, darkness was born. *Et vidit Deus lucem quod esset bona: et divisit lucem a tenebris.* God didn't make anything bad! Nor dirty. Nor perverse. Darkness created itself, as a consequence of light's creation. In the same way that a light bulb had to be invented before the shadows underneath a coffee table could appear. We are here today to bless the newly wed and to thank God for such a perfect couple. That's not why all of you sit catatonically before me. Unfortunately, some of you are here for other reasons. Perhaps the beer. Perhaps the gossip. Perhaps the sweaty dancing. Or maybe you came because you couldn't find a better way to kill boredom. [*Chuckling*] As Fray Batista, my mentor and friend used to say, boredom should be a sin. And it is! Whoever gets bored denies God. How is it possible to get bored when one can always talk to him, how when the Bible is so entertaining? *Filii Chus: Saba, et Hevila, et Sabatha, et Regma, et Sabatacha. Filii Regma: Saba, et Dadan.* When a couple weds, God smiles. And when God smiles, a rainbow is born, as Fray Batista used to say. And how not to smile in front of such a pretty couple? In a time when shadows in the form of divorce and Hollywood threaten the sanctity of marriage, Severino e Inés swear to love one another for the rest of their lives. On an island where only, what, sixty years ago, on a September twenty-third just like today, a group of lost peasants attempted, in this very town, a town of sons, a despicable attack against she who gave us language, culture, and civilization, (Spain!), Severino e Inés lock their lives in holy matrimony. Their revolution takes place not in a bar, but in a church. Not through violence but love. Love is the opposite of violence. Today the kings of Spain celebrate from their tombs the union between Severino e Inés. It's awkward to say Severino e Inés, don't you think? It would be a lot easier to say Severino y Inés, wouldn't it? Most do. Most accept the mental effortlessness required to say "y Inés." Why confuse yourself, most say, and not say "y Inés"? Why such a stupid rule, changing the "y" for the "e"? Today I'm telling you why! Because language was not invented today, nor yesterday, nor the day before yesterday. What we speak today took centuries, what centuries, millennia, to become what it is now. The same is true for God's law. It wasn't invented yesterday. It wasn't invented in Spain or North America or Ponce. God's law is . . . universal. I'm sure one or more of you wonders, "Why not say Inés y Severino, instead? Why not say her name first and avoid the 'y' dilemma altogether?" For God's sake! His name comes first! Then a conjunction, in this case "e"! Then *her* name! Why? *Faciamus Hominem ad imaginem, et similitudinem nostram: et præsit piscibus maris, et volatilibus cæli, et bestiis.* Because God created man first, the way he created light, and by default women were created.

1.2 *AUGUST 1951*

[FRANCISCA *enters examining an unopened letter. She is followed by* INÉS.]

FRANCISCA: It doesn't look like a love letter to me.

INÉS: And on the inside?

FRANCISCA: You mean I can open it?

INÉS: Without reading it.

FRANCISCA: To open a letter without reading it is like undressing without touching. What's the point? [*Opening the letter*] The handwriting of a madman . . . dated "the end of August . . ."

INÉS: Why would Severino write me a love letter, and why date it the end of August and not a specific day?

FRANCISCA: His hand was shaking when he wrote it, look.

INÉS: Don't read it, it's mine.

FRANCISCA: The fate of all things written is to be read.

INÉS: Not love letters.

FRANCISCA: Especially love letters. These are written so the recipient, in this case you, can show them to her friends, her children, her grandchildren.

INÉS: Of course not. They are written for the lover to keep them locked in a chest, treasuring them from afar and reading them only in times of grief, under covers, by candlelight.

FRANCISCA: I'll read it then and once you start grieving, let me know.

INÉS: Give it to me, it's mine!

[INÉS *tries to go after it, but she hurts her ankle.*]

FRANCISCA: Are you OK? Inés?

INÉS: Keep the letter, for all I care. Severino is an idiot anyway. This time I really hurt my ankle.

FRANCISCA: It hurts, I believe you, it hurts so bad. Oh, how it hurts!

INÉS: You're so indifferent to other people's pain.

FRANCISCA: Not to other people's, to *your* pain. It always takes place in your ankle. [*Giving her the letter*] Come here.

[FRANCISCA *caresses her hair while singing "Parlez-moi d'amour" softly.* INÉS *reads the letter.*]

FRANCISCA: And?

[INÉS *hands her the letter.* FRANCISCA *reads.*]

FRANCISCA: How trite.

INÉS: But cute.

FRANCISCA: Of course he doesn't know how to write, why would he if instead of going to college he joined the army. He probably doesn't know how to read.

INÉS: Going to war wasn't his fault. He's no less smart than any of his mates.

FRANCISCA: Are there no books in war?

INÉS: You are so judgmental.

FRANCISCA: It's hard to be a smart woman in this town. We have no other option but to end up with fools like him.

INÉS: At least he's handsome.

FRANCISCA: If by that you mean skinny and sick looking, then yes, very handsome . . . and why does he write you a love letter now that he's moving to New York?

INÉS: He'll be back.

FRANCISCA: Those who leave never return.

INÉS: Haven't you seen *La Carreta?* They come back in the end.

FRANCISCA: You're right. Like in *La Carreta*. What a great play! They come back in the end. With no jobs, no money, and missing a son. Poor Luis, dying stuck inside a machine.

INÉS: He's only going to build a foundation for himself and then start something else here. He'll be back in a couple of months. Time flies.

FRANCISCA: And you believe that?

INÉS: You're jealous because no one has ever written you a love letter.

FRANCISCA: I don't get them because I don't need them. I could write them myself if I wanted to and imagine they were written by a sophisticated, well-mannered French expatriate who writes to me from a deserted island where he can only eat raw fish and think of me.

INÉS: You'd be lying to yourself.

FRANCISCA: We all lie to ourselves, the most when it comes to love. [*Snatching the letter from* INÉS] Don't answer.

INÉS: I have to reply something.

FRANCISCA: Why take on so much responsibility so soon? Don't answer, thus you force him to write something better next time, something less common, something original, something he himself could've never imagined he was capable of writing. Something unique.

INÉS: But if I don't answer he will lose interest.

FRANCISCA: How little you know about men and their man-world. They love rejection. We do, too, although I'm about to change that . . .

INÉS: How?

FRANCISCA: That'll be the second part of this story. [*Pause*] This scribbled rag he calls a letter we're using to start a fire.

INÉS: No!

[FRANCISCA *runs away,* INÉS *runs after her.*]

FRANCISCA: Your foot doesn't hurt anymore. A miracle!

INÉS: Give me the letter!

FRANCISCA: You're right, it might be excessive to burn it.

[*She puts the letter inside her mouth.*]

INÉS: What are you doing?!

FRANCISCA [*the whole letter inside her mouth*]: He doesn't deserve you. This letter doesn't deserve you.

INÉS: Are you crazy, stop!

[FRANCISCA *chews on the letter and spits it out.*]

INÉS: How could you? My first love letter ruined on the floor.

FRANCISCA: Now it'll be easier to pretend you don't care.

INÉS: But I do!

FRANCISCA: You do.

SCENE 1.3 *SEPTEMBER 1951*

[SEVERINO *enters, followed by* CELESTE.]

CELESTE: Calm down!

SEVERINO: Stop telling me to calm down!

CELESTE: Drink, water, breathe.

SEVERINO: I don't want to.

CELESTE: Then stop pacing like a madman.

SEVERINO: That's how I feel.

CELESTE: You walk like a character in a René Marqués play.

SEVERINO: In his plays nobody feels what I feel. In a play, especially one by René Marqués, the characters poeticize, exaggerate their feelings, mythify them, but no one *feels* them the way I do.

CELESTE: That sounded quite poetic to me.

SEVERINO: I am in love, for fuck's sake, and it doesn't matter how I say it, how I define it, how I describe it, it always sounds like cheap poetry, and believe me I try and try and try not to sound like a fool but there is no way. I want to jump into a river and die of a cold.

CELESTE: Don't let me stop you.

SEVERINO: That was a joke. Remember the time I used to be funny?

CELESTE: No.

SEVERINO: Yes, you do. Everything I said used to make you laugh.

CELESTE: Remember that time we thought of the fifties as the future?

SEVERINO [*crying*]: Exactly! It's already September and she hasn't replied a word.

CELESTE: You're quite good at melodrama. You should have been an actor.

SEVERINO: I don't understand how people love to fall in love, read, write, talk about love. It's dreadful.

CELESTE: Only because you are being rejected, but requited love is divine. Although in your case I think you enjoy the role of the rejected. Never have I seen you this sprightly.

SEVERINO: I could have sworn she loved me back. Or at least that she liked me. A bit. She used to look at me and stay still, as if she were standing alone in the middle of a bridge that has collapsed without her noticing. She's still there, standing on the memory of a bridge that has collapsed, staring at me, her stare is what keeps her on her feet.

CELESTE: What a poet!

SEVERINO: Let me be a poet if I want to be a poet or an actor if I want to. I don't understand why she doesn't like my letters, with all the references I make to the night sky and the moon.

CELESTE: Maybe she doesn't get poetry.

SEVERINO: Inés is brilliant. Back in school her English was better than Mrs. Albors's. They hired her to teach English the moment she graduated. I'm sure she reads my letters and laughs.

CELESTE: I think she likes them so much they scare her. I bet she's hung all of your letters across her wall and that she reads and rereads them until she falls asleep. I bet she caresses herself with them in the morning, when she wakes up covered in sweat and moist.

SEVERINO: Celeste!

CELESTE: And afterward she dries herself up with them and she smells them and smells them and makes out with them.

SEVERINO: Stop filling my head with filth.

CELESTE: Let's write her another one.

SEVERINO: What for? She doesn't care.

CELESTE: She will care about this one, you'll see.

1.4 *SEPTEMBER 1951*

[INÉS *has finished reading a letter. She cries on the floor.* FRANCISCA *smokes.*]

FRANCISCA: I don't understand what the big deal is.

INÉS: He hates me. Thanks to you.

FRANCISCA: And that's exactly what we wanted.

INÉS: Is this your idea of fun? Seeing your sister on the floor, sobbing miserably? What are you, a monster? Why do you like to see me suffer? Is it because I'm prettier than you?

FRANCISCA: I'm used to it.

INÉS: Is it because I'm smarter?

FRANCISCA: That's debatable.

INÉS: My English is better than yours.

FRANCISCA: Let's change the subject.

INÉS: Why do you play these games and why am I so stupid that I let you get away with them?

FRANCISCA: It might not seem to make sense now, but in the long run, it's a good thing he hates you.

INÉS: Do you like women? Is that why? You like women, don't you? And you hate men. I've read about your kind. You were emotionally castrated as a child because I got all the attention from Dad and from all men.

FRANCISCA: I don't like women.

INÉS: You can tell me, you know. Is that why you wear pants? You wish you were a man?

FRANCISCA: Pants fit me better than skirts, that's all. And since no one else would wear them around here . . .

INÉS: A lot of people say you wish you were a man.

FRANCISCA: A lot of people think Puerto Rico will be a state one day. Does that mean it'll happen? No.

[*Pause.*]

I can't believe you told me that.

INÉS: It's true. They call you dyke and butch princess. They also make fun of your witch makeup.

FRANCISCA: People resent me for having style.

INÉS: Keep on telling yourself that.

FRANCISCA: You do too. But you lack the balls to dress the way I do.

INÉS: I don't want to have balls.

FRANCISCA: What else do you want this guy Severino for if not his balls?

[INÉS *laughs but gets sad again immediately after.*]

FRANCISCA: I know you're hurt, I know you grieve, but things are about to get better, and this time they will stay that way. This letter Severino wrote is proof that my theory about men, about love, really, is true. You've truly broken his heart, that's why he hates you. But hate is nothing more than love unattended. I bet he will be coming begging for you, crawling for your forgiveness.

INÉS: You know what? I'm going to do the opposite of everything you've told me to do. This is about my love, not yours. I'm going to find Severino and I'm going to apologize for not responding to any of his letters.

FRANCISCA: Blame me if it helps.

INÉS: I'm going to explain to him how much I love him and if he doesn't love me back I will follow him on my knees until he finally does notice me, and when he does, I will look deep into his eyes and I will not blink until saltwater pours out of my face and then . . . he will pity me. Pity leads to love.

FRANCISCA: Too true, I can see him from here.

[INÉS *freezes.* FRANCISCA *waves in his direction.*]

INÉS: Don't wave at him!

FRANCISCA: I'm waving at his sister. Oh, how convenient, she's leaving him alone. Now or never, Rat's Ass.

[INÉS *exits.* FRANCISCA *smokes.* CELESTE *enters.*]

CELESTE: Pass one.

FRANCISCA [*giving her a cigarette*]: What are they doing?

CELESTE: Talking. Going for a hand, it seems.

FRANCISCA: And what does he do?

CELESTE: He gets closer. And closer.

FRANCISCA: Then stop looking.

CELESTE: Where did you find these? They're weird.

FRANCISCA: Daddy brought them from his last trip to Europe.

CELESTE: Does he go there often?

FRANCISCA: That's what I'm supposed to say. A friend of his sent them from Cuba.

CELESTE: Your dad has friends in Cuba?

FRANCISCA: Yes, but that's not talked about.

[*Pause.*]

Now what are they doing?

CELESTE: Kissing.

FRANCISCA: This I want to see.

[*They both stare offstage.*]

FRANCISCA: They have so much to learn. Look at the way your brother sticks out his tongue.

CELESTE: They'll learn.

FRANCISCA: If you put two illiterate kids on an island with tons of books on it, do they learn how to read?

CELESTE: They learn how to fuck.

FRANCISCA: Badly. You need a reader to teach you how to read.

CELESTE: Easier said than done, but as far as I know, you've never kissed anybody.

FRANCISCA: That you know. I don't tell you everything.

CELESTE: You don't? I do.

FRANCISCA: I wouldn't be so sure.

CELESTE: She's grabbing his ass.

FRANCISCA: You enjoy watching that? I can't stand public affection.

CELESTE: That little sister of yours is not as innocent as she looks, her hand in his pants.

FRANCISCA: Do you think your brother has a big dick?

CELESTE: No. Maybe. I don't know, I don't think about it that often.

FRANCISCA: He doesn't need one. Inés lacks the experience you have.

CELESTE: It went out. Pass me the lighter.

[FRANCISCA *hands her a lighter.* CELESTE *lights her cigarette.*]

They're good. Gauloises. That doesn't sound like Spanish to me.

FRANCISCA: Because it's French.

CELESTE: Oh. They left.

FRANCISCA: Finally.

CELESTE: I hope it lasts.

FRANCISCA: And what if it doesn't? Not everything has to last.

CELESTE: You're so jaded, Panchi.

FRANCISCA: I've told you to never call me Panchi, and it's not jadedness, I simply don't understand everyone's obsession with permanence. Things change, the world changes, people change, and there is nothing wrong in accepting change as is, in what endures and what doesn't.

CELESTE: You talk as if you've been married five times and all you had left were your memories.

FRANCISCA: Maybe I was married in another life.

CELESTE: I can't picture that no matter how hard I try.

FRANCISCA: Why not? Because I wear pants?

CELESTE: No, silly, I love you in pants. It's just hard to see you in a situation that demands such responsibility.

FRANCISCA: Au contraire, that's exactly what I like about marriage. The mutual level of responsibility. The living proof that everything we do affects other people.

CELESTE: I have something to tell you.

FRANCISCA: I realized that the moment I saw you.

CELESTE: I think Clemente got me pregnant.

FRANCISCA: That's easy. Can you get twenty dollars? I can lend you ten.

CELESTE: The thought alone makes me want to throw up.

FRANCISCA: Doña Alejita is very good, discreet and very safe too.

CELESTE: I couldn't do it.

FRANCISCA: Don't tell me you're planning to have it?

CELESTE: I thought, something to do.

FRANCISCA: Is Clemente going to marry you?

CELESTE: I don't want to get married. When one can touch the world?

[FRANCISCA *opens her mouth in surprise.*]

FRANCISCA: I can't believe it.

CELESTE: Why do you look so happy?

FRANCISCA: You used to be such a nonentity and look at you now, how subversive.

CELESTE: I got it from you.

FRANCISCA: You're going to be a single mother! Who needs a man, after all?

CELESTE: You don't think it's such a terrible idea?

FRANCISCA: I think it's the best idea in the world. Finally something interesting is going to happen around here.

CELESTE: I'm going to be a single mother! I'm not sure if I want it to be a boy or a girl.

FRANCISCA: Either way we'll win in the end. If it's a girl, she'll grow up to take care of you, and if it's a boy, he'll grow up to take care of me.

CELESTE: How come?

FRANCISCA: Because I'm going to marry him.

CELESTE [*laughing*]: You're insane.

1.5 *SEPTEMBER 1951*

[INÉS*'s bedroom.* SEVERINO *stares around.*]

INÉS: Do you like it?

SEVERINO: This is your bedroom?

INÉS: I forget that I take it for granted.

SEVERINO: I love it.

INÉS: Did you see the altar to Virgin Mary?

SEVERINO: There's a flower covering her face.

INÉS: To protect her from the sun. Do you like my bed?

SEVERINO: It's really high.

INÉS: It's a special bed.

SEVERINO: How so? Aside from it being your bed.

INÉS: That's not why!

SEVERINO: Not yet.

INÉS: Grandpa Francisco got it made in Cartagena.

SEVERINO: A coastal bed!

INÉS: And with history. It was his marriage bed and after Grandma Auxilio's tragic death, Grandpa sent it by boat—

SEVERINO: Can I ask how she died?

INÉS: Not today. After her death, Grandpa sent it by boat so we would take care of it, a collector's piece. When Daddy ran for mayor the whole house became like a guest house. And so after many people had slept on it, he decided it was fine for me to have it. Even Albizu slept on it. Did you know that? Pedro Albizu Campos, *el Maestro*, slept here once or twice a year for a couple of years. Do you find that strange?

SEVERINO: Is your family . . . ?

INÉS: What?

SEVERINO: Pro-independence?

INÉS: Aren't you?

SEVERINO: I don't know. I don't think about it that often.

INÉS: But what's so weird about it, with the number of us that grows and grows everyday?

SEVERINO: That's a good point.

INÉS: So what do you think?

SEVERINO: I—

INÉS: You don't think it's a good idea for Puerto Rico to assimilate, do you?

SEVERINO: Don't you teach English?

INÉS: Answer me! You don't think we should be a colony forever, right?

SEVERINO: No.

INÉS: Do you believe in freedom?

SEVERINO: Of course I do.

INÉS: Then if you do believe in freedom as you say and you do believe in the abolition of colonial regimes as any man of our time would, then you must think it's a good idea for Puerto Rico to be a republic, free and independent from the U.S. or even Spain. Its own nation, with its own language, its own baseball team. What do you think?

SEVERINO: I don't like baseball.

INÉS: It was an example!

SEVERINO: I still don't understand how you teach English.

INÉS: For the same reason that Albizu studied at Harvard.

SEVERINO: He did?

INÉS: It is our duty to learn English, not to assimilate, but to confront the empire from within. We need to learn English so when U.S. American tourists arrive we can treat them as equal, on the outside, though on the inside we know we are better than they are because we can speak their language or not if we so choose, the way the French do. We'll win this battle if we understand their language without them understanding ours.

SEVERINO: Battle?

INÉS: That's what Albizu calls it.

SEVERINO: El Maestro. Do you know him in person?

INÉS: Of course. He used to sleep here. In this bed. [*Fixing the bed*] A bed made in Cartagena, a bed that has seen so much love and so much death bedded the father of our revolution when he visited Lares.

[INÉS *cries.*]

SEVERINO: What's wrong?

INÉS: I want this to be the bed where we make love for the first time. And the last.

SEVERINO: If we don't break it.

INÉS: We're getting married soon, right?

SEVERINO: As long as your parents and my parents and your parents' parents and my parents' parents say yes.

INÉS: Oh, god, how embarrassing!

SEVERINO: What?

INÉS: Without noticing, I asked for your hand when it should have been the other way around.

SEVERINO: My lips are sealed.

[*There is a silence.*]

INÉS: Too bad we have to wait until you come back from New York to get married . . .

SEVERINO: It's only a couple of months.

INÉS: . . . with how beautiful you're going to look lying down on this bed once we marry. [*In English*] But I understand that we'd better wait until you get back.

SEVERINO: What?

INÉS: Didn't you learn English during the war?

SEVERINO: Only a couple of phrases . . . Filth, mostly.

INÉS: Like what?

SEVERINO: Um . . .

INÉS [*in English, slowly, to make sure he understands her this time*]: It's OK. You can tell me. Am I not your future wife?

SEVERINO: Um . . . let's see. [*In English*] Open your legs wide.

[INÉS *laughs.*]

SEVERINO [*in English*]: Suck my dick. Right now.

[INÉS *laughs more, embarrassed but joyous.*]

SEVERINO [*in English*]: Feed my hungry cunt.

INÉS [*falsely alarmed*]: What!? Don't ever say that again!

SEVERINO: What does it mean?

INÉS: I don't dare repeat it. That word is so ugly.

SEVERINO: Tell me. We are going to be husband and wife.

[INÉS *whispers into his ear.* SEVERINO *blushes.*]

SEVERINO: Oh righty.

INÉS: They say the best place to learn a language is in bed.

SEVERINO: Teach me.

INÉS: We need to wait until you get back, don't we?

SEVERINO: We don't have to. We can get married right away and spend a whole month together before I leave.

INÉS: Are you serious?

[*He nods.*]

INÉS: Oh, god, how embarrassing!

SEVERINO: What, now?

INÉS: First I ask you to marry me and then I force you to marry me before you leave.

SEVERINO: Sounds like fate to me.

INÉS: But you should ask me to marry you, so that I can preserve that moment in my memory the way it should have been.

SEVERINO: OK.

INÉS: OK. Let me act like I don't know you're going to propose so my reaction comes out natural. Let me think of something else. That way when you approach me I'll be really surprised.

SEVERINO: OK. Ready?

INÉS: Yes!

SCENE 1.6 *SEPTEMBER 1951*

[FRANCISCA *smokes.* SEVERINO *paces as he puts on a tuxedo jacket. She helps him with his jacket, while he holds her cigarette. He brings it close to his mouth, almost about to smoke it, but he doesn't. It happens a couple of times.*]

SEVERINO: Can I have one?

FRANCISCA: It's going to make you want to take a shit.

SEVERINO: I've been throwing up all day, my gut is empty.

FRANCISCA: Then here. But you have to ask for it in English.

SEVERINO: No, thank you.

FRANCISCA: I'm helping you practice. You're not going to get to New York not knowing how to speak. They'll eat you alive.

SEVERINO: It's not like that at all. It's filled with Puerto Ricans. They say you can survive if you can speak with your hands.

FRANCISCA: Is that all you want to do with your life, to survive?

SEVERINO: Gotta start somewhere.

FRANCISCA: That's right. Gotta start somewhere. Ask me. For a cigarette. In English.

SEVERINO [*in English*]: Have one?

FRANCISCA [*in English*]: May I have one?

SEVERINO [*in English*]: May I have one?

FRANCISCA [*in English*]: May I have one, please?

SEVERINO [*in English*]: May I have one, please?

FRANCISCA [*in English*]: Sure. Here. Have one.

SEVERINO [*in English*]: Thank you.

FRANCISCA [*in English*]: You're very welcome.

[FRANCISCA *lights him a cigarette. He takes a drag and starts coughing.*]

FRANCISCA: I told you. It's bad for you.

SEVERINO: This is awful. Awful. It tastes awful. I will never smoke again.

FRANCISCA: The Marlboro cowboy says you can never smoke just one. [*In English*] Did you practice your vows?

SEVERINO [*in English*]: Yes, sir!

FRANCISCA [*in English*]: Can I hear them?

SEVERINO [*in English*]: No, sir!

[*They smoke.* CELESTE *enters.*]

CELESTE [*to* FRANCISCA]: Inés needs you.

FRANCISCA: What now?

CELESTE: Makeup.

FRANCISCA: I already told her what to do.

CELESTE: She's having trouble with the rouge. She wants lots of it but she's afraid she'll look too much like you.

FRANCISCA: When I'm done here.

CELESTE: Give me one.

FRANCISCA: You're pregnant.

CELESTE: My child is going to be a smoker.

FRANCISCA: No.

CELESTE: Just one.

SEVERINO: The Marlboro cowboy says you can never smoke just one.

CELESTE: Turn around, the bride's coming.

SEVERINO: I've already seen her.

CELESTE: You shouldn't have, it's bad luck.

[SEVERINO *turns, smoking and coughing from time to time.*]

INÉS [*entering, to* FRANCISCA]: Didn't Celeste tell you to come help me?

FRANCISCA: What if my hand takes over and turns you into a witch?

INÉS: None of those women knows about makeup the way you do.

FRANCISCA: It'll be a minute till I'm done smoking.

INÉS: Give me one. Severino, don't turn around!

SEVERINO: It'll give you bad breath.

FRANCISCA [*giving* INÉS *a cigarette*]: Look who's talking, after so much vomiting.

INÉS: Vomiting?

CELESTE: Did you vomit?

SEVERINO: A little.

FRANCISCA: His stomach is empty.

INÉS: Why, are you nervous?

SEVERINO: Not at all. Are *you* nervous?

INÉS: I'm not nervous, I'm in pain!

SEVERINO: Why are you in pain?

CELESTE: She just got her period.

FRANCISCA: A little early.

INÉS: I think I'm synced with you.

FRANCISCA: I used to be synced with Celeste, but now she's pregnant we are all mixed up inside.

SEVERINO: Can I help?

INÉS: Don't turn around!

SEVERINO: I've already seen you in the dress.

INÉS: It's bad luck.

SEVERINO: Why didn't you let me light a candle to Mary in your room?

CELESTE: Let's do shots. It'll calm everyone down.

[*She gives everyone plastic cups and serves them rum.*]

INÉS [*to* FRANCISCA]: Light me up.

[FRANCISCA *lights her cigarette.*]

FRANCISCA: That sweet little virgin can't take the heat.

[INÉS *and* FRANCISCA *laugh.*]

CELESTE: Great. I want to say something first, but I bet for sure I'm going to start crying.

FRANCISCA: I appreciate the warning.

CELESTE: But you guys couldn't have chosen a better day to get married. Even though it's been about eighty years since *El Grito* I don't think I've ever seen Lares so packed with people coming from all over the Island . . . Our country was free for a whole day. What better way to celebrate than with a wedding? The number of people here tells me that in a couple of years we will be celebrating not only your anniversary, but absolute separation from the Yankees. *Salud*!

[*Everyone does a shot.* SEVERINO *has turned around and stared at* INÉS *this whole time without anyone noticing.*]

SEVERINO: You look stunning.

INÉS: What are you doing? Go!

CELESTE: Severino, come with me.

FRANCISCA [*to* CELESTE]: Make him practice.

[CELESTE *takes* SEVERINO *away.* INÉS *and* FRANCISCA *stay in silence for a moment.*]

INÉS: What?

FRANCISCA: Nothing.

INÉS: Why are you smiling?

FRANCISCA: He's right. You look very beautiful with a cigarette in your hand.

INÉS [*surprised by the compliment*]: Thanks.

FRANCISCA: You must be really nervous to want to smoke. You've always criticized me for it.

INÉS: I'm not nervous.

FRANCISCA: Good.

INÉS: You'd like that, though. Because you think I'm making a huge mistake by getting married so fast. I'm not nervous at all.

FRANCISCA: I've never said anything like that.

INÉS: But you've thought it. You also think Severino is stupid.

FRANCISCA: Not anymore. Now that I know him better I think very highly of him.

INÉS: You would be so happy to see this marriage fail.

FRANCISCA: How could you say that? I want nothing more than to see you happy.

INÉS: You don't have to lie to me, sister. I know you hate that I'm getting married before you, even though you're older. You won't stop making faces.

FRANCISCA: Why are you saying these things? I have never wanted to get married.

INÉS: That's what you want people to think. And you succeed at it. But you can't fool me. You wear pants, and dress all in black, and smoke, and read books . . . that way you fool people into thinking that you're over all these mundane social constraints. But you can't fool me. You're only making up for the fact that you'll probably never have a husband.

FRANCISCA: Let's go in. I want to finish your makeup before it's too late.

1.7 *SEPTEMBER 1951*

[FRANCISCA *works on* INÉS*'s makeup. On a separate part of the stage,* CELESTE *helps* SEVERINO *with his vows.* PADRE AURELIO *appears again. The three actions—ceremony, makeup, and practice—happen simultaneously.*]

PADRE AURELIO: But for some reason unclear to me, the groom has asked to say his vows last.

SEVERINO: Because I don't think it's as you say, Padre Aurelio. I think God created man as an experiment, the way he created dinosaurs; seeing he had made a mistake, clearly, he created women, the way he created birds.

[CELESTE *hits him with something.*]

PADRE AURELIO: Don't let's argue about creation in a church.

SEVERINO: I would lose. So please don't let's argue and go on with the ceremony. God won't mind a glitch in chronology.

PADRE AURELIO [*clearing throat and going on*]: Today the kings of Spain celebrate from their tombs the union between Inés and Severino. When a couple weds, God smiles; when God smiles, a rainbow is born, and well, it has not stopped raining. This union is about to change that. Inés, repeat after me. I—

INÉS: I

PADRE AURELIO: Inés Franco.

INÉS: Inés Franco.

PADRE AURELIO: Take you.

FRANCISCA: Don't move.

[INÉS *doesn't move.* FRANCISCA *applies blush.*]

INÉS: Take you.

PADRE AURELIO: Severino Ramírez.

INÉS: Severino Ramírez.

FRANCISCA: Look up.

[INÉS *looks up.* FRANCISCA *applies eyeliner.*]

PADRE AURELIO: For my lawful husband.

INÉS: For my lawful husband.

PADRE AURELIO: To have and to hold from this day forward.

FRANCISCA: Close your eyes.

[INÉS *closes her eyes.* FRANCISCA *applies eye shadow.*]

INÉS: To have and to hold from this day forward.

PADRE AURELIO: For better, for worse.

INÉS: For better, for worse.

PADRE AURELIO: For richer, for poorer.

INÉS: For richer, for poorer.

FRANCISCA: Open your mouth wide.

[INÉS *opens her mouth wide.* FRANCISCA *applies lipstick.*]

PADRE AURELIO: In sickness and health.

INÉS: In sickness and health.

PADRE AURELIO: Until death do us part.

INÉS: Until death do us part.

PADRE AURELIO: Severino?

SEVERINO: Severino?

[CELESTE *stands next to* SEVERINO *with the vows he's written in her hand. He delivers the vows not in the actual ceremony, but more as if he were rehearsing them before the actual ceremony.*]

PADRE AURELIO: Repeat after me.

SEVERINO: Repeat after me.

PADRE AURELIO [*to the congregation*]: It's not a sin to laugh.

[SEVERINO *and* PADRE AURELIO *chuckle.*]

PADRE AURELIO: I—

SEVERINO [*in English*]: I—

PADRE AURELIO: I—

SEVERINO [*in English*]: I—

PADRE AURELIO [*clears his throat*]: OK. Since you've opted to say your vows in English, then I'll say my part in Latin. Those who don't understand should reconsider missing Latin mass, now only performed on Sundays at dawn. Severino Ramírez vis accipere Inés Franco, hic præsentem in tuam legitimam uxorem iuxta ritum sanctaæ—

SEVERINO [*in English*]: I, Severino Ramírez, take you, Inés Franco, as my wife. I promise to be good in true times.

CELESTE: True in good times.

SEVERINO: True in good times. And bad times. Even if you stop being true to me, which will never happen because we are who we are. From this day on . . .

CELESTE [*in English*]: . . . ward.

SEVERINO [*in English*]: Ward.

CELESTE [*in English*]: Onward.

SEVERINO [*in English*]: Onward. For better, rich, poor, sick, until death . . . this last phrase sounds better in Spanish, don't you think?

CELESTE: Totally.

SEVERINO: Until death do us part.

1.8

[*A wedding dance unlike anything we could possibly imagine a Puerto Rican wedding dance to be, with Elizabethan bows and steps, Victorian lifts and twirls, weaves. The majestic dance culminates with the guests carrying the newlyweds onto the bed.* FRANCISCA *is left alone. She creates a sign that reads: "Wish you could write love letters like Voltaire? Feel like a poet but never learned how to write? Talk to me." When she finishes writing the sign, she hangs it, sits at a small desk, and waits.*]

ACT 2

2.1 *FEBRUARY 1952*

[*New York.* SEVERINO *appears from under the covers, half naked. He lies in silence for a moment. He reaches for a glass of water. He sits up and drinks quietly.*]

SEVERINO: I don't want to die alone.

[*Also from under the covers,* SUSAN *appears.*]

SUSAN: What did you say?

SEVERINO: You heard me.

SUSAN: How considerate of you to say so.

SEVERINO: How come?

SUSAN: Let's see. [*Perhaps getting dressed, perhaps getting up to make coffee*] Perhaps . . . because I am here. In the same room as you. You're dying. In front of me. I am well aware that you're dying. I take care of you, some would even say I take *good* care of you. I'll probably be here and witness the exact moment when you die. So it occurs to me that maybe . . . perhaps, you're not dying alone.

SEVERINO: You know what I mean.

SUSAN: If you had wanted to die next to your wife you would have left a long time ago. You decided not to. Hence, you die alone.

SEVERINO: Don't make fun.

SUSAN: I don't. Either you stop saying you're dying alone *pronto* or I'm leaving, in which case you're seriously. Going to. Die. Alone.

SEVERINO: You wouldn't leave me here in this condition. God formed you from my rib so we could always be side by side.

SUSAN: Is that a dare? Because I'm an atheist.

SEVERINO [*coquettish*]: Maybe.

SUSAN: You think I'm not capable of grabbing my things and walking away, leaving you like this, unable to even go to the bathroom on your own or to cook?

SEVERINO: I can cook.

SUSAN: Badly. You think I don't dare?

SEVERINO: I have Russ.

SUSAN: He's as useless in life as you are on your deathbed. You think I don't dare?

SEVERINO: No.

SUSAN: Try me. Say something really hurtful to me. Make me want to leave and I swear I will.

SEVERINO: I've never loved you.

SUSAN: I knew that. Try again.

SEVERINO: When we have sex I think of my wife.

SUSAN: When we *had* sex.

SEVERINO: When we *had* sex I thought of my wife.

SUSAN: I thought of your wife as well. Anything else?

SEVERINO: I never planned to leave her. The times I said I wanted to leave her to be with you, I didn't mean it.

SUSAN: That's alright, I never believed it.

SEVERINO: You pretended so well that you believed me.

SUSAN: Because you pretended so well that you meant it.

[*She lies down next to him.*]

SEVERINO: See? I told you you couldn't leave me.

SUSAN: See? I told you you couldn't hurt me. Speaking of hurting, you've got mail. Not from your wife, though. Your sister . . . Celeste.

SEVERINO: Why doesn't she write?

[*Pause.*]

Read it to me.

SUSAN: I can't read Spanish.

SEVERINO: I've taught you enough. Let's hear it.

[SUSAN *opens the letter and skims through it.*]

SUSAN: Your wife's dead. Just kidding. I think it says you're an uncle.

[*He snatches the letter from her and reads the beginning of it.*]

SEVERINO: No, not yet. Another month. She's decided on a name, though . . . Ramón Evaristo.

SUSAN: That's beautiful.

SEVERINO: Until people start calling him Moncho.

SUSAN: Why would people call him Moncho?

SEVERINO: Because that's what you do. You take a Ramón and you make him a Moncho, obviously.

SUSAN: Anything else?

[*Silence while he reads the rest of the letter. His face loses color.*]

SEVERINO: Yes.

2.2 FEBRUARY 1952

[FRANCISCA *is writing a letter under her letter-writing station. She has added the word "Free" to the sign.* INÉS *enters, four months pregnant.*]

INÉS: I see business is finally taking off . . .

FRANCISCA: Since it's a free service I wouldn't call it business . . . but yes. Today I had a total of four clients, including a very sad woman who came for the first time, Esperanza.

INÉS: That's her name? No wonder she's sad.

FRANCISCA: She knew what to say in her letter so I didn't have that much creative freedom, but her handwriting sucked. Third grade level at best.

INÉS: Who's that one for?

FRANCISCA: That hubby of yours.

INÉS: You write him letters?

FRANCISCA: Sometimes.

INÉS: Oh. What about?

FRANCISCA: The usual. How are you, how's the job search, has your English improved? Your wife misses you.

INÉS: Don't write that.

FRANCISCA: Don't you want him to know? How you cry at night, how you treat us all like strangers, how you overwhelm your sixth graders with love poems they don't understand.

INÉS: Do you think I should have an easier curriculum?

FRANCISCA: No.

INÉS: But you think my teaching goes over their heads.

FRANCISCA: There is nothing you can do about that. You didn't raise them. Their stupid parents did. Ricardo's mom came yesterday to tell me that her sociopath of a son doesn't like my class. So? I said, I'm not here to entertain anybody. "Is there anything you can do?" Like what? "I don't know, does he really need to learn English?" No, no one *needs* to learn anything. It's very easy to stay stupid. We're having a meeting with the principal tomorrow.

INÉS: I haven't told Severino I'm pregnant.

FRANCISCA: Still? It's been four months since he left, it's February already.

INÉS: I've tried many times to tell him, but I can't do it. I'm like your new client, Libertad.

FRANCISCA: Esperanza.

INÉS: I know what to say but the words don't come out. I sit at my desk but instead of writing I just sit there admiring that desk that once belonged to Grandma Auxilio and I feel like crying but I don't. And time goes by and I get bigger and I promised Celeste weeks ago I would tell him but I haven't, I haven't.

FRANCISCA: She probably did already.

INÉS: That bitch!

FRANCISCA: She's his sister.

INÉS: So?

FRANCISCA: They have that strange brother-sister bond.

INÉS: I don't know about this baby thing.

FRANCISCA: What are you saying?

INÉS: I don't know what I want. I know what I don't want.

FRANCISCA: What do you not want?

INÉS: I don't want to be one of those lonely single mothers who gets abused by their children and are made fun of in church.

FRANCISCA: You don't have to be lonely. Celeste is going to be a single mother and I will be there to take care of her and her baby.

INÉS: I don't want to be one of those single mothers who relies on her even more single friends to take care of her child. Makes their friendship very suspicious.

FRANCISCA: Does it now?

INÉS: You asked me to tell you what I don't want, so I'm telling you, honestly and frankly. We have that sister bond.

FRANCISCA: Well, you don't have to endure either of those things, since you have a husband.

INÉS: I don't know how to tell him.

FRANCISCA: I can tell him right now.

INÉS: No! I know what I don't want. I don't want him to know I'm pregnant.

FRANCISCA: Why not?

INÉS: I don't want him to feel obligated to come back.

FRANCISCA: He was in the army. Obligation turns him on.

INÉS: He wasn't really in the army.

FRANCISCA: Oh?

INÉS: He—he didn't pass their health test. They recruited him to be in an office. Sorting mail, moving stuff around, alphabetizing. You're passing judgment!

FRANCISCA: I'm not the one passing judgment, you are! You'd rather raise a kid by yourself than with someone you consider a loser.

INÉS: Don't put words in my mouth.

[*Pause.*]

He used to write me love letters. One a day. Recounting all the great big city things he had seen. I used to read them and think, this is why I married you. I could never move to a city like that. I admired him. Then his letters changed. It got colder. He didn't have money for warm clothes or enough to eat. I sent him money, but more letters came and all he talked about was the weather. About how he needed stronger medicine, how he can't stop coughing, warmer coats, more food. So I sent him more money. And he still writes back blaming his terrible luck on the bad weather!

FRANCISCA: One has to fall before standing.

INÉS: He's such a loser!

FRANCISCA: All the more reason you should ask him to come home. He probably wants you to ask him. Tell him you're pregnant and he will be so happy to come back. We'll help him get a job teaching English. He'll be warm and there will be no more need to talk about the weather . . .

INÉS: Since when are you so hopeful?

FRANCISCA: I like babies now.

INÉS: Why?

FRANCISCA: I've been thinking that's the way to go if we want this revolution to ever take place. Since we started teaching we've been on the outside of it. We need to join the revolution once again.

INÉS: How is having babies a way of joining the revolution?

FRANCISCA: Think about it. They've arrested Albizu. He'll be in jail what, ten, fifteen years? If we start having lots of babies now, by the time he gets out he will have a grand army of strong, young, literate, bilingual Puerto Rican men. Our babies.

INÉS: Are you planning to have one too?

FRANCISCA: I wouldn't know what to do with it. I'll have Celeste's. And I'll even be nice to yours, if you let me.

INÉS: Without Albizu there is no revolution in sight.

FRANCISCA: You can arrest the man, but you can never arrest an idea.

INÉS: I liked you more as a pessimist.

FRANCISCA: It'll pass.

INÉS: He wrote me a letter the other day telling me he went to the Edgar Allan Poe street and saw the building where he finished writing "The Raven." I thought that was impressive.

FRANCISCA: It is.

INÉS: Not if you haven't read any Edgar Allan Poe.

2.3 *FEBRUARY 1952*

[*New York.* RUSS *enters carrying his bicycle and a bag full of groceries. He is covered in snow.*]

SUSAN: Oh, no.

RUSS: Is there any wine left?

SUSAN: You were supposed to bring some.

RUSS: Remember that time I fell on the snowy pavement while carrying two bottles of red wine? Let's say it looks like someone got shot on one twenty-fifth street, which is not unlikely.

SEVERINO: How did you manage that?

RUSS: So I'm biking, and you know, the groceries are kind of heavy, I'm not trying to rub it in anyone's face, but the fridge has been empty for a couple of weeks, no big deal, I don't mind grocery shopping in the snow, though you can't really see what's ahead of you, which is kind of exciting, suddenly a guy opens his door right in front of me—

[SEVERINO *laughs.*]

RUSS: Very funny. Have me bring the groceries—and the wine!—while you guys indulge in illicit romantic relations.

SUSAN: That's good for a title.

RUSS: I have news.

SUSAN: Good or bad?

RUSS: Yes. I got fired.

SUSAN: What happened?

RUSS: At around seven or eight at night after working overtime for four or five hours, the elevator gets alarmingly, inexplicably crowded to the point that I can't reach the control panel, me and a bunch of suits stuck on the sixth floor, complaints ensued . . . I couldn't help it.

SUSAN: What did you do?

RUSS: I farted. Really loud.

SUSAN: Russ!

RUSS: It was too tempting. You don't know how boring an elevator on Park Avenue can be. It worked! People moved out of the way and I was able to reach the buttons. A couple of them even laughed. But someone complained to the manager and I got fired.

SEVERINO: He fired me for a lot less than that.

RUSS: He reminded me about it. He also said I might be the only white man in town willing to be an elevator man, that I dressed like a dude. That hurt.

SUSAN [*to* SEVERINO]: Why did you get fired again?

SEVERINO: We were caught switching elevators. We had a rule that whenever we met on the same floor, we had to run and swap places.

RUSS: And do a high five.

SEVERINO: High five!

[*They do a high five.*]

SEVERINO: I got fired. He didn't. Can you believe I miss working there?

RUSS: I already don't. To not have to dream of the same doors closing and opening . . . I'd rather work door to door. The wine!

[*Pause.*]

SEVERINO: Did you check the mailbox?

RUSS: I wish I had three hands, but—

SUSAN: I'll go.

[SUSAN *gets the keys, which are hanging from a nail on the wall, and exits.* RUSS *starts putting the groceries away.*]

RUSS: I'm making spaghetti tonight.

SEVERINO: Let Susan make it.

RUSS: I make good spaghetti.

SEVERINO: Hers is better.

RUSS: I better learn. She won't always be here for me.

SEVERINO: You guys won't be friends after I relocate?

RUSS: Me friends with her?

SEVERINO: You could become lovers.

RUSS: I couldn't do it without feeling like I'm sleeping with you.

[SUSAN *enters.*]

SUSAN: Nothing.

SEVERINO: Bitch.

RUSS. Seriously?

SUSAN: Nothing. Maybe her letters are getting lost in the mail. The whole hire-the-handicapped program. Maybe they'll hire you, Russ, you need a job.

2.4 MAY 1952

[INÉS *is getting ready for class. She is seven or eight months pregnant.* FRANCISCA *enters, holding a letter.*]

FRANCISCA: Have you seen this?

INÉS: Who's Susan?

FRANCISCA: No, this.

INÉS: "Hire the handicapped. It's good business"?

FRANCISCA: To do what?

INÉS: It's addressed to me.

FRANCISCA: Who's Susan?

[FRANCISCA *shrugs and exits.* INÉS *opens the envelope using a pair of scissors and reads the letter. The bell rings. Students file into the classroom.* INÉS *puts the letter away.*]

INÉS: Hello, children.

STUDENTS [*in unison*]: Hello, Mrs. Franco de Ramírez.

INÉS: How are you today?

STUDENTS [*in unison*]: Fine, thank you. And you?

INÉS: Very well. Today we are going to continue with Edgar Allan Poe. Before we begin, please pay attention to the quote on the board. Esmeraldo, can you read it out loud, please?

ESMERALDO: "Poetry has not been a . . ."

INÉS: Purpose.

ESMERALDO: ". . . purpose, but a passion."

INÉS: Read it again.

ESMERALDO: "Poetry has not been a purpose but a passion."

INÉS: Beautiful. Who would like to respond to the quote first?

[*Silence.*]

Genoveva, how would you respond to it?

GENOVEVA: I love it.

INÉS: Why?

GENOVEVA: Because it talks about how his poetry is about passion and not purpose.

INÉS: Your pronunciation has really improved, Genoveva. Can you say that again without using the same words the author uses? That would be the basic principle of interpretation.

GENOVEVA: Yes. [*Thinking for a moment*] For me poetry is about sentiments, like love and sadness.

INÉS: Versus?

GENOVEVA: Versus being the kind of poetry that has a . . . purpose. I mean, that tries to say something different from what we feel in the inside.

INÉS: Poetry is an emotional response, you say, as opposed to an intellectual response to the world.

GENOVEVA: Exactly.

INÉS: And I completely agree with you, Genoveva. Poetry, no matter how perfect its sentences, how schematic its structure, is an emotional art. For what good is a poem without a heart? You might be too young to understand this, but passion is what drove Jesus to the cross, passion drove Columbus to *cross* the Atlantic when he had no idea of what he would discover, although some people say he didn't discover a thing, that this land was already discovered, it wasn't. Columbus discovered America, we all know that. Sure, Indians lived here already, sunbathing and chanting. I for one wouldn't count either of those things as a huge discovery and can say with utter peace of mind that Columbus did in fact discover this land. But you know all this already, don't you kids? History class?

[*They nod their heads.*]

Ms. Ayala is a good teacher, isn't she? Does she ever cry in class? No, why would she? Ms. Ayala is a great teacher. Have you noticed how she can't spell? Not a big deal, but I tell you . . . spelling . . . [*writing the word "spelling" on the board*] Spelling will take you far. Most people who don't know how to spell are failures and you don't want to be a failure. You want to be a . . . professional, successful human and success is, success is a very tricky word to spell because it has two *s*'s and two *c*'s. Back to Edgar Allan Poe. The first poem we are reading by him is his most famous, his most beloved. It's called "Annabel Lee." That's with a double *n* in Annabel and a double *e* in Lee. Repeat the title with me: "Annabel Lee."

STUDENTS: "Annabel Lee."

INÉS: And who is Annabel Lee, you might wonder? I won't give it away, but let me tell you that "Annabel Lee" is my favorite poem. Until we get to Robert Frost. He's a . . . he's a classic. A new classic. He will be a classic. Let's read it to ourselves first.

GENOVEVA: I want to read out loud.

INÉS: Later! With the pink crayon you are going to underline the words that you don't know. New words! With the green one the words that you don't know how to pronounce and with the blue one, you are going to mark all the times the author uses the word "*love*." Poets have always loved love, it's so easy to spell. Although as we are about to see, it doesn't always work out or in the case of "Annabel Lee" it is very sad since she dies. A cold wind comes in and kills her, leaving the poet alone. She dies before they even . . . I'm not ruining the poem for you, you can tell from the very beginning . . . "a wind blew out of a cloud by night killing my Annabel Lee." Chilling, not killing. She dies and he's left alone. That's exactly what passion is. Being left alone to write about your Annabel Lee. If you are a man, of course. If you are a woman, well, you'll have to come up with your own version of "Annabel Lee." That might be a fun project, actually, to have you guys write your own version of the poem. I don't know if I can get it approved by the department, but wouldn't that be fun? To write your own version of this beautiful tale about losing the thing we love the most? Oh, my god, my ankle is really hurting today. We're going to have to stop right here. Don't be alarmed, I'll be fine. Put your heads down. It's better to stop now while I can still walk. Sometimes it gets really bad . . . you don't want to hear about that, sometimes I can't walk at all . . . the bell will ring soon. Have you noticed how the bell seems to be a little early these last couple of days? Not today. Today it won't catch me in the middle of a sentence, no, no. [*Suddenly extremely condescending*] Keep your heads down. We still have some thirty minutes left? Let's take it easy today. Let's not burn our heads with too much learning in one day. Education is important but it's not everything.

2.5 *MAY 1952*

[RUSS *enters, covering his face.*]

SUSAN: Are you OK?

RUSS: What does it look like?

SUSAN: What happened to your face?

SEVERINO: Did someone punch you?

RUSS: What does it look like?

SUSAN: Sit. I'll get some ice.

[*He sits.* SEVERINO *examines his face.*]

SUSAN: Are there any cuts?

SEVERINO: A small one. It's not that bad. Do we have any Band-Aids left?

RUSS: Let me cut your face and you let me know if it's not that bad.

SEVERINO: Not a bad place to have a scar. Could have been your nose, right against the concrete.

RUSS: Who bought flowers?

SUSAN: I did.

SEVERINO: Was he black?

RUSS: He was white. White people are awful. I said I don't want to talk about it . . . and why does it have to be a he? A woman could have punched my face repeatedly against a wall in Riverside Park.

SUSAN: What were you doing in Riverside Park?

RUSS: It's the end of May! Trees are blooming, birds are singing, humans are sunbathing . . . I laid down on the grass, peacefully. I don't want to talk about it. Is there any wine left?

SEVERINO [*giving him his glass*]: Here.

SUSAN: I stole it.

[*He drinks.*]

RUSS: Looks really cheap for something stolen.

SUSAN: We were in the middle of a celebration.

[*Pause.*]

Aren't you going to ask us what are we celebrating?

RUSS: You're going to tell me anyway.

[*Pause.*]

Fine. He's married already, so that can't be it.

SUSAN: Right.

RUSS [*to* SEVERINO]: You are getting better?

SEVERINO: Not at all.

RUSS [*to* SUSAN]: You're pregnant?!

SUSAN: Close.

RUSS [*to* SEVERINO]: You're pregnant!

SEVERINO: I'm a father!

RUSS: Oh. Oh. Oh.

SEVERINO: You're supposed to be happy for me.

RUSS: Wasn't he due in June?

SEVERINO: A couple of weeks premature. I was born a little premature too.

RUSS: And look what good it did you. What's his name?

SEVERINO: Claudio.

RUSS: Cute.

SUSAN: That's what I said.

SEVERINO: I hate it.

RUSS: Why?

SEVERINO: My father's name was Severino . . . so was my grandfather's.

RUSS: She did him a favor, then.

SUSAN: That's what I said.

SEVERINO: Fuck you both.

RUSS: You might never get a chance to meet him, who cares what he's called. He can start a new cycle. Here, you drink more wine. You deserve it.

SEVERINO: I really do. I'm coughing blood again too.

RUSS: For real?

SEVERINO: No, pretend blood.

[*Silence.*]

RUSS: You should have gotten two bottles.

SUSAN: I only have two hands.

RUSS: You shouldn't have bought flowers.

[*They drink wine in silence.*]

2.6 *JULY 1952*

[*A red-carpeted living room.* INÉS *sits quietly.* CELESTE *enters.*]

CELESTE: Is there coffee left?

INÉS: I thought you weren't talking to me.

CELESTE: Is there?

INÉS: Some from this morning.

CELESTE: I know your foot hurts, but can you please bring it to me?

INÉS: Ankle.

CELESTE: Black. No sugar.

INÉS: I know.

[INÉS *stands up with some difficulty and heads toward the kitchen.* CELESTE *sits down slowly.*]

CELESTE: I am never going to drink alcohol ever again. I know I always say that, but this time it's true. Why did I agree to do shots?

INÉS [*offstage*]: You always do.

CELESTE: Why do I always?

[INÉS *arrives with a cup of coffee.*]

CELESTE: It was fun though. Everyone asked about you.

INÉS: What did you tell them?

CELESTE: What you told me to tell them, that your foot hurt. Ankle. You should have been there.

INÉS: It wouldn't have made a difference.

CELESTE: It's so easy to hide, and you pass that stuff on.

INÉS: I'm not going to argue about this again.

CELESTE: The best part was when Lolita Lebrón spoke. She's so feisty. And elegant too.

INÉS: What did she talk about?

CELESTE: She said . . . [*Struggling to remember the exact words*] At least we now know exactly what we are. A colony. It is written.

INÉS: We've been saying that for years.

CELESTE: And now that we know, we can move forward. And then she talked about the importance of risking one's life for independence and that made me think we haven't done anything risky in a while. You should have come.

INÉS: My ankle was hurting.

CELESTE: You only had to walk to the square, which is the same as going to the bathroom and back.

INÉS: I'm not going to argue about this again.

CELESTE: Me neither. My head hurts.

[*She sips coffee.*]

Then everyone got really drunk, we danced, and I might have made out with Julio . . .

INÉS: Did Francisca make out with anybody?

[*They both laugh.*]

CELESTE: It hurts to laugh. Are you writing to Sevo?

INÉS: Huh? He who doesn't give doesn't receive.

CELESTE: He told me he hasn't gotten any letters from you in months.

INÉS: That would mean one of us is lying . . . you decide which one.

CELESTE: No, *merci*.

INÉS: You had no problem getting involved when you told him about Claudio Seguro.

CELESTE: I did you a favor.

INÉS: You did all three of us a favor.

2.7 JULY 1952

[SUSAN *and* SEVERINO *are naked under the blankets.*]

SUSAN: Still alive?

SEVERINO: Barely.

SUSAN: Do you want some water?

SEVERINO: Don't move. It's here. I see the light. I knew I was going to die naked.

SUSAN: I need water.

SEVERINO: Don't move. I see him, he approaches. He's—[*grabbing her hand*] wait. God is a woman?

SUSAN: She is and if she doesn't drink water real soon she's closing the gates to Heaven for eternally ever after.

SEVERINO: Don't close those heavenly gates yet. Not while I'm still living.

[*She starts to put some clothes on, leaving her pants on the floor.*]

SUSAN: Is that your passport on the floor?

SEVERINO: Yes, sir!

SUSAN: You might not want to lose that.

SEVERINO: I might not need it again, sir! Can you pick it up on your way here?

[*She's getting herself a glass of water.*]

SUSAN: If you can screw you can pick up a passport.

SEVERINO: True.

[*He sits up and looks for the passport. He finds a letter on the floor.*]

SEVERINO: What is this? I know this handwriting. Why is it addressed to you?

SUSAN [*treading carefully*]: I wrote to your wife some time ago. I wanted to know how the baby was doing.

SEVERINO: Why would you do that?

[*He starts looking through the letter.*]

SUSAN: I . . .

SEVERINO: What is Inés thanking you for?

SUSAN: Taking care of you.

SEVERINO: You kept her letters from me?

SUSAN: That was part of taking care of you.

SEVERINO: What letters is she talking about?

SUSAN: The last time you read one of her letters you were in bed for a week.

SEVERINO: How many have you hidden?

SUSAN: Vomiting blood. I was waiting for the right moment to give them to you.

SEVERINO: What better moment than still alive?

SUSAN: When I thought you could take it.

SEVERINO: I'm lucky I made it through that fuck.

SUSAN: You feel so much better without her.

SEVERINO: She's the mother of my son.

SUSAN: If you miss her so much, why haven't you left?

SEVERINO: I fell in love . . . with this city. And I met you.

SUSAN: I never asked you to stay.

SEVERINO: Never with words, but you begged me to, with your looks, your hands, with your food.

SUSAN: You always told me not to get too involved. That once you had enough money you would leave. I haven't seen you make any effort.

SEVERINO: I've been dying.

SUSAN: No, you've been living. Thanks to me.

SEVERINO: I thought she didn't want me near him—

SUSAN: *You* don't want to be near him. Meeting your son will make you realize what a failure you are.

[*He throws a punch at her. Pause. She punches him back. Pause. He coughs a little. She goes to the kitchen and pours him a glass of water.* SEVERINO *starts to cry.*]

SEVERINO: I don't deserve that water.

SUSAN: No one should be denied a glass of water.

SEVERINO: I've never been capable of punching anyone.

SUSAN: Should I feel special?

SEVERINO: I hate it. Punching, slapping, throwing, breaking. I hate violence. That's why I can't watch sports, that's why I didn't pass my army health test. I'm a pussy.

SUSAN: You are. A pussy-loving pussy.

[*He drinks water. Long silence.* RUSS *enters.*]

RUSS: Are Mommy and Daddy still fighting?

SUSAN: No, honey, you can come out now.

RUSS: I want a glass of water.

SUSAN: You can have it.

RUSS: Whose passport is that?

SEVERINO: Mine.

RUSS: You have an American passport? [*Picking it up*] Wait, this is not you. I didn't know you had a little sister.

SEVERINO: It's me.

RUSS [*with a girly voice*]: I hate violence, I can't take it anymore, I can't even watch baseball, the way the bat hits the ball is too much for me.

SEVERINO: Give me that. I do look like a girl.

[*Pause.*]

RUSS: I bet your kid is ugly as hell. With that monster of a mother he's got and you looking like a bearded fourteen-year-old girl.

SEVERINO: His mother is only a monster on the inside. Outside she is one of those people born to be stared at but completely oblivious to the fact. An undercover princess.

[SUSAN *gets up and disappears into the room.*]

RUSS: For a man who abhors violence, you're pretty good at hurting people.

[*Silence. They drink water.* SUSAN *comes back with a small pile of letters and throws them on the bed.*]

SEVERINO: Thanks.

RUSS: I don't want to be here for this. Good night, guys.

SUSAN: Good night.

[SEVERINO *starts to open the letters. As he skims through the first one, a flash of anger can be seen in him. He proceeds to read the rest of the letters.*]

2.8 *JULY 1952*

[*A confessional.*]

FRANCISCA: Hello. Hello. Can you hear me?

PADRE AURELIO: I can hear you fine.

FRANCISCA: Can you see me?

PADRE AURELIO: No.

FRANCISCA: I always thought it was the other way around, that you could see me but that I couldn't see you.

PADRE AURELIO: Depends on the confessional, how much room you have, budget cuts.

FRANCISCA: I see.

PADRE AURELIO: Someone hasn't been to confession in a while.

FRANCISCA: I only came that one time years ago, when I was ten. Remember?

PADRE AURELIO: Refresh my memory. I hear fifteen, twenty confessions a day.

FRANCISCA: How do you live like that?

PADRE AURELIO: The power of prayer.

FRANCISCA: What about it?

PADRE AURELIO: It gives me the strength to care.

FRANCISCA: Maybe you won't remember.

PADRE AURELIO: You can test me.

FRANCISCA: I told you about wanting to be a man. Sometimes. And that I entertained myself during mass fantasizing of a red devil showing up in the middle of the service, jumping from lamp to lamp, spitting fire and burning the whole thing down.

[*Pause.*]

Then I said that I never believed in God. You said it's human to doubt the existence of God and I said, "Oh, no, father. I have no doubt. No doubt at all." And then you cried.

PADRE AURELIO: I didn't cry.

FRANCISCA: You remember!

PADRE AURELIO: Francisca. Why are you here and not on your way to the cemetery?

FRANCISCA: I joined the procession for a while until I couldn't take it any longer.

PADRE AURELIO: It's really hot for a procession.

FRANCISCA: I like that. The praying, the weeping, the sleepwalking . . . I wanted to take longer to arrive, so I stopped and decided to retrace my steps. But I found myself lost.

PADRE AURELIO: You've come to the right place.

FRANCISCA: How so?

PADRE AURELIO: God loves the lost.

FRANCISCA: Why?

PADRE AURELIO: The lost of the world know not of God's love. That hurts him tremendously. We love the ones who hurt us the most.

FRANCISCA: But it was not my intention to come to church. I was using it as a shortcut. Did you know that? A lot of people use your church as a shortcut? Your church is as wide as the whole block.

PADRE AURELIO: Why come to confession if you are only shortcutting?

FRANCISCA: Isn't that the most perfect question you could ask? As I was crossing the church I decided to sit down on one of those wooden benches that are so uncomfortable wondering, why on earth are these benches so uncomfortable? Does worship need to be painful? I sat in painful silence staring at the passersby, the shortcutters. Have you ever done that? Stare at people walking? Where are they going? Why are they going where they're going and why does it look like there is a purpose to their going when most likely there isn't?

PADRE AURELIO: Do you have a purpose?

FRANCISCA: I think I do.

PADRE AURELIO: Do you want to tell me what it is?

FRANCISCA: No.

PADRE AURELIO: Can I guess?

FRANCISCA: You can try.

PADRE AURELIO: Are you involved in the burning of the flag during Severino's interment?

FRANCISCA: How do you know about that?

PADRE AURELIO: I hear twenty confessions a day. Are you involved?

FRANCISCA: I'm in charge of holding the babies in case something goes wrong.

PADRE AURELIO: Something will.

FRANCISCA: I've become that woman who holds other people's babies. I was holding Ramón during the procession today. He had no idea. He had no clue. I couldn't take that much happiness. I gave him back to his mother and came here to confess something I haven't done yet.

PADRE AURELIO: Do you want to tell me what it is?

FRANCISCA: I disagree with you, father, God doesn't love the lost. Only the lost love the lost.

2.9 *Later that day*

[*A rainy afternoon. A gazebo at the National Cemetery in Puerto Rico.* INÉS *sits in the only chair. The bed serves now as a coffin, where* SEVERINO *lies covered with an American flag.* FRANCISCA *stands next to* PADRE AURELIO. CELESTE *holds two babies.* GUTIÉRREZ *stands in the center. His uniform is a little too big on him. He reads from a wrinkled and sweaty piece of paper with carbon pencil scribbling on it.*]

GUTIÉRREZ [*mumbling a little*]: We are gathered here to honor a hero. Today, we say farewell to a man who gave a very important part of his life to the nation that gave him life. Thanks to the help of men like him, we are free to stand on this American soil and breathe the air of liberty. A comforting smell. A smell like no other in the world. [*Looking at the paper*] Severino Ramos—

CELESTE: Ramírez.

GUTIÉRREZ [*looking at the paper, clearing his throat*]: Ramírez . . . was part of the Sixty-fifth Infantry, and although he was never in combat he contributed to the fight against evil down in Panama. He was in charge of sorting the soldiers' mail. A very important job, for what's a soldier without his mail? His help is not unwelcome. It's thanks to people like Severino that the United States of America established herself at the very center of this side of the world, and the other side too. His death reminds us of how important it is to give. Give what? Everything. His death . . . is a real loss for America.

CELESTE: U.S. America.

[GUTIÉRREZ *puts a very small trumpet in his mouth. "Taps" is heard over the speakers, instead of from the trumpet that he is pretending to play.* PADRE AURELIO *laughs. A pair of soldiers begin to fold the flag, clumsily.* CELESTE *and* FRANCISCA *whisper to each other.*]

FRANCISCA: Shouldn't they be here by now?

CELESTE: I know.

FRANCISCA: Are you sure the guns are not real?

CELESTE: Old models without ammunition. They're like gardeners in military uniforms.

FRANCISCA: Give me the babies.

[*One of the soldiers gives* INÉS *the folded flag. He whispers something in her ear. The trumpet is no longer heard.*]

GUTIÉRREZ: This is the moment when, if there is anyone who would like to say some words in honor of the hero, you may.

[*Silence.* CELESTE *looks around, sees nothing.*]

CELESTE: Um . . . I was his sister.

[*Pause.*]

I wanted to say that . . . I never saw my brother as a hero . . . I don't think he considered himself that or that he even wanted to, much less in the way that you describe him. So I am going to ask you to take back your flag. We don't want it.

INÉS: Celeste, what are you saying?

CELESTE: Please, sir. Take back your flag.

INÉS: Celeste.

GUTIÉRREZ: Sure. If you don't want it.

INÉS: I want it.

CELESTE: No, you don't.

INÉS: Yes, I do.

GUTIÉRREZ: She said she wants it.

CELESTE: She doesn't.

INÉS: I do.

CELESTE: She's confused.

GUTIÉRREZ: Her husband died.

INÉS: I'm not confused.

CELESTE [*to* FRANCISCA]: Where are they?

INÉS: Who? Francisca.

FRANCISCA: What?

INÉS: Who is she waiting for?

FRANCISCA: I'm not a part of this.

INÉS: Part of what? [*To* CELESTE] Can you stop moving and tell me what's going on?

CELESTE: They had until about now to get here.

INÉS: Who?

FRANCISCA: Tell her.

CELESTE: No.

INÉS: Tell me what?

CELESTE: No.

INÉS: Francisca?

FRANCISCA: Celeste, Julio, and Pedro plotted to steal the flag and burn it.

GUTIÉRREZ: That's illegal.

INÉS: You were plotting to burn the flag? Stop looking around! Tell me.

CELESTE: Yes.

INÉS: Have you lost your mind?

CELESTE: You've burned many flags before.

INÉS: It's your brother's burial.

CELESTE: Didn't it bother you to see his body covered in a flag that's not his?

INÉS: He didn't have a flag, he didn't care about any flags.

GUTIÉRREZ: Let her keep it.

CELESTE: Nobody asked you. Inés, give me the flag and we'll burn it later.

GUTIÉRREZ: They'll arrest you for that.

INÉS: I am not burning the flag. No one's burning any flags.

CELESTE: What do you want it for?

INÉS: I don't *want* an American flag.

GUTIÉRREZ: Then give it back to us. We'll use it.

INÉS: I'm not giving you anything. I don't want it but it's mine. It's not *a* flag. It's the only thing left I have of my husband.

FRANCISCA: You have Claudio.

INÉS: I know I have Claudio. But this is different. It represents him. That's where he died. So even though I hate it I am keeping it. We are keeping it. You may continue with the ceremony, sir.

GUTIÉRREZ: We're done.

INÉS: What about the burial?

GUTIÉRREZ: We take care of that ourselves.

INÉS: What do you mean?

GUTIÉRREZ: You stay here while we put him on the truck and drive him to his hole in the ground. Have a good day. You stay here, Father.

PADRE AURELIO: I have to come bless the ground where he will be buried.

GUTIÉRREZ: We have no time for that.

PADRE AURELIO: It'll only take a couple of seconds, I sprinkle some water on the site, circle it with the incense—

GUTIÉRREZ: This is not a Catholic cemetery.

PADRE AURELIO: All the more reason. This land needs to be blessed in order to receive his body properly. I baptized him myself.

GUTIÉRREZ: This is a federal land. It already is blessed. Have a good day, Father.

[*The soldiers exit. The sound of a truck approaching can be heard.* PADRE AURELIO *practices the rite of blessing the land in the place where the body had been laying before. He does this more for himself than out of duty, almost whispering.* INÉS *cries.*]

PADRE AURELIO: Deus, cujus miseratione animæ fidelium requiescunt, hunc tumulum benedicere dignare, eique Angelum tuum sanctum deputa custodem: et quorum quarumque corpora hic sepeliuntur, animas eorum ab omnibus absolve vinculis delictorum; ut in te semper cum Sanctis tuis sine fine lætentur. Per Christum Dominum nostrum. Amen.

CELESTE [*after the sounds of the truck leaving have vanished, even if Aurelio is still practicing his ritual*]: Inés, please. Let us burn it. This is not right. It won't do anybody any harm. It will make us laugh and keep us warm. Please let us burn it.

PREMEDITATION

Evelina Fernández

Production photograph by Ed Krieger for the Latino Theater Company

CRITICAL INTRODUCTION

Grace Dávila-López

Evelina Fernández is a longstanding Chicana *teatrista* who has been involved in various aspects of theater- and filmmaking in Los Angeles—as a theater and film actress, a playwright and film and television script writer,[1] and an activist—since the late seventies. She is first and foremost one of the founding members of the Latino Theater Company (LTC), where she is playwright-in-residence. Fernández has written at least a dozen major plays, and has received accolades and prestigious awards such as the "L.A. Drama Critics Circle Award for Outstanding Writing of a World Premiere Play" (2012) for *A Mexican Trilogy*. Still, most of her plays are not yet published, or not easily accessible, and most commentaries on her work are found in Los Angeles–based theater reviews, online pieces, and interviews. The publication of *Premeditation*—its staged production described as "a Chicano-Noir inspired journey through the intricacies of marriage"[2]—is a momentous opportunity to get acquainted with Fernández's artistic trajectory, her work, and her important place in Chicanx theater.

Fernández, who was born and raised in East Los Angeles, started writing short stories and delivering speeches in elementary school, and became interested in theater during her years at Garfield High School. During the course of her studies at California State University, Los Angeles (CSULA), she got involved in the Chicano movement, and, consequently, in Chicano theater. While at CSULA, Fernández auditioned and was cast in the leading role of Della in Luis Valdez's historic staging of *Zoot Suit*, which opened in 1978 at the Mark Taper Forum. By 1981, Fernández had become a member of the legendary Teatro de la Esperanza, which at the time was located in Santa Barbara. Her experiences with El Teatro Campesino and Teatro de la Esperanza influenced her theater themes and aesthetic views, and made it possible for her to establish long-term personal and working relationships. These include Mexican director José Luis Valenzuela (whom she married), and long-time fellow actors Sal López, Geoffrey Rivas, Lucy Rodríguez, and Lupe Ontiveros (d. 2012), founding members of the Latino Theater Company (LTC),[3] all of whom she considers her theater family.[4] In 1985, Fernández relocated to Los Angeles and has been a member of this important theater group. Her plays have been influenced and molded by the collaborative work method of the ensemble, as she specifically writes for the actors in the group.

Premeditation, just like its title suggests, revolves around a plot to commit a crime. It presents two couples embittered by the frustration of constant arguing. Throughout the play, the differences between both couples become obvious. Esmeralda and Fernando are a well-educated, upscale, middle-aged couple; she is a sophisticated lady with a penchant for thesaurus words, he is a UCLA literature professor. They have recently become empty nesters. Of Mauricio and Lydia, we learn that he is a hit man, and she is a feisty, foul-mouthed housewife who doesn't need a dictionary to call things the way she sees them. Later we learn they have children, and are struggling to make ends meet. Turmoil is evident for both couples as domestic recriminations between husbands and wives overlap in what seems like rapid crossfire. Ironically, regardless of their differences in social background, both couples experience the same kind of cliché marital problems stemming from lack of interest and miscommunication. Thus, the first scene culminates in both husbands asking their wives, "What are you talking about?"—a phrase that will be repeated throughout the play. This beginning points to what seems like never-ending conjugal dissatisfaction. That is, until Esmeralda hires Mauricio as a final solution to her desperation. The rest of the play becomes an arena for the war of the sexes, and it leads to a reflection on marriage, love, and self-preservation. It also becomes a playground for comedic farce, humorous situations, and melodramatic moments that makes us wonder whether Esmeralda's actions will lead to an affair, or to murder.

First presented in the spring of 2014, *Premeditation* was brought back to the L.A. stage in the fall for Encuentro 2014.[5] A one-act version of *Premeditation* dates back to 1992, but it only features two characters: Esmeralda, the desperate wife, and Mauricio, the hit man.[6] It is interesting to note that in the one-act version, Esmeralda comes to realize her husband and her marriage are worth saving, but in the 2014 version, she is not convinced her marriage can be fixed. A constant of Evelina Fernández's plays is the presence of strong female characters and supportive female relationships. Accordingly, the addition of Lydia, who identifies with Esmeralda's marital frustrations and offers her moral support, might be crucial in the final outcome of the 2014 version. But the fact that Mauricio and Lydia are able to rekindle their love might also emphasize Lydia and Esmeralda's different circumstances. Thanks to Esmeralda's lessons in romance, Mauricio understands that for a marriage to work, "You have to set the scene. It has to be planned, thought out, well considered . . ." In other words, "it has to be premeditated." But Esmeralda's marriage has become an empty lie, which is making her crazy, as when she comments: "I look at the mirror and I don't recognize who I've become." Feeling disconnected from her true self, Esperanza realizes the real solution to her dissatisfaction does not lie in Fernando, but in herself.

The staging of *Premeditation*—as developed by the LTC, directed by José Luis Valenzuela—attests to the rich complementary relationship between Fernández's writing and the ensemble work. The play's text offers limited stage directions, but at the LTC's hands, *Premeditation* becomes a beautifully orchestrated theatrical experience. The set design, lighting, and costumes create a dramatic, "L.A. noir" atmosphere. The play's prologue, for example, becomes a sensuously choreographed tango in which the actors enter the stage individually, each one dancing at their own rhythm with the stage furnishings: a chair, a mirror, a clothing rack. The characters become fully alive, with Fernández playing the role of Esmeralda, Sal López as Mauricio, Lucy Rodríguez as Lydia, and Geoffrey Rivas as Fernando. The seductive tango music comes together to create a poetic ambience suited for the fine-tuned tempo and sensuously melodramatic acting of the ensemble. In subsequent scene changes, the actors will double their roles as hotel assistants, as well as stage crew. Throughout the play, the gigantic black and white projections—of lit cigarettes, puffing mouths, lips, smoke, eyelashes, transfixed stares, etc.—elegantly emphasize the noir style, enhancing the moods brewing in the characters' consciousness. This would be a play realistically set in the 1940s, but the plot relies strategically on the use of cell phones, specifically the iPhone, with its GPS capability and its Apple ID features. This intersection of space and time continuums adds deeply layered meanings to the conflicts represented, and it showcases the LTC's talent for humor and creative collaborative work.

Contrary to Fernández's previous plays, *Premeditation* is set in a world intentionally devoid of Chicanx-centered situations. There are no overt references to immigration, wars, or the historical present. The plot doesn't revolve around family histories or generation gaps, and there is no turmoil associated with overtly social or political issues. Also, the dialogue does not include as much Spanish-peppered language as previous plays, only a few words at most. The characters have Spanish names, but in the staged version they are pronounced mostly with English intonation. In that context, Fernando's effort to correct the hotel attendant's pronunciation from Riviera to Rivera becomes a funny contradiction. These are definitely not conventional Latinx characters either, Esmeralda prefers scotch rather than the *ron* included in her hotel room's full bar; Mauricio prefers bourbon, and he is a Trojans fan; Fernando drives a Volvo, and eats soyrizo from Trader Joe's; and Lydia's love letter is verbatim the lyrics to a Marvin Gaye song. These characters are very much at ease in their American context, which seems like an intentional breakaway from stereotypes. Nonetheless, there is an effort to disambiguate the characters' heritage. In a reference to the times when Esmeralda and Fernando were known as Esme and Fernie, Esmeralda clarifies, this was before "... we discovered our roots and reclaimed our birth names." There is also a very funny moment when Fernando, as he is defending his effort to be a good husband, says, " ... I love the opera and classical music, fine art, and I appreciate and cherish the wonderful things about being Chicano, and I love our culture"; as if to remind us, with a wink, that these are still Chicanx characters.

Premeditation exemplifies Fernández's ability to create inventive dramatic situations with character development well grounded on a solid command of dialogue, and a flair for humorous situations and playful language. The staged version of the play also attests to the Latino Theater Company's tradition of collaborative work, which is evident in the artistry in developing the noir atmosphere, and the ensemble's solid command of acting, tempo, and flawless delivery of lines. In terms of the theme, the author stays true to her commitment to create new and interesting roles for Latinx actors. Just like Esmeralda, who liberates herself from self-constraints in an experimental move, Evelina Fernández's exploration of new thematic territories keeps her work premeditatedly relevant.

NOTES

This introduction is an updated and shortened version of an introduction to *Premeditation* originally published in *Gestos* 59 (April 2015): 83–89.

1. For a list of Fernandez's filmography credits, go to www.imdb.com/name/nm0273490/.
2. This quote comes from an LATC marketing blurb about the play.
3. The group originally formed at the LATC as the Latino Theater Lab.
4. Evelina Fernández. "Evelina Fernández—In Her Own Words." latinopia.com. June 15, 2010. Accessed May 17, 2017. http://latinopia.com/latino-theater/evelina-Fernández-in-her-own-words/.
5. For a review of this event, see Jorge Huerta, "Encuentro 2014: Latina/o Theater Moving Forward," *Gestos* 59 (April 2015): 173–188.
6. Evelina Fernández, *Premeditation. Latino Literature: Poetry, Drama & Fiction* (Alexandria, Va..: Alexander Street Press, 2006). This one-act version of the play was staged at La Plaza de la Raza, Los Angeles in 1995. It was later adapted to the screen by Alberto Barboza. It received a Best Short Film Award at the Los Angeles Latino International Film Festival (2004), and it was aired on Showtime (2005).

BIBLIOGRAPHY

Coates, José Benjamín. "El teatro representado en español en Los Ángeles: lazos culturales y desafíos comunes." *Gestos* 56 (November 2013): 148–57.

Fernández, Evelina. *A Mexican Trilogy*. London: Samuel French, 2015.

———. *How Else Am I Supposed to Know I Am Still Alive? Contemporary Plays by Women of Color*. Kathy A. Perkins and Roberto Uno, eds., 160–67. New York: Routledge, 1996.

———. Correspondence via personal e-mail. January 2, 2015.

———. "Evelina Fernández—In Her Own Words." latinopia.com. July 15, 2010. Accessed Jan 2, 2015. http://latinopia.com/latino-theater/evelina-Fernández-in-her-own-words/.

———. *Premeditation. (One-act play). Latino Literature: Poetry, Drama & Fiction*. Alexandria, Va: Alexander Street Press, 2006.

Geirola, Gustavo. "Visualidad/visibilidad: la teatralidad del teatro y el fetichismo. *Luminarias* de Evelina Fernández." *Gestos* 25 (1998): 51–73.

Huerta, Jorge. "Encuentro 2014: Latina/o Theater Moving Forward" *Gestos* 59 (April 2015): 173–88.

——— and Carlos Morton, "A Conversational Review of *Solitude* by Evelina Fernández." *Gestos* 50 (November 2010): 201–4.

Kearns, Carol. "The Latino Theater Company's *Premeditation*." HowlRound. Nov. 13, 2014. Accessed May 17, 2017. http://howlround.com/the-latino-theater-companys-premeditation.

LATC [Los Angeles Theatre Center]—*Premeditation*. n.d. Jan 15, 2015. http://thelatc.org/upcoming-shows/premeditation/.

Latino Theater Company Digital Archive. N.d. May 17, 2017. www.latinotheatercompany.net.

Rampell, Ed. "Evelina Fernández and Her Contributions to *Charity*." L.A. Stage Alliance. May 8, 2012. Accessed May 17, 2017. http://thisstage.la/2012/05/evelina-fernandez-and-her-contributions-to-charity/.

PRODUCTION HISTORY

A one-act version of *Premeditation* was developed with the Latino Theater Company in 1992 and was also adapted into a short film by Alberto Barboza in 2004.

Premeditation was developed with the Latino Theater Company and premiered at the Los Angeles Theatre Center (LATC) on April 19, 2014. It was directed by José Luis Valenzuela, with set design by Francois-Pierre Couture, lighting and projection design by Pablo Santiago, sound design by John Zalewski, costume design by Naila Aladdin Sanders, and choreography by Urbanie Lucero. Henry "Heno" Fernandez was the stage manager; Esperanza America was the assistant stage manager; and the technical director was Wayne Nakasone.

The cast of the original production was as follows:

Esmeralda . . . . .Evelina Fernández

Mauricio . . . . Sal Lopez

Lydia . . . . .Lucy Rodriguez

Fernando . . . . Geoffrey Rivas

Premeditation was remounted for the 2014 Encuentro Festival at the Los Angeles Theatre Center with the same cast and creative team as above. It was subsequently presented at ArtsEmerson in May 2016, where the role of Lydia was played by Angela Moya.

CHARACTERS

Esmeralda

Mauricio

Lydia

Fernando

Waiter, played by the actor who plays Fernando

Bellboy, played by the actor who plays Fernando

Hotel Clerk, played by the actor who plays Lydia

PROLOGUE

[Music plays throughout as lights go up on an elegant middle-aged woman, ESMERALDA, *wearing a beautiful Chinese robe. She sits at her dressing table. She looks at herself in the mirror and begins to put on her jewelry: a necklace, earrings, a ring.*

Lights go up on a middle-aged man, MAURICIO, *standing before a mirror wearing pants and a T-shirt. He looks at himself and begins to get dressed: a shirt, a tie, a sharp-looking coat.*

ESMERALDA *looks at herself in the mirror, long and hard.*

MAURICIO*'s wife,* LYDIA, *with bleached blonde hair, black eyeliner, and red lips, enters, interrupting his ritual. She has a shirt in her hand.*

ESMERALDA*'s husband,* FERNANDO, *enters wearing a terry cloth robe and a towel around his neck. He wears thick-rimmed glasses and his hair is wild. He carries a newspaper underneath his arm. He tosses the wet towel on the bed.*

The music ends.

The following dialogue overlaps between both couples.]

FERNANDO: Have you seen my brown jacket?

ESMERALDA: The corduroy one? I took it to the cleaners.

FERNANDO: I just had it cleaned.

ESMERALDA: It looked dirty.

FERNANDO: But it wasn't.

ESMERALDA: So, you want to wear a dirty-looking jacket?

FERNANDO: Who cares?

ESMERALDA: I care.

FERNANDO: Why?

ESMERALDA: You're right. If you don't care, why should I? It's not a reflection on me.

LYDIA: Why do you have to be so messy? Why do you wear white shirts everyday, anyway?

ESMERALDA: But I'm sure some people will think it is a reflection on me because I'm your wife . . .

LYDIA: It's not like you work in an office or anything. I can't get these stains out of your shirt!

FERNANDO: What are you talking about?

MAURICIO: What are you talking about?

ESMERALDA: Don't say that!

LYDIA: You know what I'm talking about.

ESMERALDA: You know I hate that.

LYDIA: It's what I'm always talking about. Your dirty shirts.

FERNANDO: OK, I'm sorry.

MAURICIO: I like to look nice, OK? It's my work ethic.

LYDIA: Work ethic? You haven't worked for months.

ESMERALDA: Do you have to drop food on your clothes every time you eat?

LYDIA: Why don't you try working around here sometime?

ESMERALDA: You don't put food in your mouth, you toss it in.

LYDIA: Why don't you get your junk out of the closets or clean the garage!

ESMERALDA: That's why it ends up on your shirts and your ties.

FERNANDO: What are you talking about?

LYDIA: And don't say, "What are you talking?" You know I hate it when you say that.

MAURICIO: What are you talking about?

LYDIA: I'm talking about you always saying, "What are you talking about?" Because you know it burns my ass!

FERNANDO: Nobody's going to care about a little grease stain. Nobody's going to notice.

ESMERALDA: I did . . .

MAURICIO: You're nuts, you know that? Honestly, I think you're losing it.

FERNANDO: That's because you were looking for it.

ESMERALDA: No I wasn't!

FERNANDO: Yes, you were!

LYDIA: Losing it? I lost it a long time ago! I lost it the day I married you! I must have been crazy!

ESMERALDA: No, I wasn't!

FERNANDO: OK, fine, you weren't.

ESMERALDA: I wasn't what?

MAURICIO: Good, you admit it, you're nuts!

FERNANDO: You weren't looking for the chorizo stain.

ESMERALDA: Chorizo? Is that what it was? With your cholesterol?

FERNANDO: It was soyrizo, OK. From Trader Joe's . . .

LYDIA: That's right. I'm fucking nuts!

[*Silence.*]

ESMERALDA: Did you make the appointment to get your car serviced?

LYDIA: When *are* you gonna clean the garage?

FERNANDO: I'm going to.

ESMERALDA: When?

LYDIA: I've been asking you for weeks.

FERNANDO: Today.

MAURICIO: Weeks? Don't exaggerate. It hasn't been weeks.

LYDIA: You're right, it's been months. Two months to be exact!

ESMERALDA: You said that yesterday.

LYDIA: Ever since you had the incident.

MAURICIO: Here we go. You had to bring it up, didn't you? Not a day goes by without you bringing up the incident.

LYDIA: That's not true. I didn't bring it up yesterday.

FERNANDO: I forgot yesterday.

ESMERALDA: And you'll probably forget today.

MAURICIO: Because I was gone all day . . .

LYDIA: But, I didn't bring it up, did I?

FERNANDO: I won't forget.

MAURICIO: . . . and by the time I got home you were in bed.

ESMERALDA: How do you know you won't?

LYDIA: But, I didn't bring it up . . .

FERNANDO: You just reminded me.

LYDIA: Did I?

ESMERALDA: I reminded you yesterday.

FERNANDO: I was busy yesterday.

MAURICIO: You're not only nuts . . .

ESMERALDA: And you're not busy today?

FERNANDO: I am, but . . .

MAURICIO: . . .you're neurotic . . .

LYDIA: Aw, shut up!

ESMERALDA: Do you want me to make the appointment for you?

FERNANDO: That would be great!

ESMERALDA: Why would I have to make the appointment to service your car?

FERNANDO: Because you just offered to.

LYDIA: You don't even know what neurotic means.

ESMERALDA: It wasn't an offer!

MAURICIO: Yes, I do!

ESMERALDA: It was a question!

FERNANDO: Then the answer is no.

ESMERALDA: No?

LYDIA: You know what, forget it!

FERNANDO: If I say yes you'll get upset . . .

LYDIA: I'm throwing these fucking shirts away!

ESMERALDA: I'm already upset!

MAURICIO AND FERNANDO: What are you talking about?

SCENE 1

[ESMERALDA *and* MAURICIO*'s house.* ESMERALDA *looks at the phone for a moment, picks it up and dials.* MAURICIO*'s phone rings on the other end.* MAURICIO *answers the phone.*]

MAURICIO: Hello?

ESMERALDA: Hello?

MAURICIO: Yes?

ESMERALDA: It's me.

MAURICIO: Yes? I was hoping you'd call.

ESMERALDA: I've decided . . .

MAURICIO: Yes?

ESMERALDA: Let's . . . well, you know.

MAURICIO: OK. Where should I meet you?

ESMERALDA: The Shangrila Hotel. I'll meet you in the restaurant.

[*Her voice trails off. Music plays as* ESMERALDA *and* MAURICIO *make their way to the Shangrila Hotel as the actors change the scene.*]

SCENE 2

[*Hotel restaurant.* ESMERALDA *enters wearing a scarf and sunglasses, carrying a small suitcase and a clutch purse. She looks around, looks at her watch. She sits.* MAURICIO *enters, wearing dark glasses. He stops, looks around, takes off his dark glasses and smiles.*]

MAURICIO: Hi.

ESMERALDA: Hi.

MAURICIO: I'm sorry I'm late.

ESMERALDA: Are you? I hadn't noticed.

MAURICIO: Were you careful that no one was following you?

ESMERALDA: Yes. Were you?

MAURICIO: Yes.

[*Pause.*]

You look . . .

ESMERALDA: Yes?

MAURICIO: . . . nervous.

ESMERALDA: I am. I've never done this before.

MAURICIO: Don't worry. It'll be fine.

ESMERALDA: How do I know that I can trust you not to tell anyone?

MAURICIO: I would never do that.

ESMERALDA: How do I know that?

MAURICIO: Didn't I come highly recommended?

ESMERALDA: Yes. But she was just another desperate woman like me.

MAURICIO: Most of the women I . . . [*searching for the word*] . . . service are. Look, if you want to change your mind . . .

ESMERALDA: No. It's just that it feels so . . . planned, so thought out, so prearranged, so intentional, so calculated. It feels so . . . premeditated.

MAURICIO: It's the only way. You don't want to get caught, do you?

ESMERALDA: No.

MAURICIO: Neither do I.

[*A waiter enters with two drinks and the check.*]

WAITER: Your drinks, Madam.

[ESMERALDA *places her credit card in the check holder.*]

ESMERALDA: Thank you.

[*The waiter leaves.*]

MAURICIO: I know you'll probably feel guilty.

ESMERALDA: Of course I will. We've been married for twenty-five years.

MAURICIO: And it's understandable.

ESMERALDA: We've made a life together.

MAURICIO: That's why I told you to take your time, think about it before you decided. You have to be sure you want to go through with this because if there's any doubt, any doubt at all . . .

ESMERALDA: No, I have thought about it. I want to. I really do.

MAURICIO: OK.

[*At* MAURICIO*'s house.* LYDIA *goes through the laundry. She cleans out his pants pocket and pulls out a piece of paper. She reads it.*]

LYDIA: Esmeralda? Who the fuck is Esmeralda?

[*She dials* MAURICIO*'s number. At the restaurant,* MAURICIO*'s phone rings. He reaches for it and turns off the ringer.*]

MAURICIO [*to* ESMERALDA]: Sorry about that.

[LYDIA *sends* MAURICIO *a text.*]

LYDIA [*while texting*]: Who the fuck is *Esmeralda*?

[*At the restaurant,* ESMERALDA *slides a key card across the table.*]

ESMERALDA: Here's the key. I'll go up first and meet you in the room.

[*As* MAURICIO *reaches for the key card their hands touch. They look at each other.*]

SCENE 3

[MAURICIO*'s house.* LYDIA *dials the number on the piece of paper. At* ESMERALDA's *house, lights up on* FERNANDO *at home in front of his computer. The phone rings once, twice. He looks over at it and decides to answer.*]

FERNANDO: Hello?

[*Lights up on* LYDIA.]

LYDIA: Who's this?

FERNANDO: Who would you like to speak to?

LYDIA: Esmeralda.

FERNANDO: Esmeralda's not home. This is her husband.

LYDIA: Her husband?

FERNANDO: May I take a message or tell her who called?

LYDIA: She has a husband? That fucking bitch!

FERNANDO: Who is this?

[LYDIA *hangs up.*]

Hello? Hello? [*To himself*] That's peculiar.

[*Transitional music.*]

SCENE 4

[*Hotel room.* ESMERALDA *enters with a* BELLBOY *who puts down her suitcase, opens the curtains, and shows her the bathroom. She tips him.*]

ESMERALDA: I ordered a full bar.

BELLBOY: Yes, ma'am . . .

ESMERALDA: Charge it to the room.

BELLBOY: Yes, ma'am.

[*He exits. She goes to the table and lights a cigarette. There's a knock on the door. She goes to the door.*]

ESMERALDA: Yes?

MAURICIO [*offstage*]: It's me.

[ESMERALDA *opens the door.* MAURICIO *enters and cases the room.*]

ESMERALDA: Didn't I give you a key?

MAURICIO: I lost it.

[*She looks annoyed.*]

ESMERALDA: Let's go over the details.

MAURICIO: Again? I don't like to do that. It lessens the rush for me.

ESMERALDA: Just once more.

MAURICIO [*sighing*]: OK.

[ESMERALDA's *phone rings. She picks up the phone, then looks at* MAURICIO, *startled.*]

ESMERALDA: It's him, my husband, Fernando.

MAURICIO: Don't answer. Where does he think you are?

ESMERALDA: I don't know. He doesn't care. He never calls . . .

MAURICIO: Don't answer. Put it on vibrate.

[ESMERALDA *fumbles with her phone.*]

ESMERALDA: Vibrate? I don't know how to do that. I'm always pushing the wrong button.

[MAURICIO *takes her phone and puts it on vibrate and tosses the phone on the bed.* MAURICIO *takes off his hat and lies down.*]

MAURICIO: OK, tell me how you want to do this.

[ESMERALDA *takes a deep breath.*]

ESMERALDA: OK . . .

[*She takes a drag on her cigarette.*]

He'll leave his office at the university at approximately four forty-five.

MAURICIO: He'll go south down the hallway and probably stop off at the men's room.

ESMERALDA: It's a long drive home.

MAURICIO: He'll leave the men's room and walk out of the north wing, second floor door, walk down the stairs, and head toward parking lot A.

ESMERALDA: He has a faculty parking pass.

MAURICIO: He'll go directly to his car—a 2010 Volvo—silver, with black leather interior.

ESMERALDA: You'll recognize it because it'll be the dirtiest car in the parking structure. It'll probably have Cheetos or Doritos bags thrown on the dash.

MAURICIO: When he reaches the car, he'll open the trunk.

ESMERALDA: That's when you'll shoot him, push him into the trunk, and take his briefcase. You said you had a silencer.

MAURICIO: Yes.

[*He shows her his gun.*]

But I like it loud.

SCENE 5

[ESMERALDA*'s house.* FERNANDO *dials the phone. Lights up on* LYDIA, *who is all bunched up. The phone rings and she looks at it. As* FERNANDO *is about to hang up—*]

LYDIA: Hello?

FERNANDO: Oh, hello. I think you may have called this number a few minutes ago looking for my wife, Esmeralda . . .

LYDIA: Yeah? So what?

FERNANDO: Who is this?

LYDIA: Lydia. Who's this?

FERNANDO: Fernando.

LYDIA: So?

FERNANDO: Well, you hung up so abruptly and you seemed surprised by the fact that she has a husband . . .

LYDIA: Yeah? So what?

FERNANDO: I'm just curious as to why you are trying to reach her . . .

LYDIA: You really wanna know?

[*Pause.*]

FERNANDO: Yes.

LYDIA: Because I found her fucking number in my husband's pants pocket . . .

FERNANDO: And may I ask who your husband is?

LYDIA: No, you may not!

FERNANDO: Well, that's not playing fair, is it?

LYDIA: Playing? Who's playing? What, you think this is a fucking game? It's not!

FERNANDO: Now, now, there's no need to use profanity. I'm simply trying to obtain some information here. You called my home asking for my wife and I'd just like to know why . . .

LYDIA: I'll tell you why! Because she's screwing my husband, that's why.

FERNANDO: You're kidding, right?

LYDIA: No, I'm not kidding!

FERNANDO: My wife? Are you sure you have the right Esmeralda?

LYDIA: Well, it was her name and her number in my husband's pants' pocket.

FERNANDO: I'm sure there's a logical explanation. She's involved in many philanthropic and community activities . . .

LYDIA: This ain't philanthropic, although you might call it a community activity or a community service.

SCENE 6

[*Hotel room.*]

ESMERALDA: You'll find your final payment in his briefcase in an envelope in the very top compartment.

MAURICIO: In his briefcase? How do you know he won't find it there?

ESMERALDA: He won't.

MAURICIO: How do you know?

ESMERALDA: Because that's where I leave his daily "to-do" list and he never does anything I ask him to. He never looks there. Never. Is it clear?

MAURICIO: Yes.

ESMERALDA: Good. [*Referring to the suitcase on the bed*] The sweatshirt is in the suitcase along with your cash advance.

MAURICIO: Medium?

ESMERALDA: Pardon me?

MAURICIO: The sweatshirt.

ESMERALDA: They were out. I got you a large.

[*He pulls out the sweatshirt. It says* UCLA BRUINS.]

MAURICIO: UCLA?

ESMERALDA: Is it a problem?

MAURICIO: Well . . . I am a Trojans fan.

ESMERALDA: What?

MAURICIO: And I obviously wear a small. I'll call attention to myself if I look ridiculous.

ESMERALDA: So, what do you want to wear . . . [*looking at what he's wearing*] that?

MAURICIO: What's wrong with this?

ESMERALDA: Talk about ridiculous. Wear the sweatshirt. They'll think you're a . . . janitor or a proud father or something.

[*He gives her a look. He takes the money out of the suitcase and puts it in his inside coat pocket. He takes out a Thomas Guide.*]

MAURICIO: What's this?

ESMERALDA: A Thomas Guide.

MAURICIO: A what?

ESMERALDA: A map. You do know what a map is, don't you?

MAURICIO: I don't need it, I've cased the joint. I know where I'm going.

ESMERALDA: What if you get stuck in traffic and have to take the side streets?

MAURICIO: I know my way around the city . . .

ESMERALDA: Take it. Just in case . . .

MAURICIO: I already told you . . .

ESMERALDA: You wouldn't want to have to ask someone for directions, would you?

MAURICIO: I don't need it. I have a GPS.

ESMERALDA: Where?

MAURICIO: Where what?

ESMERALDA: Where do you have the GPS?

MAURICIO: On my smart phone.

ESMERALDA: What if you have an accident and you become incapacitated? What if the first responders find your phone? What if they look at your GPS and trace you to the scene of the crime?

MAURICIO: They can do that?

ESMERALDA: I don't know. But, I don't trust the government, do you?

MAURICIO: No.

[*He thinks, then takes the Thomas Guide. He takes a book out of the suitcase.*]

[*Reading*] Webster's New World The . . . Thes . . . what?

ESMERALDA: Thesaurus . . . [*taking the book*] it's mine. I read.

[HOTEL CLERK *appears at the front desk, on the phone. The hotel room phone rings.* MAURICIO *and* ESMERALDA *go to the table and stare at it. It stops ringing.*]

SCENE 7

[ESMERALDA's *house.* FERNANDO *sits at his computer. The phone rings and he goes to answer it. He is sure that it's* ESMERALDA.]

FERNANDO: There you are . . .

HOTEL CLERK: Hello? May I speak with Ms. Esmeralda Riviera?

FERNANDO: Rivera. Esmeralda Rivera.

HOTEL CLERK: Yes, that's what I said, Esmeralda Riviera. Is she home?

FERNANDO: No, she isn't. This is her husband, Mr. Rivera. Who, may I ask, is calling?

HOTEL CLERK: Well, Mr. Riviera, I'm calling from the Shangrila Hotel.

FERNANDO: Shangrila Hotel?

HOTEL CLERK: Yes, please let Ms. Riviera know that she forgot her credit card at the hotel restaurant and that we'll keep it for her at the front desk.

FERNANDO: The front desk? Wait a minute. I know what this is. Am I being punked?

SCENE 8

[*Hotel room.* MAURICIO *closes the suitcase and heads toward the door.* ESMERALDA *throws herself on the bed. He stops.*]

MAURICIO: Just one question.

ESMERALDA: Yes?

MAURICIO: Why do you want your husband killed?

ESMERALDA: What does it matter?

MAURICIO: If I'm gonna kill someone, I need to know why.

[*She gives him a look.*]

It doesn't have to be a good reason. Just a reason.

ESMERALDA: Oh, I have my reasons. I have lots of reasons.

MAURICIO: I just need one.

ESMERALDA: He leaves his underwear on the bathroom floor after he showers.

[*He nods, turns toward the door, then stops.*]

MAURICIO: Give me another one.

ESMERALDA: You said you needed one.

MAURICIO: That's not a reason.

ESMERALDA: It's a reason. One of many.

MAURICIO: Give me another one.

ESMERALDA: Look, you got your money and you got your reason. Now go.

MAURICIO: I can't kill a man for leaving his underwear on the floor.

ESMERALDA: What kind of hit man are you?

MAURICIO: One with a conscience.

ESMERALDA: Of all the hit men in all the gin joints in East L.A., I had to hire one with a conscience. It figures. It's just my luck.

[*She puts her cigarette out in the ashtray, hard. She thinks.*]

It's not just the underwear.

MAURICIO: What then?

ESMERALDA: It's him leaving wet towels on the bed. It's his filthy car. It's him reading the paper and pretending that he's listening to me when I know he's not. It's him ordering movies that he knows I won't like. It's him not taking responsibility for anything unless I remind him to. It's about me always having to be in control!

MAURICIO: Is that it?

ESMERALDA: No, there's more! Much more. These "issues" may seem insignificant to you, but when you have to put up with them for over twenty-five years . . . You think it's easy to have to remind someone to rotate the tires, to pick up the toilet seat and try not to dribble on the floor? Do you think it's easy to have to be on top of it all the time? It isn't! You have to kill him because he's driving me crazy!

MAURICIO: Hold on. Let me ask you something. Do you nag him?

ESMERALDA: Nag him?

MAURICIO: Yeah, I mean do you nag him about these things day and night?

ESMERALDA: Well, I . . . bring it to his attention.

MAURICIO: How?

ESMERALDA: What do you mean?

MAURICIO: I mean do you say, "Honey, can you please pick up your underwear?" Or do you say, "You left your underwear on the bathroom floor again!"

ESMERALDA: There's no point in bringing it to his attention gently.

MAURICIO: Why not?

ESMERALDA: Because he won't do it. The only way he does anything is if I bring it to his attention . . . firmly.

MAURICIO: Oh, come on . . .

ESMERALDA: It's true. Do you think I haven't tried being kind? Do you think I haven't tried positive reinforcement? Praising him when he does something that he's supposed to do anyway, like it's a big deal? It doesn't work. Do you think I like being a bitch?

[*He gives her a look.*]

Well, I don't!

MAURICIO: Do you expect me to believe that?

ESMERALDA: I don't expect you to do anything, but go kill the bastard so I can get on with my life.

[*There's a knock at the door.*]

BELLBOY [*offstage.*]: Room service.

[ESMERALDA *looks at* MAURICIO *and he hides in the bathroom. She opens the door and the* BELLBOY *enters with a full bar.*]

ESMERALDA: Thank you. Charge it to the room, please.

BELLBOY: Yes, ma'am.

[*The* BELLBOY *sees* MAURICIO*'s hat. He looks at* ESMERALDA *suspiciously. He exits and* MAURICIO *comes out of the bathroom.*]

MAURICIO: So, let me get this straight. You want me to go knock the guy off for dropping his shorts in the bathroom, not having time to wash his car, for reading the paper, and for ordering bad movies? Come on, give me a good reason here. Tell me he slept with your best friend or he beat you up or he called your mother a name or something. But don't send me out to kill the guy for not changing the oil in the car. I might as well kill myself!

ESMERALDA: Oh god, don't tell me you're that kind of guy. I bet you don't listen to your wife either.

[*At* ESMERALDA*'s,* FERNANDO *dials the phone. The following dialogue overlaps between both couples.*]

MAURICIO: I listen to her. I listen to her nag me day and night.

FERNANDO [*on the phone*]: Lydia . . .

MAURICIO: "When are you gonna clean the garage?" "Get your AK-47s out of the coat closet."

LYDIA [*on the phone*]: Yeah?

MAURICIO: "Do you have to be so messy? I can't get these bloodstains out of your shirt."

FERNANDO: I've come across some interesting information.

MAURICIO: "When are you gonna take me out to dinner?"

FERNANDO: My wife left her bank card at the Shangrila Hotel restaurant.

ESMERALDA: I don't think that's unreasonable.

LYDIA: The Shangrila Hotel? Why, that motherfucker.

ESMERALDA: When was the last time you cleaned the garage?

FERNANDO: Lydia, what are you going to do?

MAURICIO: What?

LYDIA: I'm gonna kill the son of a bitch!

[*Loud music plays as* LYDIA *goes to the closet and gets a gun.* FERNANDO *goes to his closet and gets a jacket.* ESMERALDA *and* MAURICIO *continue their dialogue.*]

SCENE 9

[*Hotel room.* ESMERALDA *is exhausted.*]

ESMERALDA: Forget it. I'll hire someone else for the job.

[*She begins to put on her coat.*]

MAURICIO: Why?

ESMERALDA: Because you're not right for it. You don't have what it takes.

MAURICIO: What do you mean?

ESMERALDA: Just that.

MAURICIO: How do you know?

ESMERALDA: I can tell.

MAURICIO: How?

ESMERALDA: I just can.

[*He gets up and paces, fuming.*]

MAURICIO: You don't even know me, lady!

ESMERALDA: Oh, did I hit a nerve?

MAURICIO: You're saying I don't have what it takes to kill somebody? Is that what you're saying?

ESMERALDA: That's exactly what I'm saying. I hired you to kill my husband, I gave you the money, gave you the plan, and you want me to give you a good reason?

MAURICIO: It's my thing, OK? I don't like to kill people behind their backs. I like to go up to them and say stuff like, "This is for double crossing Chuy" or, "You fucked with the wrong man's wife" or, "Manny says to say hello to St. Peter for him." You know, it's my thing. How can I put a gun to a guy's head and say, "This is for not picking up your *calzones*?" Come on, it's pathetic. It ain't right!

ESMERALDA: A hit man doesn't ask for a reason. A hit man does his job and takes the money.

MAURICIO [*insulted*]: Do you think I'm in this for the money?

ESMERALDA: You mean, you're not?

MAURICIO: No! I'm in this for justice, lady!

ESMERALDA: Oh, brother.

MAURICIO: I serve the people, all right? I'm the guy that comes to the aid of Mr. and Mrs. Everyman because the system has failed them or because they can't afford to hire a lawyer, but they *can* afford to hire a hit man. You know how many criminals get away with murder? You know how many people get away with screwing good, honest people? I'm a public servant, lady!

ESMERALDA [*to herself*]: My god, he's serious . . .

[MAURICIO *takes off his coat and sits on the bed.*]

MAURICIO: Now, think hard. He must've done something . . . said something . . . Have you ever caught him in a lie?

ESMERALDA: No.

MAURICIO: Has he cheated on you?

ESMERALDA: No.

MAURICIO: Does he say bad things about your mother?

ESMERALDA: He says she's a nag.

MAURICIO: Is she?

ESMERALDA: Yes.

MAURICIO: What, then?

[*She thinks.*]

ESMERALDA: He made promises he didn't keep.

MAURICIO: Like what?

ESMERALDA: He told me I would be his queen.

MAURICIO [*in disbelief*]: And you believed him?

ESMERALDA: Yes. I was born with my umbilical cord around my neck.

MAURICIO: Huh?

ESMERALDA: Only kings and queens are born with their umbilical cord around their neck.

MAURICIO: Oh, yeah? Does that include drag queens? You mean all the *queenotas* in L.A. were born with *ombligo* cords around their necks?

ESMERALDA: You're not homophobic, are you?

MAURICIO: No way! I love women!

ESMERALDA: What?

[*They look at each other, confused.*]

MAURICIO: So, he said you'd be his queen and you believed him because you were born with your cord around your neck?

ESMERALDA: Yes.

MAURICIO: Lady, the only thing that cord did was stop the oxygen from going to your brain. That "queen" thing is a line. I've used it myself once or twice. "*Mi reina, mi vida . . .*" you know.

ESMERALDA: And were they just lines?

MAURICIO: Yeah.

ESMERALDA: How can men do that?

MAURICIO: Do what?

ESMERALDA: Make promises, swear, vow, profess, pledge; only to later deceive, deny, mislead, fool, delude . . .

MAURICIO: Hold on, lady. What the hell are you talking about?

ESMERALDA: I'm talking about how you men make promises and then you break them.

MAURICIO: You think we mean to? We don't!

ESMERALDA: You don't?

MAURICIO: You know, when you're young and you're in love . . . you say things, you make promises. You say the things you think she wants to hear because you want to make her happy. It's that time, you know, when you see that look in her eyes, like you can do no wrong. When you know she'll believe anything you say. We say things. Yeah, we make promises. But, when we make them, we don't think we're gonna break them.

ESMERALDA: But, you break them nonetheless. Whether it's intentional or not it still hurts when you realize that everything you believed isn't true. That they were just words.

[*She begins to cry.*]

MAURICIO: Oh, no, come on. Please, don't cry. [*He turns away*] I can't stand to see a woman cry. No, come on, please . . . Look, give me blood, guts, pieces of brain matter, the smell of a decomposed body. But, please don't cry. I can't take it.

[ESMERALDA *looks at herself in the mirror, sees her makeup is a mess, and runs into the bathroom.* MAURICIO *runs after her.*]

SCENE 10

[*Hotel entrance.* FERNANDO *enters wearing a trench coat, a hat, and sunglasses. He sees* LYDIA *through the window, wearing a trench coat, scarf, and sunglasses. He gets up and goes to her.*]

FERNANDO: Lydia? Is that you?

LYDIA: Who are you?

FERNANDO: Fernando, Esmeralda's husband.

LYDIA: What the fuck are you doing here?

FERNANDO: I'm trying to prevent you from committing a crime.

LYDIA: Stay out of this! This is none of your business!

FERNANDO: Of course it is. You're planning on killing your husband because you think he's screwing . . . I mean, having an inappropriate relationship with my wife.

LYDIA: I don't think, I know . . .

FERNANDO: And I know my wife. She's a good, loving wife. She would never cheat on me. Never.

LYDIA: Then what was her number doing in my husband's pants pocket?

FERNANDO: I don't know. She may have been looking for someone to hire to clean up the yard or clear out the garage . . .

LYDIA: That ain't it. Believe me.

FERNANDO: What makes you so sure that he'd be having an affair?

LYDIA: A woman can tell these things. We have a sixth sense about 'em. You guys think we don't notice, but we do. Every look, every move, every word. We're making mental notes and you don't know it. I've noticed . . . He wears white shirts everyday because he knows he looks good in white. He's always primping in front of the mirror and lately he's been checking his phone for messages . . .

FERNANDO: That doesn't prove anything.

LYDIA: It proves he wants to look good. For who? Me? I don't think so. He hardly even looks at me. I mean, not like he used to. When we were young, he couldn't keep his hands off of me. He was nice, kind, funny, sexy. Now, I'm lucky if I get a "Hi" or a "Good morning." I mean, I'm practically invisible to the guy.

FERNANDO: Well, that happens in marriages over the years.

LYDIA: In yours, too? See, it's all making sense. I saw this on Dr. Phil. Two people feel unfulfilled in their marriage so they look somewhere else.

FERNANDO: Lydia, you've got a very vivid imagination and as a professor of literature I appreciate that. But, my wife is fulfilled. She's happy . . . mostly. Yes, she gets impatient with me sometimes when I'm forgetful, but I can honestly say that we have a wonderful life. She wants for nothing.

LYDIA: But, do you make her hot?

FERNANDO: Pardon me?

LYDIA: You know what I'm talking about.

FERNANDO: Well, Lydia, I hardly know you, but if it will prevent you from making the biggest mistake of your life, I will share that we do get intimate on a regular basis. We put it in our calendars, just to make sure. And we stick to it . . . most of the time. Sometimes my job . . .

LYDIA: No wonder she's screwing around with Mauricio.

FERNANDO: Stop saying that, she's not screwing around.

LYDIA: Yes, she is and I'm gonna kick her ass, as soon as I kill my husband.

[LYDIA *begins to exit.*]

FERNANDO: Wait! Wait! Look, they're probably not even here. This is all my fault. I should have never called you back with the hotel information. I wasn't thinking. Do you want to spend the rest of your life in prison? You can't just barge into a hotel room and kill someone.

LYDIA: You wanna make a bet?

[*She takes out the gun.* FERNANDO *looks around.*]

FERNANDO: What are you doing? Put that thing away!

[FERNANDO *takes the gun away.*]

LYDIA: Give me that!

FERNANDO: No! Now, Lydia, calm down. Take a deep breath before you act.

SCENE 11

[*Hotel room.* ESMERALDA *and* MAURICIO *come out of the bathroom.*]

ESMERALDA: It's painful when you realize that you are taken for granted; that you're no longer loved.

MAURICIO: No longer loved? I'm sure your husband still loves you. It's just that . . . what I'm saying is that . . . it's like . . . [*searching, looking down at his shoes*] like a pair of shoes, right? I mean, you see them, you fall in love with them, you buy them, and when they're new you take good care of them. Then, you break them in and they get really comfortable and you stop taking such good care of them. But they're still your favorite shoes.

ESMERALDA: So, what's your point?

MAURICIO: My point is that just because your husband takes you for granted, doesn't mean he doesn't love you.

ESMERALDA: Is that supposed to make me feel better?

MAURICIO: Yes.

ESMERALDA: Well, it doesn't. But you're right. That's exactly how I feel, like an old pair of shoes, being kicked around all the time.

MAURICIO: That's not what I meant. Look . . . [*Stopping himself*] Forget it. You women . . .

ESMERALDA: We women? We women what?

MAURICIO: You always do that. You take something we say, even if we're trying to be caring and sincere, and you turn it into something mean and ugly.

ESMERALDA: Comparing me to a pair of old shoes was being caring and sincere? Please!

[*She goes to the bar to pour a drink.*]

MAURICIO: Can I have one of those?

ESMERALDA: I have gin, bourbon, and rum.

MAURICIO: Bourbon.

ESMERALDA: On the rocks?

MAURICIO: Straight.

[*She pours two bourbons and hands him one.*]

Thanks. My wife does that to me all the time.

ESMERALDA: Does what?

MAURICIO: Makes me feel like I did something wrong when I know I didn't. She twists things around, you know. Like I can say something . . . anything, like, "Hey, you look real nice today." And she'll go, "Are you saying I didn't look nice yesterday? What was wrong with the way I looked yesterday?" And she'll go on and on until I'm apologizing and I don't even know what I'm apologizing for. Now, that's despiteful . . .

ESMERALDA [*correcting him*]: No, don't you mean deceitful?

MAURICIO: I know what I mean. I mean despiteful.

ESMERALDA: No, you're using it in the wrong context. You either mean deceitful or . . . do you mean despicable?

MAURICIO: I mean despiteful, lady. As in, despite what you say, I'm not changing the word, OK?

ESMERALDA: Well, it still doesn't make sense . . .

MAURICIO: See, that's another thing. Why do you women always have to have the last word?

ESMERALDA: Now, that is an unfounded allegation.

MAURICIO: A what?

ESMERALDA: It's untrue, false, misleading, specious, an incorrect statement . . .

MAURICIO: Stop! What the hell do you mean?

ESMERALDA: I mean it's a goddamn lie!

MAURICIO: What's a lie? [*Confused*] What the hell were we talking about, anyway?

ESMERALDA: You said women always have to have the last word!

MAURICIO: It's true . . .

ESMERALDA: No, it isn't.

MAURICIO: Yes, it is.

ESMERALDA: No, it isn't!

MAURICIO: Yes, it is!

ESMERALDA: It isn't!

MAURICIO: OK, it isn't! Damn, lady, I come to work for some peace and quiet, OK? If I wanna argue with someone I'll stay at home!

[*Silence.*]

ESMERALDA: Well, it isn't.

MAURICIO: Jesus Christ! You know what? I'm getting the hell out of here!

[*He grabs his things to leave.*]

ESMERALDA: Go ahead, leave! Just walk out without resolving anything!

[*He stops, turns toward her with hate in his eyes. He pulls out his gun and points it at her.*]

Oh, yeah, that's right! You can't have a meaningful dialogue, so you resort to violence. That's so typical. What happened to your conscience, your need for a "good reason"?

MAURICIO: I got a good reason! You're driving me up the fucking wall!

ESMERALDA: Exactly! And that's the reason you have to kill my husband!

[*He's caught. He lowers his gun.*]

MAURICIO: You are one sharp cookie.

[ESMERALDA *goes for a cigarette. She holds it up for* MAURICIO *to light.*]

SCENE 12

[*The following dialogue happens simultaneously in the hotel room and the hotel entrance.* MAURICIO *lights* ESMERALDA*'s cigarette.*]

FERNANDO: Albert Einstein said, "Men marry women with the hope they will never change. Women marry men with the hope they will change. Invariably they are both disappointed." Men and women are wired differently. We see things differently, that's just the way it is.

LYDIA: Yeah, yeah, I know all that. Women are from Venus and men are from Mars and *You Just Don't Understand* and all of that crap.

FERNANDO: Exactly. And . . . can I be perfectly honest with you?

LYDIA: Go ahead.

FERNANDO: Sometimes, no matter what I do, I can't make Esmeralda happy. We have a beautiful home, wonderful friends, a very active social life . . .

LYDIA: Tell me about it.

FERNANDO: Lydia . . .

LYDIA: OK, go on.

FERNANDO: . . . and no matter how hard I try, she complains. I mean, she complains about things that are so minute and, to be honest, it becomes banal.

LYDIA: Banal?

FERNANDO: Commonplace, uninteresting, dull . . .

LYDIA: Like this conversation.

FERNANDO: Look, the point I'm trying to make is that we all become annoyed with our spouses, and I'm sure your husband must have some redeeming qualities.

LYDIA: Yeah, he probably does. But I can't think of any right now because he's banging your old lady . . . I mean your wife. Sorry, Fernie.

FERNANDO: Fernie? [*Chuckling*] No one's called me that in years. Esmeralda used to call me Fernie when we were in college.

LYDIA: Is that where you met?

FERNANDO: Yes, I was a lit major and she was a political science major. The moment we met, I knew, she was the one for me. Fernie and Esme . . . we were inseparable. Then we discovered our roots and reclaimed our birth names, Fernando and Esmeralda. We went to grad school, then got married. But, to be honest, I miss Fernie and Esme. And I don't just mean the names.

LYDIA: Why do you say that?

FERNANDO: Oh, I don't know. After I got my Ph.D. and was hired by the university our lives became about other things . . . She wanted a house, we bought a house. She wanted a family, we had our son.

LYDIA: You have kids?

FERNANDO: Just one.

ESMERALDA [*in the hotel room*]: When our son was born, he took over our life. We knew we were only going to have one so we put our all into him.

FERNANDO [*to* LYDIA]: . . . He's a beautiful human being. Grown and gone now. He went to school on the East Coast . . .

ESMERALDA: . . . We read to him, sang to him, piano lessons, little league, soccer, boy scouts . . . and then he grew up . . .

FERNANDO: . . . he fell in love and never came back. We love his partner, very nice guy.

ESMERALDA: They come and visit now and then, but . . .

FERNANDO: We miss him.

ESMERALDA: Life got so quiet after he left . . .

LYDIA: The empty nest thing?

FERNANDO: I suppose.

ESMERALDA: . . . and I had to look around and face reality.

LYDIA: You work at UCLA?

FERNANDO: Yes . . .

LYDIA: Well, my husband's a Trojans fan.

ESMERALDA: There I was living with a man, a stranger really . . .

FERNANDO: What does your husband do?

LYDIA: He's a . . . uh . . . he's in between jobs right now.

ESMERALDA: . . . going through the motions of daily life.

LYDIA: He had an incident . . .

FERNANDO: An accident?

LYDIA: No, an incident.

ESMERALDA: Our life is so quiet sometimes that I can hear him breathing and chewing and snoring and burping and farting and shitting and I hate it!

SCENE 13

[*Hotel room.*]

MAURICIO: What happened to women? I remember when you would do what we said. Now, you guys are ten steps ahead of us. We gotta watch our backs.

[*He hands her a drink and sits on the foot of the bed.*]

ESMERALDA: It's called evolution . . . growth . . . unfolding . . .

MAURICIO [*interrupting*]: I know what evolution means. It means going from being a monkey to being a man.

[*Pause.*]

It means . . . changing. Like my wife changed. You know, when we first hooked up she was crazy about me. Always there for me, you know. She'd ask me what I wanted for dinner. She'd iron my clothes, keep up the house . . . Now, I come home from a hard night's work and I find a note: "There's leftovers in the Tupperware, stick it in the microwave." But that ain't the worst of it. The worst part is . . . we hardly do it anymore. The other day I tried and she says, "You wanna get me excited? Wash the dishes. And if you really wanna turn me on, take out the trash." I'm not sure, but, I think maybe . . .

[*He stops.*]

Never mind . . .

ESMERALDA: You think maybe what?

[*He looks at her, then away.*]

MAURICIO: I think maybe she don't love me no more.

ESMERALDA [*feeling bad for him*]: What makes you think that?

MAURICIO: I don't know. The way she talks to me. The way she looks at me. Like there's no *cariño* coming my way, you know.

[*He goes to the bar.*]

ESMERALDA: Are you sending any *cariño* her way?

MAURICIO: What?

ESMERALDA: Is there any romance left in your marriage?

MAURICIO: Romance?

ESMERALDA: Yeah, you know. Kissing, caressing.

MAURICIO: Huh?

ESMERALDA: Those things are important to a woman, you know.

MAURICIO: They are?

ESMERALDA: When was the last time you breathed down her neck and said "I want you . . ."

MAURICIO: Huh?

ESMERALDA: When did you last pull her close to you by the waist and travel her body with your hands, touch her inner thighs . . .

MAURICIO: What are you talking about?

[*She gives up.*]

ESMERALDA: When was the last time you told her you love her?

[*He thinks real hard.*]

MAURICIO: Uh . . .

ESMERALDA: That long, huh?

MAURICIO: I'm not that kind of guy. I mean, I'm a killer.

ESMERALDA: That's no excuse.

MAURICIO: She doesn't like that kind of stuff, anyway.

ESMERALDA: Of course she does.

SCENE 14

[*Hotel entrance.*]

[LYDIA *is confiding in* FERNANDO.]

LYDIA: And then we hardly have sex anymore . . .

FERNANDO: You don't?

LYDIA: And he doesn't put anything into it. You know what I mean?

FERNANDO: Absolutely.

LYDIA: He just goes through the motions like he's on automatic pilot, you know what I'm saying?

FERNANDO: Yes, I do.

LYDIA: You know what I wish? I wish he'd put some romance into it or something. I wanna be turned on, you know? He takes everything I do for granted. He thinks our comfortable lifestyle just happens. Like everything magically falls into place. He doesn't even look at me when I talk to him sometimes.

FERNANDO: Really? Well, that's inconsiderate.

LYDIA: Damned right, it is! He's an inconsiderate shit. He really does deserve to die.

FERNANDO: Look, I'm sure you're jumping to conclusions. You're assuming something that I'm positive is not happening. I'm sure Esmeralda left her card here because she was having lunch with a girlfriend. I bet she's done with her mani-pedi by now. Let me call her so we can clear this whole thing up.

[*He takes out his phone.*]

LYDIA: What kind of phone do you have?

[*He shows her.*]

Do you know her Apple ID?

FERNANDO: Her what?

LYDIA: Let me see that.

[LYDIA *takes his phone.*]

See if she has her "Find my iPhone" on. What's her Apple ID?

FERNANDO: Uh . . .

LYDIA: Here it is. Do you know her password?

FERNANDO: Try r-e-i-n-a.

LYDIA: Phone number?

FERNANDO: 3-1-0-8-4-9-3-9-3-0.

LYDIA: You see, the Shangrila Hotel. She's still here!

[FERNANDO *takes the phone and looks at it.*]

FERNANDO: What? That's impossible.

SCENE 15

[*Hotel room.*]

MAURICIO: I . . . I've never been the romantic type. I wouldn't know where to start.

ESMERALDA: It's easy.

MAURICIO: Yeah?

ESMERALDA: You just look deep into her eyes and say, "I love you, babe."

MAURICIO: I can't.

ESMERALDA: Sure, you can. Try it.

MAURICIO: Get outta here . . .

ESMERALDA: Come on, try it.

[*He looks at her, unsure. Then he clears his throat.*]

MAURICIO [*as if he's reciting from memory*]: I love you . . .

ESMERALDA: . . . babe.

MAURICIO: Babe.

ESMERALDA: See?

MAURICIO: Was it all right?

ESMERALDA: Uh huh. Now, try it just a little softer and breathier.

[ESMERALDA'*s phone vibrates. Lights up on* FERNANDO *as he's calling* ESMERALDA. *In the hotel room*, ESMERALDA *doesn't want to interrupt the moment for* MAURICIO *and tries to turn her phone off, but hits the wrong button.* LYDIA *and* FERNANDO *can hear them on the other end.*]

[*Demonstrating*] "I love you, babe."

MAURICIO [*imitating her*]: I love you, babe.

[*Back to* LYDIA *and* MAURICIO.]

LYDIA: That fucking asshole! He never says that to me!

FERNANDO: I'm gonna kill the bitch!

[*He heads into the hotel.*]

LYDIA: What? Wait, calm down! Have you ever used a gun before?

[*Back to hotel room.* ESMERALDA *continues the romance lessons.*]

ESMERALDA [*impressed*]: Good. OK, now come close and put your arm around my waist and pull me close.

[*He does.*]

Look straight into my eyes, brush my face with the back of your fingers ever so lightly, and then say, "I love you, babe."

[*He does as she says.*]

MAURICIO: I love you, babe.

[ESMERALDA *lets out an involuntary breath.*]

ESMERALDA: See there.

MAURICIO: What?

ESMERALDA: You made me feel . . . something.

MAURICIO [*feeling good about himself*]: Yeah?

ESMERALDA: Yeah.

[*She goes to the bar and pours herself another drink.*]

Want another one?

MAURICIO: Sure.

[*He goes to the bar and she pours.*]

SCENE 16

[*Hotel restaurant.*]

LYDIA: Wait, wait, what are you gonna do?

FERNANDO: Well, I'll confront her.

LYDIA: How?

FERNANDO: Well, I'll say, "Esmeralda, being in a hotel room with a man other than your husband is very inappropriate."

LYDIA: Inappropriate? Is that the best you can do?

FERNANDO: Unacceptable?

LYDIA: What the . . . forget it!

[FERNANDO *becomes reflective.*]

FERNANDO: What would possess her? I find it so peculiar. A midlife crisis? Menopause? I've heard that some women just go completely haywire. They lose it. They don't think straight. I'm at a loss . . .

LYDIA: Come on, dude, pull yourself together. What the hell? Let's go find them.

FERNANDO: How? We don't even know where they are.

LYDIA: Where do you think they are? In a room with a bed.

FERNANDO: How do we know that for sure?

LYDIA: Didn't she leave her credit card?

FERNANDO: Yes.

LYDIA: And didn't they call you?

FERNANDO: Yes, they did! They're holding it for her at the front desk.

LYDIA: Then, go to the front desk, identify yourself, see if she checked in, and get the key. You're her husband for Christ's sake!

FERNANDO: Good idea.

LYDIA: OK, go.

SCENE 17

[*Hotel room.* ESMERALDA *is sipping on her drink. She and* MAURICIO *have bonded.*]

ESMERALDA: When I was a girl growing up on the East Side, we'd run to a friend's house after school. In her backyard, there was a swing. Well, it wasn't really a swing, but a disk tied to a tall eucalyptus tree by a rope and the only way we could get on that swing was by climbing onto the roof of an old shed, holding onto the rope, and jumping on the disk in midair, our feet never touching the ground. I think about it now and wonder how we never broke our necks. But we didn't and we'd take turns jumping onto that swing over and over again until the sun went down, because it was so frightening and so exhilarating. That rush . . . that rush made me feel so alive. I think about that so much lately . . .

MAURICIO: We used to play chicken on the railroad tracks by our house. One time the train came so close I saw my life flash before my eyes. All three years of it.

[*They laugh.*]

ESMERALDA: So, is that what you feel when you . . . you know. Do you feel that rush?

MAURICIO: Not so much anymore. I miss it though.

ESMERALDA: How did you get into this line of work, anyway?

MAURICIO: A friend needed help. A greedy landlord wanted more rent and they could barely make ends meet. I thought it was a one-time thing . . . But, as it turned out, I was pretty good at it, a natural. The word got out and one thing led to another. Now, I've been at it so long . . . It's all I know, you know. It's not like I want to do it forever. You know, this kind of work takes its toll on you . . . Cracking skulls and breaking necks ain't all it's made out to be. You know how much a dead body weighs? When I was younger it was no problem. But now, I get home and I'm pooped. And it's not just the physical toll, it's the other stuff, too . . .

ESMERALDA: The psychological . . .

MAURICIO: . . . and the emotional . . .

ESMERALDA: Not to mention your karmic debt.

[*Hotel front desk.* FERNANDO *rings the desk bell. Back to hotel room.*]

MAURICIO: My what?

ESMERALDA: Never mind.

[*Front desk.*]

FERNANDO: My wife forgot her credit card . . .

[*Hotel room.*]

ESMERALDA: What is your wife's name?

MAURICIO: Lydia.

[*Front desk.*]

HOTEL CLERK: And your wife's name is?

FERNANDO: Esmeralda Rivera.

HOTEL CLERK: Oh, yes, Esmeralda Riviera.

[*Hotel room.*]

ESMERALDA: What does she do?

MAURICIO: Oh, she's a hairdresser. She used to forge checks, but she wanted to go legit and I respect that.

[*Front desk.*]

HOTEL CLERK: Are you checking in, too, sir?

[*Hotel room.*]

MAURICIO: She's quite a woman, my wife.

[*Front desk.*]

FERNANDO: Yes.

[*Hotel room.*]

ESMERALDA: You really love her, huh?

MAURICIO: Yeah. I can't live without her. I remember the first time I laid eyes on her. We were in high school and I was stealing stuff out of a teacher's desk, thinking nobody was around, and I look up and there's this beautiful girl, with bleached blonde hair, red lips, and lots of black eyeliner. She looked at me and smiled then she just went back to practicing signatures with her pen. It was love at first sight. We were so in love. She used to write me love poems. Beautiful ones . . . but now . . . we're in a slump.

ESMERALDA: Oh, come on. You can pull out of it. Anything's possible. I mean, look at the economy.

[MAURICIO *doesn't get the connection.*]

MAURICIO: What?

ESMERALDA: Look, if you want your marriage to work out you have to work at it. Create an environment for growth.

MAURICIO: Yeah?

ESMERALDA: You have to set the scene. It has to be planned, thought out, well considered. It has to be . . .

MAURICIO: . . . premeditated?

ESMERALDA: That's right.

MAURICIO: How?

ESMERALDA: Well, you put on some music, something sensuous.

[*She goes to her phone and plays some sensuous music.*]

You dim the lights.

[*She dims the lights.*]

You put out your hand and say, "Let's dance."

[*He shakes his head no.*]

MAURICIO: I haven't danced in ages.

ESMERALDA: What?

[*She pulls him to his feet.*]

MAURICIO: No, really . . . I don't dance no more.

ESMERALDA: Of course, you do. Now, come on, follow me.

[*He resists, but she won't let go. He begins to follow her reluctantly.*]

That's it.

[*She is smooth and sensuous as she teaches him to move.*]

Good . . .

[*He gets the hang of it little by little. They dance sensuously together until the song ends. He brushes her face with the back of his fingers.*]

MAURICIO: I love you, babe.

[*They look into each other's eyes . . . The door opens and* LYDIA *and* FERNANDO *barge in.*]

LYDIA: I knew it!

[ESMERALDA *and* MAURICIO *are startled.*]

FERNANDO: Esmeralda?

ESMERALDA: Fernando?

MAURICIO: Lydia?

LYDIA: What the fuck?

[*Loud music plays as* MAURICIO *pulls out his gun,* LYDIA *pulls out her gun,* ESMERALDA *pulls out her gun, and* FERNANDO *pulls out his gun. They all look at each other. Everyone is breathing hard.*]

MAURICIO: Lydia, why do you have a gun?

LYDIA: 'Cause I'm gonna kill you, you lying shit!

MAURICIO: What are you talking about?

[*Both* LYDIA *and* ESMERALDA *point their guns at* MAURICIO.]

LYDIA AND ESMERALDA: Don't say that!

[FERNANDO *looks at* ESMERALDA.]

FERNANDO: Esmeralda, how could you?

ESMERALDA: I . . . I have my reasons, Fernando.

[LYDIA *looks at* MAURICIO.]

LYDIA: Why are you doing this, Mau?

[MAURICIO *looks at* LYDIA.]

MAURICIO: It's what I do, Lydia. It's my job, what they pay me for. You know that.

LYDIA: You liar. I don't believe you for a second. This ain't no job!

FERNANDO: A job? Wait a minute, Lydia, is your husband a . . .

LYDIA: Yeah, but don't judge!

FERNANDO: You said he was in between jobs . . .

LYDIA: He is! [*To* MAURICIO] You're lying, Mau! I heard you say, "I love you, babe." We walked in on you . . .

MAURICIO: No, babe, I swear. It's not what you think. Esmeralda was giving me lessons . . .

LYDIA AND FERNANDO: Lessons?

MAURICIO: Dance lessons . . .

ESMERALDA: Romance lessons . . .

[FERNANDO *is confused. He puts down his gun.*]

FERNANDO: What the hell is going on here?

MAURICIO: It's not what it looks like, I swear!

LYDIA: Yeah, right!

MAURICIO: You know what? You're never gonna believe me anyway, so . . .

[MAURICIO *puts down his gun.*]

FERNANDO: I'm at a loss . . .

LYDIA: Ah, shut up, Fernie . . .

ESMERALDA: Fernie?

LYDIA: You're always at a fucking loss.

ESMERALDA: Excuse me? How would you know that?

LYDIA: Because, we've spent time together, Esmeralda, and he told me . . .

ESMERALDA: You know absolutely nothing about my marriage, my husband, or me!

LYDIA: That's what you think. I know plenty. I know he tries to make you happy and all you do is whine. Ain't that right, Fernie!

[FERNANDO *doesn't know what to say.*]

FERNANDO: I . . .

ESMERALDA: What is going on, Fernando? You have some explaining to do.

FERNANDO: I beg your pardon? You have some explaining to do, Esmeralda. What are you doing in a hotel with a stranger? Did you hire him to . . .

ESMERALDA: Yes, I did, Fernando.

FERNANDO: Why?

ESMERALDA: Because, I can't take it anymore . . .

FERNANDO: Do I make you that unhappy? Do I?

ESMERALDA: Well . . .

[*She hesitates.*]

MAURICIO: Tell him the truth, Esmeralda . . .

LYDIA: The truth? The truth about what? About you and her? [*To* ESMERALDA] You two-timing bitch.

MAURICIO: Stop that, Lydia! Don't talk to Esmeralda like that. She's a nice lady and she's been through hell with this guy!

FERNANDO: Hell? What are you talking about?

[ESMERALDA *points her gun at him.*]

I mean, I don't understand . . .

MAURICIO: You don't appreciate her, Fernando. You take her for granted! You leave your *chones* on the bathroom floor, OK?

FERNANDO: Don't appreciate her? Is that what she told you? [*To* ESMERALDA] Is that what you told him?

LYDIA: Look who's talking! You don't pick up your shorts either.

MAURICIO: I know, but we're not talking about me. We're talking about him.

FERNANDO: You've got a lot of nerve. At least I show my wife affection once in a while. Have you ever heard of foreplay?

[MAURICIO *looks at* LYDIA.]

MAURICIO: Foreplay?

ESMERALDA: Precoital stimulation.

MAURICIO: I know what foreplay is! What do you know about my sex life?

FERNANDO: A lot, as a matter of fact. You just go through the motions, no romance.

[MAURICIO *looks at* LYDIA *in disbelief.*]

ESMERALDA: But, he's getting better. He just needs a little practice.

FERNANDO AND LYDIA: What?

ESMERALDA: I mean . . .

FERNANDO: Please, Esmeralda, spare me the unsavory details about your salacious tryst.

ESMERALDA: Tryst?

LYDIA: Yeah, tryst!

ESMERALDA: Is that what you think this is?

MAURICIO: What's a tryst?

ESMERALDA: A romantic rendezvous . . .

MAURICIO: That's not what this is! She paid me! You gotta believe me, Lydia. You know what I get paid for . . .

FERNANDO: You hired a gigolo? You hired someone for sex?

MAURICIO: I'm not a gigolo!

LYDIA: Yeah, Mau ain't no man ho!

MAURICIO: I'm a hit man!

[FERNANDO *looks at* ESMERALDA, *then at* LYDIA.]

FERNANDO: A what?

MAURICIO: A hit man, bro! And you're my hit!

LYDIA: What the fuck?

[MAURICIO *points his gun at* FERNANDO. FERNANDO *puts his hands up and looks at* ESMERALDA *and* LYDIA.]

FERNANDO: A hit man?

ESMERALDA AND LYDIA: Yes.

FERNANDO: You put a hit on me? You want me dead?

[MAURICIO *grabs* FERNANDO*'s gun and ties his hands behind his back. He grabs the pillow and holds it up against* FERNANDO*'s head, points his gun at it.*]

MAURICIO: What do you want to do, Esmeralda? This changes the plan. But we can still pull this off.

[LYDIA *moves to stop* MAURICIO.]

LYDIA: No! You can't kill Fernie! He's a good guy. He's a geek, a nerd. He's a professor at UCLA!

MAURICIO: That's reason enough! Get out of my way, Lydia. This is my business and you need to stay out of my business!

LYDIA: No, this changes your plan. You said it yourself. What about the body? How can you get rid of the body? They have her name, her credit card number. They'll come after her and she'll rat you out.

ESMERALDA: I would never do that!

FERNANDO: Yes, she would. She loves to gossip.

LYDIA: Don't do it, Mauricio!

MAURICIO: I gave her my word and you fucked it up, Lydia.

LYDIA: I'm sorry. I found her name on a piece of paper in your pants and I jumped to conclusions.

FERNANDO: I told you they weren't having an affair, but did you listen? No!

LYDIA: Oh, so now it's my fault?

[MAURICIO *looks at* ESMERALDA.]

MAURICIO: Tell me what to do, Esmeralda?

LYDIA: Mau, you'll get caught.

MAURICIO: I have to do this, Lydia. You know I do.

LYDIA: No, Mauricio. It doesn't matter. Forget about the incident!

[MAURICIO *lowers his gun.*]

MAURICIO: You had to bring it up, didn't you?

LYDIA: I'm just trying to help . . .

MAURICIO: You're not helping, Lydia!

LYDIA: OK, I'm sorry I brought it up.

ESMERALDA: What incident?

MAURICIO: Nothing . . . [*To* LYDIA] You see! Now you put doubt in my client's mind.

ESMERALDA: I already had my doubts about you. What incident?

MAURICIO: It's nothing.

LYDIA: Yes, it is.

MAURICIO: Be quiet, Lydia!

LYDIA: Don't you tell me to be quiet!

MAURICIO: Then shut-up!

ESMERALDA: Look, I hired you! You're working for me. I need to know about the incident or the deal is off and I want my money back.

MAURICIO [*to* LYDIA]: You happy now?

LYDIA: What? Wait. How much money?

[MAURICIO *shows her lots of fingers.*]

Oh, shit. OK, then. You better tell her.

FERNANDO: Lydia . . .

LYDIA: Sorry, Fernie, we need the money. We got two kids to feed and a house payment.

ESMERALDA: Mauricio, tell me about the incident.

[MAURICIO *looks at* LYDIA. *She nods.*]

LYDIA: Go on, tell her, Mau.

MAURICIO: It was nothing, really. I was hired for a job. This guy wanted his wife knocked off. Something about wanting to start a new life, you know, the usual. Anyway, I case the joint and everything's going as planned and I'm about to do her in when I hear this voice . . .

ESMERALDA: In your head?

MAURICIO: No, from down the hall . . . a little kid calling out for his mom . . . and, well, she started to cry and I couldn't go through with it, that's all . . .

LYDIA: And he's had issues ever since.

ESMERALDA: What kind of issues?

LYDIA: Well, you know.

MAURICIO: It was the first time I thought about the consequences of what I do . . . and it tore me up.

LYDIA: He hasn't been able to work, either. I tried to get him to go to therapy, you know, like in the *Sopranos*. But, he didn't want to.

ESMERALDA: I really think you should, Mauricio.

LYDIA: That's why I thought he was looking somewhere else for some action, you know. [*To* MAURICIO] Why didn't you tell me you had a job?

FERNANDO: Really, Esmeralda? You hired this guy?

ESMERALDA: He came highly recommended.

MAURICIO: She was an old client . . . from before the incident.

FERNANDO: Of all the hit men in all the gin joints in East L.A., you hired this one?

ESMERALDA: Oh, stop! Don't give me that smug attitude of yours! How was I supposed to know he had a conscience?

LYDIA: Yeah, Fernie, stop being a shit! Mau's a good hit man. At least, he used to be.

ESMERALDA: Don't even bother, Lydia. Don't you know? Fernando is perfect. If you don't believe me, ask him.

LYDIA: Yeah, I could tell he was full of himself as soon as I met him.

FERNANDO: Full of myself? I was there for you, Lydia. I listened while you questioned your husband's fidelity, his manhood, while you questioned his chivalry. I provided you a safe space and practiced good listening. I had your back and now . . .

LYDIA: Aw, shut up! I listened to you, too. You ain't no prize. Your wife wants you dead. She must have her reasons.

MAURICIO: Oh, she does. Lots of reasons!

FERNANDO: Oh, really? What are they?

MAURICIO: Well . . . you don't put down the toilet seat and you dribble on the floor . . .

FERNANDO: I what?

[LYDIA *gives him a look.*]

LYDIA: And what else?

MAURICIO: And you, you don't rotate the tires, you watch bad movies, you don't listen to her when she's talking to you.

LYDIA: Neither do you. There has to be something else.

MAURICIO: . . . and, and . . .

[*He looks at* ESMERALDA.]

What else?

[ESMERALDA *mimes something around her neck.*]

He choked you?

ESMERALDA: No!

[*She goes to him.*]

[*Whispering*] The umbilical cord . . .

MAURICIO: Oh, right. You told her she would be your queen!

LYDIA: And you believed him?

MAURICIO: Yeah, because she was born with her umbilical . . . forget it.

FERNANDO: She is my queen. I treat her like a queen.

[*He looks at* ESMERALDA.]

MAURICIO: No, you don't!

FERNANDO: I try, Esmeralda. I try to make you happy. I give you flowers on our anniversary. I always kiss you "hello" and "good-bye." I try to be witty and intelligent in our conversations. I'm working on my sense of humor and I try to be an enlightened human being in many ways and I care about humanity. I love the opera and classical music, fine art, and I appreciate and cherish the wonderful things about being Chicano and I love our culture.

[MAURICIO *looks at* ESMERALDA.]

MAURICIO: He sounds like a terrific guy.

FERNANDO: What more do you want, Esmeralda?

LYDIA: Yeah, what more do you want?

ESMERALDA: It's more than that.

FERNANDO: What is it?

ESMERALDA: You live in a cloud! You don't deal with the little things in life: the yard, feeding the dog, being on time . . .

FERNANDO: My god, Esmeralda! You act like I'm the bad guy here!

MAURICIO: You mean, you're not?

FERNANDO: No, I'm not! I've worked my whole life. I've worked hard my whole life. I've always treated her well, always.

ESMERALDA: No, don't listen to him!

MAURICIO: Wait, I want to hear what he has to say.

FERNANDO: And I work hard now. It's not easy being a professor.

MAURICIO: Really, I never imagined . . .

LYDIA: Mau, we need the money!

FERNANDO: You have to write, you have to get published, you have to attend conferences, write papers, read! Do you know how much I have to read? And I'm not even talking about having to deal with students. I have to teach them, talk to them, grade them!

MAURICIO: Dang! And I thought my job was hard!

ESMERALDA: I told you not to listen to him. It's the story of my life. I know what you're thinking. You're thinking that he's the nicest man in the world and that I should be grateful.

LYDIA: I saw an episode like this on *Snapped*.

ESMERALDA: It happens all the time. "Oh, you're so lucky. Fernando is such a good husband."

MAURICIO: Hello?

ESMERALDA: But they don't live with him!

LYDIA: Nah, I don't buy his story.

MAURICIO: Lydia, I know we need the money, but come on.

LYDIA: No, no. The only way Fernie is able to do all that is because he has her. Am I right, Esme? You don't sit at home watching Dr. Phil and stuffing your face, do you? You're busy taking care of all the other crap so Fernie can do his thing. Am I right? You make sure the house is taken care of, the groceries, the trash, paying the bills . . .

ESMERALDA: . . . the gardener, servicing the car, taking the clothes to the cleaners, planning dinners for his colleagues and their spouses and pretending that I like them when I'm bored out of my fucking mind.

LYDIA: You know what they say: "Behind every good man is a . . ."

FERNANDO: What a cliche!

LYDIA: No, you're a cliche, Fernie! You're a fucking cliche!

MAURICIO: He sounds pretty good to me.

FERNANDO: I'm a good husband to her!

LYDIA: And she's a good wife! You know what your problem is, Fernie? You think you're so good that there's no room for improvement. Kill him, Mau!

ESMERALDA: But you said he'd get caught.

LYDIA: Don't worry about that! We'll figure it out. Go on, Mau, he deserves it!

MAURICIO: I'm not gonna kill him! Why should I?

LYDIA: Because Esmeralda's right!

MAURICIO: How do you know that?

LYDIA: Because that's what I do! And it's hard! It's hard to be on top of it all of the time! I get the same crap from my friends, Esme. "Oh, you're so lucky to have Mau. He doesn't beat you, he's not a drunk, he lets you work. He always looks so sharp." Yeah, he was a good hit man. But who washed the blood out of his shirts and reminded him to cover his tracks? Who reminded him to wipe off his fingerprints and made sure there was gas in the getaway car? Me! And did I ever get so much as a "thank you"? Honestly, I don't even think he even noticed. Did you, Mau?

MAURICIO: What are you talking about? [*Catching himself*] I mean . . . Come on, Lydia. Of course I noticed. Maybe I never said anything, but I noticed. You know, I'm not the, the, the . . .

FERNANDO: Expressive type?

MAURICIO: Yeah . . . but I do notice . . . Lydia, sometimes I come home and I know you've had a rough day and you're scolding the kids because they're out of control and your hair's all wacky and you're wearing an old sweatshirt and jeans and your fuzzy little *chanclas* and to me you look beautiful and I think I'm so lucky to have you and there's no place else I'd rather be but right there with you nagging me and giving me a hard time.

[LYDIA *turns away from him.* MAURICIO *looks at* FERNANDO.]

What'd I say?

FERNANDO: You did well, until the nagging part . . .

[MAURICIO *sits next to* FERNANDO *on the bed.*]

MAURICIO: What happened to her? She used to love me so much I could do no wrong. What happened?

FERNANDO: Women change, evolve . . .

MAURICIO: Yeah, yeah, I know.

ESMERALDA: So, you're not that girl who used to write love poems, huh?

FERNANDO: Poems? Really?

LYDIA: He told you?

MAURICIO: Oh, yeah, she's a great writer.

LYDIA: Well, they weren't really poems . . . they were love letters, really. Like I was so in love with Mau, I had to say something about it or I'd pop right open, you know? There was one that Mau carried around for years, didn't you, Mau?

MAURICIO: I still do.

[*He takes out his wallet and pulls out an old, yellowed piece of paper.*]

LYDIA: You still carry it?

MAURICIO: Yeah, see . . .

[*He shows it to* FERNANDO.]

Sorry about the bloodstains. Listen to this. [*Reading*] If this world were mine, I'd place at your feet, all that I own, you've been so good to me. If this world were mine . . .

LYDIA: Mau, I didn't really write that, OK?

MAURICIO: Yes, you did. I saw you write it. [*Reading*] I'd give you the flowers, the birds and the bees . . .

LYDIA: No, they're just words to an oldie I liked . . . by Marvin Gaye.

MAURICIO: You didn't write this?

LYDIA: I didn't write any of them, Mau. I just wrote down lyrics to songs I liked and you thought . . .

MAURICIO: So, you lied?

LYDIA: I didn't lie. I just let you believe what you wanted to believe.

MAURICIO: Why?

LYDIA: I don't know. I showed you one and you thought I wrote it and it made you so happy and then by the time I knew it, it was too late to tell you the truth and I guess I wanted to make you happy.

MAURICIO: Oh . . . But still . . .

[*He puts the poem back in his wallet.*]

FERNANDO: But still? It was a lie, Mau. She plagiarized Marvin Gaye. She let you believe she wrote you love poems all these years . . .

ESMERALDA: She never told him she wrote them. He assumed . . .

FERNANDO: But she let him believe it. That's dishonest.

LYDIA: I wanted to make him happy, that's all!

FERNANDO: By lying?

ESMERALDA: By letting him believe what he wanted to believe. We all do it. We do things, we say things to make someone happy . . . right, Mauricio? Isn't that what you said?

MAURICIO: Yeah, but I was talking about . . .

FERNANDO: Is that what you did, Esmeralda? You let me believe what I wanted to believe?

ESMERALDA: I let myself believe it, too . . . We do that sometimes. We even lie to ourselves. We live our lives trying to make others happy and in the end we find out . . . we're not happy.

FERNANDO: I never stopped you from anything. I never stopped you from pursuing your dreams . . .

ESMERALDA: No, you just followed yours and never looked back. I'm not blaming you. You were oblivious.

LYDIA: You still are.

ESMERALDA: But, when it hits, it hits you hard . . .

LYDIA: Like a kick in the ass.

ESMERALDA: And you don't know who or what to blame.

LYDIA: You blame your circumstances.

ESMERALDA: You blame your spouse . . .

[ESMERALDA *goes for a drink.*]

Sometimes, I look in the mirror and I don't recognize who I've become.

LYDIA: I'm not that girl who used to pretend to write poems just to make someone happy. And I think about my life and all the years I've spent trying to . . .

ESMERALDA: . . . make a home for us, a life for us, and the truth is . . .

LYDIA: . . . We still argue over the same things. We are the same people with the same flaws as when we got married.

ESMERALDA: And life goes on and I'm only going to get older and older and older and older . . .

LYDIA: All right!

[ESMERALDA *begins to cry.*]

MAURICIO: Oh, no, don't cry . . . Come on, Esme . . . Look, you're not old. You're a beautiful lady. You're smart, the way you use those big words, and you're sexy and you can dance. It's like . . . [*searching*] . . . a flower, right? When it's a bud, it's pretty, sure. But you can't really tell what it's gonna be until its petals loosen up and it begins to open. Not until then can you see that flower's true beauty. Not until then does it give off its full essence. That's when you can put your nose up to it and say, "Now, that's a beautiful thing." That's the way you are, Esmeralda, like a flower that is barely blossoming.

ESMERALDA: What a beautiful metaphor.

MAURICIO: What?

ESMERALDA: An implied comparison, an analogy . . .

LYDIA: What you said was nice.

MAURICIO: Hey, it was, wasn't it?

ESMERALDA: I think I may have underestimated you, Mauricio. Here I thought you were an insensitive, testosterone-driven male who didn't care about a woman's feelings.

MAURICIO: I am . . . sometimes. Sometimes I'm still a chump, a monkey, not a man.

ESMERALDA: Oh, come on. You're not such a bad guy.

MAURICIO: No wonder Lydia don't love me no more.

LYDIA: Don't say that, Mau.

ESMERALDA: Oh, she loves you. She just needs to know that you love her.

[MAURICIO *goes to* LYDIA.]

MAURICIO: You know, when I had the incident . . . When I heard that kid calling out for his mom, all I could think of was you and our kids and what my life would be like if somebody bumped you off and about how much I love you and how I can't live without you.

LYDIA: Oh, Mauricio, nobody's gonna bump me off.

[MAURICIO *goes up to* LYDIA, *strokes her face with the back of his fingers.*]

MAURICIO: I love you, babe.

[LYDIA *melts. They kiss.* LYDIA *looks at* ESMERALDA.]

LYDIA: You know, Esme, sometimes when you weigh your options, you find out it's better to work with what you got.

[LYDIA *looks at* FERNANDO.]

Or not. But, like Oprah says, "We're only disappointed by our own expectations." And when it comes to being happy . . . it's on us. Isn't it? I mean, no one else can do that for us, right?

[*An epiphany.*]

ESMERALDA: Right.

MAURICIO: I'm not gonna be able to pull this off, am I?

LYDIA: No. Maybe it's time to go legit.

[MAURICIO *reaches into his coat pocket and hands* ESMERALDA *his cash advance.*]

MAURICIO: Here's your cash deposit . . .

ESMERALDA: Oh, no, please keep it. It's the least I can do. In fact, why don't you rent yourself a room here tonight. It's on me. Order champagne, room service, get romantic, make wild, uninhibited love.

MAURICIO: Really?

ESMERALDA: Uh huh.

LYDIA: Thanks, Esme.

[*They head for the door.*]

MAURICIO: Hey, Esmeralda, thanks for the romance lessons.

ESMERALDA: My pleasure. Keep loving each other.

[MAURICIO *and* LYDIA *exit.* ESMERALDA *stays behind with* FERNANDO *with his hands still tied behind his back. They look at each other for a second. She begins to gather her things.*]

FERNANDO: Esmeralda? What are you doing? You're insane, you know that? Honestly, I think you're losing it.

ESMERALDA: I lost it a long time ago.

[*She picks up the suitcase and heads toward the door.*]

FERNANDO: Esmeralda . . .

[ESMERALDA *stops.*]

I'm sorry . . .

[ESMERALDA *puts down the suitcase and looks at him.*]

ESMERALDA: I am too.

[ESMERALDA *goes to him. They kiss. She pushes him away.*]

But there's no going back. We both know that. And to be honest, I'm frightened to death. But I haven't felt this exhilarated; this intoxicated, this euphoric in ages. My heart is pounding. I feel a . . . rush. That all-elusive rush . . . Life is such an enigmatic conglomeration of opposing forces, male and female, testosterone and estrogen, the yin and the yang, clashing, battling, combating one another in search of that delicate balance called understanding. And as elusive as it may seem, as difficult as it is to find; when you do, it is such sweet bliss.

FERNANDO: What are you talking about?

[ESMERALDA *reaches for her gun and points it at* FERNANDO. *Then, she lowers it, tosses it on the bed, picks up her suitcase, and opens the door. A bright light shines through the door as* ESMERALDA *steps out into tomorrow.*]

CONCLUSION
Looking Back, Moving Forward

For thirty days, the Los Angeles Theatre Center was alive with the pulsating energy of more than a hundred artists who filled the grand lobby and each of the five theater spaces on a daily basis. It also garnered national attention from Steven Leigh Morris in *LA Weekly*:

> The work of these U.S.-based Latino companies turned out to be a fair representation of American nonprofit theater at large. There was experimental theater, solo performances, ensemble-devised work and playwright-driven work. So where's the distinct identity? In the politics, of course . . . Encuentro put to rest the condescending bias that ethnic theater is somehow lesser than mainstream work, and therefore not really worth discussing . . . With the range of aesthetics, and the caliber of performance, Encuentro 2014 made its case that Latino theater cannot be ignored in any serious discussion of how the United States is evolving.

One of the Latino Theater Company's primary objectives for producing the Encuentro festival was to reinvigorate a national network connecting regional Latinx theater artists and companies to expand the potential for collaborations and the dissemination of their work.

Years later, the impact of the festival continues to grow and become more and more apparent. This can be seen in a revitalization of the festival tradition in the Latinx Theater Movement including INGENIO Milagro in Portland, Oregon; Latinx New Play Festival at San Diego Repertory Theatre; and Sin Muros Latinx Theatre Festival at Stages Repertory Theatre in Houston, Texas to name only a few. These events join a cadre of ongoing festivals and gatherings such as Two River Theater's Crossing Borders Festival and Oregon Shakespeare Festival's Latinx Play Project.

The seeds of many of these collaborations have roots in the connections and resource sharing engendered through the work of the Latinx Theatre Commons. As these examples demonstrate, the Encuentro and subsequent LTC convenings and events have not only provided an avenue for viewing art but also a platform for providing valuable tools for replicating these models in people's own communities. At their core, these festivals celebrate the ephemeral nature of performance but also activate a collective remembrance of our Latinx histories and mythos. Festivals can also serve as a call to action for communities to question the status quo and their place in the landscape of the American Theater. Anthologies such as this one are crucial to combat erasure in the historical record and serve as an archive of embodied knowledge while also creating the possibility for future reimaginings of these works.

Reflecting on collaborations and the dissemination of work from the festival, some of the post-Encuentro highlights include: the presentation of Caborca Theatre's *Zoetrope: Part I and II* at Pregones Theater (January 2015); *Properties of Silence* at the Carrie Hamilton Theater at the Pasadena Playhouse (March 2015); Rubén C. González's *La Esquinita, U.S.A.* at Pregones Theater (December 2015), Aurora Theater (July 2016), and Su Teatro Cultural Performing Arts Center, which also included Rickerby Hinds's *Dreamscape* (April 2016). The Latino Theater Company's *Premeditation* was presented at Arts Emerson in Boston in the spring of 2016 as a direct result of the Encuentro festival and was accompanied by Marissa Chibas's *Daughter of a Cuban Revolutionary. Premeditation* was featured in the Spring 2015 edition of *Gestos* journal, and *Daughter of a Cuban Revolutionary* was included in the 2017 anthology, *Contemporary Plays by Women of Color* (second edition), edited by Roberta Uno. Additionally, some of the Encuentro plays themselves have gone on to be produced by other Encuentro companies, namely CASA 0101 Theater in Boyle Heights which produced Karen Zacarías's *Mariela en el Desierto/Mariela in the Desert* (November 2016).

Several of the companies also strengthened their artistic partnership with the Latino Theater Company after the festival by returning to the stages at the Los Angeles Theatre Center (LATC). In the Spring of 2015, Teatro Luna returned to LATC with the coproduced, world premiere of *Generation Sex*, and Rickerby Hinds's *Dreamscape* was also featured in that season, to much acclaim, and garnered multiple NAACP Theater Awards.

Theater Mitu's *Juárez: A Documentary Mythology* also returned to LATC with a three-week run as part of the 2016 Fall season.

Another profound influence of the Encuentro Festival is the very real human impact, which can be challenging to trace and categorize. Festival artists, audiences, and Latinx Theatre Commons conveners attest to the ways in which the festival had an impact on them personally, artistically, and professionally. For instance, artistic partnerships, such as the collaboration between Karen Zacarías and José Luis Valenzuela on Zacarías's play *Destiny of Desire* and its tour of the regional theater circuit, are but one example of the artistic impact of not only the festival but of the Commons as a whole. The Encuentro Fellows have also all gone on to much success, illustrating the abundance of new collaborations between Encuentro artists. Ultimately, the Encuentro was about the artist experience, and these testimonials from the participants reflect its impact:

> "For fifteen days I lived in a microcosmic world where everyone loves the arts and honors the artists. Collaboration trumped competition, multiple generations learned from each other. The young honored the elders in that old-school way that feels like the kind of respect that can save the world. High school students jumped to their feet in wild standing ovations for the early morning shows performed especially to welcome them."
>
> —Magdalena Gómez (author of "Shameless Woman" and Pregones Theater's *Dancing in My Cockroach Killers*)

> "My sister asked me 'So, what did you find?' I looked at her puzzled. 'At the Encuentro,' she said. I thought about it . . . We found each other."
>
> —Nicolas Valdez (Su Teatro)

> "It has been an honor and a pleasure to network, meet, hang, talk, build, laugh, and share the space with everyone this time around. This was my first time at a conference/festival such as this, and I must say, it left me wanting more and more. Much love, respect, *luz y progreso para todos.* THANK YOU ENCUENTRO!!"
>
> —Nicky Laboy (Pregones Theater)

> "Being at the Encuentro is a once-in-a-lifetime opportunity: *It is like coming out of the shadows of invisibility and silence.* Ex-

> periencing all these vibrant voices carried by young people is a promise for the future. There is a camaraderie and lack of competition that is refreshing. INTAR offered their set to us out of the blue. Everything is so well organized. Everything screams 'WELCOME HOME.' This is our culture, our voice, our expression. It is really an encounter. We talk, we work together, we see each other's work. No criticism, only uplifting dialogue and camaraderie. My play, *Maria's Circular Dance*, is about cartel violence. It had to cross the border, out of silence. I am proud of my work and of my actors."
>
> —Eva Tessler (Borderlands Theater)

> "What we all shared is beyond measure. We all shared our work, our ideas, our stories, and our passions. People/artists from multiple generations would gather and share music, share our hopes and dreams, share our booze, share our scripts, pretty much whatever we had, we shared. In this process of sharing we opened each other up to new ideas, new perspectives, new methods or even old ideas, perspectives and methods that can still cause an impact. It seems like the world is a new place, a bigger place and those conversations about being a Latino in America are ongoing and it's up to us to raise our voices, collectively and have our say. As Luis Valdez said 'There is no US America. There is no Latin America. There is only one America *y tenemos que luchar por ella*.'"
>
> —Archie Villeda (Su Teatro)

As these testimonials demonstrate, there is power in the communal experience of creating, witnessing, and participating in theater festivals. The dream of revitalizing a network of Latinx artists and companies across the U.S. continues to be realized with each new production, tour, and convening. These connections have deepened established relationships while also creating new ones. For example, in 2017, the network expanded its reach to Latin America with the Latino Theater Company's *Encuentro de las Américas* festival and the LTC's first international convening, a project the coeditors of this book are also anthologizing. As José Luis Valenzuela declared in the 2014 Manifesto, Encuentro artists emphatically claim our place here and now in the new American Theater.

ABOUT THE AUTHORS

Trevor Boffone is a Houston-based scholar, educator, writer, dramaturg, and producer. He is a member of the National Steering Committee for the Latinx Theatre Commons and the founder of the 50 Playwrights Project. Trevor has a Ph.D. in Latinx theater and literature from the Department of Hispanic Studies at the University of Houston, where he holds a graduate certificate in Women's, Gender, & Sexuality Studies. His first book project, *Eastside Latinidad: Josefina López, Community, and Social Change in Boyle Heights*, is a study of theater and performance in East Los Angeles, focusing primarily on Josefina López's role as a playwright, mentor, and community leader in Boyle Heights. His writing on contemporary Latinx theater has appeared in *Theater, Theatre Journal, Latin American Theatre Review, GESTOS, Label Me Latina/o, Gender Forum, The Rocky Mountain Review, El Mundo Zurdo 4, Voces del Caribe, Upstage,* Café Onda, HowlRound, and *Arts+Culture TX.*

Mariana Carreño King's plays include *Miss 744890* (2014 Winner, MetLife Nuestras Voces National Playwriting Competition, Repertorio Español, 2016, and picked for publication in Italian as part of the American Playwrights Project); *Dance for a Dollar* (a dance-theater collaboration at Miracle Theatre in Portland, Oregon); *Ofelia's Lovers* (Mabou Mines Residency); *Rare Encounters, Darkroom, The Wake,* and *Fool's Journey* (INTAR's NewWorksLabs); and *Adela* (Autonomous University of Queretaro, Mexico), among others. Mariana is also a director, part of the Advisory Committee for The Lark Play Development Center US/Mexico Playwrights Exchange, member of LAByrinth Theatre Company, and alumna of the Hispanic Playwrights-in-Residence Lab (HPRL) at INTAR.

Grace Dávila-López is an adjunct professor of Spanish at the Department of Romance Languages and Literatures at Pomona College. She specializes in Puerto Rican theater, and she has published in the *Latin American Theatre Review*, *Conjunto*, and *Gestos* (1986–2015), of which she was a founding member. As a resident of Southern California, she is interested in the work of the Latino Theater Company and the Los Angeles Latino theater scene.

Evelina Fernández was born and raised in East L.A. and began her career in Teatro Chicano. Her first professional job as an actor was in the original *Zoot Suit* at the Mark Taper Forum. She is a founding member of the Latino Theater Company, where she has developed most of her work for more than thirty years as an award-winning playwright, screenwriter, and actor. She received the L.A. Drama Critics Circle Award for *A Mexican Trilogy*. Her plays have made the L.A. Times Critic's Choice list: *Solitude* (2009); and *Dementia* (2010). She received a Best Playwright Ovation Award nomination for her play, *Hope: Part II of A Mexican Trilogy*. In 2003, *Dementia* received four L.A. Stage Alliance Ovation Award nominations. *Charity: Part III of A Mexican Trilogy* was Back Stage's Critic's Pick in 2013 and *Faith: Part I of A Mexican Trilogy* premiered to critical acclaim. She is a member of the Advisory Committee for the Latinx Theatre Commons.

Javier Antonio González was born in 1980 in Vega Baja, Puerto Rico. He is the Artistic Director of Caborca with whom he has made: *Distant Star* (Abrons Arts Center); *Hamlet* (Jersey City Theater Center); *Zoetrope* (LATC/Pregones Theater); *Open up, Hadrian* (Magic Futurebox); *El correo de la noche* (IRT); *FLORIDITA, my Love* (IATI Theater); and *Barceloneta, de noche* (IATI Theater). Most recently, his first feature film, *The Entitlement*, premiered at Manhattan Film Festival 2018. In 2016, he directed his own translation of *A Midsummer Night's Dream* at Teatro en el Parque in the City of San Juan, Puerto Rico.

Rubén C. González received his training at The London Academy for Performing Arts, Circle in the Square Theatre School, El Teatro Campesino, and The University of California, Davis, and he has performed on stages across the country. His solo works (*Diary of a Mad Mexican*;

The Messiah Complex; and *La Esquinita, U.S.A.*) have received much critical acclaim. The latter was named Equity Production of the Year by the *Phoenix New Times*. His film credits include *Selena*; *The Master*; and *La Mission*. He is married to the lovely Sonora Vasquez, and they have two children, Jaden and Mateo Imix.

Rickerby Hinds has the unique ability to challenge conventional notions of the stage while remaining respectful of its long history and traditions. A native of Honduras who immigrated to South Central Los Angeles at age thirteen, he has found a voice through the stage that he could not have imagined given his beginnings. Possessing an M.F.A. in playwriting from UCLA's School of Theater, Film and Television where he was twice awarded the Audrey Skirball-Kenis award for best play, Hinds's visionary creations span the gamut of human experiences through his unconventionally innovative storytelling style using hip-hop as its foundation.

Jorge A. Huerta is Chancellor's Associates Professor of Theatre Emeritus at the University of California, San Diego. A founder of El Teatro de la Esperanza and other *teatros*, he is a leading authority on contemporary Chicanx and Latinx theater as well as a professional director. He has published a number of articles, edited three anthologies of plays, and written the landmark books *Chicano Theatre: Themes and Forms* and *Chicano Drama: Performance, Society, and Myth*. Dr. Huerta has directed in theaters across the country and has lectured and conducted workshops in Chicanx theater throughout the United States, Latin America, and Western Europe. He is a member of the Advisory Committee for the Latinx Theatre Commons.

Tiffany Ana López is director of the School of Film, Dance and Theatre in the Herberger Institute for Design and the Arts at Arizona State University. She specializes in fostering plays about violence and trauma and has worked with the Oregon Shakespeare Festival, Mark Taper Forum/ Center Theatre Group, Arizona Theatre Company, Cornerstone Theater Company, The Los Angeles Theatre Center, CASA 0101, and Breath of Fire Latina Theater Ensemble. Recent production dramaturgy includes: *Mojada: A Mexican Medea* by Luis Alfaro, directed by Juliette Carrillo; *The River Bride* by Marisela Treviño Orta, directed by Laurie Woolery; and

Romeo and Juliet, directed by Dámaso Rodríguez. She is a member of the Advisory Committee for the Latinx Theatre Commons.

Irma Mayorga, a native of San Antonio, Texas, is a Chicana scholar and theatermaker. With collaborator Virginia Grise, she conceived and wrote the celebrated solo work *The Panza Monologues* (University of Texas Press, 2014), which dramatizes links between gender, race, and obesity in Mexican American communities. Her play *Cascarones* earned the Jane Chambers Playwriting Award and went on for development at the prestigious Eugene O'Neill Theater Center's Playwrights Conference. Her creative work as a theatermaker also includes directing and dramaturgy. Her scholarship explores contemporary theater and performance by U.S. people of color and Latinx expressive culture. She is a member of the National Steering Committee for the Latinx Theatre Commons.

Teresa Marrero is Professor of Latin American and Latinx Theater in the Spanish Department at the University of North Texas. Her scholarly publications include the anthology of plays *Out of the Fringe: Contemporary Latina/Latino Theatre and Performance*, which she edited with Caridad Svich. Her journal articles have been published in *Theater*, *TDR*, *GESTOS*, *Theatre Topics*, and *Latin American Theater Review*, and in the arts and humanities digital publication *Argus-a*. In 2010 her Spanish language play, *La familia*, premiered in Dallas at the Bathhouse Cultural Center. She is a critic for www.theaterjones.com, and a member of the American Theatre Critics Association. She has served on the National Steering Committee since 2013 and is now an Advisory Committee member of the Latinx Theatre Commons.

Beatriz J. Rizk is Colombian American. She is a professor, critic, promoter, and researcher. She has published numerous articles and essays on Latin American and Latinx theater in specialized magazines. She has edited eight issues of *Tramoya* (Universidad Veracruzana) on Latinx, Indigenous/Indianist, Brazilian, Colombian, Central American, Bolivian, and Dominican Theaters. Among her thirteen published books are: *Latin American Popular Theatre: The First Five Centuries*, (1993); *Posmodernismo y teatro en América Latina* (2001); and *El legado de Enrique Buenaventura.* (2008). She is a Smithsonian Institution's Latino Senior Fellow. She directs the Educational Program of the International Hispanic Theatre Festival of Miami, and is a member of Teatro Avante.

Chantal Rodriguez is the associate dean of the Yale School of Drama and a lecturer in dramaturgy and dramatic criticism. From 2009 to 2016 she was the programming director and literary manager for the Latino Theater Company, the operators of the Los Angeles Theatre Center. Chantal holds a Ph.D. in theater and performance studies from UCLA, and her work has been published in *Theater*, *Theatre Journal*, *Latin American Theatre Review*, *e-misférica*, and *Theatre Research International.* In 2011, the UCLA Chicano Studies Research Center Press published her monograph, *The Latino Theatre Initiative/Center Theatre Group Papers*, which was nominated for three Latino Literacy Now International Book Awards. She serves on the Advisory Committee of the Latinx Theatre Commons, and on the National Advisory Board of the 50 Playwrights Project. Chantal is a recipient of the Los Angeles Women's Theatre Festival's 2016 Rainbow Award, and was recognized as a Young Leader of Color by TCG in 2011.

Olga Sánchez Saltveit, originally from New York City, is Artistic Director Emerita of Milagro, the Pacific Northwest's premier Latino arts and culture organization. Previously, she served as a cofounder and artistic director of Seattle Teatro Latino. An actor, director, devisor, and emerging scholar, her creative work has been seen throughout the U.S. and Latin America. *Tricks to Inherit,* her translation of *Astucias por heredar un sobrino a un tío* by Fermín de Reygadas, provides access to a unique work of New Spain Enlightenment theater. Her article "(Afro)Latinx Theatre: Embodiment and Articulation" was published in *Label Me Latina/o.* She is a member of the National Steering Committee for the Latinx Theatre Commons.

José Torres-Tama is a 2015 MAP Fund recipient for his *Taco Truck Theater/Teatro Sin Fronteras* radical theater on wheels performance that challenges the anti-immigrant hysteria gripping the United States of Amnesia. An NEA Regional Artist Project award winner for his hybrid genre shows, *Aliens, Immigrants, & Other Evildoers* is *"a sci-fi Latino* noir" solo that exposes the labor exploitation of immigrants in a country that readily dehumanizes them. Vanderbilt, Duke, Cornell, and other institutions have presented his solos, and internationally, Roehampton University in London; Bluecoat Arts Centre in Liverpool; and performance festivals in Poland, Slovenia, and Mexico City have presented his provocative work.

José Luis Valenzuela is the artistic director of the Latino Theater Company (LTC) and the Los Angeles Theatre Center (LATC). He is a distinguished professor and head of the M.F.A. Directing Program at UCLA's School of Theater, Film & Television. Valenzuela has been a visionary advocate for Chicano/Latino theater and film for more than thirty years. Notable contributions include creating the Latino Theatre Lab at LATC in 1985, and establishing the Latino Theater Initiative at the Mark Taper Forum in 1991. Most recently, he directed Karen Zacarías's *Destiny of Desire* at Arena Stage, South Coast Rep, the Goodman Theatre, and Oregon Shakespeare Festival. Together with the LTC, he produced the 2014 Encuentro Festival and the 2017 Encuentro de las Américas festival at the LATC. He is a recipient of the Ann C. Rosenfield Distinguished Community Partnership Prize and the Hispanic Heritage Month *Local Hero of the Year* Award. Valenzuela serves on the Advisory Committee of the Latinx Theatre Commons.